BOOKS BY JAMES W. HALL

Fiction

*Under Cover of Daylight**

Poetry

The Lady from the Dark Green Hills
Ham Operator
The Mating Reflex
False Statements

*Published by
WARNER BOOKS

TROPICAL FREEZE

JAMES W. HALL

James W. Hall

WARNER BOOKS

A Time Warner Company

WARNER BOOKS EDITION

Copyright © 1989 by James W. Hall
All rights reserved.

This Warner Books Edition is published
by arrangement with W.W. Norton & Company,
Inc., 500 Fifth Avenue, New York, N.Y. 10110

Cover design by Jackie Merri Meyer
Cover illustration by Alain Chang

Warner Books, Inc.
1271 Avenue of the Americas
New York, N.Y. 10020

 A Time Warner Company

Printed in the United States of America

First Warner Books Printing: March, 1991

10 9 8 7 6 5 4 3 2

FOR MY PARENTS

J. Noble Hall, Jr.
Anne Welborn Hall

Here are your waters and your watering place.
Drink and be whole again beyond confusion.

—ROBERT FROST
"Directive"

TROPICAL FREEZE

1

On Friday night, January the third, Thorn put on a clean T-shirt and cutoffs and drove his '69 VW convertible to Coconuts, a new waterfront bar behind the Holiday Inn. He ordered a beer, and the bartender brought him a Tecate, a slice of lime on the top of it. He sipped it, watching the pretty tanned women swirl around the dance floor and the bar.

Thorn had gone to Coconuts because his loneliness had begun echoing too loudly, and he thought he wanted to fill himself up with rock music and empty chatter. It was the first weekend of the new year. He thought maybe he was ready to come home with a warm body.

He'd been there only a few minutes when a dark woman with her hair clenched back in a ponytail took the stool beside him. She swiveled around to face him and began tapping her Corvette key chain on the bar.

"I'm a dentist," she said. "Does that bother you?"

"Not yet," he said.

She smiled at him and he smiled back. She tapped the key chain against the bar, keeping the beat to a loud song he didn't recognize.

She laughed and set down her frothy red drink.

"You know it's funny," she said. "A guy like you, all raggedy, sunburned, and unshaven, if I saw you up in Miami, I'd probably say to myself, Look at that syphilitic loser. But down here in the Keys, damn if you're not romantic. You're a water bum, living on your sailboat, and I'll probably wind up in the sack with you tonight, getting my eyeballs fucked out."

Thorn rose, picked up his Tecate, and moved down three stools.

A green-eyed blonde in a black Danskin top and a denim skirt was sitting next to him. She sighed, shook her head, and turned on him. She told him she'd used her Christmas break to drive all the way from Minnesota to Key Largo to scuba dive on the reefs and she was shocked by the decay of the coral and the degrading of the water. The damn locals were doing a lousy job of protecting the ecology. This place was a national treasure, and they were letting it get ruined. Thorn nodded, set aside the lime wedge from his new beer, and tried to interest himself in her eyes. A warm light seemed to be filling them.

She looked back at him, getting quiet, leaning slowly toward him, peering strangely at his face. He was about to speak, to ask her if she'd like to analyze the moonlight from his hammock, when she reached out and touched his cheek with a cool finger.

She said, "You really ought to have that crusty red patch looked at."

He stared at her.

She said, "Melanoma. You know, the big C?"

He got the bartender's attention, paid his bill, and left Coconuts. He drove south a couple of miles and turned into a dark street where the palm fronds stirred against the one working streetlight. Papa John's Bomb Bay Bar was at the end of that dark rutted street, past a weedy trailer park. The bar was in a sagging shack on the edge of the Atlantic.

He parked the VW next to a shrimp truck and went inside. No women there. No dating rituals or ferns or foreign beers. The only decorations were some framed black-and-white photos on one wall.

It was a rogues' gallery. A much younger Papa John stood out on anonymous docks with his cronies: politicians, baseball players, movie stars. All of them sunburned, posing beside their marlin or holding up a string of game fish.

Thorn leaned against the bar and watched Papa John in his white captain's hat and rumpled white shirt going about his work, drawing beers for the two shrimpers sitting at the end of the bar. Both of them wore stained undershirts, tattoos on their arms, baseball caps; one had dog tags. Thorn nodded to the men, and they nodded back. One of them said his name.

When Papa John brought Thorn his Busch, he asked Thorn how the fly-tying business was doing.

"I'm carving plugs now," he said. "Cutting back on flies."

"Plugs," said one of the shrimpers. "Shit, whatta you want to waste your time carving plugs?"

"Silhouettes," said the other shrimper. "That's all the goddamn fishes care about. They see a shape they like, they'll hit it. Fish don't give a shit if it's made out of wood or plastic."

"Well, I give a shit," Thorn said.

Papa John said, "Hell, I'm with Thorn. Give me wood every time. That plastic crap, man, a good-sized fish hits plastic, the thing blows up on you."

Papa John and the shrimpers started in on it, who knew more about catching fish. As Thorn washed away those Tecates with his Busch, he watched the three men. They were in their sixties, and there was still a pioneer gristle in their faces. But the flesh on their arms was loose, their fingers thick and clumsy with gout or arthritis. Thorn knew these shrimpers, and he knew their sons. They were paler than their fathers, less hardy specimens, men whose only calluses came from golf, or tapping buttons.

He drank his beer and watched these men argue. These men who had done every rough and difficult thing a man might be expected to do in the Keys. Everything but replace themselves.

In a few minutes Papa John came over to him again and asked if he wanted another beer. Thorn said he reckoned he'd done enough celebrating tonight. He dug some change from his pocket.

Papa John squinted at Thorn, gave him a long, searching look. He said, "You know what, son. I believe I could use somebody like you around here."

Thorn laughed.

"I'm serious, Thorn. I am." He looked back at the shrimpers, then leaned forward into confidential range. He said quietly, "I could teach you some things, Thorn. I could."

"What? How to be a scoundrel?" Thorn said. He put the change down on the bar. "A rapscallion?"

Papa John smiled. "Yeah," he said. "That, and a lot more."

"No, thanks, John. I got myself a vocation already."

"Carving plugs," Papa John said.

"It keeps me busy," said Thorn.

He said good-night to the shrimpers, nodded to Papa John, and left.

When he got home, he wasn't feeling sorry for himself anymore. He was feeling sorry for Key Largo, for Florida, for North America. For men and women everywhere. For the race of lonely creatures that walked upright.

He knew what his problem was. It'd been too damn long since he'd been in love. It was three months ago that he'd kissed Sarah Ryan good-bye. She'd moved to Tallahassee, taken a job with the Sierra Club to fight for the rights of the manatee and wood stork.

All through that September she'd talked about it, what a

chance it was, a bigger impact on things, no more Miami public defense work. Let the slime and sleaze fend for themselves. Thorn said yeah, it sounded great, a great job. Both of them acted this through, some tears, some long hugs. The damn job splitting them up. Thorn even started to believe it at times.

But he knew when she drove away that afternoon, waving into her rearview mirror, he knew that was all shit. They'd burned it up, whatever had fueled their love, making it so bright and hot and fast. All though September they'd raced through the motions. Sexual seizures, biting, pinching each other as if to squeeze out that extra drop. Gripping tight while the G-force died, while their rocketing hearts slowed back to normal. Then even slower than that.

And since that afternoon Thorn had been living aboard the Chris Craft, relearning the language of his own solitude, while he and Jack Higby rebuilt his house, plank by plank, peg by peg, leveling, squaring up the edges.

Back in August his house had been destroyed. A bomb meant for Thorn had blasted it, sprayed his belongings across the entire five acres of Thorn's property. And now and then, as he and Higby worked, one of them would stumble across a charred and twisted tool, an old reel singed by the fire, the door from the broiler, and Jack might hold it up, trying to figure out what it had been, and Thorn's heart would flare, miss a beat.

It'd been in August that' he'd tracked down his foster mother's killer, untangled a snarl of greed and hate. And now strangers came up to him, patted him on the shoulder, standing there in the Largo Shopper on the produce aisle, saying, all right, bud, way to get 'em. Like it'd been a baseball game and he'd hit a grand slam. Six people dead. A lot of damn blood on the stage at the end of it. And every hand patting his shoulder left a burning print.

It was getting close to midnight. Thorn's beer buzz had died to a hum, and a sharp headache was easing up the back of his neck. He was on the *Heart Pounder,* his thirty-two-foot Chris Craft, anchored in the basin at the end of his dock on Blackwater Sound. He sat at the swing-up table, listening to the hiss of the Coleman lantern.

He was sanding a six-inch piece of hickory that he'd cut from a broom handle. For two days he'd been whittling on that hickory. It was to be a replica of a ballyhoo, that oily black demon with a two-inch sword, the prey of dolphin, sailfish, marlin.

His craft had always been in tying flies. Steady fingers, miniature knots, attaching sprays of fur or horsehair with garish synthetic threads. But that was before. That was six months ago, before things went from quiet to deafening.

He still filled the orders he got from fishing guides and a couple of friends who ran local tackle shops. Those flies still paid his meager bills. But it was a labor now. He'd lost the heat.

The fishing guides still came aboard, made small talk, told their quiet stories of scorched reels and melted ball bearings, from the lightning first run of bonefish or permit. And when Thorn brought out those flies and handed them over, the fishermen still touched them with a cloaked reverence as if they were handling icons.

But it was just mechanical. His passion had drained off. The surge, the hot focus as he worked, the afterburn that lasted into the evening of a successful tying day. All of it had evaporated. So he had taken up plugs.

He had worked first on darters. A blunt-nosed, stubby plug, it was shaped to dig into the water and then dart when the rod was jerked. Darters imitated distressed fish back in the channels and canals. Those popeyed snook would watch from their safe cages of mangrove roots, thinking no, no, no, no. Until sometime during the final retrieve, because they believed the wounded minnow had recovered and was swimming away: Yes!

He'd moved on to poppers, the torpedo-shaped dancers, then floaters and divers, and crawlers. He had a drawerful of them now, some without their final treble hooks, several half painted, some still naked wood. None had been in the water yet, to have their chance to trick or fail. But that didn't matter. What mattered was that he felt eager and fresh, learning this new craft.

In the distance Thorn heard the muttering of a small outboard. He drew back the red-and-white checked galley curtain and saw the running lights of a bonefish skiff.

As it approached Thorn's dock, he made out Captain Bradley Barnes, probably on his way back from a night of drinking up at Senor Frijoles, running home to Rock Harbor. Barnes was a cranky retired M.D. who chartered his sixteen-footer, the *Lucy Goosey*, out of Papa John's Bomb Bay Marina. Barnes had erected a sign on the lintel over his dock that said, DISCOUNTS FOR THE SPEECHLESS.

Thorn took the lantern outside and met Barnes on the dock and helped him make fast. They sat on the edge of the dock and looked out at the black harbor, at the moon muffled deep in clouds.

"Those Grizzlies you tied are knocking them dead," Barnes said, whiskey and green peppers on the breeze.

"So I hear," said Thorn.

"Had an angler this afternoon, he hooked himself what must've been a fourteen-pound bonefish. Just inside Dove Key in about a foot of water. He wrestled that bone for half an hour and got tired and wanted to give the rod to me. I wouldn't take it, so he kept on cranking, got it up to the boat, and that horse broke off soon as it saw the net. That Grizzly still in his lip."

Thorn said, "Probably showing it around tonight. What to watch out for."

"I lost all four of those you made for me. My angler snagged two on the bottom, logs or some such." The doctor smiled, his lips blistered, his blue eyes bleached by the sun. "So, I'm here to buy a dozen more."

Thorn told Bradley he was out of the materials for the Grizzly. There weren't going to be any more of them.

"What exactly were they?"

Thorn was silent. In a minute Bradley laughed into the dark.

"Can't shoot me for asking," he said. "Like asking the pope what he spiked that wine with. Well then, hell, I'm going back out there tomorrow, see if I can't find those logs those flies got snagged on. See how long I can hold my breath. I got my heart set on that fly-fish trophy at Old Pirate Days this year."

"That'd be four in a row, wouldn't it?"

"Four's a good number," he said. "I got a fondness for it."

When Barnes was gone, Thorn went inside and opened the drawer beneath his bunk, where he kept his materials. The piss yellow swatch of polar bear fur was there, still enough of it left to stuff a football. He could make enough Grizzlies to flood the market, catch every bonefish left in the Keys.

Twenty years ago the fur had been a gift from his foster mother when she'd returned from Alaska after a month of fishing up there. He'd found it at her house, in his boyhood room last August, when he was cleaning out the place to ready it for sale.

He had tried using a pinch of the fur on a standard fly, something close to the Bonebuster, two silver eyes, a crimson belt of Mylar that cinched in the pinafore of polar bear fur, the hook curling out the spray of skirt like a single disfigured leg. He'd named it the Grizzly.

And now the impossible had happened. The lure was consistently firing their brains, bringing them to the surface with an eerie regularity. It'd been happening now for two months, the longest string of luck any of his lures had ever had.

Thorn tried to imagine what strange collision of scents this was, how the fur of that Arctic beast could catalyze these tropical spooks. What was it they saw? This invader from a universe of ice twitching in their marshy pool, igniting some ancient rage perhaps, some hatefulness for the outsider, the alien.

Thorn took the wad of polar bear fur out on deck, dropped it into the departing tide. He watched it as it floated across the basin, and in a while into a slick of yellow moonlight, then into the path of a shrimper on her way out, disappearing finally below the hull, churned to particles by the prop.

Benny Cousins stood on the lower deck as the forty-five-foot Bertram idled across the flats. The water here was less than a foot in places, laced with sandbars and coral heads. It's why he'd hired this jerkoff captain to bring them in. Guy by the name of Murphy, who'd worked this shoreline for the Coast Guard for twenty years. Murphy was retired and living down in Grassy Key, making do on his pension and Social Security. So you'd think he'd be happy to make five hundred bucks to do a little boat handling for Benny, just keep his mouth shut and steer them to shore. But no, this tightass wanted to know everything. Like he was going to file a float plan with the fucking Supreme Court.

Benny said don't worry about it. I'm picking up a friend of

mine about twenty-five miles offshore, bringing him back to the Keys for a weekend party. All you need to know is the loran coordinates for the meeting and the location of our landing in Key Largo.

But this guy wouldn't give up. He kept bugging Benny all the way out from the docks in Islamorada. This isn't some kind of drug run, is it, Cousins? Hell, no. I look like a drug runner to you? You can't tell, the jerkoff had said. Everybody's into it these days. Well, I'm not fucking into it, Benny said. I hate drugs, drug runners, everything they fucking stand for.

So Murphy gives it a rest for a few minutes. They're out there in the dark, cruising out to sea, Benny looking up for the couple of constellations he can name, and this guy starts in again. How come your friend didn't fly in? What's all this boat shenanigans? It don't smell right. And Benny left him up there on the bridge and climbed down to the deck, where his two men, Donald and Joe, were smoking cigarettes, sitting in the marlin fighting chairs. Let that jerkoff Murphy guess all he wanted. Fuck if Benny was going to say another word to the guy.

But Murphy did have a point. Benny could've brought Claude in by plane. Walked him right through Customs, done it under their noses. But what fun was that? He liked playing up all this clandestine bullshit. It impressed the clients, helped spread the good word among their kind. If he made it look too easy bringing these guys across, they might think it wasn't worth the price.

Right after midnight the thirty-foot Donzi showed itself, made its three shorts, one long flash with its searchlight. The off-loading worked fast and quiet. Not a word. The Haitian, Claude, climbed aboard with his suitcase, wearing a flowered shirt, white pants. Benny waved at the man on the Donzi, and the boats separated. Start to finish, the whole thing was a minute, a minute-thirty tops.

And now they were idling across the flats, heading to Dynamite Docks in North Key Largo. There was no development at this end of the island, nothing but hundreds of acres of mangroves and alligators and scorpions. And this one cement dock that ran out a couple hundred feet. The place was a legendary drop-off spot for smugglers. It's why Benny had picked it. Nobody used it anymore because the DEA had built one of their outpost stations a few hundred yards from the docks. That was just the kind of heavy-handed symbolism they liked. Hey, look what we're doing! Shaking the bushes real loud as they snuck up on you. It was one of the reasons, just one, that Benny had quit the DEA.

He liked the irony of bringing Claude ashore here, within spitting distance of his old colleagues. And Dynamite Docks had the reek of history. He could imagine the wagons of rum creaking down a sandy path out to some old jalopy on the highway. And he could picture the hippies back in the sixties, VW vans gridlocked back there in the woods, waiting for their bale of grass.

They were about fifty yards from shore when Murphy called down that there was a boat and some activity at the docks. Claude moved alongside Benny, staring at him in the dark.

"You said it was all arranged," Claude said.

"Hey," Benny said, "I can account for every fucking DEA boat, Customs, Coast Guard, you name it. If it's one of ours, I know its present location. And they aren't around here." Benny strained through the dark toward the darker shoreline, the Bertram still gliding forward.

"What do I do?" Murphy called down.

"Keep going," Benny said. He told Claude to get his ass down below and stay there. Then he got Donald and Joe arranged flat on the front deck. He told them to keep their Mac-10s trained on the shore. Benny shook his head and snapped the slide shut on his Smith automatic. All right then, gentlemen, start your engines.

Murphy slid them neatly up to the edge of the dock. The other boat was a eighteen-foot Boston Whaler. Benny could see the black gleam of a plastic-wrapped bale. He could even smell the shit. Nobody was around.

He hissed at his guys, waved them back to the stern deck. Claude was glaring at him through the parlor window, making slit eyes at Benny. He probably scared normal people with that look.

Donald and Joe made the Bertram fast to the pilings, and Benny stepped onto the dock. There was a black Ford van parked about twenty yards off, near the trees. Benny motioned for Donald to go one way, Joe the other way, surround the van.

When they were in place, he walked across the sandy ground and stood facing the rear doors, raised his automatic, and was about to fire when the door came open a crack and a boy's voice said, "We surrender."

"Get the fuck out here," Benny said. All that DEA adrenaline soaring through him again. "Now, motherfuckers!"

It was a boy and girl with matching frizzy blond hair, both in blue jeans and black T-shirts. Rock stars in training.

Donald and Joe came around the van. The teenagers edged away from them. Benny opened the van door. In the half-moon glow, he could make out two or three bales.

"How old're you two punks?" he said, closing the doors.

"Eighteen," the girl said.

"Ken and Barbie," Benny said, "out in the spooky woods at night with a ton of illegal drugs. How does that happen? Huh? Where in hell did you develop fucking values like that?"

"We have the right to remain silent," the boy said. "The right to have an attorney present."

Benny snorted, turned to his men. Donald smiled. Joe was eyeing the girl.

"What is it?" Benny said. "Your old man a lawyer?"

"As a matter of fact," the boy said, "he is."

Benny shook his head and said, "Jesus Christ, that's the way it's fucking going."

He shot the boy in the knee. And when the kid was on the ground writhing, Benny moved over to him, stepped on the ankle of his good leg, and shot him in the other knee. The girl screamed for him to stop.

A brown Mercedes rolled up the narrow path.

"It's about fucking time," Benny said. He shot the boy through the chest and turned to the girl. "You wouldn't ever do anything like this again, now would you, sweet pea? Seeing what can happen."

She swallowed, mouth quivering. She said, "No, sir. No, never."

He pressed the barrel of the Smith against her left breast. Rubbed the barrel against the cotton, until he felt her nipple harden. He trapped the tip of her nipple inside the barrel. She wasn't wearing a bra. Yeah, it figured. It went with the rest of her values.

"You promise now?" Benny said. "You give me your sacred word of honor you won't ever participate in this kind of filth again?"

"I promise," she said. "I promise."

Benny squeezed off two quick rounds into her left breast. It blew her backwards a couple of yards into a bush.

"Jesus Christ, Benny!" Donald said. "Why'd you do that?"

Benny put the Smith back on his hip, turned, and looked at Donald. He said, "To teach her a goddamn lesson."

2

Thorn was idling in his driveway, looking for a space in the traffic on U.S. 1. It was Friday, the tenth of January, and the winter Winnebagos had arrived, and the bright rented convertibles, and dusty station wagons from Indiana. All of them streaming through Key Largo, on their annual hunt for paradise. Thorn had been waiting there for five minutes. He needed a wide break in traffic, because his VW had lost its will to rush.

He was on his way up to Miami to get a blade for the Lakowski 175 sawmill he was using to rebuild his house. A hardware store in Hialeah was the only place for a hundred miles around that still stocked blades for that electric monstrosity.

When he saw a space coming up right after a brown Mercedes, Thorn slipped the shifter into first, revved it hard. But the Mercedes slowed, pulled into the gravel along the shoulder, and tucked into the drive beside him.

It was Gaeton Richards who got out of the car. He was wearing a blue windbreaker, madras plaid shirt, jeans, and tennis shoes. He'd grown a mustache since Thorn had seen him last, sandy blond, like his hair. Thorn got out of the VW. They shook hands; then Thorn laughed and opened his arms, and Gaeton stepped forward into an embrace.

When they stepped apart, Thorn said, "It's been what, over a year?"

Gaeton said, "It was Old Pirate Days last January."

"Yeah, yeah," Thorn said. "We made conch fitters over at your trailer."

"And you got drunk, sang Christmas carols."

Thorn said, "Yeah, it's coming back to me."

He'd noticed a man sitting in Gaeton's car, not looking over at them.

Gaeton said, "Well, hell, let's do it again this year. Dress up this time, get polluted, kidnap a maiden. Hey, we could make your VW into a float, ride in the parade. Really do it up right."

"Yeah," Thorn said, smiling.

Gaeton said, "You're on your way somewhere."

"I was going up to Miami, but I can do it later."

"No, that's perfect," Gaeton said. "I got to take this guy up there anyway. Come with us, zip this guy by the car showroom for a minute or two, run your errands, come on back. Give us time to shoot the shit."

"You were coming to see me?"

"Yeah," Gaeton said, his voice lower. "I needed to talk."

"OK, let me stash the VW." Thorn turned to get in his car, then turned back. "Up and back, right? No side trips."

"My word on it."

Their passenger was a quiet gentleman. He had a mat of crinkly yellow hair that he brushed straight back away from his face, cheekbones that could slice ten-pound test line, and raw pinkish skin. If he wasn't an albino, he'd climbed out of the same gene pool. He sat in the back seat, wearing a blinding yellow

shirt with blue hula girls on it, and white pants. He looked like
nobody'd ever shown him how to smile.

As they crossed the Jewfish Creek Bridge out of Key Largo,
Gaeton launched into a story about his final assignment with the
Miami field office of the FBI. Seems there was an elephant
shipped into the Metrozoo from the Far East. The unfortunate
pachyderm had been stuffed full of garbage bags of heroin. Just
as the *federales* were closing in on the zoo handlers who were
plucking bags out of the elephant goop, the elephant started
having intense seizures. Must've digested one of the bags during
his voyage. And there he was, rearing up, threatening good guys
and bad guys alike.

"Ever see what a three-fifty-seven magnum does to elephant
hide?"

"It's been awhile," Thorn said. "I forget."

"Not a whole hell of a lot," Gaeton said.

Gaeton went on with the story, while Thorn glanced into the
back seat at this man. Those green eyes clicked onto Thorn's and
held him for a minute. The guy had something burning in there.

They strolled around the lot of a Porsche and Ferrari dealer-
ship, the two of them following behind the man in the hula girl
shirt as he stalked down the aisles of cars. After a while they
attracted a young salesman. He sized up the three of them and
spoke to Gaeton.

"Looking for some speed and luxury today?" the young man
said.

"Our friend Claude is." Gaeton nodded ahead to the other
man.

"He speak English?"

"I couldn't tell you," Gaeton said. "I never had the occasion to speak to him."

"Well, we'll let him look a bit," the salesman said. He seemed to be used to this, three guys shopping together but not knowing each other.

Claude had stopped in front of a black Porsche. He tried the door, but it was locked.

Gaeton called out, "Find one you like?"

Claude looked back at Gaeton. No car buyer's flush in his face. Just that heavy-lidded look, like a snake about to doze off or strike. It was hard to tell.

Gaeton said, "Get us the keys to that one, will you? Our friend wants to sniff the leather."

In a few minutes the salesman sauntered back with the keys. He was wearing a black polo shirt with a red alligator on it, a white coat over that, white pants. Dark wraparound sunglasses, loafers without socks.

"The Carrera has very silky steering," the boy said as he unlocked the driver's door. "And a top end of one hundred seventy-four." He turned his sunglasses on Claude and said, *"Me entiendies?"*

Claude let a few seconds pass, then said to the salesman, "You may speak to me in your language. I understand it well."

"Well, then," the boy said. A fidget appeared in his right hand, drumming on his pants leg. He nodded his head at Claude.

Claude said, "I want to experience this top end you speak about. This one hundred and seventy-four. I want to feel this."

The boy glanced at Gaeton and Thorn to see if they were smiling. They weren't. The salesman created a smile anyway. "We'll go around the block, a mile or two, then swing back and talk." Getting a patronizing authority in there.

Gaeton yawned, looked off at the traffic. Thorn watched a jet rise from Miami International a mile or two to the north, its rumble vibrating through the asphalt lot.

He'd been running into this same type of kid a good bit lately. The boy had a nasal haughtiness, as if he'd been to some college where he'd been educated beyond his character, given a glib view, a sketchy understanding of the great ideas. And now there was no job on earth that wasn't beneath him.

Claude got into the driver's seat and started the Porsche. Raced the engine. It sounded like he was holding it at redline. The kid ducked into the passenger side, and Thorn and Gaeton headed back to the Mercedes.

At Frog City they reached the last traffic light on the western edge of Miami, the current border of the Everglades. The salesman turned in his bucket seat and made a frantic wave to Gaeton and Thorn, who followed in the brown Mercedes. It was his third since they'd left the car lot. Gaeton waved back.

A hundred yards ahead of them the four-lane highway narrowed to two as it entered the Everglades. The last of the housing developments behind them now, just the shadowy tunnel of pines ahead.

"They must've run out of conversational topics," Gaeton said.

"They don't seem to have a whole lot in common," said Thorn.

"First dates are tough."

The light turned green and the Porsche's rear tires squealed and Gaeton crushed the accelerator pedal of the Mercedes, lugging after them.

Thorn said, "You see that? He had hold of the kid. Had him by the scruff, like you hold a dog back."

In a minute Thorn leaned over to check the speedometer. Eighty-five and the Porsche was pulling steadily away.

"By the way, Gaeton, who is this guy? A pharmaceutical king?"

Gaeton Richards leaned back, one hand on the wheel, the other brushing a strand of hair off his forehead. He looked over at Thorn, the trees flashing by behind him.

"I'll tell you, buddy," he said. "I don't know who the hell that guy is. And I sure wish I did."

"Come on." Thorn laughed. "Who is he?"

"All I know is I'm supposed to take him on a shopping spree, see he gets whatever he wants, not let him out of my sight."

Thorn eased his hand up for a good grip on the door handle, braced his feet flat against the fire wall.

"Why do I have the feeling I'm not going to get that blade today?"

Gaeton was quiet for a few moments; then in an almost dreamy tone he said, "You ever remember Saturdays, going to the *Guardian* office?" Nearly closing his eyes as he recalled it. "How we would play with the bars of lead type and make up our own newspaper stories about people around town. Get ink on our clothes."

"Yeah, I think about it. Those were good days," said Thorn. "I remember the headlines we made up. BILL NICKERSON FOUND ASLEEP IN HAMMOCK WITH DEAD SNOOK, things like that."

The *Guardian* had been Gaeton's father's newspaper, the only paper at that time in the upper Keys. It was a one-man affair that he ran out of the downstairs of a Conch house in Tavernier, on a squeaky hand-set press. Gaeton senior had been the reporter, the publisher, editor, everything. He was a calm, quiet widower, who subscribed to a dozen New York magazines, read cowboy novels, smoked a pipe. His hands were always inky and knuckle-busted.

Thorn thought of him often, of his voice especially. How steady and rich it had been, never straining, no matter how angry he might be, or disappointed. Holding that solid timbre, always clear and direct. It still resonated in Thorn's inner ear, a kind of middle C, a reference point. The man could stand in the blast of a hurricane or the easy wash of a summer trade wind and speak with the same calm and grace.

"I was just thinking about those days," Gaeton said. "How we thought things were back then, how we pictured the world."

"It was a simpler time," Thorn said.

"Yeah, simpler."

Thorn watched the asphalt hurtling underneath them. In the distance the Porsche smoked to a stop.

Gaeton said, "He's testing the brakes now. If you're going to drive that fast, you need good brakes." Gaeton brought the Mercedes down to just a little over legal speed. The other car was still a half mile ahead.

The Porsche took off again, its tires burning.

"Here we go," Gaeton said, accelerating.

"You're telling me you don't know this guy? We're playing tag at a hundred plus and you don't know who he is?"

"I'm working on it," Gaeton said. "That's what I wanted to talk to you about. I wanted you to meet him, see what I'm into."

"Looks like you're still in the bad guy business. Not a big change from the FBI."

"If you're going to help me, I thought you should know how it is, see one of these jokers."

"Help you? Who said I was going to help you?"

"You will," Gaeton said. "I just haven't asked you yet."

"Ask me, so I can tell you no right now and get it out of the way."

Thorn watched the steering wheel shimmy in Gaeton's hands. He kept himself from leaning over to check the speedometer. The black Porsche was just a speck now at the end of a long straightaway. They had to be doing over a hundred.

Gaeton glanced over at Thorn, caught his eye, and smiled. He said, "I remember when we were kids, you and me, Darcy, Sugarman, always around this time of year, we'd get into that pirate thing. Dueling. Eye patches, that whole number."

"I'd forgotten," Thorn said.

"Dad never liked it. Glorifying bad guys, he used to say. He'd say things like that and I thought he was being tightass and fussy. I never knew what he meant. Not back then."

Thorn was silent. He was trying to put this together. Claude, the *Guardian,* pirates. This whole day.

Gaeton said, "You're rebuilding your house now. That's taking all your time, right? Getting yourself back together. I shouldn't be bothering you with my bullshit."

"You in some kind of danger, Gaeton?"

Gaeton held his eyes to the road. Empty now for as far as they could see. The pines and melaleucas blurred past. He shook his head as if trying to focus his eyes on the here and now.

He said, "You ever hear of Benny Cousins, the guy I work for?"

Thorn said he hadn't.

"Well, he was a hotshot with DEA, till he quit few years back, started Florida Secure Systems."

"Now he's your boss."

"Yeah," Gaeton said, thinking about it. "My boss."

"So, what's the problem?"

"I wish I could tell you the whole thing, Thorn. But I can't."

"You can't tell me, but you want me to do something."

Thorn willed his right foot to relax, stop stamping on the imaginary brake. Gaeton looked over at him.

"Oh, hell, Gaeton, you need me, I'm there," Thorn said. "You know that."

"Yeah, I knew that." Gaeton smiled at him. "But it's still good to hear you say it."

The wheel was shaking hard now. Gaeton was working just to keep them in their lane. He squinted down the three-mile straightaway at the disappearing Porsche. Then he cleared his throat and looked over at Thorn, his eyes full of trouble.

"Benny's looking for somebody to show him the fishing spots, show him how it's done. Simple, basic stuff, where to cast his line, like that. I suggested he talk to you."

"You did?"

"See, the thing is, Benny plays it very close to the vest with me. So, I thought, well, if you were out with him, fishing, shooting the shit, just you and him, you might be able to fill in some gaps for me. Might get some privileged glimpses."

"Glimpses into what?" Thorn said.

"His business dealings," Gaeton said.

"This is very vague, man."

"I know it is, but it's the best I can do at the moment."

"All right," Thorn said. "Let me get this right. You volunteered me to take this guy out, put him into some fish. I listen to what he says, tell you about it later. That what you mean? Help you investigate your boss."

"Yeah," Gaeton said. "Listen, but don't try to wheedle anything out of him. The guy's very cagey."

"Jesus, Gaeton. You could've asked me first."

"Yeah, I should've. But Benny brought up the fishing thing all of a sudden, and I just blurted out your name. And he's fastened on to it, keeps bringing you up."

Thorn looked out his window at the Everglades, at that sweep of watery prairie, the gnarled cypress, the crisp distances. A great white heron, all wings and neck, floated between the trees out there, making lazy strokes.

"We can talk more about this later," Gaeton said. He patted the dashboard. "We better catch up to our friend here."

The Mercedes crept up to one-thirty, the Porsche disappearing around a curve, and by the time Thorn and Gaeton rounded it, the Porsche had gained a half mile on them.

The road ahead made a sweeping turn through the saw grass and palmetto. Flocks of egrets perched on the bare branches of the cypress, and the vast marsh stretched away to every horizon. They drove ahead for five more minutes, rounding a gentle curve and facing down a long, empty stretch. They could see maybe five miles ahead, and there was nothing.

"Shit," Gaeton said, bringing the Mercedes down below a hundred. "He must have turned off somewhere."

"That, or he's in California by now."

He told Thorn to hold on, and he braked hard, swerving the car into a rest stop. There was a van load of nuns sitting at the cement picnic tables. They held their drumsticks still and watched as the Mercedes slid across the lot. Gaeton made a full one-eighty and fishtailed back onto the asphalt, giving Thorn a wink.

It took them twenty minutes of backtracking, but they found the Porsche parked in the lot of a Miccosukee Indian village. Gaeton parked beside the Porsche. In front of them was a gift shop in a rotting wood building. A hand-lettered sign propped beside the door advertised airboat rides and cases of cigarettes.

Thorn was about to get out of the car when Gaeton put a hand on his arm.

"I been meaning to give you this thing."

He pulled a small knife from his pocket, held it out for Thorn.

"What? A bribe?"

"Kind of," Gaeton said.

"That your dad's?" Thorn said. "His Buck?"

Thorn took it, examined it. It was a one-bladed Buck with a black, deep-grained handle.

Gaeton said, "I don't have any use for the thing anymore. And I thought, what with you into carving plugs now, maybe you'd like it."

"I don't know, Gaeton," Thorn said. "I appreciate it, but—"

"Take it, Thorn. Don't embarrass me."

"Well, thanks, man. Thanks very much," Thorn said. He opened the knife, tested the blade with his thumb. A razor. "I'd forgotten he did that, whittled."

Gaeton said, "You know, it was mainly trick stuff. Wood chains, balls in cages, stuff like that."

Thorn glanced at the old Indian woman watching them from the admission window.

"I know he'd like you to have it," Gaeton said. "Me, I've been carrying it around for years. I never use it but to clean my nails."

Thorn held the knife and was about to ask Gaeton to quit

bullshitting him and tell him what this was really all about, but his friend had turned and was getting out of the car. Thorn slipped the knife into his pocket and followed.

Gaeton explained to the old Indian woman in the admission window that they were looking for the owner of the Porsche. The woman stared at Gaeton, said nothing for a moment, then inspected Thorn. Finally she pointed into the compound. Gaeton pushed through the turnstile, and Thorn followed, past an even older Indian woman weaving a hat from palmetto fronds, through double swinging doors into a dusty yard.

There was their man. Claude was counting out some bills onto a weathered picnic table in front of a band of Miccosukee Indian boys. They were in jeans and dirty flannel shirts. Long, greasy black hair, cowboy hats and boots. Fat Samoan faces. They were slapping each other on the back, grinning.

Twenty yards away was the alligator pen. A young Indian boy was standing in front of a half dozen sleeping alligators. He was holding a pole about eight feet long, shaved to a sharp point. Another Indian boy was lashing the left wrist of the Porsche salesman to the side of the alligator pen. Naked and flat on his butt in the dust of the pen. His other wrist and both ankles were already roped to stakes. His bright clothes were strewn about. One tan Weejuns was in the corner of the mouth of one of the larger alligators. The reptile seemed to have fallen asleep midmunch.

"Would you fucking look at this," Gaeton said.

A couple of the Miccosukee boys noticed Gaeton and Thorn and moved to confront them. Protecting their cash position here.

"Hey, Claude," said Gaeton. "What the hell're you doing?"

Claude reached out and put an arm on the biggest boy's shoulder and halted him.

"No, these are my associates," Claude said.

Claude was standing in the shade of a chikee hut a few yards from the alligator pen. A few Indian women stood nearby, watching Claude, silently disapproving of all of this.

The car salesman hissed at Gaeton and Thorn. Apparently afraid to shriek and wake the gators. The boys who had tied him up had climbed out of the pen and were examining the pile of money on the table nearby.

"Hey, Claude, look," Gaeton said, putting his hand on the man's arm. "I think we got ourselves a cultural misunderstanding here. I mean, maybe in Jamaica, or wherever the hell you're from, you know, you guys are a little more heavy into the torture angle." Gaeton sent Thorn a look: Get ready to hit somebody. "But you know, we Americans, well, when we go out and buy a car, well, normally the guy that sells it to us, we like to let him live. At least for a while." He gave Thorn a quick smile. "I mean, I don't want to lecture you, God knows, but we're real close here to having a deceased citizen on our hands."

Thorn watched as the alligator that'd been chewing on the shoe came to life and took a few sluggish steps toward the naked man.

"Oh, shit, look out now," one of the Indian boys said. "That's Maximilian."

The Porsche salesman had decided to play dead. He was gazing back to Thorn and Gaeton, giving them a sad and painful face. He was ignoring the alligator, though surely he could hear the reptile dragging itself along, maybe already feel its breath on his ankle.

"Get some garfish," the oldest boy said to one of the others. "Hurry up, asshole." The young boy ran back into the main building.

"Me and my friends, we can dispose of the body," the oldest

boy said. "For another thousand."

"OK, that's it," Thorn said, pushing past the Miccosukees. He picked up the sharpened pole the young boy had used. Took a breath and climbed over the fence.

Maximilian was two yards from the car salesman when he fell asleep again. The loafer still hung out the corner of its mouth. Thorn squatted beside the man and began to work at the knot at his right wrist, holding the lance with one hand, untying with the other.

He had one wrist loose and had moved around to untie the other when the smallest of the alligators lifted its body and took a steady aim at Thorn, crossing the five yards of dusty ground with surprising speed.

Thorn jabbed the point at the reptile's mouth, dancing away to the right to draw it from the Porsche guy.

"Stick him in the nose," Thorn heard someone say. "In the nostrils!"

The gator paused, gathering itself, looking over the battlefield. Thorn glanced quickly over at Gaeton. He had his Colt out and had it leveled at the gator, a look for Thorn. No jokes. Just say the word.

Thorn looked back at the gator, drew the pole back carefully, and made a savage strike, but hit only teeth and gums. The car salesman had his left wrist free and was working frantically on his ankles. Thorn edged backwards, poking the air just between the eyes of the gator. It surged forward and got inside the striking point of Thorn's pole. He stumbled backwards, fell, and the alligator lunged at him.

A fish landed in the dust a yard from Thorn's face, and the alligator hesitated for a moment, cut its eyes toward the fish. It lowered itself and snapped it down. Thorn rolled to his left, got his feet back, and followed the car salesman across the fence.

They stood gasping, looking back into the pen.

"My shirt. My fucking jacket," the Porsche guy said.

Thorn stared at him.

"My goddamn outfit. Jesus Christ! Look at it."

Thorn kept staring at him.

Gaeton came up beside Thorn, putting away his Colt. His shoulder harness showed under his windbreaker.

"I would've shot," he said. "Except I couldn't remember if these things are endangered or not."

Thorn turned his stare to Gaeton.

"Hey," Gaeton said. "Just kidding. Just kidding."

And the man, Claude, was there, too, standing behind Gaeton, those green eyes, with their quiet burn, their lazy power. Then the man smiled at Thorn, but it wasn't a smile you smiled back at.

"Can we get that damn saw blade now?" Thorn said, turning to Gaeton, letting go of those green eyes, of that smile that was no smile.

Thorn drove the Porsche back to Miami, following the three of them in the Mercedes. By the time they reached the car lot, the salesman was yes-sirring Gaeton, almost bowing as they walked over to the showroom.

Thorn stood around in the showroom, while the salesman, Claude, and Gaeton sat inside the sales manager's office. The manager spoke with somebody on the phone. He talked for a while, then handed the phone to Gaeton. Gaeton spoke a few words and hung up. Everybody walked out of the office smiling one smile or another. Even Claude seemed docile.

Gaeton came across to Thorn, handed him the Mercedes keys.

"Go get your saw blade and go on home," he said. "I got to

clean up a couple more things here."

"That's it?"

"For now," Gaeton said. "We'll talk some more later."

"Well," said Thorn, "thanks for the entertainment."

4

When Thorn pulled the Mercedes into the grassy two acres where his house was going up, there was a white Monroe County Building and Zoning station wagon parked next to Jack Higby's rusty pickup. Jack had been helping Thorn rebuild the stilt house since September. They were about a week away from putting on the tin roof.

Jack was sitting out at the stone picnic table under the sapodilla, giving a sip of beer to his skinny black dog. There was a man in a white short-sleeved shirt and gray pants up on a stepladder inspecting the subflooring, scribbling on a clipboard. He glanced over as Thorn was getting out of the Mercedes.

Jack rose and came over to Thorn. Barefoot, his jeans bagging on his skinny body, and his long black beard flecked with sawdust. The building inspector started down the ladder.

Thorn waited for Jack by the car. The dog, Garfunkel, loped over to Thorn first, plunged his nose in Thorn's groin, and gave him the pubic lift. Thorn stooped and scratched the hound's throat. Jack checked out the brown Mercedes, lifted an eyebrow.

"Don't ask," Thorn said.

Jack said, "Well, we got us a problem here, partner."

"What is it?" Thorn said. "We too far over code?"

"Well, you talk to him," Jack said. "I hadn't done us no good with the man."

Thorn met the building inspector in the middle of the yard.

"George Carmel," the man said, putting out his hand. Thorn shook it. "You got yourself a real interesting house here, Mr. Thorn. Real interesting."

Thorn waited. The man was red-faced. He had an unhealthy glow, as if things were stretching to their limits just below his surface.

"Hey, could we get out of the sun?" Carmel said.

Thorn led him over to the shade the house was throwing. The man sat on a stump, shook out a cigarette, and gestured at Thorn with the pack. Thorn shook his head.

"I never seen wood like this before," Carmel said. He'd picked up a small piece of nara the size of a pencil box. "Weighs like lead," he said. "Must be hell to nail into."

"We're not using nails," Thorn said. "You didn't notice?"

Carmel smoked his cigarette and eyed Thorn.

He said, "Where's wood like this come from?"

"Borneo," Thorn said.

"Jesus," the man said. "Borneo. Where the headhunters are."

Thorn said nothing.

"How you come by it?"

"Port of Miami," Thorn said. "We take apart the cradles the Taiwanese use to ship their cheapo boats in. They're cutting down their hardwood forests to ship us plastic knock-off yachts."

"They charge you up there for that?"

"We're doing them a favor," Thorn said. "Saving them having to haul it off and burn it."

"That's where all of this comes from?" Carmel asked.

"Is this official?" Thorn said. "Some new regulations?"

"You're so touchy," the man said. "I see this strange wood, I just want to know where it all comes from. Like that siding you're using. That tamarind? From around here."

"Some of it," Thorn said. "There's mahogany, green heart; there's some Jamaican dogwood, buttonwood. Whatever we can scrounge."

"From developments?" Carmel said.

"Look," Thorn said. "These woods are legal. If somebody bulldozed a protected tree and left it along the highway and I come by and pick it up and shave it into planks, it's no crime."

"Well," Carmel said, "I'm no lawyer. But . . . You know, I'm just trying to spare you some aggravation. People spend a few years building their dream house, and they move in, tack down the carpets, switch on the TV, and then they find a red tag on their front door. They cheated here or there on the codes, or sometimes they just didn't even know the codes. There're so many little things to keep up with. And next thing they know, the whole thing has to come down. They're crying as the bulldozers roll into their yard. See? I'm just trying to spare you that."

"So spare me," Thorn said. "What's it take to spare me?"

"You married, Thorn?"

"No." Thorn looked over at Jack, sharing more of his beer with Garfunkel. A heron watching from the shoreline, waiting his turn.

"Well, you don't know then," Carmel said, shooting a look toward the Mercedes. "Wife wants to buy this and that, make the nest pretty. You know what Tupperware costs? Those plastic things? And the kid. Hey, if you're in the tenth grade, you can't just wear a pair of jeans. No, you got to have some red threads running this way and that. And birthdays, and anniversaries, and you have to take the old lady out to eat once or twice a week, keep her lubricating sufficiently."

"How much?" Thorn said.

"Two hundred," the man said. "You know, a couple of pair of jeans for the boy. Tupperware. Keep the veggies fresh."

"Get off my land," Thorn said.

"Yeah, yeah," the man said. "A man with morals, I like that."

"Sure you do."

Carmel stood up, brushed off his gray pants. His face had gotten redder in the shade. He flicked his butt into a oleander bush nearby.

"Give you one more chance," Carmel said, uninterested now. He drew his ball-point out of his shirt pocket, clicked it a few times.

"If you're not off my land in about thirty seconds, you're going to be picking exotic Far Eastern hardwoods out of your lower tract."

The man looked at Thorn and squeezed his face into a sour smirk. He dashed off a quick scribble on his clipboard, took a thumbtack out of his shirt pocket. He stepped over to one of the cedar telephone poles, the stilts that Thorn and Jack had augered into the coral bedrock. The man fastened a red tag to it.

"You're officially out of business," Carmel said, looking into the bureaucratic middle distance. "You want a list of your violations and methods of compliance, you come to the county building anytime Monday through Friday, ten to two. But let me tell you something, wild man. You so much as start up a power saw on this place, and you're bunking with the sweethearts at the county jail."

He walked back to his station wagon, got in, and drove away.

Jack and Garfunkel came over.

"Well?" Jack said.

"Let's take the afternoon off, Jack. Go rip the faces off some barracuda. How 'bout it?"

"Whatever you think," Jack said. "Whatever makes you happy."

Darcy Richards stood in front of the WBEL weather map and pointed to the satellite photo of a front pushing down from Canada. It was the first major Arctic invasion of the season, a five-hundred-mile-wide glacial arm stretching through the Midwest and into North Georgia, its wispy fingers already tickling Atlanta.

"Well, the radar boys tell me this is a fizzler. They say it's going to run out of momentum in Jacksonville. But I say this is the real thing, a genuine Siberian express hiding in a dip in the jet stream." Darcy smiled into the lights. "Right on schedule, second week in January. So, I'm warning you, get out your camel hair coats. It's gonna get damn cold this weekend."

The national temperatures flickered into place behind her, and the producer whispered into her earphone, "Temps, temps."

Darcy said, "You know, the station pays a fortune for these electronics, but to tell the truth, that's mainly to trick you folks into thinking we know what we're talking about."

"Come on, Darcy," said the voice in her ear. "Easy now."

"What I think is, we've blown it. I think we've put too much fancy jargon between us and the weather. Low-pressure ridge, tropopause, adiabatic changes. We've gotten as bad as lawyers. As my daddy used to say, if you want to change the world, first thing you got to do is start calling things by their right names."

The voice said, "Eight, seven, six, tossing it back to Jill and Mike, five . . ."

Darcy stepped toward the camera, to the edge of the set. She stood there for a moment and smiled at the cameraman, who was smiling at her. Right with her.

"So, I'm saying it plain. It's gonna get damn cold."

The young man and woman sitting at the WBEL's news central desk grinned like maniacs as Darcy took her seat again next to the black sportscaster.

The male anchor turned his bright teeth on Darcy. "Well, we can always count on you, Darcy, to tell it like it is."

Darcy nodded to him and then nodded into the lights.

The female anchor started in on the Hollywood news notes, something about a young actress dating one of the Kennedy boys.

Ozzie Hardison switched off the television set and stood there, getting his breath back. Bonnie, his old lady, was hammering on the front door, but Ozzie didn't move. He was holding on as long as he could to the weatherlady's face, her body. For months now he'd been planning on liberating a VCR from some weekend house around Key Largo so he could tape her and play her back, put her on freeze-frame, slo-mo. Count her freckles.

"You dorkus, open the door!" Bonnie got one eye up into the little window near the top of the door and yelled at him. "You dickbrain!" She hammered some more, clacking her beer bottle against that little window.

Ozzie walked into the bedroom, wiped some sweat from his lip. He was still feeling weak. Man, the weatherlady had looked good tonight. A dark blouse, light skirt, her thick hair simple and straight. Just the way he liked it. Hippie chick hair, bangs coming close to her eyes. The color was more red than blond. And tonight she'd even licked her lips once; that drove Ozzie right across the line, made him grab his hard-on through his jeans and squeeze.

Bonnie banged and banged on that door. A neighbor across in the Bomb Bay Village trailer park yelled at her to shut up. She screamed back at him to piss up a palm tree, and she went right back to pounding on the door, down to a good steady rhythm.

It was Friday, so the weatherlady would be pulling into her trailer in a couple of hours, spending another weekend in Key Largo. Shacked up with that blond asshole. Ozzie didn't know what she saw in that white bread guy. Mr. Neat. Mr. Haircut. But then it didn't really matter. 'Cause Mr. White Bread wasn't long for this earth. Ozzie could just tell.

Darcy drove her Fiat Spider up Biscayne Boulevard, watching the wind shake the cabbage palms. She breathed in that hint of ozone, an electrical turbulence from the first collision between the strands of cold, dry air and the sultry high-pressure ridge over Florida.

The squall line would arrive by Sunday. A wall of boiling black fog, storms breaking out along the edge where the two air masses clashed. Those squalls could be more turbulent, do more damage, than some hurricanes.

And these were the charged hours before it happened. When the first opposing scouts met and struggled briefly and quietly at twenty-five thousand feet. All that icy air piling into a rounded prow as it advanced. The air closer to the ground slowed down by friction against the earth. Stringy gray nimbostratus clouds reaching out, the upper air unstable.

As usual she had had an early hint of it, something like the tartness of green apples in the back of the throat, a quiet burn in the sinuses. It was something no radar could trace and no normal person would even give words to. But it was her work and the nearest thing to a gift she had.

It wasn't a sense or a superstition, didn't reside in the nose, the bunions, or any section of her viscera. It was the weight and color of the air, the taste in her lungs, the vibrations her bones could hear, the odor of light. Weather moved through her as if she were permeable, and she extracted from the currents their messages, whispers of where they had come from, where headed.

She drove the Coconut Grove route tonight. Wangled through a complicated intersection governed only by yield signs. Nearly got hit by a Ford, honked at by a black pickup truck. Yield signs! Deputy sheriffs were unloading footlockers of cocaine at the Port of Miami at noon. What made anybody think yield signs still worked?

She'd heard that almost every bill above a twenty in South Florida had been found to be dusted with traces of the drug. Little white footprints, ghost tracks. Death dust everywhere. It was in the air, maybe giving everyone a faint high all the time, getting in there and making the synapses fire a little hotter. Maybe that was causing the quicker pulse on the streets. The silt of cocaine on every bill. It got into the blood and simmered on low, rendering the brain down little by little to a thick broth of its former self.

As her front wheels hit the rough asphalt of the Bomb Bay Village trailer park, all the automatic streetlights in the village switched on. She drew the Fiat up onto the cement slab outside Gaeton's silver Airstream. The place had become her weekend retreat for the last few months.

A brown Mercedes was parked in front of the mobile home and Thorn was lying in the recliner on her porch, shaded from the twilight by a green and white awning that was attached to one side of the Airstream. The lights switching on like that, Thorn over for a rare visit, the first major front coming. Darcy felt a foolish surge of happiness. Signs, signs, a world of signs. Things on the verge of change.

Thorn was her brother's friend really. He and Gaeton had been grade school and high school buddies and she'd been the tag-along sister, three years younger, but because even then she had an instinct for the weather, the tides and resulting movement of fish, they'd let her come along, a kind of human barometer.

How does this feel, Darcy? Over there by the sandbar?

No, farther, by that stand of mangroves.

Thorn had always asked her how she did it, trying to learn it in the way you'd learn to read the depths by the tint of water. But it wasn't anything *out there*. It drifted somewhere in her consciousness. Something so wispy that the moment she began to try to describe it to him, it would vanish.

Thorn smiled as she opened her car door. He always seemed to pick up the pace of her pulse. He was rawboned and tanned. His eyes looked at you. They didn't slide off. They were blue and deep-set beneath thick blond eyebrows. He'd let his sun-singed hair get a bit shaggy, and there was a mistiness in his eyes she didn't remember, but considering all that had happened to him lately, he was still Thorn. The only guy she'd ever trusted enough to tell about her gift. The only guy who even came close to being the fisherman she was.

5

"Hey, stranger," she said, settling into the recliner beside him. She looked at him more closely. "Thorn, you OK? You look spooked."

"Yeah, yeah, I'm fine," he said. "Really." He smiled to show her how fine he was. "Just came over to drop off Gaeton's car." He nodded at the Mercedes.

"Oh, boy," she said. "What've you two been up to?"

"Well, now that's a story," Thorn said. He had a Budweiser in his hand, four empties on the cement beside his recliner. He'd been picturing that alligator, its jaws wide, its eyes empty. It made him very thirsty.

Thorn tore out the last beer from the six-pack and offered it to Darcy. She took it, drained a third of it, gasped, and said, "I could use a good story."

He took a small sip and looked up at the last shreds of daylight. A sulfurous golden glow, like honey swirled with blood, shone in the west through a tangle of telephone poles and palm fronds. From down the row of trailers, Bruce Springsteen began to wail. The old couple sitting out on their porch across the street stood up, glared down the street, then across at Thorn and Darcy as though they were accomplices, and went inside their trailer, and turned on their chuffing air conditioner.

He told her about the morning, keeping it light, and when he was finished, she was quiet. He took another sip from his beer, watching the last light take the red in Darcy's hair, leaving a flicker where her eyes were.

She said, all business, "And did you stay around, see how he handled the Porsche guy?"

"Yeah," Thorn said. "They made some calls, worked it all out."

Darcy sighed.

"This company Gaeton works for, it's what, a rent-a-cop thing?"

"No," she said. "It's bigger than that. It's international." There was something odd in her voice, as if she wanted to say more, maybe debating it.

"Gaeton asked me to help him with something he's working on."

"Well, now that's just great."

"What're you so pissed about?" Thorn looked at her through the final stages of twilight, tried to read her face. But the parts that mattered were gone.

She sighed again, said, "I just don't like to see him mixing you up in his business, that's all."

"It's OK, I need a break," Thorn said. "I been working nonstop on the house. It's good to get out, see how the world's going."

"Yeah, yeah," she said. "Maybe you two deserve each other."

This was a new Darcy. Not little sister Darcy. Not Miss Congenial, Miss Monroe County, Runner-up Miss Florida. That Darcy, who never froze her smile into place like the other beauty queens but really seemed to enjoy it, standing up there in a bathing suit, as if it were too goofy not to enjoy. Only reason she was runner-up to Miss Florida was that Darcy had not really given a shit about the whole thing, and when they asked her what she wanted to do with her crown if she won, she said to nail it on the wall just below the 110-pound tarpon she hauled in last summer. That was that. It got a laugh. And second place.

But this new Darcy had a tang of bitterness in her voice. A nervous impatience that Thorn assumed came from working in Miami all week, only getting back home on the weekends. As if she were taking on the accent of the fast-lane Miami hotshots she had to work with.

"I'm sorry, Thorn." She reached over, touched his hand briefly. "Don't mind me. I'm just going through something. I don't know. Maybe it's El Cambio. Hot flashes, loss of procreative urge. General aimlessness."

"Maybe it's just a tropical depression," he said.

"I'm serious, Thorn," she said. "I read about this. It's like a disease that everybody gets, middle-age measles. It's on page one twenty-three of that book, whatever it's called. A person turns thirty-six, the longing genes switch on. You start thinking about Yeats, him saying that life was a long preparation for something that never happens. You just got to wait it out. Twenty pages farther in that book, your genes are going to throw something else at you. May take a few years, but it happens."

"And while you're waiting?"

"That's what I'm working on at the moment," she said. "A whole new career. I'm sick of predicting the future. I'd like to *cause* the future, make something happen."

Thorn said, "If your genes are going to change you anyway, why do anything? You could just lie around, watch the clouds for five years till life had meaning again. Rediscover your navel."

He liked being a little boozy. You could have conversations like this. He couldn't remember the last time he'd said "life" and "meaning" in the same sentence. Maybe never.

She said, "Even you, Thorn. You're not immune. You roll a rock in front of your cave, but that won't stop the changes. That's my point. It doesn't matter what you do, whether you're striving or not striving, you still change."

"All I'm striving for is to finish my damn house," he said. "Live on land again. I'm sick of that boat. I turn around, I hit my head on something. I turn the other way, I hit the other side." He sipped his beer, and they were quiet for a moment. She kicked off her leather pumps, and Thorn watched her wiggle her toes, playing scales in the air.

She said, "Sometimes I think, just quit your complaining, Darcy. You're the weatherlady. You're the vivacious beauty queen with the big knockers. What're you bitching about?"

"Big knockers?" Thorn said.

"Yeah," she said. "I had large breasts once. You never noticed? I had them all through high school. It's how I got hired at WBEL. Out to here." She motioned in the dark. "A couple of years ago I had an operation, had them reduced. I was sick of them. My back hurting all the time. You men don't know about big breasts."

"We're always happy to learn."

She was silent. Down the row of trailers, Bruce Springsteen was getting weepy about steelworkers and their bars. Pushing his voice down into his throat, between a grunt and a C flat.

"Size doesn't matter," Thorn said. "They say it's not the size of the dog in the fight, it's the size of the fight in the dog."

"You guys got a million of those," she said. "I heard 'em all. It's not the length of your wand, it's the magic with which you wave it. Horse pucky."

"OK, we're in touchy territory here. I'm sorry, I thought we were still joking."

"Yeah," she said. "We are, I guess."

They listened to Bruce going on about the shot-and-a-beer guys, Thorn thinking he could use a couple of shots just now.

She said, "Only guy I ever knew who didn't feed me one of those lines had a dick like a sequoia. So figure it out."

Thorn said, "I don't think I know you well enough to be having this conversation."

"I don't know *anyone*," she said, "well enough to be having this conversation."

The moon was a smudge of light behind thick clouds out in the Florida Straits. Thorn took a fast ride out there, cruising weightless along his line of sight. It was a boyhood game he'd played on those nights when the island fever burned too hot. He stayed out there for a moment or two, got some order back in his head, then came back slowly to that island, that trailer park, that chair, that body grown heavy with drink.

The bathroom in the mobile home was smaller than the head on Thorn's Chris Craft. And the racket he was making in there, mainlining five Budweisers into the john, blotted out Springsteen. When Thorn was finished, he washed up, checked his face in the mirror. The beers had taken root in his eyes. He experimented with a happier look, lifting his eyebrows, forcing a momentary shimmer to his eye, raising the corners of his mouth. But it was grotesque, a drunk's cockeyed smile.

Darcy was waiting for him in the dark living room. She was leaning against the doorsill, looking out at the sky, holding on to the brass door lock chain.

"Another front coming?" he said.

"Yeah," she said. "But a high-pressure ridge's deflecting it at the moment."

He came up to her side. Snagged the toe of his boat shoe on the edge of the rug and stumbled into her shoulder. She turned and put out her hand to steady him, and it slipped into his shirt, grazed across his chest. She smiled and began to slide it out, but Thorn covered it with his hand, kept it there. One of her finger-tips pressing against his nipple.

"I'm a little drunk," he said. But he didn't release her hand.

She brought her other hand up slowly and touched his face. Fingertips reading the stubble on his cheeks, braille, a message there. Then a slow tracing of his eyebrows, nose, upper lip, up the cheekbone, and brushing the hair at his temples. Thorn felt a flood of warmth rise inside him. His eyes swimming. The muscles in his neck relaxing as well. He gave himself over to this ticklish tour.

Her hand circled his neck, back-combed up through his hair, and cupped his head. He let her have some of its weight. Holding there, cradling his skull.

"Are you drunk?" he said. Drowsy, his head floating in her palm.

"No," she said. "Stone cold sober."

"Good."

After a time he opened his eyes, looked at her now, at the moonlit face, sideburns of down. He lifted a finger, brought it to that dust of hair on her cheek, ruffled it against the grain of the light till it was a milky powder.

He brought his face to hers, their mouths aligning, but not a kiss. Holding off the hunger. Their lips grazed, adjusting, making the slightest calibrations of angle and shape as if they were whispering into each other's breaths. Both of them trying to make this first kiss, this one which Thorn did not even realize until now that he had been waiting for for a very long time, to make it as close to perfect as possible.

And it was.

6

"I didn't kill anybody till I was twenty-eight," Papa John said. "What's your hurry?"

Ozzie said, "I'm thirty-two, for christ sakes."

John lit another Camel and rubbed the thumb of his smoking hand across the beard stubble on his throat. He eyed Ozzie through the smoke. Ozzie was wiping down the bar with a wet, greasy rag, putting a fleeting shine on the mahogany. The guy wasn't at all what Papa John had had in mind. He was a Florida Cracker for one thing. Worse than an ordinary redneck. You couldn't teach Crackers anything. They had undescended brains.

It was three o'clock in the morning. It'd been another slow Friday night. Used to be that the Bomb Bay Bar was the axis of the universe in Key Largo. You didn't come to this island and not squeeze into Papa John's place some time or other.

But something had happened. Some tilt he couldn't quite figure out. Now just an occasional tourist might stick his head in Papa John's place, maybe even step inside, but then he'd stop and give him a little embarrassed wave and he'd leave. Was it some smell he couldn't smell? Fuck if he knew.

It wasn't the money that bothered him. He still had enough scams going down, enough cash stacking up out on his boat. No, what bothered him was the lie of it all. Here he was, the original thing. A Conch, sixty-three nonstop years on the islands. Half of that he'd spent running Papa John's Bar in Key West, the rest of it bouncing around the Keys, making some smuggling runs, pot, rum, Uzis once, always on the lookout for a place with the fishing camp feel that Key West had lost. And then fifteen years ago he'd found it in Key Largo.

Now Key Largo was losing it. The hot tubs and wooden decks, pastels had arrived. Fancy stores were festering along the highway, full of plastic geegaws you wouldn't believe. Turning shit to chic. Everybody trying to snag the tourists on their way to Key West. Now the island was full of fern bars with brass railings and speakers seven feet tall. Bars with names of tropical fruits, Mangoes, Pineapples, Papayas. And the tourists dancing the night away while some guy did his Jimmy Buffet calypso imitation. All of them thinking this is the real Key Largo. Hey, let's boogie. It bothered the fuck out of him.

And then just this week John had heard talk that the Rotary Club was looking around for another Captain Kidd, the honorary king of Old Pirate Days. Papa John had had a lock on that for the last twelve years. He'd ride at the head of the parade, toss out gold foil-wrapped candy, while he swigged from his rum bottle.

For a lot of the last decade Papa John had Monroe County by the balls. He'd made decisions right there on that barstool that had changed the island, shit, the whole chain of Keys forever-fucking-after. His photo had even been in the Chamber of Commerce brochure. Colorful local characters. Now look at him, at this place.

"When I was thirty-two, I'd already done a ton of living," John said, looking around at the photos on the walls of his bar, trying to find 1953, tickle his memory a little. He pointed his Camel toward a photo near the women's bathroom. "There it is."

The photo showed Papa John standing on the docks in Key West next to Ernest Hemingway and one of Hemingway's pals, some guy from New York, an editor or agent. Behind them, hanging from the rack, was an 388-pound blue marlin. Papa John was standing a foot to the right of the great man, holding the 40-pound rod that Hemingway had used. Papa John had led them to the spot, walked Hemingway through the whole thing, had practically swum down there and stuck the rigged ballyhoo in that marlin's face.

Papa John said, "You don't kill somebody soon, you could wind up like that guy, blowing his head off with a shotgun. Guy had a lifetime hard-on to kill somebody. Kept going to war, never got a shot in. Best he ever got around to was on safari, water buffalo or some shit."

"Who is it?" Ozzie was using that greasy fucking rag to wipe the sweat from his forehead. John groaned to himself.

"Who is it?" Papa John said. "Good God, boy. You made it to the what grade?"

"Fifth," Ozzie said, a hint of anger showing.

"That's Hemingway. Ernest Hemingway. The great man. The guy who made me rich, people looking to sit on the barstool where the great man farted. He was a farter, too."

"I know who fucking Hemingway is. I'm not stupid." Ozzie wiped at the bar. He looked up and said, "I *did* kill a colored man once. But I just left him for dead, so I don't count that."

John sipped his beer and dragged some more smoke in on top of the cool burn. Maybe he was wrong. He'd kept Ozzie around for the last few weeks 'cause of this feeling that the kid was capable of something bigger. It would come and go. About the time Ozzie seemed hopeless, he'd come out with something like this, and Papa John would go, well, maybe he's got potential after all.

Ozzie told his story. How he'd been out driving and he came up behind this black man in a pickup and got the black man to pull over. Out on one of those farm roads around Tallahassee you can't believe they ever bothered building in the first place 'cause it doesn't go anywhere. So he gets this black guy alongside the road and he gets out of the car and he goes over to him and the black guy is all, yes sir, no sir. And he's got a yappy white dog with him, never stops barking. So Ozzie, and he's with some other guy, another loser, tried to go to Vietnam but his arrest record was too long, so this guy is pissed at everybody, and Ozzie starts getting pissed at this little dog, yapping.

"How'd you get a nigger to pull over like that out on some country road?"

"I used the siren and the lights."

"What siren?"

"I was driving a police car."

"What!"

"Billy Dell's, that's the boy I was with, his stepdaddy was deputy sheriff. We took his car and we're out chasing people. Spooking the spooks."

"Jesus Christ, Ozzie, a police car." Now that's why he kept the kid around.

So Ozzie reached across this black man and grabbed that dog. What else was the kid leaving out? The dog a pit bull? The black guy six feet seven? Papa John made a note to work on the boy's storytelling. I mean, that was what this was all about anyway, wasn't it? John wanted to leave behind somebody to sit where John was sitting and talk to the tourists late at night, holding them by the lapels like the Ancient Mariner in that poem, dragging them back to when men were full-size.

So Ozzie had the guy in the ditch by the time John got back to it. He and his buddy were holding the black man's face down into a little ditchwater. The other guy was going a little berserk, talking Klan talk, kill talk. And Ozzie was holding on to the black man, sounded like just for more or less symbolic contact.

The other guy found a Coke bottle lying nearby the ditch and gave the black man a blast to the back of the head. Then another one and a few more. And he handed it to Ozzie, and Ozzie was scareder of his buddy by that time than of the bleeding body, so he took a couple of turns.

"And we got back in the car and drove off," Ozzie said.

"You mean you got back in the police car. Were the lights still flashing the whole time? Did you turn them off while you were killing this guy? You still holding the fucking dog or what? There's some details here, some shit that you need to say to set the stage."

Ozzie looked at Papa John, eyes blank and watery as soap bubbles.

"The fuck difference does it make, the lights were on or off? We left this guy for dead. That's the story. That's the point. We drove off and left the guy and his dog. I broke the dog's tail just as we were leaving."

"Holy shit," Papa John said, and he stubbed out his Camel in the mother-of-pearl shell. "That's what I mean. You broke the dog's fucking tail. That's a detail. That's a weird fucking fact should be in the story. In the main part of it. Not some afterthought. You broke the dog's fucking tail. I mean, I never heard of that before. Never seen it, heard of it, nothing."

Ozzie said, "So what? I'm supposed to tell every little diddley-squat thing that happened? The guy had garlic breath, I'm supposed to say that? He was wearing a gas station shirt, his fingernails were greasy, shit like that?"

This wasn't going to be easy. Papa John finished his Bud. He gripped the longneck bottle by the throat and smacked it against the bar. Ozzie took a step back. Papa John held up the jagged remains like it was a microphone and he was about to interview this Cracker, see what made him so stupid.

"What? What?"

Jesus, the kid's eyes got slimy when he was scared, like oily tears were building up in there.

Papa John stood up, walked a few steps so he was just across from Ozzie, the bar between them. He lunged the bottle at the kid, drove him back against the cash register. He took another swish at him. He didn't know if he really wanted to cut the kid or not. Probably yes.

Ozzie was panting. His eyes sparking. Probably a little curl of shit appearing.

His voice came to him finally. "So, I don't tell stories as good as you think I should. That what's got you so pissed?"

Papa John held that ragged bottle out, making his face take on a crafty look, feinting a little with that hand. He felt as if he had a direct line to the boy's pulse. Up, up, up, up.

"Is it so fucking important I broke the dog's tail or didn't? It's my story, ain't it? Can't I tell it how the fuck ever I want to, can't I?"

"No," Papa John said, getting every bit of bass he had into his voice. "You got to know how to tell a goddamn story. The right way. You can't learn that, then forget all the rest of it. You're no use to me. I can get any cripple covered with weeping sores in off the highway to sell my pot and do B and E for me. You think that's what I want you for, that petty shit?"

Ozzie held that rag, stared at John, a hazy smile coming and going.

Papa John said, "You got some of the skills you'll need to work with me. But you haven't got them all. Sooner you just admit to that, sooner we can get on with your fucking education. Is that goddamned clear enough for you?"

"It is," Ozzie said.

John put the bottle down and sat back on his stool. Ozzie

finished wiping everything down, glancing over at John and that broken bottle. He put all the beer steins back on the shelves behind the bar. He got everything just like Papa John had shown him and shown him again. Ozzie was learning the rules even if he was about as bright as an escapee from the moron farm.

When he'd finished cleaning the bar, Papa John was still sitting there smoking his Camels, drinking another beer, watching the dark spaces around the rafters.

Ozzie stepped up behind him, holding his guitar.

Ozzie said, "I know who it is I'm going to kill. I picked him out."

John closed his eyes. Maybe if he counted to ten thousand, his blood pressure would go down. He opened his eyes and looked at Ozzie. His personal albatross. He'd been looking for a son, and the gods sent him this poor doofus.

"Yeah?" Papa John said. "You going after a poodle this time. St. Bernard?"

"He's that blond guy, lives around here. Shacking up with the TV lady."

Papa John smacked his open hand on the bar; then he caught himself, took a breath. Was the kid joking him with all this murder talk?

"Look, Oz," John said, letting more smoke out as he spoke, "you want to earn a merit badge with me? Then keep your old lady quiet, OK? I'm getting nothing but complaints from the trailer park. It's the fucking noise from your place, the screaming and bitching. They can't hear 'Hollywood Squares' 'cause of the noise. You want to kill somebody so bad, kill Harriet."

"Her name's Bonnie."

"Harriet," Papa John said. "It's a joke. Ozzie and Harriet."

"I don't get it."

Papa John sucked a deep drag on the cigarette, let it drift back out his nose, squinting at Ozzie the whole time, not sure if the boy was putting him on or not.

Ozzie said, "So, now I can play, right?"

Ozzie switched on all the spotlights first, got them aimed just like he liked them. He climbed up on the four-by-four stage where back a few years ago the topless dancers had wiggled all night. Ozzie hitched his guitar on and spent a minute tuning it up. John shook his head. Jesus, the kid was twelve years old.

Ozzie pretended to switch on an invisible mike, lowered it a few inches, and screwed it tight. Tapped it. The mood was coming on him now; all the shit he'd taken from John just seemed to whoosh out of his head. He strummed that opening C, then found G.

> It was forty years ago, he came to town
> riding on a shrimp truck through the middle of the night,
>
> looking for a fight, smelling like a hound,
> driving through the dark to that neon bright.
> That neon island in the sea, the dark dark sea.
>
> It was forty years ago, he came to town
> riding on a shrimp truck in the middle of the night,
> a lover of whores, a fighter, and a clown. . . .

Papa John watched the boy looking soulfully out at the empty bar, watched him strumming that scarred-up guitar and tapping his flip-flop out of rhythm to the song. He was no Hank Williams, but he had a passable voice. Not much style, but John was giving him advice there, too. Look mean, get more smoke in your voice. Say a few words before you start in hammering on that guitar. Stuff like that.

Ozzie was a good-looking boy in a cheap, shifty way. He'd

brought that song in one night, proud as could be. And he'd gotten up there and sung it to Papa John, just the two of them in the bar. And damn if John hadn't felt the hot burn of tears rising inside. The boy had him hooked.

Now he let Ozzie get up there and sing the song every night, a sort of taps. Times like this Papa John thought maybe he was being too hard on the boy. Maybe it was time to give him a little more responsibility than driving the ice cream truck. Sometime soon maybe he'd even take the boy out on his boat, do some target practice, see if the boy had any kind of eye.

7

To the north the sky was jammed with the alternating light-dark scales of a mackerel sky. A few fat cumuli hovered to the south, their edges whipped into feathery mare's tails. A sign the wind had shifted up there and soon would switch down below.

Thorn watched as Jack Higby parked his pickup next to the VW. Since August the convertible top on the VW had been stuck in the open position. He didn't see much point in fixing it. Maybe he'd just drill a hole in the floorboard when the summer rains began.

Thorn was working the lathe. Since daybreak that Saturday morning, he'd had it going. He was turning one-and-an-eighth-inch squares of mahogany, bringing them down to one-inch pegs. He had found a soothing, dead-brained motion, dropping one peg every minute or so into a straw basket. Those pegs were holding the house together. Stronger than nails, they'd give it flex enough to keep it from snapping apart in a hurricane and sailing off to Yucatán.

That particular chunk of mahogany had come from a tree knocked down by Hurricane Floyd that he'd found at the county dump. He hadn't paid a nickel yet for wood. In fact, they were about a third done on the house and were only up to three hundred dollars total. Most of that was for gas to Miami and some blades. Higby was going to take his wages out in fishing trips on the *Heart Pounder*. Thorn figured he owed Jack about six years of good hard fishing by now.

Jack came over and watched Thorn work for a minute, then yelled over the bray of the lathe, "What about them red tags?"

Thorn shut the machine off and stepped away from it, dusting the spray of sawdust from his arms. "I'll go down the building department Monday, see what the jerk wrote us up for. We could just catch up today, the pegs, whatever you think."

"Well, then I'm going to tackle that sink again," Jack said.

As Thorn got back to work with the pegs, Jack fastened the big chunk of lignum vitae to the standup Blaisedell lathe. It was a machinist's drill press that Jack had converted. It had a Model A five-speed transmission and must've weighed a thousand pounds. Jack had gotten the idea that Thorn should have a wood sink in his bathroom. He'd cut off an eighteen-inch section of the trunk of that tree and was smoothing a basin into it. It was becoming a pretty thing.

A welder down on Big Pine Key had hauled that lignum vitae tree up one afternoon a month ago. He said it'd been struck by lightning and had been lying out in his backyard for five years. The man had stood there, ready to leave, looking at the tree he was leaving behind. He told Thorn, if he wanted to bring back the smell of that wood, nice honeydew aroma, he'd have to treat it like a woman he'd been married to for fifty years. All the smell's still in there, he said, but you have to rough her up a little to get it back.

Thorn watched Jack turning that sink for a few minutes, then stepped back and looked at the skeleton of his house. It was at a stage now, there were a dozen projects to choose from. He could mill the siding boards or spend the day doubling up the top plates for the roof trusses. Or set up the builder's level, that telescope on a tripod, and shoot all the levels, going from corner to corner, making sure everything was dead even, shimming up the low spots.

Or he could stretch out in the hammock, have a beer from the cooler. He could watch Jack work for a while. Lie back and feel the new stirring in his chest that Darcy Richards had set off.

Deputy Sheriff Sugarman rolled into Thorn's yard at that moment. In his patrol car, and in uniform. And as he got out of the patrol car, Thorn could see he was in a bad mood. The way he huffed when he had to open the door again and pull out a wad of papers. The stiff, military way he walked across the yard toward Thorn. The sharp nod he gave Jack as he walked past the scream of the lathe. The tug he gave the zipper on his jacket.

Normally he was a handsome man. Dark eyes, straight, thin nose, *café con leche* skin. A short Afro. Harry Belafonte as a young man, riding the lobster boats ashore. A couple of inches over six feet, just taller than Thorn. But you wouldn't call this man stalking across the yard handsome, not today.

Up close, his anger was even more obvious. He glared at Thorn, shoulders heavied down, an almost imperceptible shake of his head. If they hadn't been closest friends since they were six years old, Thorn might've run for cover. As it was, he said, "What'd I do now?"

"Nothing," Sugarman said.

"Whew, that's a relief. I was getting palpitations."

"No, no, buddy. This nothing is a bad nothing. This nothing is a nothing that should've been something."

Sugarman looked off at the dark line of clouds to the north.

"Thorn, you didn't file for a permit, you don't have a licensed contractor, you got no proper plans."

"I have plans," Thorn said. "Yeah, I do, over there."

He hustled over to a stack of mahogany siding boards beside the stone barbecue pit, looking for that book of poetry by John Ashbery. Thorn had found it in a remaindered bin at the Book Nook. He'd bought it because he liked the name, Ashbery. But the poems seemed to be encrypted by the insane. So Thorn was using the printed pages to start the nightly charcoal and the blank end pages to sketch on.

He found the page with the plans sitting on the barbecue pit and brought it back to Sugarman.

"This is just a box," Sugarman said. "A box on six stilts."

"Exactly right," Thorn said. "Our plans."

"Give me a break, man. This is worthless. You need detailed blueprints."

"Look at the house, Sugar," Thorn said. "We're doing fine with these plans."

"That's not the point."

"What is?"

"Well, the point is somebody has a wild hair at Building and Zoning, and they're going to make your life shitty till you go along with the rules for once. That's all there is to it. And next time they send a cop out here it won't be me, and it won't be a warning. They'll put you in the tank."

Sugarman frowned, massaged his brow, his receding hairline.

"How's the food in the jail these days?" Thorn said. "Still serving tacos on Fridays?"

"You never quit, do you?"

"What's to quit?" Thorn said. "It's still us against them, isn't it, Sugar?"

"I'm afraid it's us against you, Thorn, this time anyway," he said. He let his eyes drop from Thorn's, studied the ground between them. "There's rules," he said to the dirt. "You either play by them, or you get screwed. That's just how it is."

The load on Sugar's shoulders was bearing down. He was shaking his head. He seemed to be doing that a lot lately. Saying oh, no, not this again. No, I don't believe this.

Thorn said, "What is it, Sugar? You look terrible."

Sugarman settled against the edge of the maple workbench. He shook his head again.

"I just helped slide two decomposed teenagers into body bags," he said. They were out in the weather at least a week, at Dynamite Docks. The raccoons'd been at them."

"A drug deal," Thorn said.

"Looked that way," he said. "Just a couple of Miami high school kids."

"That's tough," Thorn said.

"Days like this, I think it may be time for another forty-day flood. Wash it all clean and just start over."

"Yeah, well," Thorn said, looking off at the darkening sky. "The problem with that is, nowadays it's the bad guys who have all the arks."

Gaeton Richards sat on the edge of the motel bed. He watched Myra Rostovitch standing in front of the window, sipping her coffee from a large Styrofoam cup. The light was leaking in around the venetian blinds now. It was still before eight on Saturday. He listened to the traffic on Calle Ocho, the blat of motorcycles, Cuban voices arguing in the parking lot.

She ran her fingers down the blinds, flattening them a bit more. There was a shine in her curly black hair.

A year ago Gaeton would've risen from the bed and kissed her, turned her around and unzipped that gray dress, rolled down her panty hose, and led her to the cool sheets. They would've stayed the weekend, their handguns on the bedside tables.

"Adamson sick or what?" Gaeton said.

Myra Rostovitch said, "Things have changed, Gaeton. Adamson's out of it. I'm taking it over from here on."

She blew on her coffee, paced in front of the TV, sipping it.

Yeah, things had changed all right. But she hadn't. She was still inside herself. Still could work a stretch of silence as well as anybody he'd ever seen. Turn it into some kind of drama or make it sexy. He'd seen people talk for an hour and not say as much as Myra got out of a minute of dead air.

"You know I'll have to call Adamson, check this out."

Myra nodded, still pacing, staring into her coffee.

She sat down in the Danish modern chair across the room, crossed her legs, set her cup on the bureau.

"Gaeton," she said, "there's been a fuck-up. A major one."

Now Gaeton tried it, the thing she did with the silence. But it didn't have the same effect. It just lay there.

Finally he said, "A fuck-up."

She studied him carefully.

"It was a simple case of the right hand not knowing what the hell the left was up to," she said.

"Give it to me," he said. "I can probably handle it."

"Well, it all sounds perfectly reasonable when you list it out," she said. "Adamson gave us the history of it, from his point of view. Last January one of his confidential informants gives him

Benny Cousins's name, suggests Benny may be consorting with known felons for unknown purposes. Adamson is intrigued. Former DEA official up to no good. It sounded like it was worth a look. So he put you down there. It made sense it should be you. You already had a network of contacts in the Keys. You were the obvious choice. It could be a RICO case, racketeering, whatever. Adamson OK's it; you go undercover, move down there; the bureau drops some taxpayer money on it.

"And let me tell you, you did a good job. Buddied right up to Benny. In six months you were his number one man. And you've got a case on him, no question. I've seen your reports, bribery, extortion, conspiracy. Some of it is maybe a little dirty, entrapmentwise, and a trifle rinky-dink, but still, it's a case."

"Rinky-dink?" Gaeton cocked his head at her. He tried to get her to smile one of those old smiles, one of the coded ones they had. But she wouldn't snag on to his eyes. He said, "Last time I looked, bribery of a public official, racketeering, extortion, it totals up to fifteen to twenty years. He'd take some county politicians down with him and some code enforcement people."

She shook her head, looking into her cup.

"Like I said, rinky-dink."

Her gaze wandered over the budget motel room, the details of this place, the double bed, the antiseptic bathroom, the seascape painting. Once they had transformed Spartan rooms like this, made them into warm, glowing oases.

She said, "Look, Gaeton. The truth is, Benny's one of the central players in a very big, and I stress it, very big situation we've been developing for quite some time."

"Is that right?"

"Yeah, that's right," she said. "And believe me, this is out of Adamson's league. This is out of Miami's league, this comes from farther north, a good way up the road from here."

Gaeton tried to recall who he'd been when they'd loved each other. Had she seen him as a hotshot on the rise, on his way up the road, north? No. More likely, she'd known the truth all along. By thirty-five Gaeton had peaked and was already heading south. Destined soon to sink back into that slum of lower-echelon agents, bogged down in the tedium of uninspired investigations. Had she timed it so she stepped away from him just at his apogee? Gaeton starting his spiral down, no more promotions, only minimum raises, and Myra, her boosters about to switch on.

Even her voice had moved to a higher plane. It was amplified now, as if she'd retrained it from sessions at long, expensive conference tables, speaking down those polished planks to men who monitored every word she uttered for any falter.

"We screwed up," she said. "It was just a case of our going in too many directions. By the time your operation came to our attention, you were already burrowed in there with Benny." She looked over at the bathroom. She saw something in there that held her attention for a moment. Some memory. Maybe a shower they'd taken together, giddy from champagne. Something that made her almost smile, almost brought back that face he remembered. She turned to him, her features hardening back into this new face, and said, "But fortunately you never seemed to catch on to our operation. So we let you stay in there."

Gaeton smiled painfully. "If I'd been more alert, figured things out, what, you would've yanked me? That it?"

She nodded.

"Glad I could oblige," he said.

She said, "And now, Gaeton, it's time to start planning on how to bring you out. That's what this meeting is about."

"Bring me out? I'm just down the road. I'll drive up."

"No," she said, and sighed. She tugged her dress down an inch. "You're out on a limb, Gaeton. Way out. You don't know it yet, but you are."

He stared at her, remembering for a moment how that mouth had molded itself to his. How it had felt to hold that solid body. The sparkle she got in her laugh.

He said, "What limb am I out on, Myra?"

She put her tinted glasses on. She stood up, cocked her head at him for a few moments, letting the silence build a nice drumroll for her.

"It was either compromise you or compromise the mission," she said. "We chose you."

Gaeton looked up at the ceiling and closed his eyes.

He said, "You're telling me that Benny knows I'm still with the bureau, investigating him?"

"Yeah," she said. "We'd provided him with limited clearance to access FBI files as part of our operation. Apparently he used that clearance to run a routine check on everybody on his staff. Your name got flagged. He came to us and wanted an explanation."

"And you gave me up?"

"Benny'd figured it out anyway," Myra said.

"Why didn't you just bring me out then, Myra? Huh?"

"Benny insisted on keeping you," she said. "You were opening so many doors for him down there, introducing him to all your Conch cronies, Benny didn't care if you were a spy, building a case on him, he was in heaven. He loves rubbing shoulders with all the Bubbas down there. He didn't want to lose you."

"Goddamn, Myra."

She said, "So we informed Adamson, and since our operation had priority, Adamson agreed that even though your cover was exposed, you weren't in any real danger. As long as you didn't try to move on Benny, you were safe."

"How long has Benny known?"

"A few months," she said.

"Jesus shit, Myra. You mean, I'm there busting my ass, trying to make a case on this guy and Benny's just toying with me? I don't believe you fucking people. The things you think you can get away with."

"It's a war, Gaeton. Wars get complicated."

"God Almighty. I fucking can't believe it."

"It gets worse," she said. She took a deep breath and said, "Benny's flipped on us. We set him up in one kind of business and he branched out into another kind. A kind that could do us all a great deal of harm. Not just careers or reputations. But lives. Other missions." She took her purse off the dresser and snapped it open and drew out a small automatic. "He could do us a great deal of harm. Especially in an election year."

Gaeton rose.

She stepped over to him and held the pistol out by the barrel. He hesitated for a moment, then took it.

"What's this?"

"A very clean ten millimeters," she said.

"What the fuck, Myra?"

She said nothing but turned and went back to her coffee. She drank the last of it and watched him standing there.

"The bureau wants me to use this," he said. "To take out Benny? Is that what you're saying?"

"The bureau wants you to continue to use your training and imagination."

"Kill a guy for conspiracy to bribe public officials? Huh? We doing that now? I didn't know."

"Don't be that way, Gaeton."

"I don't believe you, Myra. Handing me a gun, telling me to go shoot some guy. Somebody owes me a very big explanation."

She dropped the coffee cup in a trash can. The light hit her hair again. Her skin backlit, creamy, the mole at her upper lip. Even in the midst of this, Gaeton noticed it, felt the warm growl rising from his stomach.

He tried to calm his voice.

"You think I'm going to shoot a guy and not know why?"

"The more people who know the specifics of this operation, the more jeopardy for everyone."

"OK, well, let me guess then. Just nod if I get it," he said. "It's about Claude and these other guys, right? They're not looking for burglar alarms. Anybody can see that. They're getting out of the business. Giving you people a little testimony and getting paid off in Porsches, nice houses. They might give you names, drug routes, bad cops. Benny's the go-between. Huh? Is that it? Am I close?"

She said nothing, gave no indication.

"Myra," he said, "I got to know. You owe me that."

She said, "I've told you what I can, Gaeton. Probably too much. Benny's a loose cannon. He's using his training as a federal agent, his contacts inside the government, and the computer access we gave him to accomplish some very bad things. The problem is, because we assisted him in setting up part of his shop, we're complicitous. Politically, it'd be devastating, impossible to bring this to court."

She let a few moments of silence work for her again. Then said: "The man knows things, he's threatened to say things that could topple people. Lots of people, and from very high perches."

"I don't give a shit about toppling people," Gaeton said. "Let him topple away. Maybe they should get toppled."

She stepped up close to him, gave him a workover with those new conference-table eyes. The ones she'd won from staring down androgen junkies.

"We're going to give you two weeks," she said. "To convince yourself I'm right and to take care of him. You accomplish it, you've got complete immunity, witness protection, whatever you want. We'll send in helicopters to pull you out if we have to, whatever it takes. The full deal."

"And if I don't?"

"You will," she said. "You'll call Adamson. You'll check with whoever you want to at the bureau. You'll see what I'm telling you is true. This is extremely volatile. It's a boil that has to be lanced. And you, because you're inside his security already, and because he thinks he has the upper hand with you, everyone agrees, you're the logical person."

"Logical," Gaeton said.

She thought about it a moment more and said, "And because it'll mean the bureau will owe you one, Gaeton, a very big one. It could turn things around for you, put you right back on the fast track. You should think about it."

"I'm not taking this fucking thing." Gaeton flipped the pistol onto the bed.

She looked at it. Picked up her purse, moved slowly to the door, and turned.

"Then leave it here. Maybe the maid can use it."

After she'd gone, he sat on the side of the bed for a few more minutes. He could hear the morning news coming from the TV next door. Something about mines and harbors. He listened to that till he got back the strength to stand.

8

"Whatta you mean, Thorn's not interested?" Benny said.

"Forget Thorn," said Gaeton. "I've got somebody else."

It was near midnight on Saturday. They were sitting in a booth in the back room of the Green Turtle Inn on Islamorada. Benny in a sherbet concoction. A rumpled raspberry jacket, lime pants, a white T-shirt advertising a Jamaican beer. He was experimenting with an earring tonight. A gold conch shell dangled from his left ear. It's what could happen when you spent twenty years in standard-issue Sears suits.

"You must not've put it the right way to this asshole," Benny said. "Give me his address. I'll take a shot at him."

"I'm telling you, I got you a much better guy," Gaeton said. "The guy I got in mind, he's a great fisherman, and plus, he's got the goods on every politician in the county. He'll break you up."

"What's his name?"

"Let me talk to him first, see if he's interested."

The late-night diners were clinking and clanking out front. The waitresses had lost all their hustle-bustle, now just smoking in a booth by the kitchen, watching the dawdlers. Benny was smiling from the four White Russians he'd had. He kept touching the fringe of black hair that circled his slick bald dome. He was getting all the hairs lined up to meet the constituents, the ones Gaeton had worked so hard setting up for him.

The barmaid came back again.

"Do us all again, sweet pea," Benny said. "The boys in the booth, too." He nodded at the three guys across the room,

Benny's tabernacle choir. All three still with their cop haircuts, square jaws. Their thick forearms resting on the table. All of them in guayaberas, one yellow and two whites.

Benny swept his eyes across the darkened parking lot. A couple of retirees going home with their Styrofoam doggy box, fighting their way through the heavy wind.

Benny said, "You sell me on Thorn, then you take it all back. What's the deal?"

"He's busy, building his house," Gaeton said. "Don't worry, Benny. The guy I got in mind for you, he knows the water down here as well as anybody. You'll love him."

Benny was still looking out the window. Or no, was he adoring his own reflection? Gaeton took a sip of his Budweiser.

Benny fingered the gold conch shell at his ear. He brought his eyes away from the window, and said, "You give up too easy, Richards." He smiled. "I haven't met the man I couldn't hire."

They traded looks. Gaeton felt a trickle of sweat sprout in his armpit.

When the red-headed man in a plaid shirt and navy pants moved cautiously to the edge of their conversation, Gaeton broke connection with Benny's eyes, waved the man over.

"Benny," Gaeton said, "this is Charlie Boilini. Charlie, Benny Cousins of Florida Secure Systems. Charlie owns Boilini's Liquors up in Tavernier." No one offered to shake hands.

"Oh, yes," said Benny. "The man who wants the stoplight."

Mr. Boilini stood awkwardly at the edge of the table.

"Well, the thing is, Mr. Cousins, it's a real bad intersection, accidents, near misses. I've petitioned the county commission, Department of Transportation. And they tell me they've got to do a study of the area first, and they—"

Benny said, "Hey, hey, hey, listen, Boilini, I'm no fucking

politician. You don't have to bullshit me with your humanitarian concerns. We clear on that?"

"Yes, sir."

"OK. So you want to put a stoplight out front, slow the tourists down. They're stuck in traffic, they get thirsty, they pull off, you get rich. Is this the story you want to make happen?"

Mr. Boilini shrugged like yeah, well, maybe.

Benny said, "So you got a problem with red tape. Every day of the week you're choking to death already on regulations, paper work. And then a simple thing like a stoplight, it's like taking a case to the Supreme Court. Am I right, Charlie?"

"Yes, sir. It's a nightmare getting anything done anymore."

Benny said, "Now, it so happens I know a man at Department of Transportation. He's a bureaucrat as bad as the next one. But he's still a good ol' boy and a friend of mine. And I think he could be persuaded to help here."

"Could you let me pay you something for your trouble?"

Benny brought his eyes up and looked Mr. Boilini over.

"Boilini, I'm no doctor, but to me, you look like you got lotsa years left." Benny took a sip of his drink. He put it down and said, "Think of it, every three minutes your new stoplight blinks and another guy's walking out with a fifth of Jim Beam. Add that up over a lifetime, you know, and that's a chunk of change. So if you were to try to pay me what that stoplight's worth to you, well, I don't think you could get together that kind of cash, now could you?"

"No, sir."

Benny said, "And anyway, Charlie, I'm one of the last of the red-hot altruists. I don't want your money. I'm motivated by the higher virtues. Quid pro quo. Things of this nature."

Boilini nodded, cocking his head slightly for the punch line.

Benny tugged on his earring again, staring down at his White

Russian. He said, "Like, I understand you're big in the Rotary Club down here, the Masons, these civic organizations."

"Yes, sir, I'm involved in a good many community activities."

Benny said nothing, waiting for Boilini to catch on. Looking at him, almost counting the seconds out loud.

"Oh," Boilini said finally. "I'd be happy to propose your membership in some local clubs. It'd be my pleasure, Mr. Cousins."

Mr. Boilini offered his hand, and Benny shook it without taking much of a grip. Bringing his face around finally to give Boilini a look at his bullshittiest smile.

"How'm I doing?" Benny asked Gaeton when Boilini had left.

"Well, you shouldn't get them on their knees. Treat them so smug." Gaeton took a sip of his beer. "Conchs are proud."

"What? That? On his knees?" He squinted at Gaeton. "Hey, Mr. Manners, when I get somebody on their knees, they don't get up. They don't walk away." He leaned across the table toward him, getting a sizzle in his voice.

Gaeton said, "These people, they've been dealing with Bubbas and payoffs for a hundred years. You want to have some impact down here, you're going to have to be a little less of a smartass."

"Gaeton Richards's charm school."

Gaeton said nothing.

Benny drew out an envelope from his inside front pocket. He passed it over to Gaeton. Gaeton looked at it for a moment, then picked it up and opened it. Seven cashier's checks. Five thousand apiece. They were made out to two past mayors of Key West. Three former county commissioners. A judge. The owner of a plumbing and construction company in Marathon. Gaeton had given Benny their names last week when he'd asked who the oldest families in the Keys were. The Conch aristocracy, he'd called them.

Gaeton slid the envelope back and said, "Yeah? So?"

"I want you to deliver these," Benny said. "Campaign contributions."

"These people aren't running for anything," Gaeton said.

"I know that," Benny said. "But I am."

Gaeton put the envelope in his shirt pocket.

Benny said, "And tomorrow sometime, take that Porsche back up to Miami, to the place you got it from."

"Why?"

"Claude's leaving town, and he decided he doesn't want it after all. OK? And don't always be questioning me, hot rod. I got my reasons for things. Just do what the fuck I tell you, OK?"

"Whatever you say, Mr. Cousins."

A slender man approached their table from the parking lot exit. He had a close-cropped beard. His clothes nicely creased. He glanced around, noted Benny's men; a light of disdain came and went in his eyes.

"Benny," Gaeton said, "this is Ralph Marris. Mayor Ralph Marris of Key West. Ralph, Benny. Benny, Ralph."

"Mayor Marris?" Benny said. "Here, have a seat." Benny patted the red leather upholstery beside him. He scooted over, shooting Gaeton a look. You're so hot for sincere. Here's sincere.

Ozzie Hardison was in the Tropical Freeze ice cream truck parked in a gravel lot about fifty feet from the front of the Green Turtle Restaurant. He was watching through his binoculars Darcy's blond boyfriend talking to some short, bald guy. He'd followed the guy from the trailer park about two hours ago. The guy'd been in there all that time talking to a string of people.

From this range Ozzie could hit this asshole, bang, shatter-slump, and be out of there in no time. Get home, put a notch in the rifle, and then wander over and maybe put a notch or two in the weatherlady.

This dingleberry boyfriend of hers was a lifeguard. It's what he called them cause of all that blond hair, the dark tan, and how they looked at you, like they were sitting up in their white chair. They talked to you like cops did; only these guys had to be a little more polite. 'Cause they didn't carry guns.

Ozzie put down the binoculars, slid the door open to the refrigerated part of the truck, and ducked in there. He opened the ice cream box and pulled out the .22 rifle. It had a cheapo sight on it and was generally a piece of Monkey Ward shit. But it was all he had, and it'd do just fine.

He was moving kind of slow, not scared really, considering how long he'd waited for this kind of situation. He was savoring this, chewing it slow. The air had a certain tang to it for the first time in a long time.

Then shit! Something whacked on the side of the truck and Ozzie jumped and banged his head on an overhead cooler.

Standing at the service window was a fat woman in a yellow muumuu. She was wearing a scarf over her curlers. And peering in at Ozzie, the wind out there whipping her scarf around.

"Hey, I see you in there."

Ozzie set the .22 in the slot between two of the coolers, rubbed his head.

"Hey! You in business or what?"

The fat lady had a fat kid wearing a baseball hat and a T-shirt and shorts. Ugly as her. Looked like the bulldog family taking themselves out for a walk.

"I'm going to tell Papa John about this. Ignoring paying customers this way."

Ozzie threw open the window. The wind rushed in and nearly knocked him back.

"Whatta you want, you got to break my window for? Huh? Huh? Say it, you fat old whale."

She moved up close, got her face in the window. She had bad skin, whiskers coming out of a mole on her chin, chili breath. Ozzie felt around back there for the rifle. Got it by the barrel. Maybe do her first, then the lifeguard.

Her whole ugly face filling up the window. Jesus, some poor shriveled-up son of a bitch had shot a load into that woman once. Imagine that. Her kid squawked behind her.

"I want a nutty-buddy. A nutty-buddy."

"Elton wants a nutty-buddy," she said, mean and slow, as if she were reading Ozzie's mind.

Ozzie had the .22 just below the counter, holding it by the stock. His other hand dropped out of sight, fit into the trigger guard.

"And Elton's momma wants four marijuana cigarettes and two Fudgsicles."

"It's after midnight, for christsakes," Ozzie said. "I'm off work. The freezers are all locked up."

"Papa John's gonna have your ass," the woman said.

"I want my nutty-buddy *now*." Elton was there behind her, having the sugar conniptions.

"Say please," Ozzie said.

"You do it, and you don't get no please and thank you, either." She used her mother voice on him. Playing dirty.

"Shit," Ozzie said. He banged the butt of the .22 down. Then leaned it against the cooler, and got her her ice cream and her four joints, put them in a brown sack, and brought them to the window. She had her money spread out on the counter.

Ozzie watched as Elton went to work on his nutty-buddy, walking back over to the apartments. The fat woman peeled one of her fudgsicle wrappers off and wadded it and flicked it at the open window. The wind caught it and took it at thirty miles an hour up the road. Ozzie slammed the window shut. Then he remembered the fucking lifeguard.

Not at the table anymore. The waitress was clearing things. Ozzie swept the binoculars around the lot, found a group of guys getting into a brown Mercedes. Four of them leaving and one staying behind. The Mercedes pulled away. The one staying behind turned finally so the parking lot light hit his face. Bingo, bango, bongo.

Ozzie waited till the Mercedes was out on U.S. 1 and he was sure nobody else was in the lot. And he switched on the roof top speakers, cranked them up loud. "See how they run, see how they run. They all ran after the farmer's wife, she cut off their tails with a carving knife, did you ever see such a sight in your life, as three blind mice." It was a scratchy tape, sounded like Richard Nixon singing it, but it got the lifeguard's attention.

A big wallop of thunder came just as the guy turned, and stared at Ozzie. Some rain began to ding the roof.

Ozzie got his face ready. Trying to adjust to this new situation, meeting this guy up close and personal. Actually, this was better than the .22. The .22 was chickenshit. The hands-on approach was always better.

Ozzie slid his hand down beneath the service window for his sawed-off Louisville slugger. He got it and reached into the cooler and took out a nutty-buddy, carried it and the bat up to the cab, keeping the slugger hidden behind his right leg. Then, standing in the doorway, he called out to the lifeguard. Said, "Hey, mister, I got something for you."

Gaeton approached the rusty ice cream truck. On its side palm trees waving, flamingos in flight. PAPA JOHN'S TROPICAL FREEZE stenciled on the service window. "They all ran after the farmer's wife." He was reaching into his windbreaker for the .357 when he saw who it was. That redneck Ozzie Hardison standing in the doorway, a big smile, saying, hi there, partner. And Ozzie reached out to hand him what looked like an ice cream bar. Gaeton nodded his head no. Ozzie said, "You don't like sweets?" And Ozzie fumbled with the ice cream, juggled it in Gaeton's direction, and lost control. And as Gaeton bent quickly to catch the thing, he saw in his peripheral sight the billy club coming down.

Then the gravel was rising to meet him. The numb thud, the flash of a blue light. She cut off their tails with a carving knife. Gaeton listened to the echo of that as he drifted away into the airless dark.

Benny Cousins opened the door to the bedroom, stuck his head in, asked if Claude was decent.

Claude said nothing. He was lying on the bed, dressed.

"Well, it's my house," Benny said. "I guess I can come and go where I want."

Benny sat in a leather wingback beside the bed, locked his fingers together in front of him, then put them behind his head.

"So tell me," Benny said, "I want to hear why you got such a case of the hots for Palm Beach. That particular house."

"It is a villa," Claude Hespier said, "not merely a house."

"Yeah, whatever. So what's the fucking attraction for a guy like you, live in a place like that, in Palm Beach?" Benny smiled.

Claude was wearing a yellow shirt with blue hula girls, white sailcloth pants. He was barefoot. Benny was still in his pastel outfit, packing his little double-barreled .32 Intratec. The thing fit right in his back pocket, no bigger than a chunky wallet. You just never knew when you were going to need artillery, walking around in the Islamorada moonlight, just him, Claude, and a nice ocean breeze. All the boys off for the night.

Claude puffed up the pillow against the headboard and leaned back against it.

He said, "I have already discussed my wishes with you when I first made contact."

"Refresh my memory," Benny said. "I like to double-check. Remind myself what makes you guys tick."

"Villa Luna," Claude said, and took a breath through his nose, "is Miss Tracy Seagrave's mansion. It has remained closed since her death. Now, since the dispute over her estate has been settled, I want to purchase the property. I want to live there."

Something about the way he breathed, or maybe it was the puffiness and shape of his lips, something about him pissed the hell out of Benny. That Caribbean way he had of enunciating instead of talking. Third world hoity-toity.

"You want to live in her house, what? To dig some of her leftover muff hair out of the drains."

"Don't mock me," Claude said.

"Yeah, well, everyone has their little quirks. I got mine, you got yours. I'm sure Tracy Seagrave even had hers."

Claude said, "It is important that we act on this investment immediately. There could be other interested parties."

"Right, right," said Benny. "Oh, and hey, tell me something else. What the hell was that shit with the Porsche kid yesterday, tying him up like that, offering him to the alligators?"

"The boy insulted me," Claude said. He was examining the palm of his right hand.

"He insulted you." Benny smiled. "How'd he do that?"

"He called me a Negro," said Claude. He picked at a callus.

Benny said, "And you're not a Negro?"

Claude raised his eyes and met Benny's. Benny was smiling.

Benny said, "Hey, I don't care how you slice it, Cheez Whiz, you got a very definite dose of the dark meat."

Claude brought his feet to the floor. He stood up.

"Claude, baby," Benny said, "I got nothing against darkies. No shit. I don't have a prejudiced corpuscle in my body. If this is a sensitive topic for you, we'll just drop it."

Claude slowly shifted his weight off the balls of his feet. He blinked, took a full breath.

"Good," Benny said. "Now, hey, since you're up already, what say we grab some air? Continue our chat. We give awful good moonlight down here in the Florida Keys."

Benny turned his back to Claude, opened the door.

He said, "I could show you my prize royal palms. The suckers set me back five thousand apiece. Can you believe that? For trees?"

He held the door open for Claude. The albino watching Benny very carefully. Benny just smiled. This was the part he liked. The moonlight walk. Put his arm around their shoulder, get them started on all the evil shit they'd pulled over the years, and let his blood percolate listening to it.

As they walked down the stairway, Benny said, "I'd like to hear all the gory details about your criminal past, Claude. And don't be shy and hold things back, man, 'cause I got to know exactly what it is you've done if I'm going to be successful at undoing it."

9

For about the hundredth time that Sunday morning, Ozzie took a look out the window of his concrete-block stilt house at the shed where the lifeguard was his prisoner.

It'd been raining all night, thundering and lightning, and there was water pooled up on the cement slab that the aluminum shed was mounted on. The guy was probably damp in there. Probably getting a little wrinkly while he waited for Ozzie to figure out what the fuck to do with him. Then build up the nerve to do it.

He turned back to Bonnie.

"How's this sound?" Ozzie tore the notebook paper off the pad and waited till Bonnie looked over, giving him her not-this-again eye roll. He cleared his throat and sang, "I love you more than my flip-flops, my Colt 45, and my old coon dog. I'm sorry I busted your lip last night, it'll never happen, aaa-gain."

"Sounds like the same old shit," Bonnie Drake said. She took a hit from her Budweiser and brought the clippers back to her toes. Snipping them into sharp little points, like he'd heard water polo players did. So far that was one weapon she hadn't used on him.

Ozzie Hardison wadded the page up and threw it at the refrigerator.

"What do I know?" Bonnie said. "I never heard one line of that hick music I liked. What the hell you asking me for my opinion anyway?"

"Who else am I going to ask? Think I should call up the

president, stop some bozo on the street? What?"

"Get an agent or something. I don't know anything about the music business. I don't even listen to that shit. Hell, you could be Kris Kristofferson for all I know."

"I don't want to be Kris Kristofferson."

"Yeah, well, whoever it is then. Whoever it is you want to be."

"You know who it is." Ozzie stood up from the dinette table and walked over to the wad of paper, stepped on it, and made a flat little circle out of it.

Bonnie put on her prissy grin and said, "Johnny Cash, Johnny Cash, Johnny Cash."

"Go ahead," Ozzie said. "Say something sarcastic."

"You should call yourself Ozzie MasterCard. Mr. Plastic Cash." She made her wheezy whiskey laugh.

Ozzie stroked his stomach, staring at her, sitting there in her green tube top, her hair greasy, her panties pulled up into her crotch so the hair sprouted out the legs. She was listening to her bitchy channel today, getting the word from the gods of smartass and ballbusting.

"You been watching 'Donahue' again?" he asked her.

She glared at him.

"What was it this time? How to have an orgasm with a sack of carrots?"

He could see the muscles in her forehead working. He'd never seen anybody with fucking muscles in her forehead before.

"How to give your man a vasectomy in his sleep? Huh? What?"

She threw the clippers at him sidearm. Dinged him hard in the neck. And they richocheted off and hit the fretboard of his six-string leaning against the bottom cupboard.

"Why don't you read your stupid songs to the weatherlady?

She's so smart. She's so beautiful and rich. Why don't you bother her with that shit you write?"

"Leave her out of it," Ozzie said.

"Your girl friend. Jesus, what a dickbrain you are."

"Stop it, Bonnie. I'm warning you now, you stop talking to me that way."

Bonnie went on filing at her nails, didn't even look up, saying, "She doesn't know you exist, boy, and if she did, she'd laugh right in your face. And you, you're writing her love songs, mooning around about her."

Ozzie said nothing, trying to decide how to retaliate.

Bonnie said, "You never even had an old coon dog. You're just lying to make yourself sound redneckier than you are."

He picked up the clippers, looked at his own nails. "There's a whole hell of a lot you don't know about me."

"I know more than I want to already," she said.

It sounded like a title to Ozzie and that made him calm down a bit. I Know More Than I Want to Know Already. About a man who was a loser from the age of fourteen. Living with whores, knife-fighting at the pool hall, and some woman, a good church woman, gets hold of him and tries to turn him around, give him good white-collar love, but he doesn't have the disposition for it, seen too much split fuck already to believe in that innocent bullshit. Beer diluting music. Yeah, yeah.

He sat there for a few minutes, and Bonnie was painting her nails some awful color of purple, stuffing little cotton balls between her toes, and did she know what he was doing over there? Did she give a rat's ass about his talent? Hell, no.

Ozzie went into the back bedroom, threw some of Bonnie's dirty clothes off the bed into the corner by where the TV was sitting on a Jack Daniel's box, and he settled onto the bed in an Indian squat.

He got one line into it, "He dropped out of school in the seventh grade, graduated to a rusty switchblade," and Bonnie was stomping down the wooden outside stairway, shaking the whole house.

Jesus, did Johnny Cash have to put up with this shit? Here it was less than a week till Old Pirate Days, and the talent contest, and he had just that one song, Papa John's ballad.

First prize in the contest was 250 bucks. But it wasn't the money that had his blood warm. It was the exposure. It was standing up in front of God knew how many people, on the stage at the Waldorf Shopping Center, and letting them hear what was seething inside him. Blowing the rest of the local phonies right out of the water. That is, if he could get over his stage fright in time.

Ozzie stood up, went over to the window, and looked out at the ocean. Pretty damn nice view for free. Papa John was letting him off on the rent, using that as his pay, plus a twenty once a week for walking-around money.

There was a yacht maybe a mile out, heading south, slicing along like that, leaving that zipper of white suds behind it, white against all that blue. It gave him a hollow ache in his gut. Almost like seeing a beautiful woman walking toward him on the street. He wanted it awful bad. All of it.

But he was the kid in his song. Dropped out of school at fourteen, fifth grade. And those women on the sidewalk, they knew. They knew from the way his eyes looked, how he parted his hair. Hell, Ozzie didn't know how they knew, but they knew. And they were switching and swaying to the goddamn docks to climb onto that yacht so it could slide by out there like the white peak of a fiber glass iceberg. And here he was, stuck with the likes of Bonnie.

Bonnie, shit. Bonnie was history. She'd just been phase one.

The third week in town he'd met her at the Caribbean Club. He'd gotten her drunk with his very first twenty dollars from Papa John. He'd sung to her there at the bar. Christ, now he couldn't believe he'd ever sung to that bitch. Then let her move her stuff into his house the next afternoon. No, Bonnie was nothing. She was just the gutter he was going to rise out of.

Phase two was Darcy Richards, maybe even three and four. And he was nearly there. Talk about luck. Here he'd been in town for two months and already apprenticed to Papa John Shelton, learning the ropes from the dark prince himself. And then it turns out that living just fifty yards away in John's trailer park was a genuine TV star, a woman with every single ingredient on Ozzie's dream woman list.

She had bozooms for one. Nice round ones. He'd even gotten a peek at her nipples. One afternoon, when he was cutting the grass in the little lots in the trailer park for John, she'd come outside her trailer and given him a Coke. He'd hung around, not saying anything, not wanting to blow it, drinking the Coke, while she pulled up some weeds growing around her driveway slab, stooping over in a loose white blouse. Ozzie angled for the right shot, finally got it, both nipples. Pink and small. Perfect.

He liked her voice. Even better in person than on TV. It warmed up something inside him. She had a flowery smell to her. And she had blond hair, with a good bit of red in it. He even liked her name, though it was a damn hard name to find rhymes for. *Larceny* was about all he'd come up with. So he hadn't used it in a song yet. But he would.

He'd liked her the first time he'd seen her, but then somebody had told him she was a weatherlady, and he'd started watching her every day, giving the Miami weather. But it wasn't really till that day drinking her Coke, smelling her shampoo, that he was in love.

He was at the point now, he'd been shadowing Darcy on the weekends, bodyguarding her, he called it. And thinking about her when he couldn't be watching over her. At the point where if she said, swallow this bag of broken glass, he'd lick his lips.

Four or five times now he'd cut her lawn. Always on Saturday, when he knew she was down for the weekend. Her lifeguard boyfriend, coming and going a couple of times, had taken a couple of hard looks at Ozzie, not saying anything but giving him the lifeguard stare. But Darcy always had a Coke for him and would talk to him. Talk to him like he wasn't some creep, the way Bonnie did.

Finally Ozzie had gotten over his shyness, and just last week he'd told her how he was a songwriter, just working at odd jobs till he got his break. And did she smirk at him, did she rag his ass like Bonnie? Hell, no. Darcy said, "That's like me. Paying the bills with one hand, trying to be immortal with the other." Man, Ozzie liked that. He thought maybe he could use that line in a song, if he could just figure out what the fuck it meant.

Ozzie put on a green sweat shirt and went outside, walked down the rickety stairs. He stopped and looked in on Bonnie in the garage, bent over the workbench breaking colored glass into small pieces with a ball peen hammer. In a while she'd fire up her blowtorch and start to piece together her designs. Flowers mostly, but sometimes unicorns or fish, shit like that, out of that colored glass and melted lead or solder or something. Hang in your window, dress the place up a little. Tourist shop shit.

Bonnie said she was trying to better herself. A businesswoman selling her glass things to the shops around the island. And now she was taking art classes at the community college. A fucking college girl, too, all of a sudden. She said it was in case she needed something to fall back on.

Other than a mattress? Ozzie said.

He walked across the straggly grass, sandspurs sticking to his frayed tennis shoes. He'd slung a painting tarp over the black Porsche. Last night he'd brought the lifeguard home in the ice cream truck and had to turn around and hitchhike all the way back to Islamorada in the rainstorm to pick up that car.

Lifting an edge of the tarp now, Ozzie felt the shine come to his blood. That car, that fucking car. It made him shudder thinking of what he had to do to that car.

Ozzie got out the key he'd locked the Yale with. And goddamn it, his hand was rattling around like it was him that was the prisoner. He glared at his right hand, took a breath, and brought the key to the slot. He slid back the double doors. It was almost noon, and the air temp was still in the seventies; but the stinking air that came rolling out of the shed must have been near a hundred. And it smelled like the smart guy's five-day deodorant pad had shriveled up and rotted away.

Shoo-ey. It didn't matter how many years of college you had. Stink was stink. Ozzie smiled to himself and took a little suck of air from outside before stepping into the shed and drawing the doors closed behind him. His heart wallowed around as if it'd come loose.

Ozzie had the guy rolled up in a ten-by-ten patch of yellow linoleum. The stuff had come unglued from the cement floor of the storage shed, so Ozzie had moved all the lawn mowers and wheelbarrows out into the yard and had just peeled up the linoleum the rest of the way.

And last night, when he brought this guy home, unconscious, all he did was lay him down on one end of it and roll him three turns, keeping the stuff tight against him. His chin was just barely out of one end, and the glue of the linoleum was sticking it all closed. Just to be safe, Ozzie had tied a length of nylon rope around the middle of the roll.

Ozzie stepped inside the shed. The lifeguard was awake, giving Ozzie his best evil eye. A yard of duct tape was keeping his mouth shut. And the linoleum was holding just fine. The guy's feet were a good yard up inside there, and his arms were flat against his sides. Like a corn dog, getting plump and juicy inside there.

About the only reason Ozzie could ever remember feeling sorry he'd dropped out of school so early was that he'd missed those frog classes. The ones where you cut its leg off and stuck some electricity to it and it twitched.

10

Gaeton Richards had crushed the palmetto bug with his chin, and now its yellow goo was running down his neck. But the roach's head was still stuck to the edge of the rolled-up linoleum and the antennae continued to wave. Gaeton could identify.

Truth was, he wasn't even sure he could give his feelers a good wave at this point.

He'd been inside this roll since just after midnight last night. It felt like early afternoon now. The dehydration was weakening him badly. He was dizzy and his throat hurt. He'd lost touch with his arms and everything below the sternum sometime early this morning.

Gaeton wondered if the palmetto bug was having an after-death, out-of-body experience. Moving toward the bright light, a transfusion of serenity, the blue doors of heaven swinging open, all those angelic feelers waving: hello, come on up, it's great up here, always dark, crumbs everywhere.

Ozzie shut the door. He was a blocky guy, big teeth, black hair cut in a burr. Large bones that carried a little extra meat without making him seem fat. And there were those eyes, a foggy gray. They probably came from his low-protein diet, Budweiser and Twinkies. He looked as if it wouldn't take a full moon to set him off. A sixty-watt bulb might do just fine.

Ozzie stepped across the linoleum roll, bringing with him some of that crisp outside air. Ozzie said, "You're stinking this place up." He unwrapped the silver duct tape from Gaeton's head and drew the white sock out of his mouth.

Gaeton dragged in a few breaths, stretched his mouth, worked his jaw. He waited till his pulse had slowed to a jog and said, "Oswald Daniel Hardison of Quincy, Florida."

Ozzie jerked around as if somebody'd goosed him.

Gaeton went on, "Worked for three months at Golden Years Retirement Home in Panama City and got eighteen months at Loxahatchee for stealing rings from old ladies there. And bills from their change purses. Ozzie, come on, man. Grandmothers' wedding rings? Ten-dollar bills folded up to squeeze in a rubber change purse?"

"Where'd you get this shit, you slut?"

Gaeton took a deep breath and tried to blow the roach head off the edge of the linoleum. Didn't faze it. The feelers still twitched, trying to locate the crack it had come in through.

"Papa John's going to be pissed when he finds out what you're doing to me."

Ozzie put his jacket on a sawhorse. He bent and scooped up his dumbbells, began working on his biceps, right arm up, left arm down.

"You take all this time just to think that up? Scare me with what Papa John might do, that old man? Shit, that's lame, dingleberry."

"Now look, Ozzie? You know why I got the skinny on you? You know why that is?"

He shifted to shoulder shrugs now. What little cockiness he'd summoned had evaporated. He was quiet, but the machinery of his thinking was almost audible in the tiny room.

The fact was, Gaeton had noticed Ozzie hanging around, taking an unusual interest in Gaeton's comings and goings. He was always glancing at Gaeton's trailer when he was cutting somebody's yard. Darcy even spoke to him some. That was when Gaeton got serious and found out his name from one of the neighbors, had Adamson run the boy through the FBI computer.

He'd checked out normal. Normal for a sleazeball.

Gaeton said, "It's because where I work, it's our business, knowing about people, looking things up on them. You have any idea who I'm referring to here? Who you've got rolled up here."

"Yeah, right. You're Mafia. You're Al Capone's little brother. Right, right. I'm not as dumb as I look, dingleberry."

"Not mafiosi, Ozzie. The other side. The good ones. The guys with the morals and the tin stars. You've just waded hip-deep into shit here, buddy."

"What a crock," Ozzie said. "Listen to me, dickbrain, you're fucking with my woman, and I'm pissed," Ozzie said, his eyes out of gear, concentrating on pumping that iron.

"Who we talking about here?" Gaeton said. "Your woman."

"You know fucking well who we're talking about."

Something in Gaeton sagged. This had nothing to do with Benny. Some relief there. This was something else. This looked to be some serious miswiring in the kid's medulla oblongata.

"Could that be Darcy Richards?" Gaeton said. "Your woman?"

"You got it, corn dog."

"She aware of this? That you're her boyfriend?"

"She will be," Ozzie said. "Soon enough. When I'm ready."

"Hey, Oz. You better find yourself another roll of linoleum for her then."

Ozzie sat down on the roll, about where Gaeton's knees would be, set the weights aside. "Jagoff like you, in the position you're in. Me, I wouldn't be in a talking mood."

"So I'm supposed to be your rival?"

"You got it," Ozzie said.

"Oh, Jesus," he said, barely a sound. "Ozzie, Ozzie."

"So what is this deep shit I'm supposed to be stepping in?" Ozzie gave the roll a little turn, rolling his butt back on it, and the linoleum revolved a quarter of a turn to the left. Gaeton got a sudden close-up of the cement floor.

Gaeton said, "Ozzie, the lady you're hot for, she's my sister, man. My little sister."

Ozzie brought the roll back upright.

"Sure she is," Ozzie said. "What a bullshit artist." But Gaeton could hear the last of the cockiness bleeding away.

"Go ask her, Oz. See if she has a brother. She comes down to visit him on the weekends, stays in his trailer. Ask Papa John or anybody around here. You're making a major fuck-up here." Gaeton tried to keep his voice slack, not let this bozo see the anger.

"You'd like that, huh? Me go over there and ask her and then everybody'd know who done what to who." Ozzie rocked the linoleum roll back and forth, looking down at Gaeton, running all this around inside there.

"Ozzie, you're no murderer. I look at you and I see a guy trying to work his way up the ranks. You found yourself a great teacher, you're probably learning some good scams. But I don't see a murderer. That's a whole different order of stupidity. People still care about that."

That got a slow turn of his head. A squint in his eyes and lift of eyebrow, theatrical slyness.

Gaeton said, "Yeah, that's right. I know a good bit about you. Heard it on the coconut telegraph. It's an island, Oz. Somebody takes a deep breath on one side of this town, somebody's eardrums pop on the other. You forget, man, I lived here all my life. I seen Papa John's boys before, coming and going. I know what kind of shit he gets you boys to pull for him."

"What a lying sack." Ozzie stood and picked up one of the barbells, dangled it over Gaeton's face. "Don't give me any more of this bullshit, or I'll do you right here and now."

Gaeton said, "He have you popping Pirellis at the restaurant parking lots? Slapping bald ones on his rims, while the guy's inside guzzling martinis. The Grander brothers still buying them off Papa John? Huh? He still into that?"

Gaeton took a breath, swallowed. He could feel the quirkiness in this boy, his impulses clashing with what intelligence he had. The boy was teetering, and Gaeton wasn't completely sure which way to nudge him. He wasn't sure anymore if he was in more trouble or less of it than if Benny was behind this.

Keeping his voice as mellow as he could make it, he said, "I want you to listen carefully to what I'm telling you. All you have to do is ask anybody in Key Largo. You find out I'm her brother, you come back here, unroll me. I'll get up, and get back to the job I'm doing. Charge this up to an unfortunate mistake. But if you go ahead with what you're planning, you're going to get caught within twenty-four hours, and you'll never see Darcy again. You won't see your balls again either."

Ozzie's eyes seemed to dim from the power drain of the thought.

Gaeton said, "And hey, while you're checking this out, you don't want me to die, right?" Ozzie stared down at Gaeton with a sleepwalker's bland face. Yes, master. What shall I do? No wonder Papa John liked this boy. "So, Ozzie. Go outside and bring me back some water."

Ozzie left and in a few minutes returned, dragging the hose into the shed. He aimed it carelessly toward Gaeton's face, squeezed the trigger. Gaeton had to twist to take a bite out of the scalding jet. It'd probably been heating in the sun for a week. But hell, it'd keep him alive for a few more hours, and it washed away that damn roach head.

It was Sunday afternoon, not much after one. Thorn watched the low, leaden clouds. They'd drained the blue from the water. The bay was a drab silver. No horizon line. The forward edge of the front had passed through last night. Today, as the drizzle stopped, the cold would settle in. Chapping weather.

He watched from his stone picnic table as a pelican coasted at fifty feet. A slight dip of the wing to touch up its flight. Then the big bird scudded, backstroked to a stall, and plunged in a stream-lined mass into a boiling school of baitfish. In a few seconds it bobbed to the top and tipped its head back, riding the small chop its splash had made. It floated there long enough to let the pinfish slip into its throat, then dragged itself into flight again. The water quickly calm, the sky empty. Nobody had screamed. No one was weeping, not that you could see.

A brown Mercedes pulled into the yard, parked next to Thorn's VW convertible. The driver looked at Thorn for a minute or two and got out.

He was about six feet and had black hair and was wearing a shiny blue Adidas warm-up suit, with new white running shoes. He'd left the motor running in the Mercedes and was walking down to the dock where Thorn was working on the ballyhoo plug.

He'd used Gaeton's knife, putting some nice gill grooves in the side of the plug. The Buck knife had felt immediately natural. The right size, right heft. He hadn't made a slip with it yet.

After he'd gotten the gills right, he'd begun to paint the plug silver. For the last hour he'd been trying to get a shimmer on its belly. But in that light everything was dulled. Hard to tell how he was doing.

The man stopped a few feet from the table. He seemed uncomfortable, in those clothes, in this spot. A long way from the cocktail lounges, shiny gray suits.

"Mr. Cousins got your code violations fixed," the man said. He handed Thorn some forms from Building and Zoning. Thorn looked at them and put them aside.

He wiped the last drops of silver paint back on the rim of the small paint bottle and rested the brush on the edge of the picnic table.

"Mr. Cousins wants to talk to you." The guy spoke with a lot of extra flesh muffling his words. He sounded like a retired boxer who'd specialized in the rope-a-dope.

Thorn said, "I'm working."

The man looked at the ballyhoo plug, then at Thorn, as if he hadn't been programmed for this many variables.

"He fixed your tickets," the man said. "It's courteous to go meet the gentleman."

"Listen to that," Thorn said, lifting his head. It was the repeated shriek of an osprey. The bird, a saltwater eagle, had built a nest in his neighbor's satellite dish around Christmas. Both the osprey and its nest were federally protected. And the man was a past president of the local Audubon group. Click, gotcha. So now his neighbor couldn't even rotate his dish. It might dislodge the bird. Thorn had been watching the nest's progress just above the treeline, maybe a half mile off.

Thorn said, "When you can see your neighbor's satellite dish, it's time to move on. Know who said that?"

"The smoke from your neighbor's chimney, is how it goes," the man said. "And it's from the *Ching Tao*."

Thorn looked at him more closely. The guy was smiling inside there, inside all that phlegm and muscle and monosyllable.

"I thought it was Davy Crockett," Thorn said.

"Crockett stole it from the *Ching Tao*," the man said.

Thorn wasn't sure now who was conning who.

The man put out his hand, said his name was Roger.

"How'd he fix my tickets, Roger?" Thorn shook his hand.

"I guess he has ways," Roger said. "He seems to've taken an interest in you."

Thorn said, "They were just issued Friday. County offices aren't open weekends. How'd he do that?"

"Mr. Cousins's wired in," he said. "Offices opened, closed, it doesn't seem to matter to him. They don't shut the electricity down on the weekends."

"They don't?"

Roger smiled uncertainly.

"Mr. Cousins is very big on computers, one computer talking

to another one. He runs his business that way. He must've got his machine talking to their machine. Something like that."

"I can handle my own business," Thorn said. "I don't need someone fixing things for me."

"Why don't you just be courteous, talk to the man?"

Thorn looked out at the water for a moment, back at Roger.

"All right," Thorn said, rising. "Let's go have a look at him."

"You'll like him," Roger said. "He's nuts."

11

On the drive down to Islamorada Thorn asked Roger if he knew what this was all about. He said not exactly. He was a little new in town. He said that until last week he'd worked out of the Palm Beach office of Florida Secure Systems, doing surveillance camera setups and maintenance for the beachfront mansion set. His job was watching winos fall asleep on somebody's stretch of sand and then rousting them. He was about to quit when he was transferred down here. In the company, working in Islamorada was considered a promotion, becoming the palace guard.

Just south of the Cheeca Lodge, Roger turned off the highway and onto the old road. He went north a half mile and turned again down a long, narrow lane. The road made a couple of twists and emptied them out on a long, stately drive. A few fifty-foot royal palms lined the driveway at the entrance. At the edge of the drive was a John Deere like the one Thorn had used a month before, augering in his stilts.

"Planting trees down here," Roger said, "you need nuclear devices, get them into the bedrock."

It was a three-story stilt house, tin roof. Wraparound porch, shutters, French doors, the light gingerbread of upper Keys Conch houses. But the house was a queasy pink. All the windows mirrored.

"Fucshia? Magenta? I'm not real good on colors," Thorn said.

"Electric Strawberry," said Roger. "That's what they told Benny, the painters did. But listen, don't say anything bad about his house. The man loves his house. The thing's a copy of some pioneer house that used to be around here."

"It's hideous," Thorn said.

"It grows on you," Roger said.

"Chancres grow on you," Thorn said.

Two other brown Mercedeses were parked in the grassy lot. And Thorn could see beyond the house a large wooden deck, a swimming pool with ocean view, people in chaises out there. The Atlantic shaking with the dull afternoon light.

They got out of the car, and Thorn followed Roger across the grassy lot.

"For a guy in the security business, he's not very security-conscious."

"Whatta you mean?" Roger said.

"No walls. No dogs. Just wide open like this."

"Don't let it fool you. Somebody inside the house at this moment knows how shriveled your pecker is."

"That's comforting."

Roger led Thorn to the pool area. A redhead was sunning nude on a recliner. A candidate for breast reduction. Thorn thought for a minute he could see blurry waves of heat rising from her. Two of Benny's men in windbreakers were having their lunch, big submarine sandwiches at a table very near the redhead. Take a bite, take a look.

Thorn sat down in a cast-iron chair by the Jacuzzi, and Roger joined his buddies at the table across the deck. Thorn watched the hot tub churn. The water jetting in, the fast ping of bubbles.

Benny made his entrance in five minutes. He was a squat man. He came hurrying out of the house in a white linen suit. Pink sweat shirt. He carried a tall green tea glass, moving like one of those small professional tackles from twenty years ago. Thorn thought, fireplugs, bowling balls, all those short, hard things with low centers of gravity. Bad things to smack into.

"Mr. Thorn, Mr. Thorn," he said, smiling, not switching the tea glass, but putting out his left hand. Thorn used his left, too, and Benny took it, directing him back down into his chair. Thorn kept a polite look on his face. But he'd already started forming pictures of Benny fully clothed, bubbling away in that hot tub. Maybe keep the guy in there for a few hours, a regular Mr. Wizard experiment. Shrivel testing.

Benny sat across from Thorn. He took a huge breath and blew it out, as if it might be his first of the day.

"So tell me, guy. You and Gaeton, you kissing cousins or what?"

Thorn considered it a moment.

He said, "If I was going to kiss a man, it wouldn't be a former federal agent."

Benny smiled. He said, "But the two of you are close, no?"

"Mr. Cousins," Thorn said, "I've never been anything but self-employed. The only reason I'm here is 'cause of Gaeton. So, yeah, you could say we're pretty close."

Benny hummed to himself, giving Thorn a curious stare. He shook his head, and said, "OK, then. Let me get right to the point with you. I hear that money isn't a thing with you. Takes other things to make you hop. OK, I respect that."

"I bet."

Benny closed his eyes, shook his head. He leaned forward on his chair, elbows on his knees. He said, I hear you know the lay of the land down here. Hell of a fisherman. Things of this sort. You check out good."

"What does that mean? Check out good?"

"We brought you up on the screen," Benny said. "What? You thought you were anonymous?"

Thorn watched a trio of killdeer flash overhead, riding a fresh breeze from the northwest, steering wide around that phony house. Thorn on a computer? Thorn, without so much as a Social Security number or a driver's license. Hadn't registered for the draft, hadn't ever paid taxes 'cause he'd never gotten a paycheck. Nothing special about that in the Keys. Living in Key Largo had until recently been like living in a foggy hollow in the Ozarks down a three-day Jeep trail. Revenue men had been as rare as frost. But in the last few years they'd been everywhere, along with their relatives, the FBI, DEA, all the initialed enforcers pushing the boundaries of law down that strip of U.S. 1.

Benny fiddled with the tiny conch shell dangling from his right ear. He said, "I like to know a guy before I get involved with him. So I read up on you, and I liked what I saw. You're a guy who wants something done, he finds a way to do it, kosher or not. A man not tainted by a lifetime of law enforcement activities. 'Cause see, in the security business you can't be too fussy about who you deal with. Some of my clients, they haven't always been good little boys and girls."

No, maybe the hot tub was the wrong approach. Maybe he should lay Benny out and run him through the sawmill. It'd be messy. But worth it. Thorn smiled at the thought of it. And Benny smiled back.

"As for you, Thorn," Benny said, "at the moment, I'm personally looking for the right guy, like a private tutor, you know, show me how to hold a rod and reel, simple stuff. Finding fish. The difference between this fish and that one. Shit like that, so I don't look like Willy off the pickle boat."

Thorn mustered another smile.

"I'm throwing myself into this laid-back Keys shit," Benny said. "I mean, I'm offering you a job, but it's like, you come to work with us, you can dress how you want. Let your fingernails go six inches, an earring. Whatever you're into."

Thorn looked at his fingernails.

"Go without underwear?" he said.

"Hell, yes." Benny smiled and tapped his middle finger on Thorn's knee. "You're exactly what I'm looking for. The real thing, an authentic. You can show me things. 'Cause you're it, Thorn. An authentic."

"Thanks," Thorn said.

"I was something of a maverick myself," Benny said. "Man, I hated government work. So I started my company, and ding, my life changed. I became an entrepreneur, and all the songs on the radio started making sense. Sunny skies above, don't fence me in." The guy was starting to get rhapsodic, swaying to the music of his ego.

Thorn watched the redhead rise, jog quickly to the edge of the pool. She looked around, waited till all her flesh came to rest and she was certain everybody was watching. Everyone was. She dove in, and as she broke back into the air, she squealed.

Benny reached out, gripped Thorn's knee, and said, "Three years ago we were doing nothing but rent-a-cop work for weddings, bar mitzvahs, dances. Shit work. But listen to this: Last year we grossed over eighty mil.

" 'Cause we broadened our scopes. Nowadays we do it all, employee surveillance, security procedures, counterespionage. Things as simple as weapons selection, guard dogs even. We'll take a guy, set up his entire security program for him, small business, international. We do labor disputes. Say a company wants to stay operational in the face of some union bullshit. We do home-away-from-home service, uniformed guards, negotiators, even bedding, laundry, recreational gear, the whole schmear."

"You guard scabs."

"That's one way to say it," Benny said. He looked warily at Thorn. "And seclusion enhancements are also big these days."

"Seclusion enhancements," Thorn said, feeling his mind fog. He said it again. Thorn cleared his throat and said, "Guys you used to put away, now you're coaching them. That's how it is?"

Benny shifted in his chair and sighed.

"See, what I'm trying to show you, Thorn, is you give me a couple of weeks of your time, let me pick your brain now and then, if it works out between us, there's a lot of slots a person could fill with this company."

Benny leaned back, his eyes panning around his property, snagging for a second on the redhead shivering, toweling off.

He bent forward, his voice dropping a few decibels, a rough imitation of confidentiality. "Fact is, Thorn. I'll give it to you in full honesty. I'm in love with these islands. I want to relocate my home office down here. But you know, the place is lousy with disorganized clowns, loners, and losers stepping all over each other trying to get things done. One of my goals is, I'm going to bring this county into the twentieth century, man. That's the long and short of it. You don't have anything against the twentieth century, do you, Thorn?"

"A lot."

Benny smiled vaguely and said, "I have guys working for me, they hunt elk in Montana every fall and just work the winter season." He seemed far away now, not sure what was happening to the thread of his sales pitch.

"Hunt elk," Thorn said quietly. "With the antlers."

"Or wild boars," said Benny. "Whatever you're into."

"Could I shoot people?"

"Not regularly," Benny said with the same flat voice.

"I'd miss shooting people," Thorn said. "If things got dull, could I shoot at you?"

"All right," Benny said, his voice suddenly neutral, finally catching on. He turned a twisted frown on Thorn. Things jumped in his temples. The gold conch shell flickered.

One of Benny's men was striding over, carrying a portable phone, wiping his mouth with the wax paper from his submarine sandwich. He handed Benny the phone. Benny held it, still glaring at Thorn, tapping his finger on the edge of the table as if counting off the seconds.

Thorn made him count off a few more, then stood, moved to the edge of the hot tub.

He kind of enjoyed the rumbling sound of the hot tub. It reminded him of one of those cracks in the ocean floor he'd read about, where the lava superheats the water, bubbles out, filling the water with its dark fertility. The fish growing huge, the plants monstrous. He liked that, a fissure between this world and that one. A place where you could go to see the two worlds clashing and bubbling and the fish feeding on the bounty.

Benny came close to Thorn, looked down at the bubbles. "OK, so I was wrong about you," he said. "But let me tell you something, hot rod. You wouldn't have lasted with us anyway. I'm looking for men. Guys got uranium in their balls."

"You know," Thorn said, turning and taking a good grip on Benny's lapels, "person like you needs to learn to relax. Get your blood pressure down in the double digits. Slosh around, open the pores." Thorn had him on the edge of the steamy Jaccuzi. Benny helpless, at arm's length now from Thorn. Roger was on his way over from the gazebo to protect his boss, not exactly in a hurry. "Guy like you puts so much stress on himself, it's got to be bad for your arteries. I feel mine get tight just looking at you."

Thorn let Benny go. He looked down at him there, splashing around, the guy not relaxing after all.

12

Gaeton had dreamed through the afternoon. It was his horny dream about lush jungle women. Brazilian, Peruvian. He wasn't sure. He'd been having it now for weeks. The setting and the women always the same, but the story line different. Probably it was his libido sending tomtom messages to his brain. Cut out all this thinking and figuring, get back to the glandular truths. Now he wished he had.

In this afternoon's dream he had cruised batlike through a tropical rain forest, steam rising from rivers. Sharp outs in the emerald shade of palms. He'd seen the iridescent blues and reds of macaws, lizards. Deeper and deeper into the green shadow of the jungle until he coasted into a clearing.

And there he was suddenly sitting on a golden throne. He had tribal markings on his face and arms. Naked village maidens were lined up to present themselves to him, one by one. Good-looking maidens, too. Sonia Bragas, every one of them. That hair, those swollen hips. They lay down on the grassy earth, opening themselves to him.

He could feel his erection pushing against the linoleum. It

brought him almost back to consciousness.

Then a blast of light. Sonia gone. The macaws flying into the brightness.

Gaeton swiveled his shoulders as much as he could to see the silhouette standing in the doorway of the shed. It was late afternoon. The door closed on an ominous sky. Probably five-thirty, maybe six. Sunday. Less than a week till the Old Pirate Days festival.

He'd always loved that time of year, even after it got so touristy. The seafood festival, the kissing booths, four days of everybody in Key Largo dressed like Blackbeard. Hey, me hearty. The treasure hunt at Harry Harris Park. The silly parade with pirate beauty queens in prom dresses and eye patches. The volunteer fire department throwing out rubber swords and headbands. It was goofy and small-town and commercial. But for three days in the middle of every January everybody on the island was smiling. And shit, when did you ever see that anymore?

Gaeton made himself look up into the shadow. He couldn't make out the kind of pistol, but he could tell it had a silencer screwed on the barrel.

Benny leaned over and pulled off the tape and pulled out the sock. Gaeton had tested his range earlier in the day, rolling a half turn to his right, coming back, taking a breath, another fierce roll. But what then? Bite Benny's ankle till he gave up?

Benny stepped close. Gaeton drew in a quiet breath.

"Oh, hey, Benny, it's you. Jesus, how'd you find me? Let me tell you, man, it's good to see you."

"Cut the shit," Benny said.

"What?"

"You know what, you Benedict Arnold."

"Well," Gaeton said up into the dark, "at least I tried."

"That you did," Benny said.

He had imagined this moment, pictured it in different ways. But never like this. It was Ozzie. Poor stupid Ozzie stumbling into it. That unpredictable swirl of weather that fouled up even Darcy's forecasts. You could see the big patterns, shifts in the jet stream, fronts, and make probable calls based on them, but it was the little local dips and eddies in the atmosphere that might just lash up a tornado that would scatter a mobile home park. Hard as hell to see them forming.

"You're a real smoke blower, you know that, Richards," Benny said. "From day one I knew what you were doing. You came in here, smiling and winking and thinking you're putting one over on me, finessing Benny Cousins. But from the first fucking minute you proposed it to the bureau, I knew. I always thought of you, Gaeton, as my pet. My pet mole.

"And then Larry, guy I had keeping tabs on you, he tells me you were knocked over the head by a guy in an ice cream truck and had taken up occupancy in this shed. And I'm like, what? This a special recipe for Eskimo Pie or something, grind up FBI undercover guys? Tell me, man. The fuck is going on with you? You in some kind of neighborhood dispute here? Some kind of sex thing? Man, it's too weird even for me."

Benny nudged the linoleum again, brought it back.

"How'd it happen, Benny?" Gaeton said. "You get some slime in an open sore? What flipped you?"

"Jesus, Richards. I thought more of you than that."

"So what did it then? Tell me. You weren't always a crook. Were you?"

"I'm still not," he said.

He sat down on a wooden keg and sighted the pistol at Gaeton. He sighed and brought it back down.

He said, "See, Richards, you're like most people, you got no sense of history. You never sat down and thought about what it is we're doing, like in the big march of time." Benny leaned his shoulder against the workbench, setting the pistol there. He said, "I'm a student of history. I read about crime. How it was, how it's changed. How it is now. I mean, everybody acts like it's all still 'Honey, excuse me, I'm going to lift your money.' Andy Hardy bullshit.

"Yeah, maybe there was a time back a hundred years ago, it was please and thank you, raise your hands, no profanity. There were rules. Everybody knew them, everybody used them. Cops could afford to be polite back. Make our nice little laws, all that goody-goody horseshit."

Gaeton was quiet. His throat had almost closed anyway. And there didn't seem much point to smart-mouthing.

He could hear a lawn mower, a baby crying. He held on to those sounds. He drew in the cut-grass smell, the aromas of the shed, oily concrete, something mildewing.

Benny said, "But come on, man. The dope czars, they got Silkworm missiles in their trunks, they got more people praying at their knees than the pope, and whatta we got? A piddling Smith and Wesson? The worthless fucking Bill of Rights?

"These guys got auras the size of New Jersey. They got armies and satellites and more money than the Saudis. This isn't happytime Eliot Ness shit. You don't Boy-Scout these fucks. What we need these days is guys on our side as big and bad and dangerous as their guys. And as rich. We been castrating ourselves with our decency and our Judeo-Christian this and that. But what we need, man, is good guys as big as they are. And ready to do whatever the fuck ugliness it takes. Guys like me."

Gaeton said, "Tell me the scam, Benny. What the hell it was I died over, huh?"

"Fuck that noise," he said. "I wouldn't tell you jackshit."

Gaeton dragged in some air.

Gaeton said, "It's just you, isn't it? Joey, Roger, the other guys. They don't know from shinola what you're into, do they?"

"I'm a loner," Benny said. "Those guys are plumb lines, man. Fastest route between two points, every one of them."

"OK, so what is it, Benny?" Gaeton said. "You supplying hitters for the Italians, playing with wise guys, is that it?"

Benny laughed, shaking his head in disgust. "That's what you think? You work almost a year, and that's what you come up with? Jesus, no wonder the FBI dumped you out here in a no-win situation. Guy as dumb as you, they were probably glad to get you out of the office."

"Well, what then? You're going to do me, what's the harm? Tell me."

Benny rose from the wooden keg. Picked up his silenced .38.

"You know, this is real convenient for me. You being rolled up like this. This is a real lucky circumstance. Because I been wondering just how I was going to step you across. But I like this, this is weird, rolled up like that. Some guy is working his own vendetta on you, and I'm just fortunate enough to be able to assist him. Man, some times, your karma kicks you out something like this, you know it must be from all the good you been doing. You see what I'm saying, Richards?"

"You're a goddamn disease, Benny," Gaeton said, trying to find Benny's eyes in the darkening room, to give him a look to remember. But all that was left of him was a gleam from his bald head, another glint from that gold earring. Gaeton said, "You're standing there giving me a twisted history lesson and I'm supposed to smile and nod my head. Get enlightened from a bag of self-righteous rat puke like you. A guy with a spine full of pus, a guy, he screws his country, and has delusions he's a goddamn hero."

The first shot tore into the edge of his belly. And Gaeton

began to sink away into a gray sea inside himself. Then slowing, stopping, beginning to rise, coming up into his body again.

Benny looked down at him from a mile away. And with blood rising into his throat, Gaeton said, "Higher, asshole."

The next shot crushed his sternum, knocked the breath from him. And he flickered on the edge of consciousness.

"Jesus Christ," Benny said. "Those fucking checks. You're still holding those, aren't you? Huh, asshole?"

Then Gaeton could dimly make out Benny bringing his head down, reaching his arm into the linoleum roll, his hand slipping farther in, wiggling the fingers into Gaeton's shirt pocket.

Gaeton collected his dwindling strength, focused it, let it gather as Benny dug the checks out. And as he was pulling his hand out, Gaeton grunted and jerked his head off the cement and bit into Benny's ear. Snagged the earring in his teeth and gave his head a final twist. Benny screamed, fell onto the cement beside Gaeton. And Gaeton sucked the earring into his throat.

Far away he heard Benny cursing. And in a moment he felt the the burning circle of the barrel press against his forehead. Branded. The Circle O Ranch.

And then it was cool and exquisitely dark, and for the first time in a very long time, he wasn't thirsty.

Benny, fighting back the pain, dropped the pistol onto the cement floor. He tore off the yellow rubber gloves. Once again keeping his hands dishwater safe. He wadded them in the pocket of his crumpled white coat. Then he squeezed his ripped earlobe tight in his right hand. Blood on his sleeve, on his shoulder. He stood there cursing himself, cursing the dead jackoff.

With his other hand, he slid the cashier's checks into his inside jacket pocket. His goddamn earlobe was pulsating with about a hundred megawatts. Benny chanted his curses, a twisted mantra of goddamns and shits.

He stooped over the body again and opened Gaeton's mouth. He stuck his fingers in there, probing between gum and cheek, under his tongue, down into his throat. A fucking first, giving a guy a postmortem mouth feel.

There was nothing in there. Benny stood up, wiped the saliva on his pants legs. Maybe he should slice him open. A little work shed autopsy. But shit, what was the point? He'd like to see the medical examiner who could match up earlobe samples.

Benny Cousins looked down at the shadowy figure of Gaeton Richards. Then he bent forward and cleared his nose, one nostril at a time over that stupid man. Dead men were always so stupid. Even worse than the living.

13

"I'm not riding with some fucking corpse," Bonnie said.

They were in the shed. Bonnie had rolled out of bed wearing a black sweat suit. She was standing there holding a Budweiser, looking down at this guy, some of his forehead gone. It was about two-thirty in the morning. Dead calm. Some sand fleas chewing on his neck, but Ozzie couldn't even work up strength to brush them off. There in that shed, the one yellow light bulb was showing this guy's brains stuck to rakes and hoes.

He couldn't goddamn believe it. It made his head swirl. At the bar that Sunday night he'd waited till Papa John went to take a piss and he'd asked Crump Berry about Darcy, if she lived with her brother. Crump drove a shrimp truck out of Tavernier.

He came into Papa John's Bomb Bay Bar every night. Crump said, yeah, sure, the brother was FBI or something like that. Straight as they come. And his sister used to be a Miss Florida beauty contest girl. Everybody knew those two.

Ozzie had to put his hands under the bar, they started shaking so bad. About then Papa John came back and said he'd gotten a call from some lady down in Islamorada about Ozzie insulting her and her kid last night when all they wanted was some ice cream and a few joints. Ozzie said, yeah, yeah, all his fault. He'd gotten his period or something. Sorry, never happen again.

Ozzie finished cleaning up the bar, a zombie, and wobbled out of there somehow. He sprinted through the cold the two hundred yards back home. The whole way thinking, well, the lifeguard offered me a deal, right? Let him go, forget the whole thing.

And then Ozzie got to the shed panting. He couldn't believe it. The fucking door was jimmied open. And as he opened it, right off he smelled the gunpowder. And something worse. But he stepped in anyway, reaching up for the string to the light, feeling the stickiness on his flip-flops. Jesus.

Then he'd run upstairs and shaken Bonnie, rattled her eyes around. Ozzie thinking, that bitch offed this guy just to trip him up. But she'd barked at him. Man, Bonnie could turn Doberman, snarling, snapping, clicking out her claws. And then Ozzie had to tell her the whole story. Who this guy was, why he was out there rolled up in linoleum. It woke her right up and got her to quit snapping at him.

She said, "You pathetic dickhead."

Ozzie said, yeah, yeah. Agreeing, taking her shit. Ready to take everybody's shit tonight.

He led her down to the shed, showed her the stiff. He picked up the Colt lying on the floor and looked it over. Nice pistola.

That made three of them he'd gotten out of this. A .357 Smith in the lifeguard's shoulder harness. On the front seat of the Porsche, a ten-millimeter Colt, looked like a midget .45. And now this one. Ozzie was thinking, man, you shake one of these lifeguards and guns come clattering out.

Ozzie by then was wondering, what the hell, maybe he'd killed him. He could've blacked out, walked in, and shot the guy. But no, that morning he'd driven around the neighborhoods in Key Largo selling ice cream till late afternoon, working his way down to Tavernier and back. Then he got some hedge clippers out of the toolshed and walked through the trailer park, pretend-ing to clip this and that, but actually circling in closer and closer to Darcy's trailer, trying to work up the stomach for going in there and asking her . . . but what? What the fuck could he say? Is it your brother or your boyfriend I got rolled up back of my house? So he clipped and snipped and wound up doing nothing.

Then he spent the evening trying to write a new song, used up ten sheets of paper and got nowhere. Then, at one in the morn-ing, he went to work. He took his raft of shit from Papa John and asked Crump about Darcy. That was the whole day. Nobody killed in there anywhere. Much as he wished, he couldn't claim this one

Ozzie said, "I'll be right behind you in the truck."

Bonnie said, "Eating Fudgsicles while I have a date with a dead guy."

"It's ten miles is all it is. It'll take fifteen minutes."

"Some cop stops me, what am I going to tell him?"

"Go the speed limit, who's going to stop you?"

"I'm going to say what? This bozo sucked on a forty-five 'cause I wouldn't come across for him."

"Sounds good to me," said Ozzie.

"Jesus Christ, I can't believe I'm doing this."

But Ozzie could hear it. A little respect in her voice. The woman was starting to see who he was. What he was made of.

"Hey, I'll buy you breakfast afterwards."

"Yeah, sure, right. Maybe a nice rare steak."

Ozzie started to unroll the guy. God, he hoped the lifeguard was still limber enough to wedge him into that car.

Out there in alligator country, the lights of Miami made a reddish haze in the sky off to the north like the city was on fire. Probably was. They were in north Key Largo, down one of those rutted roads that led west off 905. The place was crisscrossed by canals back there. Ozzie's hands still herky-jerky.

Bonnie pulled up to the edge of the canal and killed her headlights. Ozzie got out of the truck, came around to look. It was colder out here, with a raw wind stinging right through you. And shit. The canal was full there, too. Cars, stoves, refrigerators. The Porsche would be sitting up out of water. The canal must have been twenty, thirty feet deep, and it was brimming over.

He told Bonnie and she cursed at him.

"I can't do anything about it," he said. "It's not my fault."

"Well, just take your flashlight and walk along the edge till you see an open spot, why don't you?"

So he did. Damn. This place had gotten so popular. Not like three years ago. He'd brought a Toyota out here and dumped it. In and out in five minutes. He'd gotten two hundred bucks for it. A Cuban he'd met in a bar at Vacation Island. That night Ozzie'd gotten out of the car, gone around to the back of it, rocking it back and forth to push it over the edge, and Jesus, then he knew what the deal was. The stench coming from the trunk. Whew.

That time he'd had to walk the ten miles back down to Key Largo. But he'd learned things since then. Get a partner, even if she was a Doberman. This time things were going better. Except he couldn't find a space. Another one of the goddamn problems with overpopulation. All the garbage.

Ozzie walked along the canal edge. Cars, cars, trucks. Insurance, insurance. He felt like putting in a call to the TV people to expose this. Make the cops get off their fat asses. They were so busy ripping off cocaine dealers they ignored these canals out here. Oh, they knew about them, and every six months or so when they needed to get some press, they'd bring a fleet of wreckers out here and haul all the stolen vehicles out. But with half of them working part-time for the drug guys, things were getting out of control. It made it hard on everybody.

Finally he found a spot. He blinked his flashlight at Bonnie, and she started up the Porsche and hauled ass down to him.

She parked it right on the edge of the canal, put it in neutral, brake off, got out in a hurry, and right away she started trying to rock it into the water.

"Wait a minute, goddamn it. Wait a minute."

Something had come to Ozzie as he'd been driving up from Largo. How he could maybe squeeze a dollar or two out of this. Long as he was in this far, what the hell. He went around to the passenger side and opened the door. He'd noticed the ring before, thought of just stealing it and trying to pawn it. There was some kind of blue stone in it, a wide gold band. It'd bring maybe fifty bucks. But no, this was better. Ozzie was learning. He was proud of himself, getting smarter finally.

Ozzie took Gaeton's hand out of his lap and twisted off the ring. It was the first dead guy he'd touched since that black field hand in the ditch. He kind of liked it. It put a zoomer in his bloodstream for a minute. He hadn't felt his blood race like that since Bonnie had squeezed off a couple of rounds at him last month.

He slammed the door of that Porsche and looked over at Bonnie. She was cursing him, stringing together all the names she'd been calling him lately. Maybe he could get that into a song. Something about touching dead guys, living with a Doberman.

You know your honey loves you when she aims too high. Something along those lines.

The two of them pushed that car. They got it going fast enough to get it over the edge and splash into the canal. Ozzie almost lost his balance and went in with it. But Bonnie, goddamn her, caught him by the neck of his sweat shirt, yanked him back. They watched it settle into that water, find its spot, get comfortable, let go of a couple of bubbles. And that was fucking that.

They were sitting in the ice cream truck in the dark parking lot of the Holy Fisherman Episcopal Church. Bonnie stood in the front of the truck. Ozzie sat in the driver's seat, staring out through the window. She'd been heaping shit on him all the way back. At this point he needed a scuba tank.

Well, if Ozzie hadn't killed this guy, who had?

He didn't know.

He didn't know shit. He didn't know what anybody in all of Key Largo could've told him. That these two were brother and sister. The weatherlady and the FBI agent. So come on, doofus, try thinking for once. Who did this guy? Who left him there for you to clean up?

Fuck if he knew.

Who? Didn't he see it? Didn't he have the brains God gave a green apple?

No, he guessed he didn't.

It was something the FBI guy was working on. Some case he was doing. And the bad guys some way or another saw what Ozzie did to this guy and came for him, did him and left him for Ozzie to fucking explain.

That made sense. Or maybe not. He'd have to think this one out. Ozzie looking out at that church, wondering why she'd told him to stop here. What were they going to do? Pray? Repent? Oh, shit. That's how far down he was right now, he was willing to consider that even. Whatever she said.

And Bonnie went on with her reasoning. So who are these guys, do you suppose? Who would an FBI guy be chasing around down here? Huh?

Ozzie worked on it. He was feeling sleepy, though. All that frizz in his blood for the last few hours, it'd died out and left him wanting to stay in bed for a week. He couldn't remember her question. He tried, but he couldn't remember it, so he just said what he always said when that happened, how the hell should he know something like that?

Drogas, Bonnie said. You dimbrain. Colombians. Or Cubans or Jamaicans. Smug drugglers. She'd said that. Smug drugglers. Shit, ever since Bonnie had started going to those community college classes, she was talking different. Making jokes he didn't get. Her voice coming down on him from a little higher up. Smug drugglers. Shit.

So? Ozzie had said. Big deal. They hit their guy, it's all done. We did the rest of their job for them. They should be happy. They should pay us something is what they should do.

"What I'm saying is, Ozzie, you've got us in some stinky shit, man. These kind of people, it's a wonder we're still alive at this moment." Bonnie leaned against the dashboard, brought her face around so Ozzie would have to look at it if he looked up from his lap. He kept his eyes down. That was it? That was her whole thing? That they were hip-deep in the cesspool? Big surprise.

"Now come on," she said. "We're going to get that window."

Oh, that. How'd he forget about the fucking window? A big stained glass thing at the front of the church. Jesus surrounded by lambs and children, some disciples and other guys standing around behind. Big mother of a window. It had enough stained glass in it to keep Bonnie in business for the rest of her life. She was guilting him into helping her do it.

Ozzie hated churches. His father'd been a preacher, part-time. The other part he worked as a roofer. Always saying it was his way of staying as close to God as possible when he wasn't actually preaching.

Ozzie thought churches were dangerous places. The place where people had fits and old people fell on the ground and cried. The place where his father would cuss and scream at everybody in the room just like he did to Ozzie and his mother at home.

So when Bonnie'd said she wanted that window one day a couple of weeks back, Ozzie had just pretended not to hear her. But now here they were, Ozzie owing her one.

Bonnie grunted at him to help her get some of these boxes empty. Shake out the Fudgesicles, ice cream sandwiches. Something to carry it all in.

"What about the priest or whatever he is, lives back there?"

"What're you, scared? You got the drug world after us, and a priest is scaring you?"

He helped her empty a few boxes, and they climbed out of the truck and crossed the dark lot to the front of the church. Bonnie bent over and started loosening up a cement parking marker. In that moonlight it could've been petrified elephant flop. Ozzie watched her rock it loose and raise it up and set it on her shoulder. Half a shot put. He was feeling a little warm toward her just now. Strange as it seemed, all the shit she'd been giving him. But there she was, kind of like him. What artists wouldn't do for their art.

She carried the rock over to the window, hefted it up, checking its weight. Then she backed up a couple of steps and started hopping toward the window to make her toss.

"Drop that stone!" a man's voice said.

It came off Bonnie's shoulder and went about a yard into the hedges surrounding the church. Ozzie raised his hands, and Bonnie turned and raised hers, too. A guy in his pajamas and robe was there holding out his gun in the moonlight. He had a beard and short gray hair. And though he wasn't wearing his collar, Ozzie knew just from the way his voice had commanded Bonnie to stop, that this guy had the power of God streaming through him.

14

Thorn and Sugarman were eating silently. Thorn could feel the hum of some leftover tension from Saturday. It had been the first time Sugarman had ever used his police voice on Thorn.

They were sitting at a waterfront table at The Pier, Key

Largo's latest hot spot. The place featured cosmetic redwood beams in the ceiling, big-screen TV in the bar showing an exercise program, potted palms everywhere. Last year at this time the building had housed an auto body shop.

Thorn wore a faded blue work shirt and khaki trousers, a leather flight jacket, and his good boat shoes. It was his dead-of-winter look.

He watched as a couple of guys in wet suits tried to windsurf out on Tarpon Basin. They coasted three feet, then fell off, got back on, hauled up the sail, and lost their balance as soon as the wind began to drive them forward.

Thorn had ordered the hamburger. He knew it was a mistake when the waitress asked him how he wanted it cooked. On a griddle, he thought of saying. With a long steel spatula, and scrape the grease off into the gutter. But he said, medium well. The young waitress wrote that down.

Then it came out smothered in avocados, alfalfa sprouts, half the state of California. It would probably make Thorn live an extra six months just smelling the thing. Sugarman didn't seem to notice, plowing through his, focused on his plate.

Today Sugar wasn't wearing his Monroe County Police green and grays. He had on a pink polo shirt and a pair of new jeans, red stitching around the pockets, running shoes, no socks.

Thorn put aside his burger.

"I don't remember ever seeing you in pink before, Sugar."

"Speak softly and wear a loud shirt," Sugarman said.

Sugarman took a small bite out of his cheeseburger. Alfalfa sprouts stuck to his chin, like a wispy Chinese beard.

"I didn't have time to change," he said. "Had this private job last night, up in Miami."

The cook had left the potato skins on the french fries. Big

thick-cut chunks. The things probably had sea salt on them. Add on another six months to live. If he ate here every day, he'd have the bowels of a teenager in no time. Thorn made a note to tell Gaeton about this place. Next time you had a hankering for alfalfa sprouts, I got the place for you.

"Beware of work that requires new clothes," Thorn said.

Sugarman shook his head. Cut him some slack, easy on the jokes.

Thorn reached out and took the alfalfa sprouts off Sugarman's chin, looked at them for a moment, and ate them. Sugarman finished his Coke, shook some crushed ice into his mouth, and started chewing on it.

"I wouldn't do this kind of work, but I'm pinched for cash," Sugarman said. "It's like fancy car repo stuff. Stealing cars from drug scum. These guys, they're cheapskates like you wouldn't believe. They go into a fancy car place, a couple of hundred thou wadded up in their pockets, and they count out ten, fifteen thousand, plunk it down on a fifty-thousand-dollar car. They got great credit 'cause they own some bank around town, one you never heard of, but it's still full of money. So, they drive the Lamborghini away, or it's a Rolls, cars I can't even pronounce their names. And these slobs just forget about paying the other forty. They're sneerers. They like taking advantage."

Thorn watched as one of the windsurfing students acquired a sudden fit of balance and began sailing out toward a mangrove island. He waved triumphantly back at his friend, and fell forward into the sail.

Sugarman said, "It can turn into dangerous shit. Because for one, these guys always got six linebackers around them, everybody armed like Israeli commandos. Anyway, so the law says you can't climb over their wall and hot-wire the thing. They practically stole this car, haven't made a payment on it in five months, and the most you can do is try to steal it back, but only out in neutral territory.

"So, I'm sitting down the street from this one guy's twenty-five-room house, in the company car, a piece of crap Chevette, and I wait till this fancy Dan comes roaring out to eat supper at midnight. I follow him till he gets to a red light and pull up behind him and just flat-out ram him in the back bumper. Fender-bender thing.

"He pops out, looks at the damage. And I get out like I'm looking at it, too. The guy looks me over, how I'm dressed, and he thinks, hey, maybe he's one of us. It gets his guard down a little. And I hand him a business card, and while he's looking at it, I'm in his car, locking the door, feeling around for the ignition key. And Christ, it's there. Thank God. So, I go lurching off in this thing, I can barely find the gearshift it's got so many extra gizmos. This guy meanwhile, he's yelling at me, brandishing a firearm but not wanting to shoot at his pretty car. I take a deep breath and look over, and there's a blonde in a red rubber dress right there in the seat beside me."

"Yeah." Thorn smiled, watching his buddy. "What'd she say?"

"She smiled at me, blew me a kiss. Freaked me out."

"Maybe she's used to it. Like a baton, getting passed on to the next guy running full speed."

"It freaked me out. Miami freaks me out. Nonstop."

"If you've got to moonlight, couldn't you find something down here?"

"This pays too good to miss," Sugarman said. "Even if it is in Miami. And plus, if I hang in there long enough, the company is branching out down here."

Thorn twisted in his chair. He thought he knew the answer, but he asked it anyway.

And Sugarman said, "Florida Secure Systems."

Thorn picked up a spoon and swiveled it in and out of the light. He said casually, "Benny Cousins's company."

Sugarman kept his coffee cup at his lips, staring at Thorn.

Thorn said, "He pays good, does he?"

Sugarman set his cup down and cocked his head.

"OK, what is this, Thorn? I don't like how this sounds."

"I'm just curious. I like to know things."

"I'm curious why you're curious."

"Hey," Thorn said, "humor me a minute. Tell me something about this company."

Sugarman sighed and frowned. A small smile in his eyes.

He shook his head and said, "I know it's very big, based in Miami, but they do work all over the world. They guard factory bosses, oil sheikhs, guys afraid of being kidnapped. They do fancy burglar alarms, James Bond stuff. They're into antiterrorist things, too, I hear. They've just generally got a great rep. A couple of guys from the sheriff's department applied but got turned down, so I consider myself lucky getting on with them."

Thorn picked up another french fry, dabbed it in ketchup, but put it down. His gut was feeling a slight chop, all this funny food.

"Now you talk to me," Sugarman said.

"I don't know exactly what it is," he said. "But something smells funny, and it's blowing in from Benny Cousins's direction."

Sugarman craned forward, squinted at Thorn.

"You're weird, Thorn. You and Higby been breathing too

much South American sawdust. You're starting to imagine things."

"Sugar," he said, "your boss, Benny Cousins, fixed my red tags. Overnight. You're going to arrest me Saturday, and on Sunday afternoon my house is a A-OK legal. Dosen't that sound strange to you?"

Sugarman lifted his eyebrows, gave Thorn a long, dismayed look.

"The man offered me a job, Sugar. He tried to bribe me into working for him, be his personal fishing guide, put him into some fish, show him how to cast his line."

"He did?"

"Did you know Gaeton is working for him?"

"I heard he was," Sugarman said. "But I haven't seen him in a long while." He pushed his plate to the side. "Thorn, you got that look again. I don't like that look."

"The guy's crooked, Sugar. He fixes things at the courthouse so somebody owes him one. He recruits his staff like that."

Sugarman shook his head and said, "Not Benny Cousins. The guy's an ex-fed, for christsakes, about as far away from a crook as you can get."

"You're not listening to me, Sugar. He fixed my code violations."

"Well, if that was true, it'd change my feelings about him," Sugarman said. "I got like a pet peeve about that sort of thing. I hate it when I'm there, doing my job, filling out every goddamn form they throw at me, and then somebody comes in and winks at the right secretary, gives somebody a fifty-dollar handshake, and man, the rules disappear. I get so ticked off it makes me just want to pack it in sometimes. Just hang it up."

A screech came from below the table and Thorn dropped his french fry.

"Just my beeper," said Sugarman, reaching to his belt to shut it off. He rose from the table. "Got to call in." He gave Thorn a helpless look. Eyes half closed, shaking his head.

The waitress appeared after Sugarman had left. She had no makeup, straight brown hair. Her eyes were merry and bright. He bet she'd never worn a pencil behind her ear, or called a customer honey in her life, or laughed while she swatted away a pinch.

As she began clearing the plates, all full of the pep she'd learned at hotel school, Thorn tried to fight off his grouchiness. It was just that he'd never seen pep in Key Largo before. Sloth, yes. Lethargy, certainly. All the pores wide open. That was Key Largo, all the Keys. About as close to pep as you could get was some New Yorker on his first day on the island, all manic to go here, do this, see that. But give them one night breathing that air, snorkeling on the reef, and next day at breakfast, they're staring out at the water, face slack, not looking around for the waitress.

But pep had arrived, like some kind of retrovirus, bringing its feverish, empty excitement. And here she was, with her bouncy step, her eager smile. A cheerleader for the New Age.

She began to bubble out the dessert choices. Thorn's mind shut down after the granola-blueberry yogurt and the white chocolate mousse. When she'd finished, he asked her if she had any peppermint patties. She cocked her head, gave it her best effort; then with a blank shake of her head she said no.

"Two cents, in a bowl by the cash register? Those things."

She smiled sadly as if she were embarrassed for him. For wanting something so meager, for mistaking this classy place for some diner.

"The check then," Thorn said.

That brought her back to life. A twitch came back into her

walk. She gave Sugarman a peppy hello as they passed. A guy she could relate to, Mr. Pink.

Sugarman sat down at the table and drew in a long breath.

"Who was it?"

"Jeannie."

"She beeps you?"

"She likes to tell me when she's had an insight."

"She had an insight," Thorn said.

"Yeah, she's been having a lot of them. Psychological insights. She's been going to see Don Meagers, the counselor at the elementary school. He does adults at night."

Thorn opened the lid of his hamburger, scraped some of the exotic vegetables off the meat, and took another bite.

Sugarman said, "She's decided she's an adult child of a co-alcoholic mother who hates men because they love her too much. Or . . . is that it?" Sugarman nudged his french fries and put his wadded-up napkin beside his plate. "No, but it's like that."

"It doesn't matter," Thorn said. "I get the idea."

"I mean, I understand a lot of it," Sugarman said. "I do. This business about how you wind up repeating your parents. Or trying to, and the other person is doing the same thing only with their parents, so you get into these fights 'cause it's not just the two of you married, but it's her parents and your parents and the two of you." Sugarman took a slug of his ice, crunched it for a moment. "Six goddamn people fighting, four of them ghosts."

They both looked out at the windsurfers for a minute or two. The guys were hopeless. They looked like they might have trouble standing up on land.

"Was everything all right?" The waitress was there, holding the leather binder, the check sticking out. She was looking at Sugarman. Thorn had stepped across into the alternate universe for her. Not there, just the husk.

Sugarman handed her a twenty, and she left.

Thorn felt a rumble in his belly. Six-point-one on the sphincter scale. Tectonic plates grinding. Tidal waves moving.

"Sugar," he said, "I know if you hear anything suspicious about Benny, you'll tell me."

Sugarman rose, looking out at the windsurfers.

"In my next life," he said, "I'm going to choose my friends better. Find some dull normals who get excited about checkers."

"Whatta you mean?" Thorn said. "I'm about as quiet a guy as you'll ever meet."

"Yeah, right," said Sugarman. "Uh-huh."

15

Who was he kidding? He didn't have anything to say to Gaeton, bothering him on a cold, blustery Monday afternoon. He was at the trailer park because of Friday night. The kiss. Because something in him had swung open, and he didn't want it to lock up again. He was there to see his friend's little sister. Go on, look it in the face.

The window unit was chugging hard as Thorn knocked on her door a couple of times. When she didn't come after a third round of knocking, he pushed the door open. Stepped into the stuffy room.

He smiled. So, she was one of those. Never used air conditioning to cool. But when the temperature dipped into the sixties, she switched the reverse cycle on high. If she wasn't sweating, something must be wrong.

She glanced up from the book she was reading on the couch, waved him in. She was in a long-sleeved gray T-shirt and red running shorts and sandals. Her hair was stacked in no particular order. Bobby pins helter-skelter. She was holding a paperback, wearing a Walkman. She smiled, took off the earphones.

"I tune in between the stations," she said, "get some white noise and dig into a hot read."

"What is it?" Thorn said.

She showed him the cover. *Moby Dick.* Her finger held her place halfway in.

He said, "I got an old high school report on that you could read, save you the trouble."

"Yeah?"

"I think what I said was that Ahab had the wrong kind of tackle. Whole problem was he was using those harpoons with short lines, trying to tire the whale out from hauling around boats full of men. When he should've used a lot more line, let the drag on the line do the work. Let Moby run all he wanted and stay back. That's what I said. I think I got a C or something. Miss Antrim said I missed the point. You remember how she was."

"I think I agree with her."

"The point's to catch the whale, right?" Thorn said. "All that other stuff, the philosophical stuff, that's just what you do while you wait for the fish to get caught."

"Come on in," she said. "Take a load off your wit."

Thorn noticed her ears today. He noticed her wrists and fore-arms. The razor line on her thighs where she stopped shaving. Her neck, the way she cocked her head. The way she walked to the refrigerator, a kind of lazy sureness as if she might break into a pirouette at any moment. He noticed the back of her neck, the wisps of red hair there.

They sat at the green dinette. She put a Budweiser down in front of him and popped one for herself. His started to sweat immediately. Thorn watching it puddle around the base of the can. The humidity in the eighties.

"Balmy," Thorn said, touching a finger to the condensation.

"Maybe," she said. "But let's work up to it gradually."

"Huh?" Then he caught it. He squinted at her. She was smiling, but she might've been serious. "You're pretty quick," he said.

"So'd you come for another kiss, or what?" she said. She took a swig. Watching him the whole time, her eyes smiling as she swallowed.

"Yeah," he said. "I guess I did."

"Well, you're going to have to earn this one. You can't keep stumbling into me, pretending to be drunk every time you want a little affection."

"You're pretty cocky, too," he said.

"I'm not touching that one."

"We could go on like this," Thorn said. "Or we could talk."

"You got a topic in mind?" She was enjoying this, sipping her beer, her Walkman lying on the table, fizzing out its tiny static. That grin in her eyes, saying, I knew it, I knew it. Someday this was going to happen.

"Where's Gaeton?"

"I'm not sure. It's hard to keep up with him," she said. "What? You worried he'll walk in, find us like this?"

"Maybe," Thorn said.

"Well, he's not here. Porsche's gone. He does this, goes off for a few days. It's what he does now."

Thorn said, "Benny Cousins offered me a job. Can you believe that? Being his personal fish guide."

Her smile dissolved.

"And?"

"I dropped him in his Jacuzzi."

"Good." Her face softened, but she was still displeased.

"He said if I came on with them, I could do whatever I wanted. Grow six-inch fingernails."

"That appeal to you?"

Thorn said, "And I could shoot elk in Montana. All kinds of benefits."

"Well, that about cinches it then," Darcy said. "You always had something against elk, haven't you?"

"No, I like big animals. I got a soft spot for them." Thorn took another sip of beer, said, "It's hard to see how Gaeton puts up with the guy. A first-class dork. He says he wants to be a major player in the Keys. Makes it sound like a hobby. And Gaeton, he's helping him. Doing what, do you know?"

"Helping Benny meet people," Darcy said. "Introducing him around. I don't know exactly what else. Maybe he's giving him elocution lessons, teaching him to speak like a Conch." The impishness was gone from her voice. Her eyes heavy.

"This is bothering you, isn't it?" Thorn said.

"Benny's into something seriously illegal, Thorn. I'm not positive yet about all of it, but I'm working on it."

"You are?"

"Yeah," she said. "Yeah, I am." It seemed to startle her, saying it and hearing it out loud.

Someone switched on Glenn Miller next door. "Chattanooga Choo-choo." It rattled the silverware for a moment, till the guy brought the volume down. Thorn looked out the small kitchen window at the purple bougainvillaea vines, a croton hedge. He watched the big band buff come outside, sit on his porch rocker with a bottle of beer and a girlie magazine. Wearing an undershirt and pajama bottoms. Ah, retirement.

"I've taken my three-week annual leave from work," Darcy said. "I'll stay out longer if I have to. Because I'm going to find out what's going on, Thorn. I am."

A cluster of creases had appeared in her forehead; her eyes were hard and set. She reached out and snapped the Walkman off.

He took another sip of beer. Her eyes were elsewhere now, all the light leaking out of them. She was somewhere that seemed to frighten her a little.

She lifted her head and said, "Gaeton hates guys like that. Arrogant bastards, coming down here, trying to bosom-buddy up to everybody. He hates them. He always has, but with Benny, he's playing along, pretending he respects the guy."

Thorn was quiet, drawing squiggles with the condensation.

She said, "I'm sorry, Thorn. I shouldn't be dumping this on you. You just came over for a nice friendly whatever, and I'm dumping my toxic wastes on you."

Thorn said it was OK.

"Let's talk about kissing some more," she said. "Let's talk about G-spots."

"All right," he said. "I'm game."

She finished her beer, went to the refrigerator, and got two more. When she bent to see what else was in there, Thorn looked at the back of her thighs. The red running shorts were riding up, her hamstrings standing out. At her hairline a slick trail of sweat ran down her neck, into her gray shirt.

"I hope you're not hungry," she said, turning, catching him in his tour of her. Not seeming to mind. "All he has is peanut butter and a carton of tofu. My weird brother."

She came back to the table, bringing two frozen glass stains. She poured her beer and didn't wait for the head to die. Foam on her nose.

Thorn wondered how he'd missed her for so long. She'd been right there, on the edge of his life since childhood. But he was just seeing her. Those sharp green eyes, that straight, almost too narrow nose. The half dozen freckles spattering her forehead and cheeks. The way one reddish eyebrow arched up and the other ran flat. A small scar curled at the corner of her eye, the shape of a small fishhook.

"So," she said, "you want to begin, or should I?" Her eyes were full of tricks.

He said, "We can't just sit on the couch, let things take care of themselves?"

"There's two ways to go here, Thorn. That's one of them, but I haven't had much luck lately letting things take care of themselves. I like to get the deck cleared right up front, do a values check, how you feel about this and that, then, you know, if we wind up on the couch or anywhere else, it's with a clear head. Like making a prebliss agreement."

"You want to know my religious preference?" Thorn said. "My politics? If I like children, dogs better than cats? My favorite color. That sort of thing?"

"It'd be a start," she said.

"Well, wait a minute," Thorn said. "I have a thought. A compromise."

"I'm listening," she said, with a wary smile.

"We go over to the couch, for ten, fifteen minutes. See how it goes. If it looks good for us, things are percolating, then we go on and fill out the rest of your questionnaire."

"You think you're that good a kisser?"

"It's worth a try," he said.

She said, "You don't mind getting involved with somebody who might be totally wrong for you? A very troublesome woman."

"I don't know," he said. "I think maybe troublesome women have a higher wriggle factor. The ones with the seething look and things to hide. The ones your questionnaire would say to steer clear of, those're the ones that make my heart roar."

"You got questionable values, Thorn."

"Yeah, I know."

"It's very immature," she said, "confusing love with drama. Thinking unless it's risky, it's not passion. That's for adrenaline freaks, Thorn."

He said, "We have these conversations. I wind up thinking about them, playing them back."

"Yeah? Is that bad?"

She smiled at him, her hands laced together, chin propped on them. He took another sip of his beer, stalling.

"Talk's too easy," he said. "Talk is what you do while you're waiting for the action."

She unlaced her hands, stood up and walked over to the couch, and stood there while Thorn looked back over his shoulder at her. Her lips came apart with a soft snap. She put her weight on one leg, a subtle shift of her hips. Thorn stood.

They kissed for ten minutes on the couch. And Thorn knew immediately that not even Bettina Daugherty at seventeen when Thorn was fourteen could compare. The two of them had kissed behind the dolphin pool her parents kept to supply local tourist shows. The dolphins rolling and blatting and clicking as Thorn kissed this girl who wanted to try everything related to kissing. She'd wanted to use him to expand her oral frontiers. But still, even that, that hot, amazing flush, was nothing next to Darcy.

Darcy had sat close beside him, smiling. And that smile had come forward into his face and it became his smile and something in her opened to him, an oceanic calm. And her lips parted, her feathery tongue slid into his mouth and circled his tongue, brought his into her mouth. Leisurely and strong. And then, it was as though the two of them had cracked through the earth's crust, and they were sipping together from a vast pure aquifer.

The light had weakened when Thorn had to rise from the couch to make a stop in the bathroom. When he came out, she wasn't waiting for him on the couch. He stood in the living room for a minute, listening to the lawn mowers, Glenn Miller's boys still swinging and swaying next door. Then he walked down the narrow hallway to her bedroom.

She was lying on the bed. She'd opened the sheets and taken off her shoes. She was neither smiling nor anxious. Looking at him with interest, a hint of curiosity perhaps. The early-afternoon light through the yellow shades was glazing her legs, making her hair more honey than rose.

Thorn came across to her and squatted beside the bed. There was mint on her breath now as she brought her face close to his.

She reached out, and her fingertip strayed lightly across his lips, drew a ticklish line down his throat to his collarbone. Thorn touched her hair at the temples, brushed it from her face.

She took her hands away from him, leaned back on the bed, and ran her hands across her breasts. Her nipples outlined through the fabric. A dreamy current came into her voice.

"It's been a very long time," she said.

"Yeah, it has," he said, but not sure which of the long times she meant.

He stood, and he watched as she sat back up, reached out and unzipped his khaki pants and pulled them down. That part of him which knew nothing but its single simple rule was responding. She drew down his undershorts and reached through his legs and took a cool grip on his balls and brought him a half a foot closer to her, taking him in her mouth, that minty mouth. And he became solid there.

Darcy held him in place, her thumb and one finger circling his balls and one finger stroking the seam of flesh hidden beneath. Thorn closed his eyes and a hot rush of air filled his lungs. His heart staggered. She stayed there, using her hands, her thin, cool fingers, her nails raking lightly across his flesh, finding some new notes, pushing his blood up an octave. Thorn massaged her skull, and watched her as she rode him, sweet, strong, and happy.

In a while she stood and drew off her long-sleeved T-shirt. He rolled her running shorts down across the flare of her hips. He undid his own blue work shirt, watching her stand before him. She was watching him, all of him at once.

When he was naked, too, she stepped forward and kissed him on the mouth, her lips opening, sliding her tongue beneath his tongue. He kissed her back. The mintiness was gone. On her breath all he could taste was himself.

Thorn, up on an elbow, was touching her left nipple, a slippery ruby. He looked at her hair, spread out against the white pillow, and spoke quietly into the half-dark, "Gaeton used to say that having sex is like running a roller coaster ride." He paused, and she made a humming noise. He said, "You can tell how well you did by how loud they screamed."

"Yeah?" Darcy said, opening her eyes briefly, closing them. Only a wispy thread connecting her to consciousness. Her voice husky. "How'd we do then?"

"I think we both did good," Thorn said.

"How do you know?"

"Hear that?"

Four, five dogs yapped and howled around the trailer park.

"We did that?" Eyes still closed.

"They started when we started. An hour ago."

Halfway down her drowsy drift to sleep, she mumbled, "Is that all it was? One hour."

He touched her hair. That thick hair, much softer than it looked. And her other hair, even softer, that tangle of rosy gold. It was scented with something, a mild flower. Jasmine? That aroma was on his cheeks, every breath now.

Thorn leaned over the edge of the bed and brought the top sheet back aboard, shook it quietly into place, and tucked it in around her. She dug the side of her face into her pillow, reached for him. He lay down and she brought her head to his chest, adjusted it till she found the right fit.

They were like that when the seashell exploded through the bedroom window. Glass scattered across the sheets. Thorn rolled to the floor, thinking he was on the *Heart Pounder*, that this was August again. Darcy made a strangled scream. He pulled her off the bed and brought her down beside him on the floor. They waited, kneeling in the dark. Dogs were barking everywhere. A cool breeze flooded through the broken window.

Darcy crawled across the floor to her purse on a chair by the dresser. She dug through it and came out with a small flat .25 automatic, a white pearl handle. She crawled back and squatted beside him. They watched the window.

He recognized the pistol. Her dad had kept it in a drawer at the newspaper office, and Thorn and Gaeton had taken it out as boys, held it, aimed it. It was a Browning Baby, intricate scrollwork on its nickel plate. The mother-of-pearl grip also engraved with a pretty filigree. Gaeton's father had found them with it once, took it out of Thorn's hand, saying nothing, puffing his pipe, giving them both a long stern look, and putting the pistol away where they never found it again.

Darcy and Thorn stayed in a crouch by the bed, listened some more. Nothing.

Thorn asked her if it was loaded.

"You better believe it is," she said.

Staying away from the window and the torn paper shade, they both dressed quickly, leaving their underwear behind.

16

Some little white poodle had broken its leather leash and chased after Ozzie all the way back to his house. Yipping and nipping. At the bottom of his outside stairs, Ozzie turned on the dog and drew his leg back, punt this sucker to Cuba. But the fucking dog stood up on its back legs and started turning around and around in a circle. Like a ballerina on a music box or something, all excited, doing its stupid trick there on the cement. Like it was trying to make Ozzie feed it or something. Ozzie stood there thinking, what the hell am I doing anymore?

He shooed the dog away and jogged up the stairs.

Bonnie was sitting at the dining room table. Jeans and a man's white dress shirt. Her hair just washed and in a ponytail. Not looking half bad, for her.

"You do it?"

He was still panting. He nodded that he had.

"Jesus Christ, now we're in it," she said. "The whole goddamn FBI'll be after our ass now. Ransoming one of their guys. The smug drugglers coming at us one way, and the FBI the other way. I can't believe you. I can't believe me."

Ozzie sat down at the table, took the Coors that was sitting in front of her, and killed it, one gulp.

"What'd you use?"

"Whatta you mean, what'd I use? My arm."

"I mean what'd you throw? A brick?"

"I stole a seashell from under the fence at Shell World. If it's any of your damn business. If you're so interested, why'd you stay here like some candyass?" Ozzie got up and took the last Coors from the refrigerator. He said, "You don't like how I do things, then bug out of here. You don't get to criticize me anymore, you hear that? This is my score. You got your thing, I got my thing. And this is it." Ozzie feeling something new here, some muscle in his voice. Maybe it was 'cause he was so scared, or maybe it was rubbing off from Papa John.

"I'm in it anyway," she said. "You do something, it affects me. I want to be sure it's not totally dumbshit."

"I been getting along fine without your help so far."

"Yeah, right. You haven't done nothing but kidnap an FBI guy and dump his dead body in a canal. You don't need anybody's help. Yes, sir. You're doing just fine fucking up all by your lonesome."

Ozzie listened to all the dogs, still barking, and some voices. He went over to the window that looked across at the trailer park, and he could see through the palm leaves four, five old farts standing out in one of the dirt streets. Dogs barking, old farts putting together an old fart posse, nobody looking over at Ozzie's. And there down at the foot of his steps was that little white poodle, still on its hind legs, still turning its circles. He got a good breath down and went back to his beer.

"How much you ask for?" she said.

"Three thousand dollars."

"Jesus Christ, Ozzie."

"Now what's wrong?"

"Where do you go for your idiot lessons? You know? I thought for a minute there last night you might have half a brain cell after all, the way you talked us out of the church thing. I was actually starting to think maybe you had a fucking chance of someday being able to walk around upright, not drag your knuckles."

Ozzie had sure as shit saved them last night. He'd stood up to that priest, and before he knew what he was doing, he was telling the priest that him and Bonnie had a terrible complaint against God. That that was why they were about to throw a rock through the window. They were trying to get his attention, to send down his mercy upon them.

'Cause up to then the Lord had failed them and doomed them to poverty and a life of misery and sin. He said how him and Bonnie had called out his name on repeated occasions and the Lord had failed to come through. All this while he was looking at the barrel of that gun, watching it tilt down. Every inch of tilt giving him more juice to talk.

Having a father who'd had a backwoods silver tongue was finally coming to some use. 'Cause he knew how these God-squaders thought, that you con them with their own shit: guilt, hope, charity. Ozzie went on, pushing it farther, saying that just a few minutes earlier, right out here in the parking lot of the church, him and Bonnie had been praying to beat the band. They'd tried calling out the name of the Lord, his secret name of Yahweh. Ozzie remembered the name from all the hundred times his daddy had screamed it out in church and made all those redneck Baptists sweat.

That priest took them into the church. Led them down front. Salvation by gunpoint, Ozzie was thinking. If his daddy had tried that, he'd have had a hell of a lot more success converting those peabrains.

That church was a much nicer place than any church Ozzie'd ever been in before. Looked like there might even be a few things around worth stealing. The priest led them down to the altar, had them get down on their knees, and got down himself right alongside of them and said a prayer out loud. His voice choky. Ozzie was thinking, good grief, maybe I'm in the wrong business. Maybe songwriting isn't my gift after all. Conning preachers might be a whole new direction.

So the preacher prayed that grace and mercy would come rolling down from the heavens and fill up these impoverished souls and lift their heads and turn their hands to profitable enterprise. All the same hooey Ozzie'd heard his old man spouting, only this guy using a better class of English. Bonnie looking across the preacher's back at Ozzie, her eyes wide like the Lord was giving her a little feel, squeezing her goodies. And Ozzie winked at her. Maybe the bitch would be more respectful. Maybe finally.

But she wasn't. She was there, drinking down the Coors he'd opened, throwing her head back and gulping it. Then she gasped, slapped the can down, and started right back in the same way she'd always done: "They're going to know right off, asking for three thousand bucks like that, they're dealing with a numbnut. A loser."

"Three thousand dollars, that's a shitload of money," Ozzie said. "What're you talking about? You don't know any more about the kidnapping game than I do, what're you doing giving me orders?"

"That's chump change. That's not diddly. She gets that for a night on TV. She goes to the mall and puts that on her charge card in one afternoon."

"So? Then she shouldn't have any trouble getting it together, should she?"

"Christ Almighty," she said. "What else'd you do? You sign your name? Give 'em your address?"

"Bonnie," Ozzie said, trying to flex that muscle in his voice again, reaching down into his throat, looking for it, "you just go ahead, keep making fun of me, you hear that. You just keep saying these things. Go ahead."

"Yeah, yeah. You're so tough. You're such a Johnny Cash roughneck. Jesus, I'm getting out of here."

But she didn't move. She just sat there looking at the empty beer can and not moving. And Ozzie knew she was scared, too. He could see it. She might give him her shit some more, talk her trash, but this was it. The scales had tipped. Ozzie was boss, captain of this goddamn ship.

"Now next thing to do," said Ozzie, "is go pick out some phone booths, write down the numbers. Run the people from phone booth to phone booth. You call them, move them to the next phone booth. Make sure the cops weren't following." Ozzie thinking, like on "Cannon" or which was it, one he just saw last week? Now what'd the kidnapper done wrong? How'd he get caught? Oh, yeah. The victim got loose, that was it. The guy broke out of the basement where they had him tied to the furnace. Ozzie thinking, well, no problem there. No problem there at all.

But one problem he *was* having was he didn't like the idea of causing Darcy Richards any pain. Course, then, on the other hand, when he had the three thousand and she found out her brother wasn't coming home, she'd be ripe for some comforting. Take her money, then step in and take her love. Maybe he'd even spend some of her money back on her. Jewelry or flowers or appliances. Things women got lathered over. Ozzie could be mighty generous. All it took to get him going was the right lady.

Bonnie, chewing on the edge of a fingernail, said, "I don't like this shit. Somebody walking into our backyard and wasting this guy. I don't like this shit at all."

"I been thinking on that," he said. "It wasn't any drug dealer or shit like that. They don't leave behind their bodies. I figured out just who it was killed him. And I know why, too."

She was really gnawing on that fingernail now, staring at him, all the bitchiness and backtalking gone out of her. Ozzie loved this. It was just like Johnny Cash. All it took, you had to jab in the spurs, show 'em what balls were all about. And even the Dobermans like Bonnie ducked their heads, stuck their tails deep between their legs.

"So, who?" she said.

"Only badass I know around here that's badder than me," he said. "Papa John Shelton."

"Come on," Bonnie said. "That old cow."

"It was him, I'm telling you. And he did it to show me what's what. It's part of the lessons he's teaching me. Like he was giving me a problem. Whatta you do with a dead guy in your shed? Like in school. Solve this. It's just like him to do it."

"The two of you," she said. "I don't know which one is worse. Doing all this macho bullshit. Guys with the real balls don't have to act tough. It's the needle-dicks that are always puffing up."

Ozzie stood up.

"Who you calling a needle-dick?"

Bonnie was silent, wouldn't even look up. She was gnawing

again on that finger. Her and her psychology. Her and her college class.

A line came to him then. It just whooshed his anger away. He stood up, got the slump out of his back, and took a good breath. He was an outlaw songwriter. He couldn't forget that. Him and Johnny and Waylon and even that white bread Jimmy Buffet. Outlaws, pirates. Yeah. Yeah.

> The night you called me a needle-dick
> was the first night of the last of your life.

It was a horse conch. A big one. Brown and unpolished. It had lodged underneath the dresser beside the bed. Darcy had it sitting on the dinette table when Thorn came back inside, the pistol sitting beside it.

She turned her face to him and her cheeks shone with tears.

"Anything out there?" she said, voice scratchy.

"People next door heard the crash, and a lady, Mrs. Beesting, thought she saw someone running away. Thought it was a black kid, but wasn't sure. Nothing else. I looked around back, some aralias were broken, but that's it."

"Look at this," she said. "It's Gaeton's."

Thorn sat down across from her, and she pushed it over to him. A class ring from the University of Florida. A blue stone.

"It was wadded up inside this, crammed in the shell." She flattened out the paper with the palm of her hand. Passed it across. It was torn from a yellow legal pad. A ragged rectangle. In pencil was scrawled: "You want the finger that comes with this and the rest of this dinklebery, you get 3000 dollars of reglar unmarked money reddy by thursday this week at no later than sometime before noon."

"Shit, shit, shit," Thorn said.

He stood up. He made a slow pass through the living room. He looked at the marksmanship trophy Gaeton had won in high school. The little black-and-white TV, the Naugahyde recliner. He touched Darcy's tarpon and looked inside the terrarium with one hermit crab living inside a small whelk. There was a round glass-topped table with a navigation chart of the Keys pressed beneath the glass. All the while he was trying to get down a decent breath, trying not to put his fist through anything.

He came back to the dining area. Darcy didn't look up from the table. She held the horse conch, turning it around in her hands.

Thorn said, "I did this somehow."

"What?"

"I let him down," said Thorn. "He asks me to help him, I make it into a joke. Dump Benny into his Jacuzzi."

"No, no. You did right, Thorn. This doesn't have anything to do with you."

He sat down across from her.

"You're just guessing."

"I *know*," she said, still handling that conch shell.

"We should be careful," he said. "There might be fingerprints on that thing."

"It doesn't matter," she said. "We can't go to the police."

"Darcy."

"There's more going on than you know, Thorn." She rose and took the horse conch across to a bookshelf beside the TV. She put it on the shelf, adjusted it, making a place for it there, swiped at the dust on the shelf with her palm.

He followed her outside. Dogs were still barking. The sky clear now, scattered with stars. Venus was bright in the west.

The Big Dipper full of black sky. It looked frigid up there tonight, the stars smaller and and farther away than usual. He stood outside the door of her trailer, both of them looking up at the sky.

"I'm calling Sugarman," he said.

"No."

"You don't trust Sugarman? Oh, come on."

"Sure, I trust Sugarman. But it wouldn't stay with the local police. Kidnapping, they have to turn these things over to the FBI."

"Well, so much the better."

She shook her head. Thorn followed her as she walked carefully down the darkened dirt lane that ran through the heart of the trailer park. Blue television light flickered across their path.

Thorn walked silently beside her out to the Bomb Bay Marina. She sat on the cement seawall, and he sat beside her. Only a couple of pickups were in the parking lot of the Bomb Bay Bar. The jukebox was playing a Merle Haggard song, its lyrics whipped apart by the sea breeze.

"Last January, Thorn, I started getting worried. The way Gaeton was acting after he quit the FBI. He just dropped out of sight. He wouldn't answer my calls."

Her hair was streaming behind her. The water slopped against the rocks just below the seawall. She was looking ahead into the dark wind, only one faint buoy light off to the east interrupting the night.

"I got Malcolm Donnelly from WBEL. He's a new investigative reporter. I got him to call the FBI and inquire about the circumstances of Gaeton Richard's departure, supposedly a story on attrition in the local office. No comment. No comment was all he could get."

"Gaeton was working for Benny at that point?"

"Yeah. He went right from the bureau to Benny. Quit in January and Benny's boy in February."

Now it was Emmylou Harris. Thorn couldn't make out the words, but it was something sad. No amount of wind could distort that. Palm fronds batted against a nearby streetlamp, the light fluttering.

"So, I called a guy I used to date. He's with the Florida Department of Law Enforcement. They collaborate with the FBI sometimes, corruption cases, some drug cases. He's got regular access to the FBI computer files. Well, I had to lie like hell to him, but he called up Gaeton's employment records for me."

She turned to look at Thorn then. He hadn't realized what this was costing her. But there, in the ragged light, he could see how pinched her eyes had become, the strain in her mouth. Those soft lips, rigid now.

"Yeah?"

She was staring at Thorn as if she were just discovering who it was she was confessing to. Maybe a little amused, surprised. Her face softening slightly. She took his hand and gave it a fierce squeeze.

She said, "There was no record of his quitting."

"Well . . ."

"Hold on," she said. "There was no record of him at all. Nothing. He'd been expunged. No such person as Gaeton Richards. Blink, he's gone."

Thorn was quiet. He felt her grip slacken.

"It's what the bureau does when they're investigating the Mafia."

"The Mafia? Down here?"

"Or investigating themselves," she said.

17

Darcy said, "Weekends I'd wait till Gaeton went out and I'd drive down to Islamorada, rent a skiff, and camp out on the flats just off Benny's place, pretending to fish."

She was pointing her toes down to the water that sloshed against the seawall, stretching them as if to make contact. Thorn held her hand, feeling the current, the blood magnetism growing between them.

"I bought the longest telephoto lens I could find. And I sat out there with the camera mounted on the fishing platform, hiding it under a fishing hat, and I took shots of people coming and going at Benny's. Most of them were fuzzy, blurred. It's hard on the water, bobbing even a little, long distance like that. But a few of them were OK."

She stopped and faced Thorn.

"Do you think I'm crazy? Doing something like that?"

"Yeah," he said. "Somewhat crazy."

"Well, good," she said. "One of us should be sane."

"Let it be me," Thorn said. They were joking, kind of. But Thorn wondered now about Darcy's grip, how tight it was.

She said, "Well, the few prints that were clear, that showed people's faces, I took them around and showed them to people I know in the news business. On the QT, of course. I pretended I was helping somebody at the station do some background checking on a story. But that didn't get much. I found out that a couple of the guys were ex-cops from Miami or Fort Lauderdale. Guys that worked with Benny, hanging around the pool."

"I've met some of those," Thorn said.

"And then there were one or two guys I recognized. Miami business people, bankers, a district manager for Merrill Lynch, people Benny does security work for. Business entertainment stuff. He was just having his big accounts down for a crab salad and a water panorama, a look at some nude girls. Keys fun and games. But then I got something. It came out of far left field.

"The man that develops my prints is Haitian, lives in Little Haiti, runs a small lab. I go there 'cause it's cheap and near work. Anyway, his name is Jules, and Jules says to me, when I go in two weeks ago to pick up some prints, that I'm hanging around some not so nice people. I go, what? And he says, this mulatto with the blond Afro stepping into the hot tub with the two white ladies. He is Claude Hespier. This Hespier guy, he's the most recent one. Like all the rest of them, near as I can tell he stays at Benny's two weekends, and he's gone.

"So Jules is there looking at me funny. He says Claude lived in the mountains on some kind of plantation. Jules's sister-in-law, Lorraine, worked for the man, cleaning house. So Jules heard what this guy was up to, knew who came for lunch at his house, lots of stuff. Hespier was some kind of enforcer for the Haitian drug connection. He did a lot of local work around the islands, murdering snitches, do-gooders. Anybody that might have had any moral fiber left."

She was staring at Thorn. He could tell his expression must not be what she wanted to see.

"Yeah? I'm listening," he said. "It's a hell of a coincidence, though. This guy does your photos knows a guy in them."

"You don't believe me."

"I believe you."

"So what're you saying?"

Thorn wasn't sure what he was saying. He just shrugged. Darcy dropped his hand.

"Never mind," she said.

"What?"

"Never mind any of this. I'll just do this alone. It's too weird. Even you, Thorn, you think I'm making this up. You think I'm on some kind of wacko trip."

"No, I don't. I just think it's strange. A coincidence, that's all."

"Well, it *is* a coincidence. Of course it is. But I checked it out. I went to Haiti."

"You went to Haiti?"

"Last weekend. I flew down there, and I met Lorraine. She's got five children, a pig, and no job anymore. Lives down the mountain from Pétionville where Hespier was. His house is closed up, and all the furniture's gone, the cars. The place is stripped bare. Weeds in the swimming pool.

"Then I was at the airport about to fly back to Miami, Lorraine showed up. She signaled me to come over to the women's bathroom. She was panicky, looking around for eavesdroppers. All in a rush she tells me that Hespier had been a very evil man. She had never told anyone this. The things she knew about him. It would be a great relief to her to tell anyone."

"What?" Thorn said.

"Well, for one thing, he was a cannibal. He ate pieces of his hits. He made Lorraine cook stews for him."

Thorn took her hand from her lap. The wind was stirring her hair. Light from the parking lot was giving her skin a golden gleam. Off in the mangroves to the south a nighthawk was bleating. It should have been a romantic moment. It should have made his heart lift, his throat clench.

"And there's more."

"I can't wait."

"Well, she said Hespier was a computer nut. He talked over the phone with it all the time. And that he had a deep longing to come to America. He loved to watch American movies. Especially Tracy Seagrave movies. He watched one of them almost every day."

"Name rings a bell."

She rolled her eyes, shook her head.

"She died ten, eleven years ago. Before she died, she split her time between Palm Beach and Palm Springs."

"You've done a lot of homework."

"Thorn, most people know Tracy Seagrave," she said.

She gazed at the marker light. Thorn watching her profile.

"Why didn't you just put all this in Gaeton's lap?"

"I was scared he was in it somehow. Either undercover or gone over to the other side. Either way he would've blown up if he'd known I was snooping."

"What other side? You don't know anything's wrong with Benny. He's a schmuck and sleaze, but that's not illegal. All you know is there's a guy named Hespier that somebody says is a killer and a cannibal who shows up at Benny's place for a couple of days. I don't see anything there, any conspiracy."

"OK, OK, what I think is," Darcy said, forcing the words out one at a time, "I think Benny's laundering people. I think he's taking some very bad people and giving them some very good ID. He's setting them up in places around America. Running a kind of immigration service for desperadoes."

"That's quite a damn leap," Thorn said.

"Not really." She looked off at the water, at a narrow trail of yellow light thrown out across the choppy water by a marina light. She said, "I pulled out some bio on Benny at the *Miami*

Herald's library. There was a snippet from a few years back as his Florida Secure Systems was getting off the ground. One of the last things Benny did for the DEA was act as liaison with the Federal Witness Protection Program. Hiding people who'd testified against the drug cartel, like that. He did that for almost a year. And that fits with Hespier. Hespier wants to come, but he can't immigrate. Benny fixes things so he can."

Thorn was quiet for a moment, letting all this settle.

He said, "So it's, give me your rich, your cannibals, your killers, yearning to shop at Neiman-Marcus."

"Exactly," she said. "But it's not funny. It's not funny at all."

"No," he said. "It isn't."

"And the house in Islamorada is a way station. They probably bring the guys in by boat, no sweat, and Benny's house is the first place they stay while all the records are getting set up. It takes two weeks apparently, and then off they go, coming into your own neighborhood, shopping at your local grocery."

"It wouldn't work," Thorn said.

"Why?"

"There's just too many people looking for the top bad guys. Their faces are on the walls of too many post offices, in too many mug books. And there have to be people, agents out there watching these guys' moves. Somebody'd catch on to this."

"Don't count on it," she said. "Benny's not stupid. He wouldn't take on somebody with a big reputation. What I think is, he's very selective, he waits till the right guy comes along, somebody with enough quick cash to buy the package he's selling and with a low enough profile that setting him up somewhere in a new identity wouldn't be too risky. I'm betting he's very conservative, not really pushing this angle hard. Why should he? He's rich. He might not even be doing it for the money. He might think it's patriotic somehow. Converting the bad guys to the good life, or something."

"The guy with the alligator Friday, one I told you about . . ."

"Yeah," she said.

"He had a blond Afro, green eyes. Looked like somebody poured too much milk in his genetic coffee. That was Claude."

She nodded her head. "And today, if the pattern holds, he's off somewhere. Moved to Palm Springs, hanging out with the stars."

"So if Gaeton's still with the bureau," Thorn said, "and he's posing as Benny's sidekick, and Benny finds him out . . ."

Darcy said, "Then poof, he's gone."

A pickup truck passed by on the road behind them; a country music song, sorrowful and slow, played loud from its windows. The truck squeaked as it bounced down the rutted street. How simple the world could be. How basic and true. Slug it out in the parking lot. Drink beer, love a woman, lose a woman. Hurt in your heart. And how far it could swing away from that.

"But ransoming Gaeton for three thousand dollars?" Thorn said. "What in the hell would Benny do something like that for? If he wanted Gaeton out of things, he'd be neater than this. I mean, this is dopey. This is lowlife."

"It's probably meant to throw us off, or the police if we went to the police. Nothing else figures."

She let go of his hand and swallowed hard. She swiveled and faced him.

"I should have told Gaeton what I found out. Maybe it was just the info he was missing." Her voice was remote, shadowy. "I wanted to be such a hotshot."

He helped her stand up and they walked around the perimeter of the trailer park. Everything quiet now. The TVs tucked in for the night. Only the wind still awake.

She seemed dazed. Her step heavy.

"You were trying to help. You were doing good."

"I screwed up, Thorn. I screwed up bad. I underestimated all of this. I was playing at it, like a goddamn weatherlady."

She stopped and her body began to shake. He held her and she pressed her mouth into his shoulder, stifling her sobs. He patted her back and looked up at a fleet of small clouds brightened by moonlight. They were sailing very high, very fast to the south. A few gallons of Georgia pond water on a voyage to the Amazon. He wished he were going.

She shivered in his arms. In a few moments she grew still. Then gently forced her way out of his embrace. She sniffed a couple of times and began to walk.

Thorn said, "So, the Islamorada house is Ellis Island. That's how you see it."

"Yeah," she said. She swallowed, took a deep breath, and let it out. "He's using witness protection as his model. People who saw crimes committed and testified and are in danger." She took his hand as they rounded a corner, headed down a dark lane. "Except these guys Benny's hiding, the only crimes they witnessed are the ones they did."

"Where do we start?" Thorn said.

"I need to get three thousand dollars out of my checking account first," she said. "At least go through the motions of paying the ransom and see what happens."

Thorn was silent. The Australian pines were turning the wind to a ghostly moan. Two-hundred-foot harps, playing their harmonic tones.

"I know you're Mr. Realism," she said. "You don't think much of psychic phenomena. But I know Gaeton's dead. I've been sensing it. He's in the ocean, a lake, in water. I don't know.

But he's not swimming, he's not breathing." Her voice was shaking again. "I know he's gone. You probably won't believe me. But he's not in the world anymore."

He'd seen Darcy guide them so many times across a flat and empty stretch of ocean, right to the hole where the big grouper were hiding. He'd been out with her on many cloudless noons when she'd predicted a violent squall by three, and it always came, rolling dark and ferocious from the Everglades. Thorn, who normally trusted only in what he could heft in his hand, believed in this, this mystical thing she could do.

He nodded his head yes, let her see his faith in her.

He said, "Isn't there anybody at the FBI you know, any of Gaeton's old friends, you could go to, tell them about this?"

"There's a woman he used to be involved with," she said. "She was an agent. Myra Rostovitch. I met her a couple of times, but hell, I'm not sure anymore who's who. If he *was* investigating the bureau itself, something I did might tip somebody off. Blow the whole thing open, might put us in danger."

"Well, what then?"

"I've been thinking about it for a long time," she said. She halted and dropped his hand. "What I could do is make contact. Pretend to be a bad guy. Buy my ticket, take my ride. Get run through the process and see how the whole thing works."

Thorn asked her how in hell she'd do that, and she said, "I've got some ideas."

"Oh, shit, Darcy. That's nuts," he said. "There's got to be a better way."

She studied him in the dim light, making up her mind about something. She looked away into the dark, then back at his eyes. Some moment seemed to pass for her, some shift Thorn could see in the set of her mouth, the deepness of her breath. She had settled an argument in her mind, and her face softened as she continued to regard him. But he knew in some subtle way he had lost her. Lost the way they'd been.

"He's gone," she said, a new edge in her voice. "Gaeton's gone, and I'm not about to play it safe. Call nine-one-one or something. Hell, no. Only way to find out how cows turn into steaks is go into the slaughterhouse."

"Bad metaphor," he said.

"Yeah, well, you know what I mean." She cocked her head at him. And again her voice was calm, almost uninterested now. "It's because I'm a woman, isn't it? You wouldn't argue like this if it were Sugarman or one of your male friends. The two of you, you'd just do it. Flex your muscles and jump into it."

"OK," Thorn said. "You found me out. I'm a sexist shit. If I care about a woman, I try to talk her out of slipping a thirty-eight into her mouth. I admit it, I'm a Cro-Magnon." She turned away from him and began to walk. He had to hurry to stay with her. She'd shifted into a long stride, her face turned away.

"Well, here's a test for you," she said, still walking fast. "Let's see if it's possible for you to care about a woman who doesn't need your help."

He dropped back a little at that, following her to her trailer. She walked up to the doorway, turned, faced him. Thanks for a wonderful evening. Let's do it again sometime. Thorn watched her eyes go slack, begin to drift inward.

He reached out, put his hands on her shoulders, massaged the tension at the root of her neck. Her head sagged forward, giving in to his hands. He ran his hands down her shoulders, her arms, took her hands. She let him hold them but didn't grip back.

She shook her head sadly at him, looking at him from inside the faraway place she'd gone.

"Just get back to building your house, Thorn. Tying your

flies," she said. "That's where your heart really is. This isn't your problem."

Thorn looked at Darcy's hands, limp in his own. Then brought his eyes back to hers. A breeze stirring her hair.

"Screw my house," he said. "Screw fishing flies."

18

"So, how's your shit doing these days, Papa?" Benny asked.

Papa John Shelton flicked some ashes from his Camel overboard and turned to get a better look at Benny Cousins. The guy was holding his ten-pound rod like he was scared of it, like it might turn into a snake and slither right out of his grip.

The guy was wearing a khaki shirt with a sailfish embroidered on the back of it. Khaki short pants, white legs, boat shoes, a khaki long-billed fishing hat with earflaps and a neckflap. Throw in dark glasses with leather blinders. Everything just off the rack.

Number one, the guy had money. He had somebody guiding him to the fancy clothes aisle, number two. But number three, he was such an asswipe Papa John was ready to fire up the engine and go in, even though they were into some good-size yellowtail.

"What kind of shit we talking about?" Papa John said.

"Shit shit," Benny said. "The kind that comes out of your backside."

"What kind of question is that to ask somebody?"

"It's a personal question," Benny said. "I'm getting personal with you."

"My shit's fine."

"Well, I'm happy to hear it," Benny said. He shifted the rod around, and took another grip on it. It still looked like he was ready to drop the whole thing if a fish hit. "You haven't ever heard the saying, so goes your shit, so goes your day?"

"I may have," Papa John said. He took another couple of sandballs out of the bucket. They were a chum and sand mixture that he balled up and froze overnight. He dropped them over the side. Then he sprinkled some toasted oats on the surface of the water. That ought to fire them up, bring them to the surface.

It was about four-thirty in the afternoon, a Tuesday. The weather was warming up a little, but still nippy. Maybe sixty today, a light northwestern breeze. A moderate chop, with an empty blue sky.

This Benny Cousins had sent one of his people over to roust Papa John first thing that morning. The man was just standing there on his boat, never asked permission to board. Papa John lay in his bunk, groggy from a first-class hangover, staring at this jocko.

Normally he would've reached up and pulled down the .45 nickel-plated service revolver he kept over his bunk and pointed it at this guy and told him to get off his boat, and try starting over the right way. But this guy didn't look like he'd move. Papa John would have to shoot him a couple of times to teach him any marine manners. And what with his headache banging like it was, he didn't want to face the noise.

The guy had told him that Mr. Benny Cousins wanted to charter his boat for the afternoon. Mr. Cousins wanted to go out to the reef, catch some fishies. He'd said that, *fishies*. And Papa John had looked at him and told him to go fuck himself and Benny whoever it was and to take his white pants and his purple tennis shirt and his Rolex watch and get the hell off his boat.

The gorilla had said, "You got that off your system, now roll out and start getting ready. He'll be over at noon. He has a hard-on to see you. Don't ask me why."

At noon Benny had parked his brown Mercedes in the shade beside the Bomb Bay Bar and got out in all his khaki glory, and Papa John had looked out from the bar and said to himself, "Jesus Christ, not that guy."

Benny Cousins had worked out of the Miami office of the DEA for ten years, back in the seventies before all the white powders started coming ashore, changing things. He'd come down on weekends and hung around, sitting in the Bomb Bay Bar, shooting the breeze with the local scuzzbags who were just then considering moving out of the marijuana business and into the white powder business.

Benny drank scotch, telling war stories about Miami cops and robbers. Everybody wondered about him. Is he looking for action? Definitely. But what kind? Nobody was sure. He'd come in, acting all down-home friendly and how y'all doing. He'd sit there and tell his stories, buy a few rounds of drinks, but nobody became his buddy. People shooting looks at Papa John.

John finally had to ask the guy to stop coming in. It was hurting business. He put it as friendly as he could. John back then was buying a forty-pound bale of grass once a month, dealing out of the bar, so he didn't want some DEA agent taking a personal dislike to him. Benny had said, huh, you're kicking me out of here? But these are my people. This is my home, this bar, this stool, this town. His eyes getting wet.

Isn't nobody in here gonna be sorry if you don't ever come back, Papa John had told him. He thought he should just get the man's snout right down there in reality and let him root. And Benny's eyes had shut off. His smile just died away. Not that he was mad or anything, but like somebody had just clipped the wires to him.

And he'd gotten up and walked off, and that was it for Benny.

Took his Nerf ball and his glove and went looking for some other sandlot. Till today. And here he was, same guy.

"See," Benny was saying, "I'm a shit examiner myself. I look at it, I readily admit to it. It comes from my insatiable curiosity about all things human."

"You're a philosopher," Papa John said.

"Yeah, yeah I am. And what shit is, it's a miracle. A daily miracle. We put something in one end, it comes out the other. It's different, totally changed. You look at it and you think, Jesus, my body did that. My body. It's how this country used to operate. You put some poor illiterate slob in one end, and America takes that slob and . . . you see what I'm saying?"

"No," Papa John said.

He splashed in two more sandballs. He was half hoping that Benny's live shrimp would get smacked by a hammerhead cruising by and pull this guy overboard, haul him out to the Gulf Stream, where he could examine the turd flow from South America.

Benny said, "I look at my shit, and I make assumptions based on things, like consistency, color. Even the smell, that can tell you a lot. I'm not saying I stick my nose down in the bowl, and I don't actually probe it with a tongue depressor like the crazy Germans, looking for undigested particles, run them through again. I'm not a fetishist or anything."

John had his line running out, the one-ounce jig carrying it down nice and smooth. He was staring at Benny, wondering why he'd taken this guy's two hundred bucks and come out here fishing with him. He guessed he was getting bored, and because he'd wondered why a guy with a pet gorilla would want to see him so bad. It reminded him a little of the old days. People with bodyguards were always wanting to use his connections.

Benny said, "Like this morning, I'm standing there and it's

been a great dump, a miracle dump. And I'm buckling up, feeling ten pounds lighter, and all at once it hits me."

John's bait bumped bottom, and he brought it up a little, began to jig it, reel in a few feet, jig.

"It hit me that here I am down here, making this place my home, getting all the plugs plugged in, the keys working in the right locks. And I thought, Papa John! The main man. Or, well, the used-to-be-main-man.

"And I go, hey, Benny. You can have the mayor carrying your books home from school, you can have the commissioners doing your cuticles and the whole Chamber of Commerce trying to get their noses inside your rosy red, but if you ain't got Papa John, man, you ain't got squat."

"Uh-huh," John said. "This all came to you, buckling up your pants? I'm supposed to do what now? Curtsy? Genuflect?"

"See how it is is, I'm down here now. I'm in the Keys to stay. Benny's come home to roost. And well, till the other day, I had this guy, a Conch type, and he was setting things up for me, greasing the chutes, you know, introducing me to the so-called big shots down here. But this guy, he turned out to be a Benedict Arnold. I had to let him go.

"So I'm there thinking what to do next, and bang, it comes to me, how about if I talk to the old man, see about what it would take for him not to kick me out of the bar anymore? How many dollars it would cost for you to welcome me *into* the bar. Act like you're fucking glad to see me is what I'm talking here. 'Cause see, I've got this idea, we could be partners, blood brothers."

"You ain't got that much money, Benny."

"No, no," he said. "You see money's just part of it, man. I'm not talking about just money. I'm talking about putting you back together again, Humpty Dumpty."

John's line jerked, his pole having that little spasm of a yellowtail, maybe six, seven pounds. He hit it hard. Got it, and started reeling it up, feeling Benny staring at him.

"You caught a fucking fish, man," Benny said.

John turned and offered him the rod. Benny looked at it, at the tip bobbing.

"I don't know how to do it," Benny said.

"Just crank."

Benny dropped his rod on the deck and took John's. He leaned way back like he was hooked to a great white, tried to crank with his left hand, looking at John with his feeble-ass grin. He switched hands finally, got it around about two turns, and the fish broke off. Benny stumbled back, almost going over the port side.

"You lost it." John took his rod back.

Benny going shew, whew, wiping at sweat on his face. Give him a real fish and his heart would explode.

"Hey, I liked that. That was good. I wondered what all the fuss was about. All these years, I wondered. But that was good."

"That was shit," Papa John said.

Benny took a few minutes getting his breath back, leaning against the fish box, gazing back toward land. John bit off the tail of a shrimp, spit it overboard, and fixed the rest of it to his jig. Let it back down into the chum slick.

"See what I got in mind is," Benny said, a slight pant still in his voice, "I rent a barstool at your place. I pay you a little something every month and you introduce me around. I shake some hands, do some magic tricks. If somebody's got a problem, needs a variance, a canal dredged out, whatever, then Benny'll switch into action, slice through the bureaucracy."

"That's Key West," Papa John said. "You're off by a hundred miles. Down there's where the Bubbas are, where the county's run from."

"That's exactly my point, John. There's a power vacuum here. See, I know you used to be head pirate down here, you had some influence. You mounted some heads on your wall and all that. I go in your bar, I see all those pictures. You with this guy and that guy. And I think, man, that's sad. That's a fucking shame. 'Cause things progressed and you didn't keep up."

Benny was standing beside him then. John felt a bump on his line, or maybe it was just brushing against the rocky ledges.

Benny said, "I'm here, my man, to save your ass, help you retain, retool your skills, and move into the electronic age. You teach me, I teach you. One hand jerking off the other."

"I already got myself a lackey," John said. "I don't think I could train two morons at once."

Benny shook his head, looking down at the deck.

They had about an hour of light left, and about that long till slack tide. Siesta time down below. For that hour between tides, you could dump a ton of shrimp in the water and those fish would just watch them rot. If the tide wasn't moving, they weren't eating. Fish were programmed like that, not able to adjust. They'd gotten hard and fixed after a million years of evolution.

Yeah, John thought, like me. Ordering the same goddamn thing off the menu at Mrs. Mac's diner for breakfast, lunch, and dinner for the past five years. Christ, look at him. The most excitement in his life lately, the most change, was this fuckbrain Ozzie. Then all of a sudden here was Benny, a jumbo shrimp snapping in front of his face. Well, what the fuck.

John turned to Benny and said, "I could sell you a barstool. Wood-burn your name on it. I could take a one-time token of respect."

Benny raised his head, a horse-trading light in his eyes.

"I was thinking more of the virtues of renting, like a trial thing," Benny said. "Month to month, till we could see how we fit, how things were shaping up."

"I got more confidence than that," said John. "I'm willing to risk that you aren't going to turn into a bigger asshole. Anyway, you get any bigger, we'll have to widen the stool."

"There you go," said Benny. "I like a guy who can joke."

Benny watched John jig his line, tried to copy it. He said, "So what would it cost me, this one-time payment?"

"A hundred thousand would be about right. Though I'd take it in installments of twenty-five."

"What? Dollars?"

"You wouldn't want to hold court in the bar like it is. The roof caving in, the foundation slipping back into the bay."

"I wouldn't want that, no."

"So, let's say you ante up twenty-five quarterly for a year. You got yourself an authentic pirate hangout. A base of operations. I glue my place back together. Time to time I might even take you out fishing."

Benny said, "What kind of assurance do I get you don't throw me out like you did before?"

"You got Papa John's sacred word on it." He shot Benny a smile.

"Shit," Benny said. "For that kind of money, you don't treat me courteously, I'll have my taxidermy guys take a look at you."

"Not to worry, Benny."

"There's another thing," Benny said, "you might be able to help me on. This Old Pirate Days thing. I pretty much got my ducks in a row already, but I guess it wouldn't hurt, having you put in a word here or there."

"What Old Pirate Days thing?"

"I decided I want to be King Pirate, Captain Kidd, or whatever the fuck it is. The guy that rides at the head of the parade.

You know, wave at the public. It'll be like my coming-out party."
Benny picked up the twenty-pound rod, leaned over, and
reached into the live well and chased a shrimp around. "I heard
you used to do that," he said, looking back at John. "So, you
could give me some pointers."

Papa John said quietly, "That's the Rotary Club. They choose
whoever the hell they want. It's their parade, their festival."

"I know that," Benny said. "You think I don't know that?
They're voting this Thursday night. Like I said, I got everything
set already. But it wouldn't hurt to have a past Captain Kidd say
a word or two around town in my behalf, now would it?"

Papa John blew some smoke out his nose. He looked back at
the horizon, bobbing with the moderate chop. The sun starting
to silhouette the treeline. From this distance it might be an
uninhabited chain of islands. It might be paradise. You come
ashore, stretch a hammock between two coconut palms, doze in
the breeze.

He said, "OK, tell you what. I'll do even better than that. I'll
throw you a party. Tomorrow night. I'll make a major produc-
tion. How'd that be?"

Benny smiled. A little unsure, but the idea growing on him.

"Yeah, that'd be good. Drink with the goombas, let 'em see
the cut of my jib."

"Yeah," said John, smiling to himself. He wanted to see that.
Benny flapping his asshole mouth for the Rotary Club boys.

Papa John felt a flurry in his heart. Yeah. All he had to do was
snap his fingers and just like that he was in the middle of things
again. If it meant kissing the devil's ass, then what the hell. He
would've traded both nuts to feel a little power again.

"One other little thing," Benny said. "I had an unhappy en-
counter with a young man over the weekend. I wondered if you
knew him. Name of Thorn."

"Sure, I know him."

"So tell me," Benny said. "Which side of things is he on?"

"Which things?"

"He a Boy Scout? A do-gooder or something? Somebody I should consider neutralizing?"

Papa John stopped cranking his line.

"Kill Thorn?"

"Kill him, or buy him off, send him on a trip, whatever."

"What'd he do to you?"

"Pissed me off, made me look very bad in front of my men."

Papa John said that didn't sound like reason enough to kill a guy.

"Isn't just that," Benny said. "Him and the Benedict Arnold I mentioned, well, they were mixed up in some sensitive business of mine lately. So I'm thinking, maybe this Thorn is out to do me some kind of personal harm, maybe it'd be circumspect to unplug the boy's life support."

"From what I know of the boy," Papa John said, feeling a fish nudging his bait, "you won't have any luck *buying* that boy off, and I don't believe he likes to travel."

"Yeah, those were my exact thoughts." Benny smiled and said, "I'd handle it myself, but truth is, I'm getting such a high profile lately I'm going to have to start farming this dirty stuff out."

"Tell you what," Papa John said, then stopping to think about it a minute. Yeah, OK, what the hell. He said, "My boy Ozzie's been itching for some work of this sort. How 'bout we pad out that first twenty-five thousand to, say, forty, and I'll have Ozzie perform the procedure?"

Benny smiled again. He aimed a stumpy finger at John and said, "Thirty-two five."

John pretended to consider it for a few moments, then said, "Deal."

They fished till the tide died out. Papa John caught a dozen yellowtail. Benny held firm at zero.

19

As she rolled her wheelchair down the ramp, Priscilla Spottswood grinned at Thorn as if he were her own lost son come home at last. She was wearing bib overalls and a yellow T-shirt and a blue-and-white-striped railroad engineer's hat. Her white hair loose and long, still full of luster. Three cats chased after her, swatting at her rubber wheels, as she rolled over to him across the concrete driveway.

It was midmorning Tuesday. The sky clear except for some cumulus along the horizon. Like distant, misty Himalayas. It had warmed up now to the middle sixties, low humidity, a light northern breeze. Good breathing weather.

As Thorn crossed the yard to her, she brought her chair to a stop, shook her head, smiling, and said, "Goddamn you, boy. Goddamn you all to hell."

He bent down and gave her a hug, her bony arms clenching him hard around the neck, her parched lips on his cheek. He took in the chalky, chapped smell of her.

Priscilla had been head librarian for the upper Keys for forty years. Retired now and just in time, because her hearing was shot. Her voice so loud, she would've rattled the card catalog.

Her blue eyes had grown milky. And there was a long corridor behind them where she disappeared every now and then, coming back with a secret smile.

"I've been guilty of neglect," Thorn said. "Not hugging the ones I love."

"If your excuses aren't full of passion and drama, I don't want to hear 'em." She rolled backwards a couple of feet. "Well, stand still and let me look at you." She took him in up and down, stayed on his face for a moment. "You're in love again, now aren't you?"

"A little, maybe."

"Foshkatosh," she said. "A little, nothing."

Her houseboat, the *Miss Priss 5*, sat up on concrete blocks twenty feet from the shore. A wide gangplank ran down from the deck. In the middle of the starboard wall a five-foot gash had been cut out and was sealed over with a plastic tarp.

Thorn nodded at the boat, asked her what had happened to it.

"I'm putting in a fireplace and chimney."

"No."

"Oh, yeah, I am. I always did want a chimney and fireplace, a mantel to put all my bric-a-brac on. So I thought, well now, old woman, you haven't got but about thirty seconds left to live, you better get on with doing what you'd always wanted to do. So now I got to make myself live one more winter so I can enjoy the goddamn thing."

A black and white kitten jumped up in her lap and circled a couple of times and curled up. Priscilla petted it, smiling at Thorn, shaking her head, looking him over some more.

"Who is she, the lucky girl? Do I know this one?"

"You know her. Darcy Richards."

"Little Darcy Richards? Well, she's had a crush on you for just the last twenty-five years. And you just noticed."

"I'm a slow learner."

"You keep letting them slip through your life, you'll end up like me, married to a hundred cats and waking up at three in the morning dreaming somebody just called out your name."

"I never set out to be a recluse," he said. "It's just turning out that way."

"Well, come on inside, and see the rest of my tribe."

Thorn pushed her up the ramp and onto the deck. As they went through the sliding door into the galley, the harsh reek of ammonia made his breath falter for a moment. Cats everywhere. There might have been forty or so. And a pelican with one wing was standing on the dining room table, watching a calico that was sleeping on top of the TV. The pelican turned and stared impassively at Thorn, then Priscilla.

Priscilla took a green squirt gun, a translucent Luger, off the sink counter and fired a couple of shots at a white cat sleeping on the sofa. It woke and shook its head and slid quickly down to the rug.

"I'm training them to stay off the furniture," she said. "It's goddamn hard to train a cat. They got brains smaller than the fleas that live on them. But I love 'em anyway, 'cause of their hearts. Now, their hearts are up to size."

She fired another burst at a black tom that was just about to jump up on the couch.

"I better start coming to see you more often," Thorn said. "You're getting damn eccentric."

"I always been eccentric. Actually, I been getting better. I haven't been grocery shopping in my mermaid suit since I can't remember when."

Thorn sat on the couch. She offered him a Löwenbräu, and he took it. She had one, too. Rolled up to face him, knee to knee.

"So now," she said. "This isn't a social call at all, is it?"

"No, ma'am, it isn't."

"And you don't want me to lend you a book. Renew your card."

"Not exactly."

"You going to make me guess?"

"I've got a problem. It's like a research problem. I need to get some information."

"You want me to do something with my computer?"

"Yeah."

"Something illegal?"

"Yeah, probably."

"Now we're getting somewhere."

Thorn carried three more coral stones the size of grapefruits over to the pile and dropped them. The gloves that Priscilla had offered him were too small, so he had trusted in his own calluses for protection. But it wasn't enough. These stones were covered with barnacle edges. He'd been working for two hours, and both hands were puffy and bleeding.

Priscilla had two hundred feet of rocky shoreline along the bay. The pile of rocks she'd mined from there so far was six feet high, ten across. He could picture her wheeling down and back, scraping them up with boathook and fishnet. So this run-aground houseboat could have a chimney. What Thorn could do in an hour probably took her a week.

He'd looked in on her a couple of times. Type, wait, type some more. Thorn had told her that he wanted to make contact with Benny's business computer. He said he wanted to use one of his company's more obscure services, a service that was probably illegal, and had something to do with immigration or ID papers. That was all he could tell her right now.

"The company's name?"

"Florida Secure Systems," Thorn said.

She raised her eyebrows, a mischievous spark coming into her eyes as she revolved her wheelchair, parked it in front of the screen, and fired up the machinery with a single switch.

Thorn made another trip down to the water. There was a good chunk of stone showing at the edge of the mangroves. He pried at it with the small hand trowel she had given him. Rocking it, like a molar still rooted hard. The mud stirred, filling the water with brown haze. He should come back over later with a real shovel and a wheelbarrow and three other guys. Wrench these suckers out, one, two, three.

But for now he needed to bloody his fingers, strain his back on something. To sublimate, give himself over to this, making it rougher and harder than it had to be. So he would not think of Gaeton, imagine where he was. So he would be doing *something*.

It was nearly noon when Priscilla rolled out onto the rear deck. A gray cat riding unsteadily on her shoulder, another in her lap.

"You better get in here, Thorn," she said.

Thorn set the wide black stone he'd finally freed onto the pile. It must've weighed sixty, seventy pounds. It was some kind of shale or slate mixed in with that limestone and coral, probably an import from Georgia or the Carolinas, some settler bringing along a chunk of home for a hearthstone.

Priscilla was sitting in front of the computer when he got inside. A message blinked in the middle of the screen. Thorn moved to her side, looked over her shoulder.

Transmission interrupted. Fatal error.

"I think somebody noticed me," she said, almost a whisper.

He glanced over the array of computer hardware. Her telephone sitting in the cradle of a modem, the high whine of the disk drive, and lots of other boxes and wires.

She had taken off her railroad hat, coiled her hair into a bun. She was looking back at Thorn, not exactly a frown, maybe exasperation.

"Somebody noticed you?"

"Here's what I did," she said. "I wrote a program awhile back. A common hacker's trick. You want to find the number of a company's computer so you can talk directly to it. You find out the main number, usually some number that ends in three zeros. In this case, five-five-five-eight-hundred is Florida Secure Systems. Then the program begins dialing eight thousand and one, eight thousand and two. If it doesn't get that violin screech of a computer signal, it hangs up."

She swiveled her chair around so she was facing Thorn. He stepped back and brushed a cat from the chaise and sat down.

She said, "I suppose it's something like going to a singles bar. You try this line, it doesn't work. So you try the next one, and on and on till you make connection. It's called handshake procedure. Anyway, so it took me a half hour to get their computer on the line."

"You did? You got it?"

She said, "That's nothing, Thorn. The first faint nibble."

She sighted her green Luger at a tabby that was flicking jabs at a shredded carnation in a vase on the dinner table. She got two streams of water on his coat before he registered it and jumped down.

"The next stage is, you got to get the computer to talk to you. Same thing, the singles bar thing. Try this, try that."

Thorn leaned back on the chaise.

She said, "I did this for you, Thorn, I didn't ask any questions. But the way it is now, if you want me to do anything more, you're going to have to tell me the reason."

"Yeah, I understand that," he said. "I need to consider it, talk to somebody else before we go farther."

"All right," she said, giving him a long, amused appraisal, shaking her head at the end of it. "I don't know what you got me doing here, Thorn. It seems a long way off from what I'd expect from a boy like you."

"I find it surprising myself."

She said, "You ever think, just go up to the front door, knock, ask the receptionist for what you want?"

"I don't think this's something they advertise. I doubt the receptionist would even know about it. I thought it'd be better to knock on the back door."

She said, "OK, well, so anyway, I got the computer finally, and it gives me choices. I can check the quarterly dividend report. I can see a calendar of upcoming events of interest to clients. Air shows, arms exhibits. I looked at that for a minute. Interesting business. You know this very minute we could be in Paris checking out the latest in spectrum analysis equipment, the stuff they use, they can analyze a hair, tell you how much Budweiser you drank in the last six months."

"From one hair," Thorn said.

"These are serious fascists we got here," she said. "Next week it's the Berlin Personal Artillery Fair. Lectures on weapon effectiveness in the Falklands War, Angola, and Afghanistan."

"There's so much to know," Thorn said.

She said, "I browsed for a minute or two; then I selected the Services Menu. And there it was, one of the categories under service, Immigration Assistance."

"Yeah, Priscilla, great. That's it, that's what we want."

"I thought so. I got excited, I was about to call you, but I said no, I'll wait, get a layer deeper in and then show off for you, make it look easy. So when I select Immigration, the screen goes blank and a row of question marks starts flashing on and off. I sit there. I mean, you told me almost nothing, Thorn. I'm not sure exactly what I'm looking for, so I typed in 'Illegal.' "

"You didn't."

"It seemed like a good idea."

Thorn sighed. His pulse was thumping in his puffy hands.

She said, "Nothing happens for almost a full minute. I thought maybe the computer went down. Then suddenly it's back on, and there's a single line on the screen, says, 'Provide User's Area Code and Phone Number for Access.' "

"No, Priscilla, you didn't do that."

"No, no. Of course, I was suspicious. But I think well, OK, it might be a common business practice or something, put you on their mailing list, like that. But still, I'm nervous, so I type in the first number that pops into my mind, the number of the library in Key Largo."

"Well, that's OK, I guess."

"And the computer starts clicking and whirring for a few minutes. And when it comes back on, the message addresses me as Key Largo Library and says that I need on-line human assistance for this department of company business."

Thorn sat up on the chaise, stomach tightening.

She said, "I hung up quick. I didn't like the feel of that."

"Neither do I."

"And then this Fatal Error message came on, and I didn't like the feel of that even more. Like somebody had been tracing the call and I cut them off."

Thorn leaned forward, stroked the chest of a black tom that had taken a position at his feet. Priscilla raised the Luger again, but a calico measuring a jump to the couch thought better of it.

It looked over at Priscilla and took a prim seat on the floor.

Thorn said, "I believe we're going to have to attack this from a different direction."

"Yeah," she said. "Before it attacks us."

20

Sugarman wasn't at home. Thorn drove around his neighborhood and finally located him at the neighborhood park. A boat ramp, basin, small beach and picnic table, and dock space for ten boats. All of it on Largo Sound, a busy bay that boaters used to cut from the backcountry to the ocean.

Sugarman was sitting at the cement picnic table under a chikee hut out on the point. There was a yellow school bus parked in the lot. Red curtains fluttered out its open window. Two skinny black dogs ran out the dock as Thorn approached. He waded through them as they nosed his hands for food.

Twenty yards from Sugarman's table, three women and a man were standing in front of the neighborhood barbecue grill. The women wore halters and and cutoff jeans. The man had on a pair of tattered jeans that hung from his skinny hips. A snarled beard, long dirty hair. All of them barefoot.

Sugarman rose when he saw Thorn and waited for him.

As Thorn passed the hippies, the man separated himself from the women and made a short bow toward Thorn, his hands making some kind of salute as if he were measuring off a foot of air.

Thorn nodded back.

Sugarman was wearing a pair of black jeans, a yellow T-shirt with a French angelfish on its front. He smiled at Thorn, but it was an effort. His eyes holding back.

Sugarman gestured at the hippies.

"Flower power," he said. "Mellow yellow."

"That or Charlie Manson," said Thorn.

Thorn sat. Sugarman gazed out at the dull shine of Largo Sound, at some sailboats moored out there, their windmill propellers twirling in the northwester.

Thorn watched the hippies grilling their meat, the three women laying out plates and plastic forks on the table over there. The man kept glancing over at Thorn and Sugarman.

"New neighbors?" Thorn said.

"Vagrants. They pulled in late last night, just parked here and camped overnight. I was elected by the neighborhood association to kick them out. Me, the cop. I came down here, and I didn't have the heart for it. The head geek said to me that the Lord God Almighty owned this land, it wasn't my place to say who could or couldn't use it."

"He's got a point," Thorn said.

"That's what I thought."

"Well, they say the geeks shall inherit the earth."

"Yeah," Sugarman said, "they're getting a damn good start."

The hippies seemed to be chanting now, shoulder to shoulder in a circle, eyes closed.

"I came over here," Thorn said, "see if you got anything on Cousins."

"Figured," Sugarman said, shifting his eyes away from the hippies, giving Thorn a tired frown. "Well, it's just like I was telling you, Thorn, Benny Cousins is running for God. He's a very saintly fellow."

"That's bullshit," he said, and massaged one sore hand with the other.

"I'm trying to be patient with you, man," Sugarman said. "You're building your house, tying your flies, concentrating on your belly button, so you're not up on what's going on around the island, Thorn. But Benny's on everybody's top ten nice guy list. He donates money to the cocaine crisis clinic, the battered wife shelter. Stuff like that. He sponsored two or three fund raisers lately for Blessed House, the halfway house for problem kids. Man, the guy's Key Largo's own Mother Teresa. He may have a little Bubba in him, maybe a tendency to want to good-old-boy the good old boys, but otherwise the guy's strumming a harp as near as I can see."

"Come on, man. Have you met met him? Been around him?"

"Once," Sugarman said. "Oh, yeah, I know. Is he somebody I'd want to have over at the house? Not really. He's obnoxious. But the good he's done, you know, there's not anybody else down here really working like that, everybody's out on their boats. They came down here to forget about all that. It doesn't fit with their picture of paradise. So, this guy comes along, I don't care if he's got bubonic halitosis, he's a good guy."

"He's a barracuda," Thorn said. "This Mother Teresa bullshit, it's just PR."

"The only knock on the guy I heard," Sugarman said, "is he has people in and out of that Islamorada house, foreign types. They show up in Islamorada, Matecumbe, sometimes they'll pick up things, walk out, forget to pay for them. He had to come by the station a couple of times in the last couple of months. Get this guy or that guy out of the tank. Shoplifting, resisting arrest with violence."

"Yeah?" Thorn said.

"Turns out these guys were all diplomats of one kind or another. They stole things 'cause they had different cultural orientation or something like that. They all had immunity. A man from the State Department even called on one of them, to let him off the hook. But Benny goes by the store where they lifted something, he makes a donation. Everything's copacetic."

"You verify that? That State Department call?"

"I guess somebody did."

"And you still call that Mother Teresa?"

"I call that *clout*, is what I call it," Sugarman said. "The man's plugged in. But just because he hangs out with lepers and highwaymen . . . I mean Jesus did that, Thorn. It didn't taint him.

"OK, so what is it has you so stirred up about Benny? I mean, if it's just that thing with fixing your code violations, well, yeah, that's cheating, but it's also par for the course down here. When in Rome kind of stuff."

Thorn sighed. He watched two of the hippie women peel out of their clothes and step under the outdoor shower. They began to glide large dark bars of soap across each other. At one with their nakedness.

"The moon must be in the seventh house," Thorn said. "Time for another bath."

"Boy, you're in a bad mood," Sugarman said. "These are gentle, harmless people."

"Yeah," Thorn said. "I am. I'm in a bad mood."

"I heard you were smearing Darcy Richard's lipstick. Is that it? Being in love, that get you in a bad mood?"

"You heard that? Where?"

"It was in the paper, Thorn. Shit, come on. Everybody knows everything."

They both looked out at Largo Sound some more. Thorn listening to the faint tinkling of the halyards out there, like trays of iced tea. He thought of how far they'd gotten away from the good parts. From the hammock days, the sunset fishing. The pleasant burn of the first beer as night came on. Lying in the bed, listening to the silky rattle of the palm fronds, to the moths battling against the screened windows, turning up the flame in the lantern, opening the book, finding the place.

He looked down at the mosaic pattern in the tabletop, broken bits of colored ceramic afloat in cement. Over the years he'd seen things in that tabletop. Sometimes sober, sometimes not. Beasts, the faces of women, schools of fish. He looked for something now, took his eyes a little out of focus. And that random jumble clarified, took the shape of a .25 Browning Baby, aimed back at his own empty gut.

"You know, I've been thinking lately," Sugarman said, staring at his hands flat on the table in front of him, "maybe I need to go see a therapist myself. Get some shrinking done."

"Oh, Jesus, Sugar, not you, too."

"I been feeling pretty blue," he said. "I'd just like to know something, be sure about something for a change. I'm floundering, buddy. I mean, these days I wonder about everything, work, marriage. Why I'm doing anything at all. What the purpose of it is."

"You got the virus, it's going around," Thorn said. "What I heard is, all you can do is wait. Have another beer, call back in a year. Do whatever you can in the meantime, and things change on their own. The calendar takes you to the next stage, things get clearer. It's the best answer I've heard lately."

"Just wait?"

"I know it doesn't sound like much," Thorn said.

"No, it doesn't," Sugarman said. "But thanks."

Charlie Manson was eating his meat now. It smelled good. He was sending Thorn and Sugar a mean look. A little spasm in one eye, while his women washed, waited their turn.

One of Sugarman's neighbors pulled into the lot; she got out of her car. A white-haired woman in a brown dress. She stared at the showering maidens, stared at Sugarman, waved her hand at him, then at them. Get up, do something. He waved back at her. Yes, ma'am. Yes, ma'am. She got back into her car and sat there for a minute fuming, then drove home. Probably to call the real police.

"Tell me something, Sugar. I need to know something."

"Shoot."

"If I told you a thing that had to do with police work, a possible crime, because I needed your help, but it was important not to make it a full-blown police matter, what would you do?"

Sugarman shook his head at Thorn.

"What're you into, Thorn?"

"Answer my question first."

"What kind of crime we talking about here?"

"It's a disappearance, maybe foul play."

Sugarman pulled in a deep breath. Thorn could see a vein rising in his throat, the skin pulling tight to his skull.

He said, "I'm your friend, Thorn. You're practically my goddamn brother, man. But you tell me something that has to do with a murder investigation, kidnapping, or the like, I'm a cop. Pure and simple."

"You're out here dressed like a real guy, even then, huh?"

"I'm off duty, yeah, but my ethics aren't. Priests are for confession. They'll never tell. A cop, well, that's different."

"Yeah," said Thorn. "It's what I thought. But I guess I needed to hear you say it."

"Now, look, I don't like the sound of this shit, Thorn. I don't want you going back into the vigilante business. We don't need that, you know. We got a pretty good system of catching crooks, putting them away."

Thorn thought for a few moments and said, "You remember

three summers ago, time we played all those hoops at Harry Harris, getting ready for summer league?"

That headshake again. He said, "OK, all right, yeah, I remember. You, me, Dewey Wisdom taking on the young studs."

Thorn said, "Well, it was serious basketball. But you know, it was mostly fair. You hit somebody taking a shot, you called the foul on yourself. Honor system."

"Yeah, OK."

"But soon as league play started, and we had refs calling the games, things fell apart. Everybody got away with what they could. If the ref missed it, it didn't happen. Honesty went out the window."

Sugarman considered it a moment, looking intently at Thorn.

"What? No police?" he said. "That what you're saying? Just let John Q. settle his own grievances?"

"It might work better now and then," Thorn said. "Sometimes it's only the players who know what really happened."

"Those ideas, what, they out of a book?"

"No, they're mine. Out of my own noodle."

"Noodle's the word for it."

Thorn was quiet, watching Charlie Manson and his girls.

Sugarman said, "For one thing, Thorn, when we were playing basketball, we weren't wearing guns. There's a big difference."

"OK," Thorn said, "it's a shitty analogy. But you know what I mean."

The tribal leader had left his harem and was edging over to their table. Sugarman turned and nodded at the man. He made his bow again, a little wider this time like he was showing you how long the one that got away was. Not a lunker, but big.

"We have spoken among ourselves," he said. "And we have decided that the two of you should leave."

"Why's that?" Sugarman asked.

"You are creating negative oscillations."

Sugarman looked at Thorn for a translation.

"Bad vibrations," Thorn said.

Sugarman stood up. "Some things never change."

"It's kind of a comfort," Thorn said.

He drove over to Darcy's trailer. It was dark, and the chill settling now. Sky clear, no cloud cover to keep the ground heat in. This new air was cleaner, had a zip to it, a few more grains of oxygen maybe. It'd probably dropped fifteen degrees in the last couple of hours, and because he'd been driving with that convertible open, his fingers were stiff, nose beginning to run a little.

A light was on inside the trailer. He stood outside for a moment, gave his heart a chance to decelerate. Be cool, not show her how just walking up to her door could send it racing.

The neighborhood was quiet tonight, the watt wars observing a cease-fire. Thorn moved over to the front door. The yellow shade in the living room window was buckled and drawn down five inches short of the sill. He could see inside. There was a guy. A blocky guy with shortish black hair sitting in the chrome dinette chair.

His arms were lashed to the arms of the chair with what looked like dark stockings. Thorn blinked and stepped away from the window.

He gave it a few seconds, then leaned over for another look. Still there. The guy nodding now at someone across the table. He looked right at home, relaxed, tied up to that chair. Then he saw Darcy's hands on the table, the right one holding the .25 Browning with the pearl handle, the left drumming on the tabletop.

21

Forget it. The dinkelbary's dead and gone already. Nevrmind the money hony. XXXX

Thorn read the note again. Darcy watching him. She was rolling the Browning from hand to hand as if it were too hot to hold. She had on a light blue sleeveless T-shirt, gray jeans, running shoes. Her hair was loose, clean, and brushed. Bangs straight and even. A little blush in her cheeks, some quiet green eye shadow. Not letting her grooming slip during this crisis; in fact, seeming to spend more time at it. Finding her own way to sublimate.

Thorn stepped over to the window and drew the shade down the last five inches. He came back over to this guy.

"You write this?" He got down into this guy's face so he could read his eyes. "This your handwriting, is it?"

"He wrote it," Darcy said. "We already established that before you got here. This is Ozzie. Ozzie Hardison. He lives in a house over by the marina. He does odd jobs for Papa John. Drives the ice cream van, mows the grass."

"You know him?"

"I talked to him once or twice."

Ozzie watched this, flicking his eyes back and forth between them, cutting to the .25, away from it.

"He threw another shell?"

"I caught him before he had a chance. I was outside."

Thorn searched her face. Her expression was bland, but she

was admitting it in her eyes. They were blazing, suffused with anger, but she was holding it off. Performing calmly for this guy.

"Where's Gaeton Richards?" Thorn said to Ozzie, standing over him. Ozzie didn't look up. He glanced across at Darcy for a moment, a sheepish look, then looked into this lap. "Where is he, you son of a bitch?" Thorn gripped him by his short, thick hair and lifted his face up.

Ozzie had a fine sprinkling of stubble on his cheeks, his eyes unfocused, dulled from within. He wasn't looking at Thorn; he wasn't looking at anything.

"Easy does it, Thorn. He's scared. He's too scared to talk."

"He sure as shit better be scared."

Thorn let his hair go. Ozzie's face fell forward again.

"What the hell're you doing, Ozzie Hardison? Writing a note like this. The hell're you thinking about?"

"I already asked him that?"

"And?"

"Sit down, Thorn. Just cool off, relax."

Thorn hesitated a moment, staring at Ozzie, then pulled out the third dinette chair and turned it around and straddled it.

Darcy touched a finger to her bottom lip, rubbed it the length and back again, looking at Thorn, considering all this.

She said, "He thought this was an act of kindness. He meant it that way."

"An act of kindness," Thorn said. "That's a good one."

"I'm trying to tell you, Thorn. Who we're dealing with here, how he arrives at things."

Thorn rubbed his hand over the lump in his pocket. Gaeton's knife. Just touching it seemed to freshen his blood. He imagined holding its keen blade against this guy's throat. Carve him a new Adam's apple.

A loud rapping came at the door. Thorn jerked.

"It's the pizza man," Darcy said. "We ordered a pizza."

"You ordered a pizza."

She rose and took her purse from the kitchen counter and stepped out the door.

"We were hungry," Ozzie said.

Thorn stared at this guy, listening to Darcy outside with the deliveryman. Bouquet of pizza already floating into the room.

"We didn't know if you liked anchovy or not," Ozzie said. "So we got half with anchovy, half just extra mushroom."

"You knew I was coming?"

"She said you probably were."

Thorn shook his head. Not believing this.

"You her brother, too?" Ozzie said. Just shooting the shit, an everyday thing tied up with dark stockings, waiting for the pizza.

Thorn said, "Now listen, I don't know what's going on here, but I'm about a split second from cutting off your air supply. So just stop the mouthing, and sit there till I say you can talk. That clear?"

Ozzie nodded. No anger showing, no malice of any kind, just a schoolboy agreeableness.

She brought the pizza back inside and got some cheap china plates down from the cupboard, napkins, asked Thorn what he wanted to drink. Whiskey, he said. Asked Ozzie, and Ozzie was about to speak, caught himself, and looked to Thorn for permission.

"He's not thirsty," Thorn said.

She brought Thorn a bottle of Early Times and a glass with ice. Set it down in front of him, tore off a wedge of pizza, and sat back down to eat. Ozzie watched this, licked his lips cautiously, staring at the pizza.

"When we're finished, Ozzie," Darcy said, "you can have a piece or two."

Thorn sipped the bourbon. Finally the hunger moved his hand forward, and he tore off a slice and ate it.

Darcy was staying inside herself. One quick, light look for Thorn, warning him to cool it, then saying, hmmm, as she ate her pizza. Tapping her fingers as if a tranquil tune played inside her. Thorn tried to bring her eyes to his, but she seemed to sense it and kept her gaze floating around the room.

Ozzie said, "This guy your other brother?"

"No," she said, "I only had one."

Ozzie blinked, swallowing, looking down, but Thorn could see he'd been nut-kicked. A flush coming to his cheeks.

"I'm her friend," Thorn said. "Her good friend." And that did it, a three-point play. Ozzie lifted his eyes to Thorn's, a dead look, his mouth fighting off a sneer.

Darcy chewed her pizza peacefully.

They ate all but the last piece. Thorn looked at it, reached out, then looked at Ozzie. The sneer solidly there now.

"It don't matter," he said. "I'm not hungry anyway. So eat the damn thing."

Darcy wiped her mouth with a paper napkin, said, "Ozzie says he found Gaeton in his shed. He'd been shot. He didn't know what to do with him, so he took him out in the Glades and dumped the body. But he took off the ring first, thought he'd make a few dollars out of it. Then he changed his mind, decided it was too cruel. So he wrote this other note."

"You believe that?"

"Somewhat," she said.

"It's true, just like she said it," Ozzie said.

"Where in the Everglades?"

"In a canal I know about, up on nine-oh-five."

"I'm calling Sugarman," Thorn said.

"No," Darcy said. "Not yet."

"You believe this, this act of kindness bullshit?"

"I believe Ozzie has become enamored of a media personality, and he considered this an appropriate courtship gesture."

Thorn looked at Ozzie. He'd missed it all. A foreign tongue.

"I know who done it," Ozzie said. "And why."

"Tell us, Ozzie," Darcy said, using a voice Thorn hadn't heard. Maybe it was her TV voice. Stiffer than her real one, sounding like a second-grade teacher, sweet but full of iron.

"I can't do that," he said. "But I'm planning on setting things right. You'll see."

Darcy stood and came around to Ozzie and untied his left hand.

"Go on, have that last piece," she said.

Ozzie looked at it for a moment, then took it and began to eat it, keeping his eyes down. It only took him a minute to get it all down. Darcy brought him a Budweiser, opened it, and set it in front of him.

Ozzie drained about half of it and set it down and wiped his mouth with the sleeve of his work shirt. Now he looked at Thorn. Narrowing his eyes to make himself look tough.

"You know what, Ozzie?" Darcy said. "You can convince us you're telling the truth by describing exactly where my brother's body is."

Ozzie thought about it. His face softened as he looked at her. Darcy gathered her hair with her right hand, lifted it off her neck to let her skin breathe. Dropped it. She stroked the blond hair on the back of her wrist, breathed through her nose. She scratched lightly at the edge of her collarbone. Ozzie watched all this, slumped forward, his throat working. Breathing visibly.

It was sexual theater. Darcy's basic movements, the power she was radiating, bristling this guy's short hairs, charging the air with her heat and spark. Something in Thorn sagged. Was that all this had been between them? The con of sex. A tango of lust. One more twitch and countertwitch between woman and man. Was that all it ever was? Fine arts. Had she summoned this same candescence for him, drawn them together fluidly and inevitably?

Ozzie said, "I'm a songwriter. I'm a lover, not a killer."

"Oh, Jesus," Thorn said. "Would you listen to this."

"All right," Ozzie said. "I'll tell you just where you can find the body, but I'm not going out there again. I don't like that place."

"That's a start, Ozzie," she said. "That gets us going."

Thorn was driving the 1963 Ford tow truck. He'd called up Shep Daniels at Largo Texaco and settled on twenty dollars and a dozen bonefish flies as payment.

It was almost nine o'clock, and Darcy and he were creeping through the deep dark, down a narrow sandy road that went west off 905. They'd flushed a rabbit and two possums, a squalling white heron.

"We should've kept him tied up, Darcy."

"I think he can help us more if we let him stay loose."

"What's to keep him here? What's to keep him from hitching up the road right now?"

Darcy looked out at the narrow roadway, the underbrush almost concealing their way. Headlights so dim on this old truck that you couldn't make out more than ten feet ahead.

She said, "He's not going anywhere, Thorn. You saw him. The boy's dead in love. As long as he thinks he has a chance of that, he'll be close by."

"A lover, not a killer," Thorn said. "Good God."

"As if he couldn't be both," she said.

Ozzie was in his bedroom rubbing his wrists where the stockings had burned them. Shit, he could've stayed there for days. Tied up with her own stockings, having her wait on him like that.

Now all of a sudden he had a real hunger to look at his Johnny Cash collection: the newspaper photos he'd torn out, the headlines, and a couple of photographs from shiny magazines. He kept them all stored inside a liquor box in his closet.

He got it down and sat on the edge of the mattress and looked at each of those photos. Getting his fix. The man had had a rough life. He'd hung in there, gotten out of prison, taken his dose of shit, and then he'd climbed right up on top of the whole world and sung his lungs out. The man dressed in black. The black hair, those eyes that just said everything about being dirt poor and hating it, and fistfighting his way past all the losers. He'd gotten way out there ahead of them all, his picture in every magazine, his name on the lips of beautiful women. All because of his voice, because he could take what was burning in his heart and bring it up into his mouth.

Ozzie took each and every article out of the box and gave each one a long look. First time he'd needed to do that in about a year, since he'd come to town feeling lonely and out of it.

And at the bottom of the box were the three fancy pistols. The two he'd taken from the dingleberry lifeguard and the one he'd picked up off the shed floor. And the box of cartridges he'd bought a couple of days ago. He held up the one with the silencer on it and found a good comfortable grip on it. Aimed it around the room.

Thorn was soaked. He shivered now as the wind came into the tow truck's broken window. The sour funk of canal water filled the cab.

Darcy said, "You're sure it's him?"

"Yeah," Thorn said. "It's him."

She was staring out her window at the dark sky.

"OK, we got him out of the water. Where're we taking him?"

"Maybe to Benny's place," she said. "Just drive up and dump the body on his front steps."

"Yeah, I could beat my fists on his chest, demand a confession."

"You still don't believe this has to do with Benny, do you, Thorn?"

"I'm trying," he said. "But it's a lot of damn guessing, so circumstantial."

"Judge Thorn," she said. "He's got to have proof."

He drove down U.S. 1, towing that Porsche past the new K Mart, the old shopping center, a couple of miles south of that, and turned into the Bomb Bay Trailer Park.

She said in a quiet voice, "How'd he look, Thorn?"

He shook his head, looking straight ahead.

"Never mind," she said. "Never mind."

She showed him which house was Ozzie's. Thorn parked in Ozzie's backyard, got out, unhooked the Porsche. Darcy stayed in the cab of the truck. When he'd run the towline back onto the spool, he walked over to the Porsche.

The water had all run out now. Strands of algae hung from the chrome strips around the window. Gaeton was in the passenger seat. His face was puffy, and his flesh was gleaming rubber. His hair had been sliced back from the water. A dark ragged cavity in his forehead.

Thorn looked across at the tow truck, at the back of her head. Darcy waited, looking ahead out the windshield at an empty lot across from the water. She didn't need to come back there to look. She had him in her head, in that vision inside her, which seemed more accurate and reliable, maybe even more vivid than what Thorn could see, standing there before the fact itself.

Thorn spit. He sent it across the gravel lot. He hardly ever spit. He couldn't remember the last time. And now he felt like kicking something. He hadn't felt that in a long while either.

He rolled the Porsche backwards into a ramshackle garage, and found a white painting tarp in there, and tossed it over the car, then came back around to the passenger door. The neighborhood was still, a northerly breeze flickering through the coconut palms. It sounded like a smoldering fire in the dry underbrush. It must have been near two, three in the morning.

Thorn opened the door and stuck his head in the car and slid his arms around Gaeton's body, hauled him out. He was stiff but soggy. Thorn carried him like a bride across the threshold over to Ozzie's ice cream truck. He didn't look at his face again.

He opened the double rear doors and hefted Gaeton up onto the steel floor of the truck. A long yellow extension cord ran from the compressor on the side of the truck to the side of Ozzie's house. As Thorn was climbing into the truck, the generator switched on.

Inside one of the bins was the ice cream. In the smaller cooler on the left side there were plastic Baggies full of joints and uncleaned marijuana. He closed the double doors behind him and stood there panting, eyes burning. He blinked them clear.

The aluminum doors to the bin hinged in the middle. Thorn lifted the door out. The cooler was two, two and a half feet across. He had to do some rearranging, moving the Eskimo Pies, the ice cream sandwiches, the Popsicles to one side of the freezer case.

When he'd cleared the space, he lifted Gaeton up onto his shoulder. A cup of cold canal water gushed down Thorn's back, and something tinkled onto the metal floor behind him.

Thorn settled the body as gently as he could manage into the case. Gaeton's back rested against the icy bottom of the cooler, still in a sitting position.

With his fingernail, he scratched the layer of frost off the temperature gauge inside the cooler. Thirty-four degrees.

He had to rock Gaeton's body upright. Then, one hand on his knees, one on his chest, pushing hard, trying to flatten the body a couple of degrees so he could fit the doors back in place. It took five minutes, all the strength he had. But he got him in there, burying him under Popsicles, fruit bars, Fudgsicles.

Thorn turned and squatted, began to pat the floor to find the object. He took it outside the truck into the light from the streetlamps. Though by then he already knew what it was, rolling it around in his fingers.

It glittered in the streetlamp. A gold queen conch earring.

He took it over to the tow truck, got back inside. Darcy turned to him, and he held the earring out to her in his open palm.

"What is it?" she said, taking it from his hand.

He waited till she looked up.

"Proof," he said.

22

Sugarman came to his front door with a huge mug of coffee. He wore a red striped cotton robe and a pair of tortoiseshell glasses.

Thorn said, "I didn't know you wore glasses."

"Since Christmas," he said. He sipped the coffee. "You want to come in, or that all you wanted to know?"

Thorn asked him if he still had that sixty-second Polaroid camera. Sugar said, yeah, he did. Thorn asked if he could borrow it for a couple of days.

"Sure you can," Sugarman said. "Even though I know you're not going to tell me what you want it for."

"It's spooky how well you know me," Thorn said.

Florida Secure Systems was in the Banco Nacional Complex on Biscayne Boulevard. The building was one of those postmodern things, brightly colored loops and spirals of concrete frosting the plain white granite walls. Tack some last-minute whimsy on the dead serious. The entranceway was the stark marble of a government building, but just inside the revolving door were murals of bright pouty lips, painted fingernails, red high-heel shoes. There was a whole wall of Marilyn Monroe touching her chin to her naked shoulder.

Thorn rode the elevator, listening to the soft jazz Muzak, watching a Cuban woman in a tight green dress touching up her mascara. He had on a white button-down shirt, gray poplin pants, and his best deck shoes. Fifty miles south, in the Keys, he might be dressed for a wedding. Here he looked like a ragman.

He carried the small leather pouch where he stored his fly-tying tools. The pliers, clippers, scissors of his trade. They rattled, and the Cuban woman turned to look at him. Thorn smiled, but she wasn't having any of it. She'd met smilers before.

The elevator was glass, running up the inside of the building, giving them a tour of the plumbing and electrical circuitry.

Thorn had a pang, thinking of his house, of the stacks of timber lying out in the yard. That skeleton of wood, half done, much of it already graying in the winter sun.

The woman got off on twelve, and Thorn rode up one more floor. The doors opened into the Florida Secure Systems suite. A chrome and Plexiglas desk blocked his way. Behind it was a wall of glass that showed a sweep of Biscayne Bay, Miami Beach beyond.

Roger was sitting at the desk. He'd been working on his tan. He was wearing an aqua polo shirt with a bright blue marlin jumping over his pecs. He looked up from a copy of *Vanity Fair*.

Thorn nodded hello.

"Well, well, Mr. Thorn." Roger folded over the page of his magazine and leaned back in the receptionist chair. "I got a bone to pick with you."

"What, did he cut off your rations?" Thorn said. "Just because I dumped him in that hot tub?"

"Mister, you made the man's major shit list."

"Yours, too?"

"Fortunately, I'm not a grudge holder. But if you're here to toss the man out the window or anything, I'm going to have to be more vigilant."

"I just want to see him, say hi. I drove all this way."

"Yeah, but the problem is, the man doesn't want to be disturbed," Roger said.

"Well," Thorn said, "then he should see a psychiatrist."

Roger smiled, said, "You're the one should do that, showing your ass around here. I mean, either you're crazy or your goddamn androgen's pumping overtime."

"Both," Thorn said. He sat on the edge of the desk. "You want to buzz him or should I?"

Benny, in a charcoal suit, French blue shirt, red Oxford tie, was wearing a small dot of a bandage on his right earlobe. When Thorn came into the office, he'd seen it and taken a deep swallow of air.

Benny was saying, "Yeah, yeah, right, Thorn, I'll give you a job. Soon as the next ice age comes, when the woolly mastodons are running down Biscayne Boulevard. When you can ice-skate to Bimini. Yeah, then come see me, we'll find you a slot."

"But Gaeton said the coast was clear. You'd forgiven me."

"Gaeton Richards?" Benny said, lowering his eyes to the papers on his desk for a fraction of a second, bringing them back up. "Where is that asshole anyway? He hasn't been around since last week." Benny took a quick look at Thorn's leather pouch.

Thorn said, "You didn't know about the accident? I saw him just yesterday, brought him home from the hospital."

Very slowly Benny brought his eyes to Thorn's. Gave him a thorough exam. Thorn suffered through it for a moment or two, then turned away, continued his prowl of Benny's office.

The wall across from his desk was covered with photos. Benny and J. Edgar Hoover. Benny and a crowd of men in tuxedoes, one of them Richard Nixon. Benny with a head of hair and Kissinger. And standing next to the Russian writer with the funny beard. Benny and some Arab sheikh. Thorn was looking at that one, standing with his back to Benny now, examining this black-and-white photo of Benny on a yacht, up in the pilothouse with an Arab in a white headdress. Benny yakked at the side of the sheikh's face while the Arab concentrated on the direction they were headed.

"Hey, hot rod, you turn around, look at me," Benny said, "tell me what accident that would be."

Benny and a Miami TV star. Benny with a pencil-thin mustache, shaking hands with a former Florida senator. Thorn turned around.

"You ask me that, and it surprises me," Thorn said. "Because Gaeton told me you knew all about it."

Benny said it wasn't Thorn's goddamn business what Benny knew or didn't know about. His eyes were charged now. He drew himself up out of his chair, put his hands flat on the desk, and leaned forward. A lot of amperage in his eyes.

Thorn said, "He spent a few days at Mariner's Hospital before I even knew about it. You know him, how secretive he is about everything. He called me yesterday, I went down there. Jesus, I thought he was in a head-on, all the bandages, bruises. His face, shoulder. It looked bad, but he was up, moving around OK. Creaky, and his speech was slurred a little, but moving around."

Benny said, "And he told you to come here, speak to me? Is that what you're saying? Gaeton Richards did that?"

"Yeah, he did." He kept his voice easy while his heart had hiccups. Thorn sat down in the bucket seat next to the desk. It looked like an ejection seat. Go ahead, he was thinking, let it rip.

Benny said, "And so what you're saying to me is, you came up to Miami, see if I still desired your services? That's the bullshit you're spouting here?"

Thorn made an affirmative hum.

"You know what, Thorn?" Benny sat back down. "The business I'm in, I've met flakes and scutwads like you wouldn't believe. But this is a goddamn first. A guy, one day he tries to drown me in my own hot tub. A week later he's in my office talking bullshit to me like we were kissing cousins." Benny turned halfway around, gazed out at the sleek skyline of Miami. "I'm a believer in hiring the handicapped. I got all kinds of half-wits and dimwits working for me. Making a decent wage, too, by God. But let me tell you something, I wouldn't pay you a nickel to pick fleas off my ass."

He had his white phone up then. Punched three numbers.

He said, "Key Largo. The number for Mariner's Hospital."

Then he punched that, watching Thorn intently with a lift of an eyebrow.

Benny asked for Gaeton Richards's room. He waited, squinting at Thorn. Benny kept the phone at his ear, curled his hand underneath his desk. The office door lock clicked.

Benny's eyes shifted down to his desktop, and he said, "When was that? Yesterday?"

As he listened, Benny rose, came around the desk, stretching the phone cord behind him, moving closer to Thorn. His gray suit was tailored to take twenty pounds off him. Halfway working.

"And he was in for how long? Yeah, OK. His doctor's name was what? Oh, you can't? Tell me, why is that?" Benny edged up closer to Thorn and let him see the look in Benny's eyes, a cold light. He ran those eyes over Thorn's face as he listened to the voice on the phone.

Benny said, "Well, then never mind, honey, I'll find out myself. And hey, tell me one more thing, sweetheart, you having some serious blood flow problems between your legs, or what?" Benny listened to her answer, smiling. Thorn could hear her squawk. He'd have to apologize to Cynthia Sanderson. Doing Thorn a favor and having to take Benny's abuse.

When he'd hung up, Benny brought his eyes slowly to Thorn's and said, "You got my attention, hot rod. If that's what you wanted, you got it."

"I could put you into some good fish," Thorn said. "I know where they are. I know a hole, I've taken snook, jewfish out of it.

Next day another one swims in and takes its place."

Benny shook his head, walked back to his desk, and clicked the door lock again.

"I already settled your fate, Thorn, or you might be ticking me off right now. My friendly advice to you, son, is to start lining yourself up some reliable pallbearers." Not angry. Not anything. He sat down, leaned back in his chair and went off somewhere, thinking, or whatever he did in there.

Thorn said, "I'll tell Gaeton you asked about him."

"Yeah," Benny said, his eyes drifting back to earth. "Do that. You do that."

Thorn got off the elevator at the twelfth floor. A lawyer's office. The receptionist was the Cuban woman in the green dress he'd ridden up with. She cupped her hand over the receiver and said, yes?

"I'm here to service your copier," he said, jingling his pouch at her.

She scowled at him and told the person on the phone she'd call right back. She led Thorn down a hallway with a plush purple carpet to a stark room with five copiers. She waved her hand at the silent machines and said something in Spanish about the tainted ancestry of all copy machines.

"Do any of them work?" he said.

"Just the one," she said. She patted it cautiously. "We call and call. It is a week now."

Thorn said, "Well, you should've bought the XR four hundred series. You bought the bottom of the line. Pieces of shit like this are always broke."

She said something else in Spanish. An anatomical absurdity. When she left him, he flipped open the lid of the working machine and laid the snapshot he'd taken on the glass plate. It took him a minute of fiddling, but he got it spitting out copies in a while. He made fifty before the machine broke down.

Back in the receptionist's lobby he said, "I have to get the rest of my tools now. I'll be back, probably around the first of July."

He posted a couple of the photocopies on the elevator walls. One over the inspection permit. He rode the elevator down to the parking garage.

There were two levels, hundreds of cars. It took him awhile, but there were only two brown Mercedes. One had Oregon plates, a Save the Whales sticker. The other one had to be one of Benny's company cars.

Thorn slid some of the photocopies under the windshield wipers, rolled several up, and slid them into the door handles. He wedged them in the gas opening, in the tailpipe, punched a couple onto the antenna, more in the grille, around the hood. In ten minutes he'd used up all fifty.

The Xerox machine had reproduced the Polaroid fairly well. It showed Gaeton sitting at Thorn's picnic table, the bay glittering behind him. A copy of yesterday's *Miami Herald* opened on the table in front of him, with the headlines clearly visible. LARGEST AIR DISASTER IN FRENCH HISTORY. Shot from the side, the photo didn't show his wounds. Or the ice cream bar that had frozen itself to his right cheek.

Before he left, Thorn slid the blade of Gaeton's knife into each of Benny's tires. Left them hissing with menace.

Darcy sat on a wooden bench in the bare white room. Cheers and applause echoed from out front in the fronton. At the oak table in the middle of the room Carlos Bengoechea was hunched over, reweaving a cesta with strands of dried reeds. They grew only in the Pyrenees, he had told her. Very strong, like the people there. He chewed on an unlit cigar, moving it from side to side, as he repaired the jai alai basket.

"You are mistaken if you believe every Basque is a terrorist," he said. "These boys, they are athletes."

"I know, Carlos," Darcy said. "I didn't say that."

"I have enough trouble, equipment, wages, I don't need trouble from Immigration. If I found out one of the boys had once been in ETA, had even painted a slogan on a wall, anything like that. I would send him back to Bilbao tomorrow."

This was a necessary formality, Darcy knew that. The denial, cleansing his personal slate. But she was impatient. She'd driven three hours to Dania to see Carlos. It was after midnight.

Darcy had spent the afternoon lying on her bed, watching the paper shades flutter, going over her plan. She'd pictured every step, making it all neat. Then started over, neatening it even more. And now she was here. Her dead brother jammed into the cooler of an ice cream truck and she was at the Dania jai alai fronton.

Carlos Bengoechea must've been near seventy. Ten years earlier he'd been one of her father's closest friends. It'd started as simply a story for the *Guardian*. Florida gambling, horses, dogs, bingo, jai alai. But her father had caught the fever. Gradually it became an addiction, three nights a week at the fronton, finally smuggling Gaeton and her along a few times. Sitting out there in a padded chair, looking at that smoky hall, they watched those young dark men run at the walls, run *up* the walls, catch that speeding goatskin ball, and sling it back at the high wall, all in one sweeping motion. The cheers, the curses, the graceful passion, the brute skill. Her father on fire beside her, watching it all.

Darcy said, "I didn't know who else to ask, Carlos. Something like this, it's out of my experience."

"Your cousin with the IRA, she has murdered?"

"No," Darcy said. She hesitated, considering how evil to make this cousin. "But she has committed crimes against property."

"Yes, yes," Carlos said. "And now she has had enough of the struggle and wants to live here."

"That's right."

He snipped some reed ends, tucked them into the cross weave. He put aside his scissors and scooted his chair around to look directly at her. Carlos closed his eyes. The cheering out front rose, a smattering of boos. Stomping.

"You can buy bogus passports in Nassau, any nationality." Carlos narrowed his eyes at her. "You can buy papers here in Miami, Fort Lauderdale. This is easy, forgeries."

"She wants something better. She wants something first class, more than just a few papers, something that would stand up to close inspection. She can pay whatever is required."

He shook his head, clicked his tongue. No, no, no.

He went back to braiding the narrow stalks into place. Bent over the cesta, focusing everything on it. She listened to the cheering, the announcer calling out the names of a new set of players.

This was all wrong. Carlos was just a simple businessman. When Darcy had thought of this, frantically running through her memory of people who could help with her plan, Carlos was the only one she had turned up. Now she realized he was simply a man like her father. Solid and honest. Let the police handle such things, he would say if she told him the truth.

She decided she would stay a minute or two longer, kiss him

good-bye, go back to Miami. Maybe one of the reporters at WBEL would know the name of a quality document forger.

Finally he raised his head, looked sternly at her. He said, "Basques have known nothing but oppression. First Franco, now this socialist state. For a true Basque, it is not a question of joining ETA or not, but what work they will do.

"But sometimes, when a boy grows older, he changes, he wants no more of the struggle. Perhaps by then he has killed, he has bombed police barracks, murdered Guardia Civil, Franco generals. He was young, brave, but now he wants no more. But how does he begin over?"

She said, "A name. A phone number. Something like that would be all I need."

Carlos held the cesta out, fit his hand into it. He moved it smoothly through the air.

"My boys are great athletes. You have seen them, Darcy, what they can do. Should they be punished forever because they once fought for the freedom of Euzkadi, their homeland?"

Darcy did not reply. She watched Carlos stare at the cesta as if trying to recall its purpose.

He drew the cesta off his hand slowly. Out front in the auditorium the announcer introduced more players. Carlos's eyes, exhausted, moved to hers.

"Your father," Carlos said, staring at her gravely, "he would approve of this?"

"I think he would," she said. "Yes, definitely."

"There is a man who lives in Homestead. He raises avocados," Carlos said. "He uses the name Emilio Fernandez."

Roger threw the last of the photocopies into the parking garage trash bin. He came back to the Mercedes. Benny was counting out bills to the tow truck man. Four new radials. Roger got in and started the car.

"What was that all about?" he said when Benny got in the back.

Benny sat there, looking at the parking garage wall.

When Roger started the car, Benny said, "You ever have to shoot anybody? Kill them?"

"Yeah," he said, looking at Benny in the rearview mirror. "I killed a guy once, yeah. Missed a few, too."

"You ever hear of anybody shot with the barrel pressing against their fucking head, they survived?"

Roger looked into the rearview mirror. He said, "In the newspaper, I read about a guy shot himself in the temple and it went through, didn't kill him. He walked to the hospital, checked himself in."

"Shit," Benny said. "Don't tell me something like that."

"What's this all about?"

"Don't worry about it, Roger. It doesn't involve you."

Roger revved the car, looked at Benny thinking away back there. He said to the rearview mirror, "I seem to have a rapport with this Thorn guy. You want me to talk to him? See what's eating him?"

"I took care of Thorn already. The boy'll be back at the bottom of the food chain before he knows it."

"How you mean?" Roger said. He put the car in gear, backed out.

Benny said nothing. Roger pulled the Mercedes out onto Biscayne Boulevard, cut into traffic.

Benny said, "The guy you read about, the one botched his suicide, he must've used a small-caliber something or other, just grazed himself, huh?"

"No," Roger said. "I remember it. It was a thirty-eight or

something big. Slug went right through, missed everything. Just tore hell out of his skull. The lesson was, you want to kill yourself, you got to use a twenty-two, so the slug gets in there, doesn't come out, just Cuisinarts around, tears everything up."

Benny staring out the window, said, "I never heard that."

Roger pulled onto the ramp for the Dolphin Expressway. He said, "Makes you fucking wonder what it takes to kill somebody."

"Yeah," Benny said. "Yeah, I guess it does."

23

On that Wednesday night the parking lot at the Bomb Bay Bar was full. And not pickups, not Keys cruisers with their peeling vinyl tops, broken-out windows. No, sir. Tonight it was new Mercedeses, Cadillacs, Lincolns. It looked as if the Republicans were having a fund raiser.

Ozzie saw Papa John standing out back of the bar, leaning on the fish-cleaning table, a bottle of whiskey sitting beside him. The man was staring out at the marina, out into the dark wind coming off the ocean.

Ozzie strummed a couple of chords as he approached, getting his fingers limber.

"Bonnie says you wanted me to sing," said Ozzie.

John turned and said, "I got some people inside want to hear what you got."

"This a trick?"

"Not on you it isn't," Papa John said. "You never mind what's working here, you just stand up there and play your song the best you know how. But I want you to change the words around just a little bit first. You think you can do that?"

"What for?"

"If I told you, you wouldn't understand, boy."

"Try me."

Papa John lifted the bottle by the throat and bubbled down some of the bourbon. He gasped, set it down on the table again, and put his arm around Ozzie's shoulder, moving him up to the edge of the seawall.

"I'm selling out," he said. "I found me somebody knows what my worn-out old ass is worth, and I'm handing it over to him."

Ozzie was quiet, scrambling in his head to stay with this.

Papa John said, "I got a gentleman inside there, he's the new generation of bandit. He's what's coming next, Ozzie, my man. I thought it was you and your kind, but it isn't. It's this guy and his computer and his German cars."

Ozzie didn't understand it yet, but he knew he didn't like how it sounded.

"All the training I was giving you, showing you how the rip-offs worked, giving you a sense of history, working on your sorry-assed storytelling, well, shit. I was wrong, little buddy. I was just being softheaded, thinking I could find me a son this late in life, get a little last-minute immortality. No, sir, by God, I hate to admit it; but I seen the future, and it's in there in the bar, burping and slapping rich men on the back. A guy wanting to be somebody he ain't, and without a goddamn idea how to go about it."

Papa John drew his head down and got his eyes to within a few inches of Ozzie's. He took hold of Ozzie's shirtfront.

"You see what I'm saying?" Nodding his head at Ozzie. "You see it?"

Yeah, Ozzie did. And he didn't like it, not even a little bit.

He said, "You're cutting me out of your will."

John let Ozzie go and looked off at the marina again. He leaned against the fish-cleaning table, getting his breath back. He cleared his throat, spoke out into the dark.

"I wouldn't do that, boy, leave you high and dry. What I did is, I got you a screen test. I got a genuine talent scout from Nashville, Tennessee, sitting in there right now, primed and waiting to hear you warble, boy. Guy by the name of Benny. Mr. Benny Cousins."

Ozzie gave it a couple of extra chord changes at the end, an extra flourish or two, strumming with his veins ignited.

It was forty years ago, he came to town
riding a shrimp truck through the middle of the night,
a lover of whores, a fighter, and a clown.
Looking for a way to be free, free, free.

Looking for a way to make an American dollar.
Bubba Benny, Bubba Benny, making the pretty girls holler.
Their mommas squeal and their daddies take a big deep swaller.
Bubba Benny, Bubba Benny, bigger than life,
Toting his razor-sharp bowie knife, Bubba Benny.

Looking up into that smoky spotlight, going ooooh, ooooh, to end it all. To bring them back to earth, to settle them back light and easy on their barstools. All fifty of them.

He ducked his head out of the glare of the light to see them. Somebody whistled; a couple of them hooted and haw-hawed; there was some applause. And the conversations started again. The volume building back up to how it'd been when Ozzie got up on the stage and steadied his hand and hit that first G chord.

That was OK. It didn't matter if these clowns had thrown eggs at him or if they'd fallen over and wriggled on the floor. He didn't give a rat's ass about them. Even that other guy, the little fat, bald guy in a white suit and pink T-shirt. The one from Nashville. It didn't matter how he'd liked it either, because Ozzie'd done it. He'd stood up there in front of a crowd and had done his thing. He'd fucking beat his stage fright.

Benny was sitting there on a barstool, staring at Ozzie, like there was one more verse or something. Or no, maybe he was zonked from the music, off in the promised land, already counting up the money that Ozzie was going to make for him.

Papa John was pulling a tray full of draft Michelobs. He was smiling at Ozzie, but not a proud smile. There was a twist in it like he was about to say something shitty.

Ozzie came down off the stage, guys in their leisure suits and ironed shirts making way for him. He leaned his guitar against the bar and settled onto the stool next to Benny. The guy revolved his stool around real slow as Ozzie came over, watching him the whole time. And there he sat, knees touching the side of Ozzie's legs, still looking at him while Ozzie waited for John to crack him a Budweiser.

"What'd I tell you?" Papa John said. "The kid a scream or what?"

"A scream," Benny said.

"It's his song for Old Pirate Days, the talent show."

"It should win something," Benny said. "God knows what."

Ozzie asked could he have his Budweiser now. His throat was scratchy as hell.

John popped one and slid it down the bar to Ozzie.

"So," Ozzie said after he'd had that first harsh swig. "We gonna get rich together, or what?"

"Excuse me?" said Benny.

Papa John moved down the bar and stood right behind Benny.

Ozzie said, "You think we could release it as a single just like it is. Or maybe it needs some polish. You know about this stuff. I'm just a singer."

"You are?" Benny said.

Papa John laughed, sputtering cigarette smoke out, coughing a little at the end. Holding his potbelly with one hand.

Ozzie straightened up, had a small sip of the Bud. He swiveled on his stool and came face-to-face with this guy.

"Don't bullshit me, man. I can take it. Just tell me what you think about my song, my voice. If I'm any good."

Benny said, "I heard dead guys sing better."

Ozzie peered at this guy, see if he was joking. He stood up, though he didn't know what he was thinking of doing. He just knew if he didn't stand up, he was going to get sick on the bar. Just cover the counter with upchuck and have to clean it the hell up himself. First singing in front of half the county and now these two jacking him around.

Benny said, "Whatta you, gonna fight me now, I don't like your singing, so we're gonna duke it out?"

People quieted down around them, giving way a little. Ozzie felt the raw burn of stomach juice coming into the back of his throat.

Benny got down from his stool and loosened his neck up with a lazy twist. He cracked some knuckles in his right hand. He wasn't but a couple of inches over five feet, but when he slitted his eyes, they got sharp and mean.

"We gonna have a bar fight, you and me?" Benny said, moving out into the center of the room. "That how this is?"

"Whoa now, whoa," Papa John said. "I don't like anybody

fighting while I'm trying to drink beer."

Someone called from the crowd, "His song wasn't so bad you have to knock him down."

"Yeah, it was," somebody else said.

John leaned against the cooler, laughing without making any sound. He tried to speak, but he was out of breath from laughing.

Ozzie was edging away from the bar, feeling the barf rising inside him. And it must've been the hand of the almighty living God that got him out the door, helped him stumble across the parking lot, and get him over to the edge of a canal before it all came in a scalding roar.

And when he could raise his face again, wiping his mouth with the back of his hand, he turned and Papa John was standing a yard or so behind him. Smiling, having his fun.

Ozzie asked who those people were in there.

"They're everybody who's got more than a dollar's worth of power in this county."

"They don't look like much to me," Ozzie said.

"In this case, boy, looks ain't deceiving."

Benny Cousins came out of the bar and walked over to them.

He got up close to Papa John and said, "This the fuckhead you had in mind to do that little piece of business for me?"

"He's a better shooter than he is a singer," John said.

"You better hope he is," Benny said. "You sure as shit better hope he is."

John's head was dropping and rising. It was almost two o'-clock, everybody gone for an hour, and the old man had been gabbing on ever since. Bragging to Ozzie, telling one story, then the next one. All of them about the same thing. Him getting the best of some fat cat or another. Tricking people, taking their money or doing something dirty to them. And every time Ozzie walked past him, he'd take Ozzie hard by the elbow and ask him, are you remembering this? Are you? Ozzie saying, yeah, yeah. Getting every word of it.

Ozzie was trying to get drunk himself, but not having any luck at it. Seven or eight beers and he didn't even have a buzz. He was just too damn wired from all that'd happened today.

Now Ozzie stood behind the bar, his eyes locked on to the loose skin at Papa John's throat, catching in the light a glimpse of a couple of long whisker hairs that John had missed the last few shaves. Those hairs were driving Ozzie a little crazy.

This old man couldn't even shave himself anymore. He was sitting there so full of himself, talking to Ozzie the same way he always did, like Ozzie was dumber than a squirrel. And he couldn't even shave anymore, couldn't do much more than draw a draft beer and tell these boring-ass stories. The guy used to be able to tear phone books in half; now he could barely turn the pages.

When Papa John finally took a break and slugged down some of the CC and ginger he'd been drinking the last hour, Ozzie said, "I know what you done to me, John. And I know why you done it. You done it to test me."

"And you passed the test," John said. "You sang your song in front of the highest and mightiest."

"Not that," Ozzie said just as John was beginning to chuckle again. "The other thing. The dead guy in the shed."

John stopped chuckling. He turned his bleary eyes on Ozzie.

"Ain't you curious about what I did with him? Don't you want to know?"

"Yeah, yeah, I'm curious. Tell me." His voice was sober now. His eyes clearing up fast as he looked straight at Ozzie.

Ozzie told him about putting the body in the Porsche, dumping it in a canal. John said nothing, cocking his head slightly as if he were trying to hear better.

Ozzie said, "I got to say, Papa John, I was impressed a geezer like you still had the balls to shoot an FBI guy."

The old man looked at Ozzie, very cagey for a minute. Then he laughed. Trying a short one, testing it out. Then he bellowed. He leaned over, slapped the table.

"Boy, that was all right. Damn good. You had old Papa John going." He laughed some more, shaking his head. Then he said, "Maybe all my work, it isn't for nothing. You're halfway catching on. You're making progress. One of these days I'm going to have to graduate you to second-class moron."

"You keep joking me," Ozzie said, "it's going to make me mad."

"Ozzie, my boy," Papa John said, "you ever run across a guy name of Thorn?"

Papa John was passed out at the table by the front door. Ozzie went on and cleaned up the bar. He was making his plans. First thing was to shoot that lifeguard Thorn, collect his thousand bucks for it. Then slip into Darcy Richards's trailer, give her the the hot beef injection.

After she got a taste of that, she'd for sure want to run off with him. They'd take that thousand. They could go anywhere. Lauderdale, Delray, one of those places. Live at the beach. Keep the door locked. Order out.

He washed some beer glasses. Swept the floor back of the bar. He wiped down the tops of the coolers, wondering why he bothered. But doing it. Just something to do.

Ozzie was putting away a handful of beer glasses, opening the

cooler top with his elbow. That's when he saw it, a black briefcase. He had to set the glasses down back on the bar. He got
quiet, listening to Papa John snuffling against the tabletop over
there.

He hauled it out and snapped it open.

Hundreds. Packed with hundreds. Sweet Jesus Mother Mary
of God. There must've been close to a twenty thousand dollars.
Enough money in there, it could just flat change everything.

24

Darcy spent that Wednesday night in a Motel 6 along the
Florida turnpike. She lay on the hard bed, the lights off, eyes
shut, hugging the extra pillow. For an hour she tried to breathe
herself to sleep. Putting her mind in her navel, following her
breath down and back out. Hindu Valium. It had worked before.
But tonight she still heard every twitch and moan of the building. Every shifting gear from the highway, voices in the hallway.

Finally, she slammed the pillow onto the bed beside her, rose,
carried her purse into the bathroom, and switched on the light.
She drew the snapshots out of their plastic windows in her wallet, slid them into the mirror's chrome frame.

Gaeton holding up a gaffed dolphin, still green and gold and
blue, fresh from the Stream. Her father looking up from his
rolltop desk, his bifocals against his forehead, making a smile for
his daughter behind the camera. And her mother, who had died
bringing Darcy to birth. A fragile Irish beauty sitting stiffly in a
stiff chair. Lucy Donovan.

Darcy peered at herself in the mirror. Touched her cheekbones, her nose. Looking at the photos, then tracing the line of her own eyebrows. She gathered her hair and drew it back tight so she could see the outline of her face.

She closed her eyes, let go of her hair, and sighed. It was her mother's skull, her mother's eyes, hair, coloring. Nothing of her father. Not a thing she could see.

She went back to bed, listened to the drone of the turnpike. Shut her eyes again and tried to open herself to the future, to images of what was coming for her. But she saw nothing, only a thick, inky mist.

Homestead was in the farm belt just south of Miami, the last of the Florida mainland before the Keys. Darcy could smell the dirt out there, the air hazy with fertilizer. Maybe it was all those chemicals that were stoning her now, making her feel so spacy. Not the fear after all.

When she arrived at ten, she walked cautiously through the grove of avocados to the small white cottage. Bands tightened across her chest. Her breath came short and shallow.

She stood on the porch and saw through the screened door garish war posters on the walls of the living room. The posters were of men with blackened faces, holding automatic weapons, standing in the jungle or in waist-high water. Biceps gleaming, lit up by rockets' red glare.

She knocked firmly on the door, and when he came in his karate uniform, black belt, she backed away. He smiled and invited her inside, but she insisted on the porch.

Emilio Fernandez came outside, checking her out from shoes to hair. He sat in a black wooden rocker, and Darcy arranged herself uncomfortably in a hard wicker chair.

Emilio, with dark eyes, hooked nose, black flattop, kept peering out at his avocado trees, the long rows of bare branches, gangly and dark, as if he were on watch.

"Five thousand dollars is what it'll set you back," he said, nothing Hispanic about his accent. It sounded like Indiana. He brought his eyes to Darcy to see how she'd take that amount. She showed him nothing, or maybe a little of the irritation she felt.

"I'm in a hurry," she said.

"I never met one of you who wasn't." His eyes were on the grove.

Darcy worked a piece of broken wicker loose on the arm of the chair and said, "Maybe Carlos gave me the wrong man."

Emilio said, "I see the five thousand, I give you your cards and papers."

"It's not that simple," said Darcy.

"Sure it is," he said. A smile began to take shape.

"You're not Basque, are you?"

"I was married to one," he said. "For a while."

"That's how you know Carlos?"

"Usually I ask the questions," Emilio said. "It's not normal someone comes in here and asks me a lot of questions. I mean, I've done a good bit of work for the man. His politics suck; but he's steady, he's tough, and you always know where he is. So, I tell him, yeah, you got a broad wants some new paper, a face-lift, I can handle it. And I'm here, prepared to help you out, but, lady, I don't *do* fucking interviews."

Darcy said, "OK, let's start over. What I want is to be somebody that already exists. A criminal. Somebody you'd find on a post office wall, but not top ten most wanted."

He said, "What? You want to get *into* jail? Now that's kinky."

Emilio's smile spread. The man looked as if he'd modeled for those posters, and after the photographers left, he'd waded on through that swamp and emptied his weapon joyously into a ring of huts.

"Can you do it?"

"Well, I don't know now. Wanting to take over a criminal's identity, that's good. I *like* this."

"But can you *do* it? And I don't mean a major offender here."

Emilio kept smiling. He hadn't taken good care of his teeth. Floss must've been hard to come by in the swamps. Darcy gave him a strictly business stare.

She said, "I have friends in law enforcement." She dug into her purse and pulled out three sheets. Wanted posters. She handed them to Emilio Fernandez. "These looked good to me. The kind of thing I have in mind. The flyers don't give us a whole lot of details, but we can wing the rest."

He looked the posters over and set them aside on the table and smiled at her again, eyes excited. They stuttered here and there. On her face, out to the grove, back to the wanted posters. Nodding his head, keeping time to a fast march.

"We don't need these," he said, his smile contracting.

She said, "It's the way I want to do it. Base this on a real person. It won't work to just pull this out of the air."

He said, "I got a better idea."

"This one." Darcy picked up the poster of a woman wanted for bombing a federal building. "She's my favorite."

"No, no. I got the exact lady for you," he said. "Much better than these bitches."

"Yeah?" Darcy sat forward.

"Yeah, yeah, a serious perpetrator but not a major offender." He smiled a little more, airing out those teeth.

"The five thousand, it's not a problem," Darcy said. "I have a cashier's check with me."

He inspected his fingernails for a few moments, then laughed briefly to himself and said, "Well, what the fuck."

Darcy said, "Can you get enough information on her so I'm convincing? Just so I knew some facts about her."

"Oh, I know the facts, all right. I got facts and facts on this lady," he said. "I used to be married to the whore." His smile soured briefly but came back. "That is, before she took such an interest in armed robbery."

Darcy stared at the image in the shadowy mirror in the Airstream trailer. Blunt cut hair, two inches long. Just barely long enough to comb. She'd parted it on the right. And the dye had come out even blacker than she'd pictured. She'd shaved her eyebrows. Now they were just a slash of black pencil.

A mass of her red hair was in the sink back at Emilio's. A five-thousand-dollar make-over. Her savings account down to eleven thousand.

She looked like she was ready to sling a leg over her Harley and ride into the night, or else heave a Molotov cocktail into a Guardia Civil station in northern Spain. Her face seemed more angular now, determined. Her eyes were red from the sleepless night in the motel. It matched the impatient burn inside her. She just wanted to be there, inside Benny's fortress. Get this thing going.

And the documents had excited her, too. Emilio hadn't forged anything. They were right there in a dresser drawer. Originals. Only her passport and driver's license had photos. Emilio had spread all this out on his dining room table. Snapshots of both of them out on a boat, at restaurants, smiling, drinking wine.

"Does she speak English?" Darcy had asked him.

"Yeah." Emilio looked longingly at one of the restaurant photos. "Spanish and Basque. But nobody knows Basque. You could get by with any gobbledygook."

After Darcy had cut her hair, done her eyebrows, Emilio had taken Polaroid head shots, glued them into the originals, using a small heatpress to seal the plastic over the photos. Delicate work. The man was a professional gluer. He'd looked up at her with his horny grin, getting wired seeing this woman taking on his wife's approximation.

Darcy was out of there as soon as the glue dried.

Maria Iturralde. Age thirty-one. Five feet five. An inch shorter and three years younger than Darcy. One thirty-five. Fifteen pounds heavier. But people changed. Damn right they did.

Maria Iturralde was wanted for robberies of Quick Marts and 7-Elevens in the Midwest. And then she'd begun taking down massage parlors. She and her black boyfriend. Emilio had kept up with her even though he hadn't seen her in a couple of years. He had clippings from the papers in Cincinnati and Detroit. Five massage parlors. She'd sent him the news stories from out on the road. Like postcards home. Some kind of quirky getting-even thing.

And then some real postcards from Biarritz, San Sebastián, Pamplona. Maria had gone home, taking her money with her from American whack-off houses, funding the terrorism campaign for Basque separatism. It was good. Not perfect, but better than she'd planned. Gave her a little more confidence.

Maria Iturralde wasn't exactly in Claude Hespier's league. Not a killer who ate his kills, but Darcy didn't think Benny would care. He wasn't running a talent agency.

She'd called Florida Secure Systems this afternoon and asked for Benny. She'd gotten the runaround for a while till she mentioned Claude Hespier's name. Then click, click, she was talking to the man himself, patched into his car somewhere. And she told him in two sentences who she was, what she wanted. She would be in Mexico City tomorrow afternoon. It had to happen that fast or she'd go elsewhere.

All right, Benny had said. Have ten thousand cash dollars with you, and in ten days be prepared to transfer another ninety to a bank in Nassau. I understood it was seventy-five total, Darcy had said, thinking she should play tough, bargain. He said, you understood wrong. A hundred total. It's what Claude paid, non-negotiable. For a genuine nukeproof, good-to-a-hundred fathoms, safe package. You still interested, lady?

I'll be there, she'd said. Five o'clock. Clicking off. Then she had to call back five minutes later to agree on where.

It was nearly nine when Thorn knocked on her door. The light was on in there, thank God. He'd been over four times Wednesday night. He was afraid she'd gone, begun her plan.

But it wasn't Darcy who came to the door. Harsh black hair chopped short, black horn-rimmed glasses. A severe woman in a man's flannel shirt and baggy jeans.

He leaned back and looked up on the outside wall for the address number. One eleven. The right place.

"Darcy here?" he said.

"No," she said, her voice deep.

"Where is she?"

"Gone."

Thorn stepped up another step and then put out his arm and levered past her into the trailer.

"Hey, you!"

"Where is she?" Thorn said.

Even when she smiled, it took Thorn a moment. And even when he realized it was Darcy, it was not over for him. He had to sit in the dining room chair and rest his arms on the table.

Thorn asked her what the hell she'd done to herself.

"Calm down," she said. "It's not what you think."

Thorn went to the refrigerator, got himself a can of beer, and brought it back to the table. She was leaning against the kitchen counter, opening and closing the wings of a corkscrew.

"All right," he said, taking looks at her in small dosages, bringing his eyes back to the beer can. "So what is it then?"

"I'm going back to work tomorrow," she said. "I wanted a change, that's all."

"Don't give me that shit," said Thorn. "This's your plan."

"OK, all right," she said. She sighed and made a tired smile. "I admit it, I was toying with the idea still. Playing around with my look. But you're right, Thorn. It's too damn dangerous. We need time to let it settle in our minds. Consider what to do. In the meantime, I'm going back to work. I'm on at noon tomorrow. They'll just have to deal with the new me." She put the corkscrew down and came over and sat opposite him. She picked up his beer and took a sip.

"You telling me the truth, Darcy?"

She nodded.

He said, "We're going to consider all the options. Everything. Even keep our minds open about telling this to Sugarman."

"Yeah," she said. "I was just reacting, temporarily insane, thinking I could pass myself off, go in there, bring Benny down like that. I've calmed down. It's OK. We'll figure a way."

He looked at her now, full on, and shook his head.

She laughed and said, "Yeah, I know. It looks pretty radical. But I can soften it some. Rinse the color out for one thing."

He said, "You go to work tomorrow like that, they'll want to switch you to live studio wrestling."

She smiled. Her eyes going soft, staying with his. She asked him if she could sleep at his house tonight. See how the construction was coming. Sure, he said. He let go of both lungs of air. Sure, OK, let's go.

25

Benny was crouched in the aluminum shed, poking at the gouge in the cement that one of his slugs had made. He located the other two and ran his fingers over the ragged craters, touched the bloody stains. He stood up, kicked at the roll of linoleum, and shook his head.

He walked over to the Bomb Bay Bar. Nothing much going on over there. He was in his black jeans and a Hawaiian shirt, parrots and speedboats. A pair of canvas deck shoes.

He took a seat at the bar. The only other customer was the guy that drove the shrimp truck. Papa John brought Benny a Coors and set it in front of him.

"So, how's the pirate business, pardner?"

"Tell me something, John," he said, keeping his voice low.

"I'm not discussing my shit anymore," John said.

Benny shook his head and said, "You ever hear of somebody shot in the head, the pistol pressed flush against their skull, right here." Benny pressed his pointing finger at a place in the middle of his forehead. "You ever heard of somebody like that living? Getting up the next day and reading the newspaper?"

The guy at the other end of the bar said, "I have. It happened to a guy I knew in Nam."

"Fuck you, weirdo," Benny said. He looked back at John. "I'm serious. You ever hear of something like that?"

"Once or twice," John said.

"I'm serious," Benny said.

"So am I," John said.

As they drove to Thorn's in the VW, Darcy said, "Did you know Gaeton kept some of your flies in his office downtown, on a corkboard on the wall, right up there with his citations? He acted like they were artworks or something. And there I thought they were just a bunch of thread and Mylar wrapped around a hook."

"That's all they are," Thorn said. "Little tricks."

"Well, he fell for them," she said. "You doing them lately?"

"A lifetime ago," Thorn said. "I only barely remember them."

"When this is over," she said, "we should get back to what works for us." She rested her hand on his shoulder and touched a finger to the back of his neck.

As he turned into his drive, he said, "You dye all your hair?"

She smiled and her finger ran down into the collar of his shirt. She said, "If I tell you, it'll just spoil the surprise."

He parked the VW next to the ice cream truck. No way to avoid it. She got out and leaned against her door. Thorn came around and stood beside her, took her hand.

"We didn't have any kind of ceremony," she said quietly.

The compressor was running, a low hum.

"Gaeton wasn't much on wakes," he said.

"No," she said. "When Dad died, you remember, people came by the house, stood around, ate conch fritters, drank rum.

And Gaeton told funny stories about Dad. The time he was pulled overboard by a tarpon. It dragged him so fast Dad tried to get up and ski. Cracked everybody up. People came up when they were leaving, said things like, we had a great time, we got to do this again, I can't remember when I laughed so hard."

"Yeah," Thorn said. "I remember that. He was a funny guy."

"A no wake guy," she said.

The compressor shut off, and she slipped in under his arm, found a comfortable notch there, both of them still watching the ice cream truck.

Thorn said, "Want a Fudgsicle? Nutty-buddy?"

"Thorn."

"Well," he said. "Let me show the house then."

"It's a good size," she said, "comfortable but not too big." Her head on his bare chest, gazing through the rafters at the big dipper, Polaris. The starlight sparkled in her pubic hair.

"I can't take any credit for it," Thorn said. "I was born this way."

Darcy said, "I meant the house."

They both laughed, and she lifted her head and kissed him again. She drew a slow line from his Adam's apple to his navel. And then began a delicate journey into his pubic hair, lingering there, combing out the snarls. He shifted beneath the comforter, opened himself to her.

"Well, architecturally speaking," he said, "it's nothing much, just a little box."

She cupped him. Jiggled him lightly.

"Don't you remember, Thorn?" she said. "It's not the size of the ship that counts. It's the motion of the ocean."

While they chuckled into the chilly dark, Thorn located with his right hand the place he had found before. The place that made her shut her eyes and lean her head back. Made her throat quake. He touched her lightly there, teased it, and then lowered himself slowly, down her body and brought his tongue to her, separating the folds, tasting again that tart jasmine that was her scent.

She lifted her legs, brought her knees to her chest, and embraced them with one arm, her other arm slung out across the floor. And Thorn drew an alphabet there with his tongue, flicking it, flattening it, probing. He vanished into the damp heat of her. Gone. A twilight in his head. She writhed and began to speak her garbled commands. And his tongue answered her in this way. A guttural mumble.

She had not dyed that hair.

Darcy brought her feet down and pressed them on the floor and lifted her hips, pressing back, grinding into his mouth.

In a while he raised himself from her and looked up across her belly and breasts at that harsh foreign face. She smiled down at him, and he brought his lips back to her and fastened himself to those other lips, shaping and reshaping the fit, the pressure, the pace, until he felt a flutter escape from her, and a sudden flare of heat, and she raised her hips from the mahogany floor and he raised his face with her.

She shivered, and snarled. Began a slow crescendo of distressed cries as if she were losing her balance on a narrow ledge. And finally it broke from her, and she brought her legs back up and hugged her knees. And she started to sob, a deep rush of tears. With one hand she held his head in place as she wept.

It was an hour later. Near midnight. The sky a dark blanket tattered with stars. The marker light sent a pulse of yellow light out across the bay. They were sitting on the porch, the comforter draped over their shoulders, dangling their legs over the edge. Thorn could feel the print of mahogany grain in his naked butt. The Coleman lantern hissed nearby.

"Did you know," she said, "that for every human being on earth, there's a ton of termites?"

"You're so romantic," he said.

She smiled, said, "And when they eat wood, they give off methane gas. Methane's one of the greenhouse gases, seals in the earth's heat. Which all means that termites are changing global weather patterns in a major way."

"Well, then," Thorn said, "there you go."

She hugged the blanket around herself. The compressor mumbled down below. She was staring at the bay, eyes on something way out. He slipped out from under the comforter and lay back on the floor.

"I'm serious, damn it," she said. "Worldwide, we're cutting down forests the size of England and Scotland every year. There's never been a better time to be a termite."

"I bet this's some kind of an analogy, right? It applies to us somehow."

She shook her head, glanced back at him, fighting off a smile. She said, "I was just looking at all your pretty wood. Wondering why it made me so sad."

"Most of this wood was headed for the dump. I'm not going to feel guilty about using it. Scotland, England, I don't care."

"Before long all we'll have left is the punky trees," she said. "Melaleucas. Good for nothing but draining the Everglades."

In the lantern light her skin was flickering gold.

Darcy said, "You know, in a lightning storm the melaleucas, because their bark is so papery, they catch fire very easily. The fires spread to the hardwoods, but the melaleucas don't burn down themselves. They're too waterlogged. They have the insides of a cactus."

Thorn was up on an elbow now, watching her.

He said, "You get very passionate. About all kinds of things."

"Those melaleucas," she said, "they're overrunning the Everglades. When someone goes to chop one of them down, the tree senses it somehow and puffs out a million spores."

"I think I know how they feel," he said.

She huffed and said, "Somebody has to do something, Thorn."

He lay back, watched the starlight shimmer.

"Then we'll make it our next mission."

She said, "I want to see Benny dead, Thorn. I do, and I don't much care how."

"Yeah, I know," he said. "I do, too. And we will. We'll do it. But let's think it out, do it right."

She was quiet for a moment, wagging her legs over the edge. Then she turned and lay back beside him and propped her head on her hand. She began to draw lazy circles in his chest hair. Her breasts pressed against his ribs.

"Does anything scare you?" she said. "Really scare you?"

"Twelve-foot hammerheads in bloody water," he said. "Blind men with spearguns."

"How about women?"

Thorn turned his head, opened his eyes.

"Why do you say that?"

"I think you're afraid of me," she said. "We're involved but you're always joking, keeping me right here, measured off."

"I wouldn't call that, a few minutes ago, measured off."

"But you are, you're afraid of letting it get deeper."

Thorn touched a finger to her wrist, drew a slow line up her arm and back down. Sliding his finger in and out each of the grooves between her fingers.

"Jesus," he said. "Now the lady wants it even deeper."

She growled and wriggled her fingers into his ribs, bit him hard on the neck. Thorn pushing at her hands. She fell onto him, and they wrestled. She pinned him finally.

And gradually her bite softened. Her fingers, too. And together they scooted on the comforter slowly away from the edge, back to the center of that new floor.

Christening it. Dozing afterward, and christening it again.

Benny asked at a 7-Eleven, and the clerk said sure, everybody knew Thorn. Up two miles, across from the canvas shop, a little gravel road. No mailbox or nothing.

Benny parked in the canvas shop parking lot. He sat out there smoking Don Ciega cigars, Cuban monsters that kept the bugs away. You couldn't get these goddamn cigars anymore. But then there were a lot of things you couldn't get anymore, and Benny still managed to have them.

He sat there from midnight to three, watching the driveway, listening to some radio talk show from Miami, insomniacs arguing about gun control. Should you teach kids how to use a gun or scare the shit out of them so they'd never go near one? That seemed to be the choices. Benny had another idea. Scare the wimps, teach the leaders. Where you got in trouble was giving guns to wimps. They went shooting at guys ordinarily they'd run from. It upset the natural order of things. He thought of calling in and setting this asshole host straight, but then he realized he needed to think about his own situation, not listen to some other guy's worries. He turned it off.

From midnight to one-thirty he'd sat there, listening to that program, just watching Thorn's drive. Not expecting anything and not getting anything. Nothing going in or coming out all that time.

For an hour or so he tapped his foot on the floorboard, running it all around, debating it. Not wanting to fall for something, walk into some dumbass trap. Because that's sure as shit what it felt like, a fucking come-hither psych job.

At about three he got out, opened the trunk. Looked up and down the empty highway. Then lifted out the M-79 grenade launcher. Frankfort Arsenal. And he picked out one of the HE rounds, a forty-millimeter concussion grenade. He could lob it over to Thorn's little estate, stun every living thing for a hundred yards around. They'd still be alive, but they'd be staggering and mumbling like a 5:00 A.M. drunk. Then he could just walk over there and sort out this from fucking that.

He carried it twenty feet north of the canvas shop to a little grove of trees. The launcher wasn't much more than a big shotgun and had less recoil than a ten-gauge. He flipped up the rear sight. But fuck if he knew how far to aim. Thorn's property was somewhere between four and five acres of woods. He could fire the grenade, be off by a hundred yards one way or the other, and all it would do was make everybody for a couple of miles around piss their pajamas. And if he walked over there and reconnoitered like he should, to do this correctly, he might be walking right into that trap.

So he stood there, taking a leak beside the grenade launcher. Watering the rocks with his seventh cup of coffee. And then, more good karma luck. Here comes a lady. Short black hair, pretty good body on her, comes walking out of Thorn's driveway.

She headed down the highway on foot. Benny thinking, now what? Go in there while the guy's dick's still wet, shake him awake, get some answers. Go pick up the lady? Grill her. Or just let the whole thing slide? Let that goofus country music guy do the work?

Jesus. What was he thinking about? A guy didn't get up and walk away with a thirty-eight slug in his head. He didn't give a shit what Roger said. Or the guy at the bar. Or Papa John. So, then, what was that photocopy? Some kind of half-assed trick photography probably. That nurse at Mariner's Hospital? That'd be easy enough to arrange. It didn't matter actually. Any way you looked at it, Thorn was jerking his chain.

Benny hustled the grenade launcher back in the trunk. Shut it and got in the car and started it. Pulled out on the highway.

Jerking his chain so he'd do something dumb probably. Like walk into the pointy teeth of some steel trap with his hard-on sticking out.

No, sir. Not Benny.

He drove south, slowed down beside the lady, got a good look at her. Pretty little thing. Nice Winnebagos on her. A regular tempest in a D cup. The guy had reasonable taste in women anyway.

Benny let go of a big sigh. Shit, he guessed he'd just let it go for now. Wait and see if that redneck Ozzie did his work.

26

Benny didn't like old ladies. Simple as that. They didn't fight fair. Take this one, sitting in her wheelchair with a muddy rock in her lap and a green Luger in her right hand, a goddamn water pistol of all things, aiming it at him. Like he was sugar and gonna melt.

And this morning especially, after not getting but an hour's sleep. The call came at eight that morning from his internal affairs office telling him there was some kind of computer incursion a couple of days ago. Originating in Key Largo. Benny going, all right now, what is this shit? More chain jerking?

"Ma'am," Benny said, standing just a yard away from a huge pile of rocks, getting a little vertigo from the situation. Not what he'd pictured as he drove over here. "I'm asking you a civilized question, and you go aiming things at me. I don't think that's polite."

A thick-necked tomcat sprang up into her lap and turned and faced Benny. He didn't like cats either. In fact, animals in general, about all you could say for them was they didn't talk. Didn't let on how stupid they were.

"Can we discuss this in a businesslike manner? Sit down and exchange views, that sort of thing?"

"You don't have any views I want to hear," Priscilla said.

"You don't even know me," he said. "I can be an entertaining fellow."

"You're trespassing."

He said, "The answer to one question would do it for me. You tell me that, bang, I'm out of here."

She said, "It's the bang that worries me."

Benny smiled. Good, she was warming to him. They were getting the dialogue going. After years of studying interrogation techniques, he'd found there was still only one good way. Get them to think of you as their only rational hope in a world gone haywire.

He'd worn his Keys threads today. A green sweat shirt with a picture of a pelican sitting on a wooden piling. Below the pelican, in black it said, "Another Shitty Day in Paradise." He left his black leather jacket opened so she could read it. His stone-washed black jeans, boat shoes. Telling the world that this man knew how to hang loose.

She said, "All right, then. Put it in five words or less; then get the hell off my land."

Benny stretched his eyebrows up, trying to ease the headache that was starting to grip his head. Jesus, sometimes these Conchs made New Yorkers seem down-home friendly. He found a level spot on the pile of rocks and sat down. But the old lady fired a shot at him, darkened his sweat shirt at the heart. He stood up. Ice tongs digging into his temples.

He forced out a smile and said, "I understand you do computer work, you know, hire out to do research for people. Things like that."

"Assume anything you like. I'm sure as hell not going to tell you anything about anything."

That was it. So much for the buddy-buddy approach. The pincers were digging in. Benny pulled in a lungful of air through his nose. And he stepped around behind her and took hold of the grips and started rolling her toward the water.

When Thorn woke that Friday morning, finding Darcy gone, he walked down to the *Heart Pounder* and lay down in the bunk. But a dream came almost immediately, and it shook him awake. In it the refrigeration in the ice cream truck had failed, and Gaeton was lying there, thawing under a sticky coating of corn syrup and chocolate.

Thorn had dragged himself up from the bunk, off the *Heart Pounder*, up the dock, across the yard to where the truck was parked under the stilt house. He unlocked the door and went inside and opened the lid. There was still thick frost on his friend's eyebrows. Temperature holding steady at thirty-four.

He stayed in the ice cream truck till dawn, sitting in the driver's seat. Bones heavy, stomach hollow. A guilt hangover. He went over his final day with Gaeton, the drive to Miami, the alligators, the joking at 120 miles an hour. The look that passed between them as Gaeton aimed his handgun at the gator.

Then he let himself recall those long-ago Saturday mornings in the *Guardian* office. The smell of printing fluid, the comforting chug of the press. Gaeton senior reading, rereading, typing fast with two fingers.

Then, later on those afternoons, Gaeton senior would lean back in his swivel oak chair, pick up that knife, and begin to whittle again on a piece of oak, making those puzzles he did, a ball inside a slotted vase, a woman trapped inside a cage. While Gaeton and Thorn stacked the *Guardian*s in the baskets on their bikes, then pedaled up and down the highway, delivering papers till dark.

Thorn sat in the ice cream truck, watching the bay turn silver, then dark green. He remembered how he'd felt on those days, that radiance in his chest. Whatever name he might give it now, then it was simply that people smiled to see him coming with the paper, and in his rearview mirror they shook the paper open and began to read as they walked back to their houses.

Even in Key Largo, a town amused by its own corruption, where folks were never shocked or even mildly surprised as they read the truth about themselves and their leaders, still, they seemed happy to see him coming and read carefully when he left.

Thorn dressed in a pair of rumpled tan pants, a plaid flannel shirt. He brushed his teeth and washed his face at the spigot under the house. He combed his hair with wet fingers. By ten o'clock he had the Lakowski sawmill going, getting some nice-looking planks out of a dirty-dog chunk of white ironwood.

The tree had come from a stand of ironwoods that were bull-dozed recently, making way for the new K Mart. The county biologist had quietly protested that these were the last ironwoods anybody knew about in all of North America. The proper down-cast looks came over the county commissioners. Another loved one is about to leave us. And the vote was unanimous.

None of the locals had fought very hard for those trees. It was getting so people were bored fighting these battles. Nobody was taking the long view anymore. Thorn had begun to believe it was because there was a drop in the population of grandchildren. When people stopped having kids, it rippled everywhere. It got harder to care about what happened in the middle of the next century when nobody you loved would be alive then. To hell with the long view.

And you needed a damn long view for a white ironwood. You planted a seed, it took six years to get tall enough to tell it from the grass around it.

He reset the saw blade and jammed the last of that heart-wood into the shriek of the machine.

When he looked up, Nan LaCroix was standing a few feet away. She was the head librarian for the local library. He brushed the sawdust from his arms, switched off the big machine, and said hello. Nan was tall and thick, had the remnants of a British accent. She was dressed for work.

"Priscilla asked me to come see you," she said. "Just now."

"Yeah?"

"Someone called the library."

"What is it, Nan?"

"Well, I don't understand this, but she said you would."

Thorn took a breath, dusted more wood flakes off himself.

She said, "A person called and inquired about our use of a computer at the library."

Thorn stopped brushing at his flannel shirt.

"And you said?"

"Well, I didn't talk to him myself, but Margaret Elkins told him no, we weren't that newfangled. And the man asked if there was somebody who worked for the library who had access to a computer terminal, somebody who might be able to do a little computer research work for him. And Margaret told him that no, nobody who currently worked for the library did, but that there *was* somebody around town who knew computers and might like to pick up some extra money. Priscilla."

"You phone Priscilla, tell her about the call?"

"Yes, we did. And she became quite excited and said to come get you. To tell you to come over right away."

Thorn said, "Did anybody tell this guy how he could find Priscilla?"

"Margaret Elkins did, yes," said Nan. "Did she do wrong?"

Benny was applying some intense psychotherapy to the old lady, showing her the connection between sanity and gravity by hanging her front wheels over the edge of the seawall.

He said, "You pulled a prank. You knocked on my door and then I got up from what I was doing and came to the door and you ran away."

There was a stiff breeze coming across the bay today. Coolish, it jostled the water against the seawall. Benny tipped her forward and watched as she gripped her armrests. The cat looked down at the water and climbed up onto the old lady's shoulder and jumped back to land. So much for animal loyalty.

Benny kicked at it, almost lost his balance, and dropped her in the drink. The muddy rock she'd been carrying in her lap slid forward and splashed into the bay.

He rolled her back a bit and said, "I think somebody put you up to that. Am I right? I don't think you were just sitting around and said to yourself, think I'll call up some businesses, sneak into their computer, prowl around. You don't seem like that kind of old lady to me. Huh?" He gave her a little rattle. Her butt scooted forward a couple of inches.

She turned in her seat, raised the water gun, and got a spurt directly in his left eye. He squinted hard, rolled her back onto land, and rubbed at the eye, smearing the sight back into it.

"You ignorant crone," Benny said.

But she had rolled away, up the sloping yard back toward her houseboat. Benny shook his head. Christ, look at him. Here he was, the CEO of a eighty-million-dollar company, a man with a vision and a mission, the general of an army of ex-cops and federal agents, and he was chasing around after a crippled-up colostomy case.

He jogged up the yard and caught her as she was rolling up the ramp to her houseboat. The woman could roll. He had to give her that much. Rock and roll.

Benny took hold of the grips and dragged her back down the ramp. The gristly old dame locked the wheels with her hands, but Benny got her back to the grass. He was starting to sweat, breathing a little heavy now.

"What? You going in there, bring out a water hose, really spray me good?"

He moved around to stand in front of her. A couple of her cats came to the doorway to see the commotion. She raised that

Luger again, aimed it at him. He flinched, but she didn't shoot. Probably down to her last couple of squirts, wanted to save them.

"Hey, listen, Miss Spottswood. Save us both any more of this bullshit, would you? It might seem like a little thing you did, asking my computer about illegal immigration. But we're talking about a project here, it's top secret, classified. People like you, if they're asking questions about an area like this, then we got a leakage problem. It could mean we got a serious national security breach. Do you see where I'm taking you?"

Priscilla looked at the narrow gravel lane that led out to the highway. Her eyes lingered there for a moment; then she brought them back to Benny.

She said, "Then let me see some ID. If you're a government official. If this is all legitimate, then you show me some official ID and I'll consider being civil to you."

Benny felt the pierce of those tongs again. ID, Jesus. Everybody was so hot for ID.

He said, "It was this Thorn character, wasn't it? You just give me a nod, yes or no, and we'll call it settled between us. Thorn put you up to it. Am I right?" He stepped up closer to her, bent over so he could get his face on the level with hers.

She raised the Luger and got him in the other eye. A real stinger.

Thorn had the VW up to sixty, but he was boxed in behind a Bronco pulling an Aquasport and a Toyota full of college kids. Two bare feet sticking out the front passenger window. He honked at the college kids, flashed his lights. Got two birds back. One out the driver's window and one from a guy with a big neck in the back seat.

It was ten more miles to Priscilla's. He'd told Nan to call Sugarman and have him meet Thorn there and to make sure he knew it was an emergency. He held his horn down, and it croaked like a strangled fowl.

He kept the accelerator flat to the floor, a gap opening as he pulled even with the Bronco. He motioned to the driver to let him cut in front, and the guy scowled at Thorn and sped up just enough to pull even again with the Toyota.

He held the horn down now, straddled the center line, and mashed the gas pedal flat. When he angled in between these two clowns, both of them yelled at him, honking back. But giving him room.

He'd crept ahead twenty, thirty yards when the siren sounded. In the rearview mirror Sugarman's lights flashed. He was shaking his head at Thorn. The Bronco and the Toyota slowed, and Thorn edged over into the right lane, up to sixty-five now. Sugarman got in front of him and led the way, still shaking his head.

Darcy's Eastern flight to Mexico City had taken three hours and twenty minutes. She had chosen it to coincide with the arrival of an Iberian flight from Madrid. In the concourse she eased away from the passengers on her plane, mingling with those who flooded down the concourse. She tore up her ticket and dropped the remains into two different trash cans. She was probably overdoing all this, but she was running on such high-octane paranoia now that she couldn't help it.

At Immigration she stood behind a group of Americans, the women in bright stretch pants, the men smelling of whiskey. When one of the men turned to her and asked her if this was her first time abroad, too, she answered him in Spanish. He smiled awkwardly, mangled a quick *muchas gracias,* and turned back to his group.

The immigration officer examined her passport and took a lazy look at her. He spoke to her in Spanish, asking her the purpose of her trip. She said, a vacation. No luggage? She said no, none. The man looked again at the passport, flipped through the pages, Maria's border crossings for the five years before she'd run back to Spain.

The phone on his desk rang. He picked it up, still holding her passport, his fingers rubbing the plastic seal over her photo. He listened to the phone for several moments and said *sí,* he would. He would do that, watching her while he talked, feeling the edges of the plastic on her passport.

She wished now she had dressed more formally. She'd worn faded Levi's and a black short-sleeved cotton blouse with a button-down collar, labels removed. And a pair of old Keds.

The immigration officer hung up the phone, took one more curious look at her photograph, and said in careful English, "Enjoy your stay, Miss Iturralde."

She took her passport and moved through the turnstile into another line through Customs. She had distributed the ten thousand dollars about her clothes. Two thousand in each pocket, some more in her shoes, a thousand in her purse. But the woman at Customs simply waved her through into the main lobby. Anything Darcy wanted to smuggle into Mexico fine by her.

Darcy found a women's room. She locked herself in a stall and closed her eyes, leaning her head against the door. She began to hyperventilate.

It took her five minutes to gather herself. Then she left the stall, stood in front of a mirror next to a Mexican girl. The girl looked up at Darcy and smiled. She wasn't more than seven. An infant in a leather sling was lashed to the girl's back. A girl of fifteen came out of one the stalls, took the child by her hand, and led her away.

Darcy went back out into the noisy lobby, bumped into the same group of Americans. The man who'd spoken to her winked over his shoulder and moved along with his herd.

She went to the Pan Am information counter, where Benny had instructed her to stand. She was about to ask the attendant the time when a man in a white uniform stopped beside her. He was blond and over six feet. His uniform had no patches or markings.

"Maria Iturralde?" he said.

"*Sí.*" She stepped away from the man.

"I was told you speak fluent English."

"I do," she said.

"Well, I'm sorry I'm late. I've been circling the airport for an hour. Dadgum air traffic here is worse than Atlanta."

He had blue simple eyes. He'd been an Eagle Scout, won merit badges in innocence.

"So, how was your flight?"

"Fair," she said, breathing smoothly now. "It's a long way."

"Well, this leg'll be a lot easier."

"I certainly hope so," she said.

27

Benny wheeled her over to the rock pile. He came around in front of her and took hold of that water gun and twisted it out of her grip, shaking his head at this, at the silliness of it.

"People know," Priscilla said. "People know you're here. I called for help."

Benny dropped the water pistol on a rock and stepped on it. Gave it a good heel crunch.

He said, "Well, then. I guess we should pick up the pace."

He found a very big slab of rock in the pile. A heavy flat black thing. He grunted it up to his belly. The boulder about crushed his vertebrae as he moved it over to the old lady. He settled it onto her lap. As he let go of the full weight of it, he thought he could hear the snap of her thighbone.

Right away the lady's eyes lost their sting. She drew her head back, and the breath rattled in her throat. He came around behind her, took hold of the grips again, and headed back to the water.

"You can tell me who put you up to this," Benny said as he bumped the wheelchair toward the shoreline, "or you can keep doing this name, rank, serial number bullshit. Though, I got to tell you the truth, at this point I'm not sure I even care anymore."

On the northern edge of her property, near a dense covering of hibiscus and oleander, there was a concrete boat ramp. It was coated with green algae. Benny changed directions and headed for it.

The old lady was nodding her head slowly from side to side. Her eyes squeezed shut. She was making gagging noises, grunts. Of all the people Benny had ferried across to the other side lately, she took the goddamn cake for orneriness.

He brought his mouth down to her ear and whispered, "Was it Thorn put you up to it?"

She gagged some more, her head slumping forward now.

He brought her to the top of the slimy boat ramp. He could feel the pull of that tilt to the bay water, and he drew back a foot.

"You could tell me, and we'd just let bygones be bygones, just get back to our business. How'd that be?"

She raised her head, turned it around so he could see her profile. Her eyes were still clamped shut. "Up yours," she said.

He let her go.

The wheelchair bumped down the ramp. For a moment it teetered to the right and he thought it was going to flop on its side, but it stabilized and got all the way to the water, little front wheels going in. And it stopped. The old lady had hold of the wheels.

She was cranking them backwards, dragging herself and that hundred-pound slab of rock back up the ramp. But the slime on the ramp kept the wheels from getting a bite. She pumped them around in place, the chair not going either direction.

Benny started walking to his car, looking back at her. The pathetic old woman was trying so hard to stay dry. He got all the way to the Mercedes before her arms gave out on her, and she let go, and the wheelchair picked up speed and splashed her into the bay. He waited for the bubbles.

Yeah, well. There you go. This was no Sunday afternoon pickup game. Ask Gaeton Richards, ask Priscilla Spottswood. Any of the others. He believed he knew how the coroner or these half-assed police would read it. The lady had taken on a boulder bigger than she could handle. And she lost it on the ramp. Hidey, hidey, hidey ho.

What the old woman needed now was a set of gills.

Thorn called out her name, but she wasn't inside the houseboat. No signs of disturbance, but the cats were nervous, roaming around, slapping and hissing at each other. He ran back outside. Called out her name again. Sugarman stood by the rock pile, watching him. His eyes dark and professional. His cop face.

Thorn hustled over to him, saw the broken water pistol in the grass nearby.

He cursed and squatted and picked up a piece of the barrel.

"What? What is it, Thorn?"

Thorn showed him the crushed plastic.

"So?"

"We're too late," he said. "He's got her."

"Thorn, what the hell're you doing?"

He turned from Sugarman and loped down to the shore. The bay water was spattered with miniature suns. It was almost noon, a northwestern breeze chopping up the surface.

On the edge of the seawall Thorn called her name. A black tabby rubbed against his bare ankle, laced around his legs, and leaned against his other ankle.

Then he saw her hair. He'd noticed it a minute earlier but thought it was trash. It was spread out on the surface of the riffling water. A tangle of white yarn.

He sprinted down the seawall, leaped into the water. He scooped up her body, found a solid footing in the bay bottom muck, and brought her face up into the air. He cradled her over to the seawall and to Sugarman.

He could tell she was dead. Though he hadn't checked her pulse, he knew it, as he lifted her up to Sugarman. He could feel the similarity between her and Gaeton. The quiet hum of current no longer circulating inside her. A new skill Thorn was acquiring, the curse of a new sensitivity.

Doris Albritton of the volunteer ambulance corps arrived in five minutes. By then Thorn was woozy from blowing into Priscilla's mouth, taking turns with Sugarman. A little gurgle of bay water had erupted from her at first, but there was no sudden revivial, no flutter of eyelids. Doris's young male assistant moved Thorn aside and laid Priscilla on a stretcher, and they rolled her back to the ambulance, the useless IV bottle swaying as they went.

Thorn and Sugarman followed the ambulance in Sugarman's patrol car. Neither of them spoke. Thorn stared at the shops and restaurants of Islamorada, Windley Key, out at the Atlantic. It was glowing a dull green today as if lit from below.

Alone in the hospital waiting room, Thorn sat watching the Channel Six noon news. His flannel shirt was dry now, pants almost there. On the local news they were bulldozing drug houses. Knocking down the flimsy homes of early Miami settlers. Public officials smiled and bragged to the camera that they were getting serious now.

The weather was coming up after the commercials.

Sugarman came into the room, sat down beside Thorn, and said, "So let me get this straight. This is your chain of events. We got a phone call made by Miss Spottswood to Mr. Benny Cousins several days ago to inquire about Mr. Cousins's business enterprises. You say you witnessed that. Then we got a voice on the phone this morning calling to the library to find out about computer research. Then we have Priscilla with salt water in her lungs. Therefore, we're going to say that voice is attached to Mr. Benny Cousins. And he was responsible for pushing her into the bay. Am I following your logic here? Is this being fair to your view?"

"It's shit, isn't it?"

"Thorn, I wouldn't dignify it by calling it shit."

"Yeah," he said. "I must be losing it."

"Sometimes I'm not sure you ever had it, Thorn. I'm concerned about you, man. Priscilla's dead, and you're coming on with this Benny Cousins obsession again. Like this guy is the source of all evil. A lady drowns and it's got to be Benny held her under. If you just stand back and look at this, switch on the common sense for a minute, you'd have to say implicating a man like Benny in a thing like this is . . . I don't know. I'd call it insane maybe. Nuts."

Sugarman seemed to be measuring Thorn's pupils, see what drug he was on.

"Well," Thorn said, watching a rock star strut while he guzzled diet cola, "if you're not going to do anything, Sugar, then I'll take it from here."

Sugarman's face ripened to half a shade darker. His neck bulged around his collar. He shook his head with his eyes half closed. He was saying something under his breath. But Thorn didn't pay any attention. The Channel Six weather was on. And a 250-pound man with curly blond hair was waving a pointer at the national map, hugging himself and shivering as the temperatures in the Northeast lit up.

Thorn closed his eyes.

He got one of the other deputies to drive him back to Priscilla's to pick up the VW. For a few shaky minutes he poked around in her houseboat, the cats staring at him, moving out of his way. He found nothing unusual, nothing to indicate Benny had been there.

He refilled all the bowls he could find with cat chow, stood at the doorway, and spoke to the brood. He told them that Priscilla was away, off on a very long trip, that he would check on them for a while, make sure they were behaving themselves.

You had to keep things simple for cats.

On the drive down to Islamorada, Thorn held it under the speed limit. A couple of vacationers honked at him when they finally got a chance to pass, glaring at this burnout in his VW convertible, top down on a freezing day like this.

His arms were limp, and inside his chest galaxies collided, suns died, old women strangled on seawater. Lovers disappeared into the underground. Thorn drove on, knowing he was prepared to do something crazy, things that might get him hurt. Beyond that, he had no idea. Beyond that, he didn't give a shit.

Before they departed Mexico City, Major Herb Johnson gave her a tour of the plane, his copilot running through the preflight checklist, speaking to the tower.

She watched the copilot flipping switches, Herb saying, "It's a C-one-forty-one B, the biggest plane in the force. Used to be we employed her mainly for staging and supply missions in Europe, the Middle East."

She nodded and followed him back into the dark, empty lungs of the plane. Small red woven sling chairs hung from the walls. Wooden pallets were tied down near the rear. Nothing else. You could park a fleet of Lincolns inside there, or tanks.

Herb Johnson said, "These days they got us running pens and paper clips to American embassies." He gave her a forlorn wink then and said, "This lady's brought the bodies of heroes back from Lebanon, before that POWs home from Vietnam. And now we're carrying embossed stationery and God knows what else."

The plane was based in Charleston Air Force Base, he said. He'd be back there for supper, after they dropped Maria Iturralde off at Homestead Air Force Base. He said he was sorry, but it wasn't exactly designed for passenger comfort. And then he smiled at her and was pointedly silent. Her turn.

She said nothing, just returned his smile. She didn't want him to have to give back his blue-eyed merit badges.

Darcy was buckled into one of the sling chairs, her back against the hull. Dust shook loose from the walls of that enormous tube. Her bones rattled in their sockets.

There was no insulation to muffle the roar, and though she had used the yellow rubber earplugs that Colonel Johnson had given her, jamming them deeper and deeper into her ears, she was sure she would be deaf when they landed.

Thorn parked the car at Marlin Foodmart and walked a half mile down the asphalt road. It had once been the main highway through the Keys. Narrow and shady. There'd been days thirty years ago he had ridden his bike there and had found alligators sleeping in the middle of that road. Two, three cars might be parked, waiting for it to move on, the drivers chatting.

Now the road was known as millionaire's alley, a potholed lane a hundred feet away from U.S. 1. All the driveways were hung with gates, posted with warning signs. He didn't know anybody who lived along there anymore. Nobody but Benny Cousins.

Thorn made it twenty feet into Benny's property when he saw W. B. Jefferson operating the big orange loader. He was just finishing a four-by-four hole in line with the other royal palms.

W.B. wore a blue nylon windbreaker, khaki pants. And under the jacket was that shirt. The bright yellow shirt with the blue hula girls on it. Claude Hespier's shirt. It was buttoned tight across W.B.'s thick chest.

W.B. saw Thorn and waved, shut down the motor. W.B. had

been a couple of years behind Thorn at Coral Shores High, but they'd known each other, like everyone did, black or white, who grew up on the island in those days.

W.B. got down from the seat and shook Thorn's hand.

"I spect there's bells and buzzers be ringing right now inside that house." He wiped some sweat away from his face with a blue bandanna. "Hell, by now they know when you was born, how many illegitimate children you got."

"That shirt, W.B.," Thorn said. "Where'd you get it?"

"You like it, I'd take a dollar for it."

"I just want to know where it came from."

W.B. said, "Right here, right where I'm working. I find every kind of thing out here."

Thorn could hear voices down the drive, toward the house, a car's engine starting. W.B. was knocking dirt clods and limestone chunks off the auger blade with the edge of his thick dark hand.

Thorn said he wanted to hear about that shirt.

W.B. tied the bandanna into a scarf on his head. Then he gazed down the drive toward the house. Thorn took a breath, hearing the car crunch down the drive.

"Well, it was one morning last November," W.B. said, "I was lowering that palm right over there into the hole, and I had it hanging there, and I came over to see was it going in straight, and that's when I saw a little piece of something sticking up out of the dirt inside that hole. I got down in there, and I pulled it out, and it was a sleeve to a nice white sport jacket. Silk or some such. Not my size, but I give it to W.B. junior.

"So, now I check every time, 'fore I put the tree in. And lordy, the shit I find. Watches, wallets, every kind of clothes. I got to stick my hand in there a foot or so. It isn't the first time I seen people use their tree holes to get rid of garbage in, but my, my, what these people throw away."

One of Benny's brown Mercedeses was pulling up. A guy spoke into a walkie-talkie, got out the passenger door. He was wearing a white Adidas tennis warm-up. He said something to his twin, the driver. And the driver stayed put, his eyes on Thorn.

Thorn said, "That's where that shirt came from, buried in the dirt?"

"Just last Monday," he said quickly, almost a whisper. He nodded his big chin toward where the last fifty-foot royal palm had gone in. "It don't fit me that good. But it's bright."

The man from the car moved up to Thorn's shoulder.

The guy's Old Spice took Thorn's breath away for a moment. He stared at Thorn as if deciding which stranglehold to apply.

"Get in the car," the man said.

"I got my own car," said Thorn.

Thorn could feel W.B. moving away from this. He didn't want to muss that hula girl shirt.

"Get in the car," the man said again, quieter this time.

Thorn turned his back on the man and said to W.B., "Hey, I'll talk to you later. You stay loose, you hear." W.B. didn't answer, watching the big man coming up behind Thorn.

When he felt the guy on his right shoulder, Thorn took a quick half step backwards, planted his right foot between the man's legs, swiveled, and brought his chest to the man's chest.

The man lurched backwards, and Thorn kept walking into him. Get people off-balance and they got funny looks. Take this guy with his tipsy grin, whirling his hands like he was treading air. Thorn had him in a full-tilt backwards stumble, driving him back until he thumped against the Mercedes's driver door. It slammed the breath from him and sent his buddy back into the car.

Thorn pressed the man against the closed door while he patted down his warm-up suit. He found the hard lump he'd expected and reached under his jacket while the man got his breath back and pushed weakly at Thorn's hands. He drew the .38 out of the holster, jabbed it into the man's ribs, and heard the passenger door swing open.

His partner cocked his pistol and said, "This the day you want to die?"

Thorn's breath was burning. He'd been neglecting his aerobics lately. He turned his head slowly to look over at the other man. He was aiming a .44 across the roof. Thorn let the .38 drop to the dirt and raised his hands. His eyes drifted up to the overcast sky.

"Well, it looks like we got us another cold front coming," he said. The man started around the car, holding the .44 with both hands. "You know, it's because of the damn termites," said Thorn. "Giving off all that methane gas. You heard about that?"

The man told Thorn to shut the fuck up.

Thorn shrugged. The guy probably didn't have any grandchildren. Probably never would.

28

"You want to take a boat ride?" Ozzie asked when Bonnie'd shut off the acetylene torch. He was standing in the doorway of her workroom, wearing his white shirt with the epaulets. Admiral Oz.

"Who'd you steal a boat from? Customs? Drug Enforcement Agency?" She raised her goggles and did her smartass grin.

"Har, har," Ozzie said. "Never mind then."

He started to walk off, but she said, "Yeah, I would. I'd like to take a boat ride. I need to get out of here." Trying in her way to make up to him.

"OK. Meet me down at the bar."

His voice was taking on that husky sound that Johnny Cash always had. Ozzie was a natural tenor, and he worried sometimes that there was too much falsetto creeping into his everyday talking voice. It was like having good posture. You had to keep after it. Hold your head up, keep your shoulders back and your voice deep in your chest.

By God, it was working at the moment. She was on her way upstairs.

Papa John was taking an old fart afternoon nap when he and Bonnie came aboard. Man was pretending he couldn't pry his eyes open. So Ozzie pulled the fancy pistol out of the waistband of his jeans and showed it to the old man. It made him blink.

Bonnie stood behind Ozzie at the doorway down to the cabin. In her little leopardskin bikini. Her gut pooching a little over the brim of the bikini. Both of them had pretty much the same look. Not completely sure what the fuck was up. And not really all that afraid of Ozzie, but willing now to go along.

"Whatever you say, boy," Papa John said, getting out of his bunk, yawning. "Man draws his gun gets to go where he wants."

"Ozzie, you dickhead," Bonnie said. But there wasn't any bite in how she said it.

"Out past the shipping lanes," Ozzie said. "I want to see that Gulf Stream you're always yammering about."

"What a dickhead," Bonnie said sadly.

Ozzie hid the pistol inside his shirt. He unlashed the mooring lines, watching both of them as he did it.

They moved carefully out of the channel, heading past Rodriquez Key. When they were in maybe ten feet of water, Papa John told them to hold on, he was going to get them up on plane.

Ozzie waited till the boat had leveled out and figured it was as good a time as any. He aimed it down into the cabin and let go of a round. He just wanted to feel the jump of that pistol. There was hardly any recoil to it at all, and it made a noise like snapping a big stick in half. Put a hole in the hull, too, above the waterline. Papa John eased off on the throttle.

"Keep us going," Ozzie yelled at him.

Bonnie was backing away from him, giving Ozzie a sloppy, scared look.

"You're always calling me things," he said to her. "I never liked it. I never thought it was funny."

She said, "I'm sorry." She sounded like she meant it, but he wasn't sure she was sorry about calling him names. Maybe she was thinking how sorry she was she'd decided to come along.

They were maybe fifteen miles out; the freighters, rusty and clumsy-looking, were between them and land now. The sky was fresh paint blue. The breeze cool but not cold. It was the kind of weather that put a bounce in Ozzie's step, a quiet burn in his blood.

Papa John had cut the engine and was smoking a cigarette in the captain's chair, giving Ozzie his silent respect. And Bonnie was lying down in Papa John's bunk. She'd gotten a little seasick.

Ozzie sat on the fish box, keeping his pistol right out there where the old man could see it.

He said, "I listened to all your bullshit. All that Hemingway this and Hemingway that shit. And what a great fisherman you were, and how you put this one over on this guy and that one over on that guy."

"Look, Ozzie," Papa John said, voice scratchy but steady. The fucker wasn't too worried, despite the pistol and the shot Ozzie'd fired. John said, "You're disappointed. I can dig that. I know it's gotta be a big upset to you, me selling out."

"You don't know how I feel," Ozzie said. "You don't know squat about me. 'Cause of you never listened to me when I talked to you."

Papa John was quiet, like he was trying to figure out the right approach to take. But Ozzie knew there wasn't any right approach. This was a done deal.

He said, "You don't know what it's like growing up back on some phosphate mine road. Trucks coming past all day, getting white dust in everything, in the food, on my pillow at night. Hell, man, when I was little, I'd cough and it'd come up like grits. If it hadn't of been for country music, I wouldn't even known there was any other way of living."

Papa John said, "Hey, listen, Oz . . ."

"You listen, you old cow. For a fucking change, would you, for once? And don't tell me how bad my story is till I'm fucking well finished with it."

John flicked his cigarette over the side, reached in his shirt pocket for his pack, and shook out another one.

Ozzie said, "Five years old and I was trying to sing songs. I'd stand up on a chair singing to my mother. That's the way I always thought I'd get out of there. Listening to the 'Grand Ole Opry' every Saturday night and seeing those badasses up there flirting with those pretty ladies. That got me going. Up on my chair afterwards singing, making my momma smile."

Papa John smoked faster and faster now. He kept glancing down into the cabin, probably to see if Bonnie was going to be any help in this.

Ozzie felt strange telling this old man about his own mother. He wasn't sure why he was even doing it. It was just coming, and Ozzie was riding with it, feeling himself swell as he got it out.

Papa John said, "Listen, boy, I'm getting some money out of this deal. That man, Benny, he's paying me a considerable amount to use that bar as his playhouse. It'd only be fair if I cut you in on the cash. How would that be?"

Ozzie said, "My parole officer used to say being poor wasn't any fucking excuse, people pulled themselves up by their bootstraps all the time. Well, fuck that. We was so poor we couldn't afford no bootstraps to pull ourselves up by."

Papa John nodded like he understood. But Ozzie knew he was just humoring him. Biding his time, probably considering how to get down below to his big .45.

Ozzie, feeling stronger every sentence of this he got out, said, "I'm standing up there the other night singing to those rich fools. And I'm thinking, this ain't nothing. I been afraid of it all my life, singing in front of a crowd of people. But I get up there, and shit, it's easy. It wasn't nothing to it.

"So, I go, hell, I bet it's the same way with everything. Being scared's a bunch of shit. It's what kept my momma living with my hell-and-damnation daddy on that phosphate road. Just that simple. Being scared kept her poor."

Man, now he was starting to wish he'd brought along a recorder, get some of this down. There were some good things.

He said, "Isn't no reason on God's green earth I can't start being exactly what I want to be. You were getting me ready to be what *you* wanted me to be, so when you died, I could carry things on for you. But the thing is, Papa John, I'm ready now,

I'm ready. I'm stepping up onstage now. Today."

Papa John didn't react. Maybe he was catching on to how serious this was.

Ozzie saw a sea gull working its way toward them from over John's shoulder. It was one of those laughing gull things that squawked like a drunk. He stood up and aimed at the bird and squeezed off a round. Missed it. He looked back, and John had changed positions, moved over to the other side of the cockpit. Yeah, they were going to get into it. And it was OK. Just fine and dandy.

"How does ten thousand dollars sound?" Papa John said, his voice a little raspier than usual. Feeble old fart.

"I'm not bargaining with you, old man," he said. "I'm taking it all. Why don't you pay attention to me now?"

John was swallowing overtime. He said, "Benny Cousins and me are partners, Oz. He's gonna want to know what happened to me. You shoot that gun, you're as good as dead yourself, boy. You better consider it a minute."

"Benny Cousins wants that bar, he'll have to deal with Ozzie Hardison now. I can drive a hardass bargain myself."

"That man'll eat your lunch," John said. "Then he'll eat the rest of you."

Ozzie stood up, looked around for another sea gull. "That little shitheel? Hell, there ain't a nigger in Georgia if I can't take care of that pipsqueak."

John coughed. He coughed harder, bringing one hand to his throat.

Ozzie was looking at Papa John, and all of a sudden the old man's eyes came loose, rolling everywhere. And John, very slow, stretched his hands out, in a trance, clawing down thick cobwebs in front of him. Pawing at the air in slo-mo, he leaned toward Ozzie, a strangled look on his face, making gargling noises.

"Don't pull any shit," Ozzie said.

Bonnie was in the doorway, watching Papa John.

"He's having a heart attack, you dorkus," she said. "You're giving him a fucking fatal heart attack."

"It's a trick," Ozzie said. He had the pistol pointed at the old man's chest. "If he don't settle down, I'll give him a thirty-eight-caliber heart attack."

Papa John went down on his knees, still making puking noises but nothing coming up. He stared up at the sky over Ozzie's head like he heard the heavenly choirs starting in on his song.

Bonnie moved up next to him. She helped him lie down flat on the deck. There was some drool bubbling up out of his mouth now, and the man was squinching his eyes. Bonnie hit him hard on the chest. Then pounded him again.

"I don't know what to do," she screamed at Ozzie.

"Don't do nothing," he said. "Let him play it out."

She leaned over him as Papa John squeezed his eyes, hugged himself. And then gasped and let go.

Bonnie tipped the old man's head back, opened his mouth, pinched his nose, and pressed her mouth to his. She started trying to inflate him.

"Stop that," Ozzie said. "If he's dead, let him stay that way. Get away from him."

But she didn't. She kept breathing into him, and when she came up for her own breath, she'd hammer Papa John on the heart again with her fist. Down for another blow. It made Ozzie sick watching that. Her mouth getting slimy.

Ozzie stepped across Bonnie and the old man, glancing down as he did, and thinking maybe he'd caught a blue tint in the old man's face now. Down in the cabin, it smelled like mildew and piss. He poked under the mattress, opened all the closets. Glanced back and Bonnie was still going at it.

He tore down the calendar thumbtacked to the clothes locker, nothing behind it. And then a photo Scotch-taped up beside it of Papa John with Benny standing out in front of the Bomb Bay Bar. Benny had his arm around John's shoulder, both of them smiling to beat the band. Ozzie tore that into confetti and proceeded to ransack the cabin.

The money was in the vegetable hamper, in with a shriveled-up apple. Ozzie stuffed it in a grocery sack. It looked to be even more cash than what'd been in the briefcase the other night. Bingo, bango, bongo, there'll be dancing in the Congo.

He came back onto the deck, and there she was, Florence Nightingale, still huffing and blowing into Papa John's mouth.

The old man sputtered once, and Bonnie pulled away from him and told him, yeah, come on, you'll make it. Breathe, goddamn it.

And Papa John blew a spit bubble and popped it. And then he opened his eyes. Ozzie sighed. Relieved and pissed both.

Papa John's eyes looked up at Ozzie. The old man followed Ozzie's hand as he brought the pistol up to the back of Bonnie's head and got steady. He aimed down over her shoulder at John. Ozzie let the old man think about that for a minute, get a grip on it. He felt the trigger cool against his finger, just a curl away from being different. Being a rich man, a man the weatherlady could look up to. Could maybe even love.

Ozzie said to Bonnie, "Well, you finally found some use for all that hot air inside you."

She started to turn her head and say something bitchy, but he fired one quick shot down through Papa John's brain. Bonnie screamed, rolled off to the side. She'd probably be deaf for a month.

Ozzie stepped back and watched the blood gather beside John's bristly cheek. He stared at it for a moment, then stooped over and touched a finger to it, and brought it up to his nose. It didn't smell like much. He'd thought it should smell like Canadian Club or something.

Ozzie shook his head, trying to get his brain firing all its cylinders. Blood smelling like whiskey? What was he thinking about? He looked at his hands shaking. Over at where Bonnie was. She'd crawled backwards across the deck and was trying to make herself small under the steering wheel. Ozzie put his finger on his neck to feel the bump of his blood. Yeah, it was jitterbugging all right.

"I done it," he said to her. "I finally shot somebody. Killed him. Jesus Christ Almighty. And it was easy. Fairly easy."

Bonnie cowered there. Every bit of smartass venom she'd ever stored away was trickling out between her legs. She was sitting in a warm pool of smartass.

He listened, and it was spooky quiet out there on the ocean. He tried to think what to do now. How to handle the next part. Papa John would've known. He would've just said, do this, go there, do that. Ozzie thought for a second he was sorry he hadn't paid more attention to the old man, learned a little more stuff before killing him.

But no, he couldn't start thinking that way. He'd get in a panic if he did and start hearing his daddy's voice, or else the voice of God. No, sir, he had to get a grip.

He reached down and took hold of John's chin and turned his face up so he could see him. Papa John had an expression on his face Ozzie recognized. It was a whole lot like the look Bonnie got when she was working on one of her stained glass designs. The little smile that came over her when things were starting to fit together good.

He walked over to Bonnie, the pistol still in his hand. He stood in front of her and she looked up at him and there wasn't nothing but hangdog cringing fear in her face.

A title came to him then. God, he wished he had a pencil and a scrap of writing paper. But maybe if he tried hard, he could just remember it. It was good enough, it could be an album title.

He said it out loud to Bonnie to help keep it in his head, "You killed one, you killed them all."

29

At the front door Roger told Joey that it was OK, he knew Thorn. Knew what to do with him. Joey shot Thorn a see-you-later-asshole look and headed back to poolside.

Now Roger was taking Thorn on a tour of Benny's house. Leading him somewhere but letting him have a gander along the way. Thorn hesitated in the doorway of the living room. Roger was in bathing trunks, squeaky rubber thongs, and a shorty T-shirt that revealed his expanding gut, standing at Thorn's shoulder while he surveyed the room.

Benny's fireplace was veneered with slabs of bleached coral, pitted and veined. In the vaulted oak ceiling there were skylights shaped into stars, boxes, triangles. Bright Audubon prints crowded the walls, egrets, herons, standing in shallow water pulsed to strike. A waterfall spilled from a spout in one wall, trickled down some mottled chunks of granite and poured into a trough of green glass. A couple of sluggish goldfish swam inside.

Dark walnut antiques were arranged rigidly in the middle of the room. They had plush red velvet covers. There were wingbacks, ottomans, two couches, a love seat. Heavy burgundy drapes darkened the room.

"Subtropical funeral parlor," Thorn said.

"The man couldn't decide," Roger said. "Beach house or bordello. His two favorite places."

Thorn could feel his heart knocking. Everywhere he turned, he saw the faint afterimage of her white hair floating on the gleam of the bay. He could still taste her lips as he had tried to revive her. And now Claude's shirt. The hole in the ground. His hands quivered.

Roger said, "Mr. Cousins's just got eclectic tastes. Let's try this, let's try that."

Thorn hid his hands behind his back. He said, "Where is he?"

"I'm used to it, though," Roger said. "Twenty years with the Justice Department, you don't get exposed to a lot of good taste."

Roger led them down the hallway. Thorn glancing up a spiral oak stairway, opening himself for any sounds, scents of Darcy.

"I want to see him, Roger," Thorn said.

"He's at Rotary, putting the trim on his float."

Thorn followed him into the Florida room. Floor-to-ceiling windows looking out at the flats, out to where Darcy must have taken her photographs.

The rattan furniture was covered in prints of ferns, palm fronds. Two white paddle fans stirred the air. In one corner there was a life-size carving of a Haitian woman carrying a basket of fruit on her head.

"Buy you a drink?" Roger said.

Thorn said he wasn't thirsty. He sat on the couch.

Roger got comfortable in one of the chairs, put his feet up on a rattan stool. He chewed his gum thoughtfully.

In a moment or two he said, "You know, back when Mr. Cousins interviewed me for this job, he asked me just one question. Up there in his office, both of us in our best suits, him there behind that beautiful desk, he looks me straight in the eye and asks me, if I had the ability to suck my own dick, would I do it?"

"He's such a classy guy."

"Yeah, well, maybe you miss the point," said Roger. "He asks me that, and I'm thinking, what's the right answer? No? That's the disciplined response. That's what you'd say in the FBI. Hell, no, sir. And if I say yes, what does that make me? Is he trying to weed out fags? Or what?"

"Yeah, right," Thorn said, "this is a Zen master question. Sound-of-one-hand-clapping kind of thing."

"All right," Roger said, "all right, that's fair. I'm glorifying this a little maybe. But what I'm telling you is, I said yes, yes, I would. 'Cause yes was the truth. And Benny smiled. That's what he wanted, the truth. He stood up, put his hand out, and shook mine and told me, good, that was good. He didn't want to hire any goddamn liars or puritans."

"So you think you work for Albert Schweitzer?" Thorn said.

"Boy, are you cranky today," Roger said, frowning, smacking his gum. He leaned forward, put his elbows on his knees. "What I'm trying to say to you is, you and me, we sort of hit it off that first day, laughed at each other's jokes. That's good. I like you. In another time we could be buddies. But just now we're standing out there bad-mouthing Benny's taste, and it comes to me that maybe you're expecting me to gang up on him some way or other, or maybe not carry out something the man asks me to do, regarding you or anything else. Well, I'm telling you straight out, that ain't going to happen. I'm a loyal guy, true to my school."

Roger chewed his gum, leaned back. Thorn looked out at the blue-green dazzle of the flats. He thought he could see some bonefish tailing out about a hundred yards. The water was so shallow it looked as if a man could walk across there, clear to the horizon and not get his ankles wet. Be like walking through heavy dew.

"Tell me, Roger, you know Benny's houseguests are crooks?"

"Where'd you get a thought like that?"

"Day you turned in your badge, you turned in your morals, too? That how it went? Or did you even wait that long?"

Roger snorted.

"Listen up, Thorn. If somebody wants to buy one of your fishing lure things, you check out their rap sheet first? Does anybody down here care who sleeps in their motel, buys their rumrunner? Shit, no. A guy pulls out his wad of hundreds, you give 'im what he asked for, right? Well, that's how it works. It's America. Until proven guilty. And Benny sells security systems. All kinds of people want security. Guys from both sides. That's just how it is."

Thorn said, "Roger, you work for a hoodlum and you know it, and if you don't, then either you're a crook, too, or you're just plain stupid."

Roger was frowning at Thorn, high voltage.

"And another thing," Thorn said. "You're such a loyal guy, you're so true to your school. What happens the day Benny tells you to get down on your knees, throw a lip around *his* pecker?"

Roger brought his feet off the stool. He stood up. He looked like he was waiting for Thorn to stand up. But Thorn just leaned back against the couch, gazing out at all that turquoise and jade. From where he sat he could see the patches of white sand, the shadowy stains of turtle grass mixed in. But the bonefish tails were gone. Probably scared away by a passing cloud or a blip in the barometer. Probably in Nassau by now.

"I wondered," Roger said, "why Benny didn't get upset, you coming in his office like that the other day. Those weird photos on his car. Slashing the man's tires. That was you, wasn't it?"

Thorn said nothing.

"Yeah, well," Roger said. "It was you, and I wondered why Benny took it so smooth. But now I see it. It's 'cause you're nuts. You come across normal just enough of the time, but then it gets too much for you and you zone out. That's it, isn't it, Thorn? Benny knows it, he doesn't take you seriously. You're a fucking loon, aren't you?"

He was about to say more, do a thorough analysis of Thorn's psychological dysfunctions, when they heard scuffling in the hall. Roger moved to the French doors that led back into the house.

Joey was prodding Ozzie Hardison in front of him with his walkie-talkie. Every poke of the walkie-talkie got a snarl from Ozzie. He was wearing his yachting clothes. A white shirt with striped epaulets, the front stained with jelly. Blue jeans and flimsy tennis shoes.

Joey gave Ozzie a push, and he stumbled into the room.

"We're being invaded," he said. "This one I caught coming over the barbed wire on the south perimeter. He snagged his pants in the wire. If I hadn't gotten him down, the juice would've come on tonight and fired his ass."

"Should've waited," Thorn said.

"You know this guy?" Roger said.

"Like a cat knows his litter box."

Ozzie growled and broke from the guard and lunged at Thorn, got him in a quick headlock, and ground his arm hard against Thorn's ears. Thorn went slack, let the rage that'd been simmering for days gather for a moment; then he swiveled and spun Ozzie one quick rotation, slinging him backwards into Roger.

Ozzie clipped him in the hip, and they both stumbled back

into the rattan couch. Roger got his balance first and took a chokehold on Ozzie. And the other guy started to do the same to Thorn but thought better of it, halted, drew out his Smith instead. He stepped back and covered Thorn.

Ozzie was gasping, holding on to Roger's forearm with both hands. Roger gave his throat a little squeeze, then lowered him slowly, sitting him down on the couch.

There was something in Ozzie's eyes Thorn hadn't seen the other night. He wasn't the smily, love-dizzied guy in Darcy's kitchen. This Ozzie had lost a ton of innocence in a few days. His eyes clear now, the fog burned off. A smartass curl on his lips.

Ozzie straightened himself slightly and said, "I want to see Benny. I'm not fucking with the help."

"He's not fucking with the help," Roger said.

"You heard me," Ozzie said. "I got serious business with the man."

Roger said, "I handle all Mr. Cousins's serious business."

Ozzie shifted his eyes to Roger.

"Sure you do."

"OK, Joey, throw these assholes out on the highway," Roger said, looking at Thorn now. Shaking his head. "We're not gonna bother the boss with these fucking loons."

"All right, then," Ozzie said. "You tell the scum sucker that Ozzie Hardison was here. Every bit the man Papa John was, and then some. Tell him he's dealing with the genuine article from here on out."

"Get this genuine article the hell out of my sight," Roger said. "Put him and Thorn in the back seat, see who gets out."

As Thorn was walking through the French doors, he turned and said to Roger, "And tell Benny that Gaeton's doing a lot better. Almost back to a hundred percent. And he wants to have a sit-down with Benny about this witness protection scam."

Turning, he walked ahead down the marble hallway, Joey poking him in the spine with a three-inch barrel.

As Joey was starting the car, Thorn glanced back at the house, at the windows on the second floor. The lowering sun put a golden wash on them.

Ozzie sat beside him in the back seat of the Mercedes, breathing hard, digging his fingers into the plush upholstery.

They were rolling down the drive when a white Plymouth with darkened windows turned into the entrance.

"Oh, boy, now what?" Joey said. He pulled over.

The other man said, "Go on. It's just the delivery."

"Great, another asshole," Joey said. "All we need."

Thorn waited till the Mercedes was almost to the highway before he turned and looked back at the house. A man in a white uniform was opening the rear door for a woman in jeans, sunglasses, and short black hair. She wasn't bound. She wasn't bleeding. No one seemed to be pointing guns at her. She got out, stared up at the house.

"Whatta you looking at, dingleberry?" Ozzie said.

Thorn turned, brought his face to Ozzie's. He stared at him for a moment at that range. Looking into those lightless eyes that were as shallow as the eyes of fish. The brain behind them probably only a bundle of tropistic impulses. Feed, screw, run.

Ozzie said, "I asked you, dingleberry, whatta you looking at?"

"I'm not sure exactly," Thorn said, "but it looks a lot like the decline of Western civilization."

"What'd he say?" Joey asked.

The other man had his arm on the seat, looking back at

Thorn. He said, "I think he called the redneck the decline of Western civilization."

Joey chuckled and said, "He may have something there."

The other man said, "You ask me, both of them got a good many of their marquee lights burned out."

The two men laughed. Ozzie faced forward, folded his hands in his lap. Thorn counted the royal palms as they passed by. Fifteen. He stared at the new hole W.B. had just finished digging.

30

Thorn and Ozzie walked along the shoulder of millionaire's alley. The Mercedes idled for a moment at the entranceway, then U-turned and headed back down the drive.

Humming to himself, Ozzie walked a few yards ahead of Thorn. He stopped at a white pickup parked in the weeds along the road. "Bomb Bay Bar" was stenciled in red letters on the door. He opened the door and leaned in.

As Thorn approached, Ozzie said, "Hey, look what I found."

He straightened up out of the cab, pointing a gleaming blue pistol with a silencer fixed on the barrel.

"My magic lamp," Ozzie said. "I rub it and my dreams come true."

Thorn stared at him for a moment. Saw again Ozzie's new eyes, that feverish glaze. "So shoot me," he said, and turned and kept walking.

He made it a few more feet, then stumbled forward, caught

himself, and stared down at the shredded flesh and cloth at his left shoulder, the blood spreading through his plaid shirt. It began as just a burn, and then his arm went numb from the shoulder down. Hung heavy at his side. At his wrist a prickle began to seep in, becoming a sharp tingle as it worked up his arm. His eyes suddenly muddy.

Ozzie was behind him, pressing the hot barrel into his spine, hiding it there as a group of bicyclers passed on the road.

"I shot you, lifeguard," Ozzie whispered into Thorn's ear. "What do you think about that? I winged your ass."

Thorn said something. Or maybe not. If he did, it was almost certainly not grammatical.

As Ozzie was driving the pickup north up U.S. 1, he held the pistol on his lap with his left hand, steered with the other. Thorn tore a swatch from the sleeve of the flannel shirt and stanched the blood, pressing hard against the throb. He clenched his teeth, managed to keep his eyes open. He was feeling oddly alert. Probably flushed with adrenaline.

The bullet had skimmed him. Tunneled an inch into his tricep and come out an inch later. He wasn't going to die. But he wasn't going to be doing any push-ups for a while.

Ozzie smiled, leaned his head back against the headrest, soaking up the moment. He said, "I think I found me something I like even better than money or sex."

Thorn took a deep breath, his throat aching. He said, "The asshole's killing them. He brings them in and executes them. They want to go underground, he's putting them there."

Ozzie craned forward for a better look at Thorn.

"Who's killing who?"

He gripped his shoulder as a jolt of electricity flared there. Then a spasm in his heart. He held himself still and breathed his way past the pain, swallowed. Came gradually back to himself.

Hours passed, months. He watched Key Largo drive past. Everything out there was numb. The billboards were bleached to grays. The bait houses and motels, their signs were wavering smoke. A blur on the world.

He had to speak. To say something. He heard the words inside himself long before they surfaced. Bringing them up from his gut in a grunt as if he were lifting a tub of bricks. He said, "Planting them in his yard. Keeping score with palm trees."

"The fuck are you talking about?" Ozzie looked over at him. "You're not going to barf in my truck now, are you?"

Thorn heard himself say in a raspy voice, "Maybe she knew it. Didn't let on and went in there anyway. Suicidal guilt."

Ozzie stared at him. Thorn leaned his head against the window. His thoughts helter-skelter now. He would have to focus. Bring things into line. He'd never been shot. Never had a hot hole torn through his body. Maybe he was dying. Maybe Ozzie was driving him somewhere to put more hot holes into him. He would have to force himself to keep the edges lined up, keep the red mist that was rising inside him from fogging his eyes. Had to think. Didn't want to lie down in the refrigerated box of an ice cream truck.

His head bounced against the window as he thought about wolves. Wolves. Yeah, wolves. Deer and wolves. He'd read about them once a long time ago. Wolves and the deer they hunted.

How sometimes, as a wolf approached a herd, there seemed to be some silent transaction between hunter and hunted. The wolf halted at striking distance from the herd, seeming to ask in a voice no human could hear if there was a deer ready to die. And a deer, maybe sick, maybe just weary of the chase, separated itself from the others, answering back, all right, OK, for the sake of the herd, take me.

And the wolf, who could have brought down any of them, took the volunteer. In his best interests, too, keeping the community of deer vigorous. Maybe that's how it was. Darcy, for the sake of the herd, had stepped apart, relaxed her hold on living. A fatal altruism.

Maybe that's what had fueled Gaeton, too. And Sugarman. All cops, all heroes. A suicidal willingness to risk. Standing on the cliff edge, looking down at the surf, the swan dive beautifully executed in the mind, but some instinctive voice saying, step back, go have a rum drink, why risk it? And the other one, prodding them half a step forward, saying, aw, fuck it, man, take the chance. You're going to die anyway. Fly, for godsakes. Fly!

Maybe it was the death defiers who pushed the world forward, made it all happen, and the others, the ones digging in their heels, padding themselves deeper and deeper inside their safe husks, maybe it was their job to keep the world from lurching totally into chaos. Took both of them. A waltz of daring and fear.

Thinking this. Considering wolves. Something he'd read a long time ago, before a blast of lead had entered his body. In the time before hot holes. Before palm trees were gravestones. Before cannibals and killers were lured up close to the boat with the great bait of America. Thorn held his shoulder, the place where vaccination scars were. Gripping it hard and looking out at Key Largo, at the Winnebagos, dusty station wagons from Indiana. At this paradise gone gray and shadowy.

Thinking to himself, no, no, this deer isn't ready. They're going to have to chase Thorn, run up his backside, and bring him down. And then be prepared for a goddamn fight.

Benny liked the puffy sleeves. He liked the red vest, the black felt hat, the brim pinned up on both sides, the purple ostrich plume. He liked the skull and crossbones cuff links, the hug-your-ass knickers, the scabbard and wide black leather belt. But those goddamn shoes, pointy slippers cut shallow like a woman's. They made him feel silly, fruitcake shoes. It took the edge off the whole costume, the whole damn festival, knowing that he was stuck wearing faggy ballet slippers or whatever the fuck they were.

He got out of the Mercedes, walked into the house, and Roger was just inside the front door in his swim trunks and rubber sandals, giving Benny a look. And Benny had all he could do to keep from taking out his balsa wood sword and poking both Roger's eyes out.

"Joey tells me somebody was by," Benny said. He adjusted the scabbard.

"Thorn and some other guy. That redneck works for Papa John."

"What? They together?"

"They were when they left," said Roger.

"Jesus Christ," Benny said. "The two of them fucking fall in love or something? They're hanging out together. I don't believe it."

Roger looking off at the ceiling now.

Benny said, "What'd they want?"

"Thorn said some bullshit about witness protection," Roger said. "You and Gaeton were going to have a talk about some scam."

"Jesus Christ," he said, and groaned. Massaged his forehead. "I got this headache, it's like somebody shot *me* in the head. And it's not like I don't have enough to think about, I got to consider a guy, whether he's dead, he's not dead. A guy, he's jerking my chain, for what reason I'm not sure yet. And I come home, and the people who I pay a lot of money to look out for my interests, they're standing around with their thumbs in their butts, smirking at me."

Roger was looking out one of the windows, maybe trying to find something out there to keep him from breaking up. Benny could see his lips wriggle a little, a chuckle just under the surface.

Benny said, "What is it? You think I look silly?"

"Maybe a little," he said.

"I'm supposed to look this way. It's historically accurate."

"Well, that's different," Roger said.

Fucker still wouldn't look at him.

Benny massaged his head some more, said, "The lady arrive?"

"An hour ago."

"She give you any trouble?"

Roger said no.

Benny said, "From here on, we keep them upstairs till they move on. No shopping. No phone calls. Nothing. I've had enough of that Claude shit, catering to these assholes so they'll send a nice report home."

"Right," Roger said.

"I don't want anything else fucking up this weekend. I been looking forward to it."

"Yes, sir."

"Now, I'm going up and talk to the lady. And I don't want you to bother us. You hear noises up there, ignore it."

Now Roger looked at him. All the humor gone from his face.

"Yeah, you heard me," Benny said. "I got a thing for these Latin types. And these goddamn tight pants, they're giving me a terminal hard-on. Goddamn things're probably the reason why the pirates had to rape when they'd finished pillaging."

Benny knocked and asked if he could come in.

Darcy jerked awake from her nap, blinked. She'd been flying inside clouds, thick dark ones. Inside the leading edge of a cold front that rumbled down the continent like a C-141B, powered by heavy Arctic air. Swirling inside that gaseous mass, plowing into the moist tropical atmosphere. Explosions of lightning all around her. The thunderous clash of yin with yang.

She woke drenched. Benny knocked again and opened the door a crack and slipped his head in. He said, "You decent?"

Darcy cleared her throat, rubbed her eyes. She nodded that he could enter. No lock on her side anyway.

He was a stumpy man in leggings and red vest, his pirate gear making him seem young, harmless. A boy at play. But his eyes up close were different from anything she had made out in her long-distance photographs. A caginess. Flirting with her as he came across and sat on the edge of her bed.

"Do you mind?" he said.

"Mind what?"

"I sit here?"

"It's your house," Darcy said.

"Yes, that's a fact. It's my house."

She didn't like this. Fencing like a dating couple. No. No, like hooker and client. See who had the power.

"Good trip?" he said.

"All right."

"They treat you OK? They didn't try to pry into who you were or anything, I hope."

"They treated me very politely," she said. "Who were they anyway?"

"People I know. That's all," he said. "It's not your concern."

Benny half turned to look at her now, planted his hand near her hip to steady himself.

He said, "So tell me, we had a hard time pulling anything up on you. Anything recent. Last jobs you pulled were what, two, three years ago? Banks, was it?"

"Two years ago," she said. "That was massage parlors."

Benny nodded, said, "So, how about lately? You retired, kicking back or something?"

"I've been with ETA. It's a political organization."

"Political organization." Benny pronouncing it, smiling. He was looking across at the window, palm fronds wavering in the dusky light. "This is one of those political groups, it shoots generals on the sidewalk. Isn't it? Walk up behind them, they been at mass praying, and you say to their wives, excuse me, senora, but your husband was once a friend of Franco. Bang, bang. This political organization, it parks cars out front of bars where police hang out. Cars full of TNT. That it? You do shit like that?"

Darcy said, "You interrogating me? Is that it? Do I need my lawyer with me?"

He turned and brought one leg up on the bed. One foot still on the floor.

"It's a hobby of mine," he said. "I like to get to know you people. See who it is I'm dealing with. How your brains work."

"My brain works fine," Darcy said.

"And everything else?"

Darcy said nothing. Reminding herself now, Maria, Maria Iturralde. More than just a tough broad. A lot more.

Benny said, "Personally, I like a woman, when I bite, she bites back. Know what I mean?"

He was looking funny at her now. Something registering in there. A light coming to his eyes.

She said, "You don't want to bite this woman, mister."

Benny swiveled quickly onto her, sitting astraddle her legs.

"I saw you," he said. "Jesus H. Christ! It was you, wasn't it? On the highway." Benny leaned back, closed one eye, staring at her face. "Coming out of that fucking Thorn's place. Last night. Right? Am I right?"

Darcy was silent. Her stomach had made a fist as she remembered walking home from Thorn's last night, the Mercedes that had slowed beside her, driven on.

"Well, my, my," he said. "My, my, my. The Hardy boy and his cunt, Nancy Drew. Pulling tricks. A couple of fucking chain jerkers."

Benny smiled. His hands going to the snap and zipper on her jeans. And Darcy sat up and seized both his ears and rattled his head back and forth.

He sucked in a squeaking rush of air and slapped her hands away. She sat back against the headboard, drew her right hand back quickly, and punched him flush in the nose. Followed it with a Three Stooges eye poke, fingernails finding wet.

"Jesus!"

As he rubbed the sight back into his eyes, she twisted to get out from under him. But he kept her pinned, bearing down hard against her knees.

And when he could see again, a bitter smile came to his mouth. And he threw his sudden weight behind a right uppercut to her chin. It banged her back against the headboard. A spangle of orange and red brightened inside her eyelids. White spirals revolved.

Her head was heavy, her eyes somehow looking down at this from the ceiling. Down a long numb shaft of time, she could feel her jeans opening. And she wondered if Maria Iturralde knew what was happening to her. Wondered what she would do when she woke up and found this dime store pirate on top of her.

From the ceiling she watched as this man cocked his right arm back, held it there, saying something. And let go of a punch to Maria's chin.

Darcy, coming back to the surface, saw lights undulating above her. And she broke through to the air, gasping, blinking her eyes.

She lifted her head slowly, her teeth aching as she tried to align them right. She looked down at herself, her jeans at her ankles. Blue panties still in place. Her chin was anesthetized, and her tongue had inflated to fill her mouth.

Someone was banging on her door. Benny, standing at the foot of the bed, was fumbling with the zipper on those pirate jodhpurs. When he had them right, he went to the door, slung it open. A big man in bathing trunks and a short T-shirt stood in the doorway.

"This better be goddamn good," Benny said.

"Somebody here to see you," he said.

"I told you, Roger, not to fucking disturb me."

"It's Myra something or other," he said. "Lady used to be with the bureau, so I thought you'd want to see her. Says it's urgent."

"OK," Benny said quietly, glancing back at Darcy. "Jesus, now what do they want?"

They left, and Darcy heard a bolt sliding into place.

She closed her eyes, watched the circus of lights on her eyelids again. She knew it would be better to keep them open. It was always better to get up and walk around. That did something. She wasn't sure what. But usually you had to have somebody to help you walk around. You threw your arm over their shoulder and they talked to you and led you around in circles while you revived. But she didn't have anybody. She'd had somebody not long ago, but she'd told him she didn't need him. She'd been wrong. Now she needed him. Bad.

The lights were so spectacular. She could just watch them for a minute or two. That was a reasonable compromise. Just to keep herself entertained till Benny returned.

31

"You're not going to die on me, are you?" Ozzie said. He was tying a knot in the yellow nylon cord that held the linoleum roll closed. "Leak to death all over the floor? You wouldn't do that now, would you?"

He stood up and took the pistol from a wooden stool. He said, "What's the problem, Thorn? Fucking cat got your tongue?"

Yeah, a whole tribe of cats. They'd crawled into his mouth, devoured his tongue. And they'd stayed in there, looking around for more. Down his throat, up into his cranium.

Ozzie said, "Well, now, I got to go get dressed. Do my thing for the talent show. Anyone asks, I should be back about one, two o'clock. If the groupies don't steal me off somewhere."

He picked up a roll of silver duct tape from the workbench and pulled out a couple of feet of it. Tore a gash in its edge with his front teeth. Ripped the piece off and did three tight turns around Thorn's head, across his mouth.

Trapping the cats inside. All those cats. Or were they wolves? Now he couldn't remember. Wolves? Cats?

He breathed hard through his nose. Drawing in the sugary aroma of rot.

Ozzie tested the tightness of the cord, then gave the linoleum roll a half turn so Thorn was staring at the concrete floor, an inch away. The gamy scent even stronger.

"Don't do anything I wouldn't do, dingleberry," he said. "And if you do, name it after me, you hear?"

Thorn heard the shed door close, the snap of a lock. He stared at the cement. A column of ants was detouring around his nose, carrying particles above their heads. Hurrying back to their burrow. Or what was it, a hive? A nest?

A hive with a tin roof. Made of Far Eastern hardwoods. A nest with an open porch and a view of the sunset, the mangrove islands. Scurrying home with little chunks of meat. To grill, then eat, then lie in their hammocks and consider the prism of sunset, the crepuscular essence.

Crepuscular? Where'd he get that? He'd never heard anyone say the word. He had no idea how he even knew it. Or exactly what it meant. But the ants probably knew. Ants had a very wide vocabulary. He'd read that somewhere. They communicated with wolves. No, no. It was wolves that communicated. With ants? No, that was antlers. Wolves talked to the things with antlers. The things Benny had offered him a chance to shoot.

Crepuscular elk.

"For one thing," Myra Rostovich said, "there're too many citizens mixed up in it."

She was sitting across from Benny out beside the pool. The wind starting to pick up, sky turning blue-black to the north over Miami. Almost six-thirty. In an hour he had to be over at the Rotary, suit up for the kickoff events, the talent contest, a couple of speeches. Firing the cannons. Yadda yadda yadda.

Myra said, "And number two, it's an election year. Paranoia's going around again."

Benny said, "I bet number three is somebody's up for promotion and she doesn't want anybody finding out she was running Murder Incorporated on bureau stationery."

Myra looked at the six Styrofoam heads Joey had brought out. Toupees on each one. Benny was going to have a head of hair for Old Pirate Days. He hadn't decided yet which look to go with.

She wore a loose white T-shirt and jeans. Dressed like a boy. Big round sunglasses with white frames. The things covered her up from eyebrows to cheekbones. She had her dark hair tucked up inside a man's panama hat. The lady didn't want to get too well known by his people.

She said, "I don't know how we got into this in the first place, what anybody was thinking about."

Benny tried on a John Kennedy. Checked himself out in the round chrome mirror. Naw. Made his face too round. Looked like that baby face Beatle, Paul what's-it.

He said, "I'll tell you, Myra, exactly how it happened. You came to me, you said, hey, we had an idea. There're these guys, if we tried to extradite them, forget it, never happen. They're in their fortresses. They got all the judges in South America pissing their pants.

"But somebody thought, why don't we lure them here with this make-over bullshit? You remember now, Myra, what a great idea you thought it was? Everybody was smiling. This big trick on the dope sultans. Get some positive ink for the FBI for a change."

She said she remembered that part just fine.

He said, "I like refreshing your memory. It sets this all straight. So we don't have two different pictures of how this is."

He tried on a blond wig. Down to his shoulders. Doris Day thing. When he set the black pirate hat on top of it, it didn't look all that strange. But he could just hear what Roger would say. Going to have to start being careful with Roger. He might be losing the man's respect. Once that happened, you could have trouble. It started to spread, and before you knew it, your guys wouldn't squeeze the trigger when you yelled shoot.

Benny said, "Well, when the grand jury released that first cowboy, you knew what I had to do. If I didn't snip him, he'd fly home and bad-mouth your little scam. Boomerang the whole thing back on me. And then, there, right at that moment, I was up to my nipples in the shit you guys created. So I did him."

Benny picked up the hand mirror, checked out his profile. No, no, he had the wrong skin tones to be a blond.

He said, "And then I'm motivated. I'm there, forced to do some fast thinking. I figure out a plan. I get everybody together, a roomful of people, you remember those people, I don't need to say all their names, and I make a new proposal. Bring the cowboys in, same as before, promise them the moon, whatever their weakness is. Say we're going to set them up in a Manhattan penthouse if that's what they want. Blonds, redheads, little boys, little girls. Tell them for a hundred thou we can give them the best fucking make-over money can buy. Give them the whole streets-of-gold bullshit.

"I mean, Myra, I thought all this out, very careful. 'Cause I'm running a legitimate business, doing just fine at it, too. I don't want to endanger that, have some congressional committee chewing my balls. And there I am, finished with my pitch. And everybody's looking at their fingernails, not saying anything one way or the other, lily livers that they are, so I assume this is the high sign."

Myra said, "That's not exactly how I remember it."

"No?"

No," she said. "All we wanted was one of them, a single big fish. It was to be a one-time-only sting situation. You offer one of the czars this identify change deal, work on him slow and easy, court him, get him one foot over the border, and slam, bang, he's ours. Nobody ever had anything like this in mind. Never, not for a second."

Benny took off the blond wig and snugged on a red Mohawk. Pulled it tight around his ears. Held up the hand mirror for the side view and squinted. No, too flaky. One of those punk rockers or whatever.

Myra looked off at the water and said, "Did you have Gaeton done?" She turned those glasses on him. "Did you, Benny?"

"I didn't *have* him done. I wiped him myself."

"Jesus Christ," she said.

"Hey," he said. "What'd you think? I was going to let him blow the whistle?" He patted the bristly flattop and said, "Anyway, it was strange circumstances. I saw an opportunity, and I took it. I didn't see a lot of alternatives. Chalk it up to the cost of doing business. One guy on our team for a dozen on theirs."

"It's got to stop," she said. "All of it."

"OK, the fact is this, Myra," Benny said, "I'm thinking lately, Jesus, do I really want to be in the asshole smuggling business? Is it worth a hundred K to put myself at this kind of risk? I'm having serious second thoughts here. Considering getting back to basics, just run my company. Diddle around with the politics down here. But if I decide to get out, then I'll decide when and how. Me, alone."

Myra said, "It has to stop, Benny."

"I don't see you all have a whole lot of leverage. You try to bring this out in the sunshine, Myra, nobody's going to get promoted, not ever, not to nothing."

Benny pulled off the punk rocker and tried an early Elvis. Deep black, ducktails. Benny smiling at it.

"My bucket's got a hole in it." He sang it, moving his shoulders. "My bucket's got a hole in it. It don't *work* no more." Then to Myra: "I bet you didn't know that. Flip side of 'Ain't Nothing but a Hound Dog.' I heard that first on my old man's Victrola. Down there in that freezing Chicago basement, cranking up that Victrola. My bucket's got a hole in it."

Myra leaned forward, waited till Benny brought his eyes back to her. Got a lock on them.

She said, "Where's Gaeton now?"

"He's biodegrading," Benny said, "evolving into fossil fuel."

He didn't like how he'd said that. His voice had sounded thin. But he looked at her, and she seemed to have bought it. Then he considered for a second asking her if she'd ever heard of a guy surviving a shot like that. But Christ, no. He wasn't so hard up yet he had to ask Myra for help.

Benny shook his head and looked out at his luxurious view. The silver ocean, coconut palms in the dusk, a pelican drifting by. Real postcard shit.

He had to get a fucking hold on himself. This Gaeton thing was starting to spook him, thinking any minute he'd turn around, there the guy would be, a zombie, holding out his arms, saying, ooooh, Benny. Why did you shoot meeeee? I thought I was your friiiiiend."

He took off the Elvis and put it back on the Styrofoam. He rubbed his slick head and took another careful look at his property. No zombies anywhere. His goose chills dying out. Headache down to a throb.

He said, "Look, Myra, don't get your bowels in an uproar. Gaeton Richards was inside our long johns for months. It was just a matter of timing when to do him. He was your fucking fault anyway. If I had to wipe him, it was because of you."

She took off her glasses and scowled at him.

Benny said, "You were banging this guy, what, a year or two?"

She didn't answer him.

Benny said, "He's there in your bedroom, the lights are out. Sweet nothings are getting said. You're both drowsy and maybe there's some wine in your bloodstream. Maybe you let something slip. Let him get a look at something he shouldn't have. The guy a little more of a straight arrow than you."

"That's not how it was, Benny."

"I'll tell you what I think," Benny said. "I think you were playing this both ways. Having me run your sting operation for you, and then sending Dudley Dooright down to make sure you got an inside view of things. Telling me one thing, Gaeton another, your superiors something else."

"Think what you like, Benny," she said. "The point is, we're calling this off."

Benny picked up Myra's white sunglasses, put them on, checked himself out in the mirror. Liked what he saw.

He pulled over another Styrofoam head. Dreadlocks.

He said, "Well, I'll consider your suggestion, Miss Myra. I'll think long and hard on it. Let you know soon as I come to some decision. For the moment, though, I think I'll stand pat. Extradite a few more of these guys. Cash their checks, punch their tickets. You know, this public service stuff grows on you. You should think about it, trying it sometime."

"I'm evidently not making myself clear enough," she said, looking off at the eastern sky. "We're not giving you a choice." Myra brought her gaze back to Benny. "By Monday things are back to business as usual. Strictly by the rules."

"Or else?" Benny said.

"That's right," she said. "Or else."

Benny looked into the mirror again. No. Dreadlocks were out. Even Benny didn't have the balls for that.

32

Thorn was on his back now. He'd twisted and lurched and brought the linoleum around a half turn. His shoulders were hunched forward from the pressure of the roll, arms numb. Probably should be grateful for that.

A bruising wind lashed at the shed. On the workbench the pages of a yellow legal pad fluttered. He watched a steady strobe of lightning under the door crack. A few raindrops had begun to tick against the roof.

And swaying on its cord, the single yellow bulb washed its ghastly light over the jumble inside the shed.

He tried making his right hand into a fist. But there was no room where it lay, mashed flat against his thigh. By edging it into the cavity between his legs, he could do it. Gripping hard and letting go. Repeating that. Pumping, pumping. Luring the blood back to his veins.

Then he shifted his hip to the left. A very subtle movement. An inch difference at most. But enough to wedge his open right hand back along his upper thigh, inch by inch. The hand with life in it again.

He jimmied it across his thigh until it pressed against his right pocket. And yes. It had not been a fantasy. He had carried it with him, snug and closed and deep inside his pocket. Gaeton Richards's Buck knife.

He worked his hand upward, nudging the knife with his fingertips higher into the pocket. Straining his shoulder up. When he had raised his hand as far as it could go, his fingers were still a few inches below the brim of the pocket.

He closed his eyes. Concentrated on breathing. He listened to the palms clatter outside, the rush of wind into the shed. He heard something falling over out there. A ladder, a bicycle. Then the rain began its thick muffle.

The knife was there. It was just a few inches away; the right physics would get it out. A slight yoga move inside that unyielding cylinder.

Thorn wedged his hand up to the pocket again, hooked his thumb over the brim. He pulled down, levering his elbow against the linoleum. He grunted and heard the seams give. Curling his fingers up to push the knife higher as his thumb tore down, until the knife slid cool and heavy into his palm.

Yeah, well. Now to breathe. Then to open the sucker.

He slithered his hand back to the gap at his crotch. He knew if the knife slipped from his grip, it would fall between his legs and be lost a few impossible inches away. So with meticulous slowness, Thorn tweezered the blade. First finger and thumb, pinning the casing against his groin, his sweaty fingers slipping on the steel and slipping again.

The first tremors of a muscle cramp pierced his palm. He groaned, held still. And willed the hand to relax. The air through his nose was burning now.

It took a few moments, but he held off the cramp and went back to work. He opened the blade a quarter of the way, held it there. But as he readied himself, the oil of his sweat broke the connection and the blade shut.

He cursed and rearranged the knife in his hand. He pinched the steel, spreading it a quarter, then a third of the way open. His hand beginning to quiver slightly. He held the blade open against the pressure of its spring, trying to find a better purchase on the slick metal. But the butt of the casing slipped from his groin, and the knife sliced shut on the meat of his thumb.

He dragged in a gallon of air.

Squeezed his eyes. He touched a finger to his thumb and could feel the lid of flesh connected by only a flap of skin. A bright burn there.

But at least, Thorn told himself, breathing hard, at least the blade had not snapped all the way closed.

He twisted his thumb around and jammed the wounded flesh against the sting of the blade and got it, got it all the way open.

Dexterity, he thought, the mother of extraction.

Yeah, Yuk it up. Give him a minute to coagulate his thoughts and he'd come up with a dozen of those. Funny guy, Thorn. The guy with a missing thumb tip. Guy with a very sloppy vaccination scar. The goddamn Houdini of linoleum. Hadn't seen a roll yet that could keep that man trapped.

Against his leg he pressed the cap of his thumb back into place. Grimacing. The blood draining from his consciousness. The shed went away, came back. He held the thumb hard against his thigh, trying to focus on the corrugated aluminum ceiling, the hush of the rain.

When the pain began to dwindle, Thorn took hold of the knife again, gripped it hard, and stabbed the blade up, then wiggled it through each layer of the linoleum. Rocking it till the blade tip surfaced through the burlap backing. He forced it forward and cut what felt like a slow, wavering line.

He lifted his head for a look. It was less than an inch. No, even less than that. He'd just put a new edge on the blade the day before. He knew it would do the job. An inch an hour perhaps. But it would work.

He wasn't at all sure of the time anymore. After Ozzie had left, Thorn might have passed out for a while. He might have drifted for hours. It could be three in the morning. The way his head felt, the soreness in his throat, hell, by now it might even be July.

He cut. In a while he lifted his head again to check the progress. The gash was still less than an inch. It had taken a decade.

He needed to make a circle large enough to reach his hand through. Cut the nylon cord. It was a simple operation. Didn't take much subtlety. Just the stamina to saw the blade up and down, pushing it forward with all the force he could summon.

Thorn eased his head back down. At least he didn't feel the hurt in his left shoulder or his thumb anymore. That, he supposed, would come later. When he tried to manage what he would have to manage when he was out of the roll of linoleum. If he got out. If he got out before Ozzie returned, Thorn jammed that blade ahead.

"Mr. Cousins do that to your face?" Roger asked her.

"What?" Darcy said. "You think I arrived this way?"

She couldn't bring her teeth together. An eye-clamping ache when they touched. Her jaw was probably broken. She lay and looked out the window, at the tangled arteries of lightning printed bright against the black. Then gone. The thunder echoing down the long canyons of the atmosphere. Even with the windows shut, wind stirred the lace curtains.

Roger stood at the foot of her bed, glanced out the window as a stroke of lightning hit nearby, the shock waves rattling the glass.

"He'll be back soon." Roger took a seat in an oak rocker next to the window. "I'll talk to him," he said. "You need a doctor." He swallowed, looking at her.

Roger wore a white polo shirt, the tail outside his faded jeans. No watch or jewelry. He looked like he was halfway down a slide into Keys sloppiness. He kept bringing his eyes back to her chin, her right cheek.

"You want a drink, vodka, anything?"

"You don't need to good-cop me," she said. "I don't have anything to hide."

"I'm not doing that," he said. "I'm concerned about you, is all."

Darcy nodded her eyes.

Outside, lightning. And the sky blew apart and compacted into the vacuum just as fast. It boomed. Tidal waves of air pounding the shore of the solid world. The tuning fork inside her began to hum.

Roger said, "He gets home, he'll be drunk. I'll see he goes right to bed. His own bed."

"You're telling me," she said, "you're going to stage a coup?"

Roger sat in the leather wingback by the window.

He said, "I'm not going to let him hurt you anymore. That's all. I draw a line there."

"A good American male," she said around the swelling in her mouth, "protecting their women. Trying to do what's right."

Roger said nothing. Looking at her, waiting.

She said, "You ever meet Gaeton Richards?"

He looked at her carefully.

"It's possible," he said. "I may have."

"Used to work for Benny."

"All right," he said. "What about him?"

"He was a good American," she said. "Trying to do right."

"I have no reason to doubt that."

Darcy said, "He was the man, if something happened to you at two in the morning, a heart attack or just a bad dream, a suspicious sound outside, you knew you could call him up, he'd come. Always. Every time. A neighbor, a man down the street. Even if you were a stranger. He'd come. He was that kind of person."

Roger said, "Maybe you shouldn't be telling me this."

"People think they can do things alone," Darcy said. "They think they're braver than they really are, and then they cut themselves off from people because they think they've got the gristle, the smarts, they can do it all alone. All of it.

"They don't think anybody would help them anyway. They've lost their faith in humanity, maybe. Everybody's a scofflaw, driving through red lights. After a while you begin to think you're the one doing wrong if you stop and obey. So, it happens, you get cut off. You think you got to do it all by yourself."

"You're into something," Roger said, "in over your head."

She nodded that she was. Way over.

"And I assume you're not who Mr. Cousins thinks you are."

"I'm not who anybody thinks I am," she said. "I'm like a soul got caught migrating, trapped between bodies. Just out here floating. Waiting for something to open up."

Roger smiled. He looked out at the lightning, at the coconut palm tossing just outside the window. He said, "I think I know how you feel."

Darcy said, "You think you can control him? Benny."

"Sure," he said. "He's just a short, fat, bald guy in a pirate suit."

Thorn hadn't made a circle. Closer to a V. But hell, it was even better. A flap to get his hand through. Just needed one side of it a couple of inches longer. So the flap would flap.

A little earlier the electricity had blinked on and off. Then off. But that didn't matter. He was doing this by feel now. He knew it would only be another minute or so—that is, if his hand didn't cramp up anymore.

When the lock on the door rattled and clicked open, Thorn had his hand outside the flap, trying to pry the opening wider. At the noise he jerked it back inside. Twisted, rocked, twisted again, and got the roll moving and brought it back around. He was facing the cement again. His friends the ants.

Ozzie came inside and stamped his feet. Going b-r-r-r.

He pulled the string on the light, pulled it several times.

"Figures," he said. "Like every other fucking thing tonight."

Thorn gripped the knife hard. The way he felt, all the juice he had in his blood at the moment, he might just be able to levitate to a standing position, take a breath deep enough to break the nylon cord; he'd spring out, slash Ozzie's throat.

After the hours listening to that storm, breathing through his nose, his thumb aching, his shoulder. After all that, and thinking about Darcy, then making himself not think about her, but the images bubbling back up, scenes of her inside that house. Of all those men. Of Benny. After all that, Thorn could feel the lava backing up inside. Ready to spew. He held the knife at the flap, the point pressed against the concrete.

"There's a goddamn bulb around here somewhere," Ozzie said.

He was rummaging through the boxes on the workbench.

"I want to see your face when I do you, dingleberry," he said. "That's half the fucking fun."

Ozzie searched for another minute, then came over to Thorn. "Well, shit," he said. "I can't find it."

He stepped over to the door and kicked it open. The cool air flooding in. Some dawnlight in the wet trees.

He felt Ozzie sit on the roll, around the center of his spine. Then the barrel pressing against the back of his skull.

"You know, lifeguard, almost nothing works out like you expect. No matter what you do. It doesn't matter who you bribe, who you shoot, how much you think things out. It's like there's always some little thing, something looking to trip you up."

Thorn's forehead was pressing into the cement, a rough grit embedding in his flesh. The pressure of the barrel increasing.

"I handed out hundred-dollar bills tonight like they was nickels. Bought some fat cats color TV sets so I'd be sure to get treated right in the talent judging."

Ozzie took the gun away, rocked the linoleum back a quarter turn. The flap rising from the floor.

He said, "I figured it was the Keys and everybody was bribing everybody else. But the fuck of it is, I must've spent a couple thousand dollars and sang my heart out and still came in second goddamn place."

Ozzie rose, stepped outside the shed, and came back in with a two-foot trophy. He set it beside Thorn's face and revolved the the linoleum roll so he could see. It was a silver cup on a wood pedestal, sparkling with rain.

Thorn tugged on the inside of the flap, bringing it flush. His hand poised behind it.

The nylon cord was a few inches below the flap. If he could slide his hand out, he could saw it in half and spin to his right and roll free. It might take a half a minute. Or two minutes. Either way, Ozzie could simply stand back, aim, and fire.

Ozzie had his right foot up on the roll like a hunter posing with his slaughtered tiger. Thorn's weight pressed against his good shoulder.

"The goddamn fix was in," Ozzie said. "Some high school twat played the banjo and sang some piss-poor bluegrass, she got the first-place trophy. Must've been the goddamn granddaughter of some Bubba or something." He sighed, went over to the door, and looked out at the rising light. He said, "It don't matter really. 'Cause I took down the little twat's name and I'm gonna pay her a call when it gets light this morning. See what she'd take for that thing."

Ozzie stooped beside him, brought the linoleum around so Thorn was on his back. Ozzie unwrapped the duct tape. Up close, Thorn could smell the whiskey, see in the vague light Ozzie's exhausted face.

"Wondered why you was so fucking quiet."

Thorn worked his jaw. The flap fully exposed now.

Ozzie planted his bottom on the roll, looked at Thorn, and said, "Nothing ever happens how you think, does it, lifeguard?"

The flap was under his right thigh. Thorn hesitated, then began to peel back the three layers of the V, straining, trying to keep his face calm.

"Like you," Ozzie said. "You started off today thinking you was just going to live and live and live. Playing house with my girl friend, tickling her goodies. All that shit. You had no way to know when you woke up this morning that Ozzie Hardison was going to be sitting on your stomach tonight, pointing a big-assed pistol in your face. Now did you?"

Thorn plunged the Buck knife into the back of Ozzie's thigh.

Got it in deep and stirred it around in there. Minced the guy's hamstring pretty good. He felt the blood running down his hand, his wrist, as Ozzie lurched to his feet, howling. His big-assed pistol clattered on the cement just a foot from Thorn's face.

"That's Benny," Roger said. He rose from the chair.

In the dawn now. Dawn outside, dawn over the whole planet.

He opened her door, stepped out into the black hallway, and said, "I'll just put him to bed. Then call you a doctor." He left.

Darcy closed her eyes, sailed off. Ionospheric swoops. Across the dark plateaus of the upper atmosphere, cloudy summits. In a misty half sleep, drifting high and weightless inside herself.

Maybe this was the dark she'd pictured. The inky mist. If that's what it was, then it wasn't so bad. Nothing to fear. She could feel the winds up here, cool and rich. Reviving something in her, some sweet song that she'd heard long ago and forgotten.

Then a gunshot roared in the dark.

It came from far down below. Down on the earth, where bodies were weighted with bone and meat. Down where footsteps echoed through the dark hallways like excited hearts.

33

Ozzie fell back into the rakes and shovels. He howled.

Thorn watched him writhing there for a moment, then jammed his hand through the flap, widening it until he could reach his blade to the nylon cord. He began to saw at it.

Ozzie was struggling back to his feet. Through his tears he began to hobble across the floor. Bent over. Looked like the one leg wasn't working at all. Might never work. He dragged it, extending his right hand for the silenced .38, while he clutched the back of his thigh with his left.

Thorn was only halfway through the strands of the cord. Going slower than he'd expected. Ozzie stooped beside him, reaching out with a spastic hand for the pistol. Then he came down to his knees, sliding his hand across the cement for the pistol.

Rolling right, Thorn brought the linoleum on top of Ozzie's hand, pinning it against the floor. He craned his arm around and slashed the Buck knife back at Ozzie's arm, nicked him deep on the wrist. He screamed. And Thorn rolled off his hand.

"Jesus, Jesus, Jesus." Ozzie fell onto his butt and dragged himself backwards over to the rakes and hoes, moaning. His eyes groggy, head sagging. He sat there and watched Thorn's hand sawing at the cord.

In another minute the cord parted and dropped away. But the sticky backing on the linoleum held it shut.

"You're still caught, dingleberry," Ozzie said, faintly. "Har, har."

Thorn rocked and turned against the grain of the roll, and the tacky glue crackled, loosened, and opened up. And quickly he uncoiled himself, coming to rest almost at Ozzie's feet.

"You stuck me, goddamn you," Ozzie said. His voice furry, his eyes holding on by a wisp.

"Yeah, I did," Thorn said, "and I enjoyed it." He stood up cautiously. He retrieved Ozzie's pistol and put it under his belt.

"Get me to the hospital," Ozzie said.

"Yeah, sure," Thorn said. "Right away."

"I'll bleed to death, you leave me like this."

"Speak to the wolves. Tell 'em you're not ready. I hear they're very understanding."

Ozzie squinted at Thorn.

He hauled Ozzie to his feet and tied his hands behind him with the nylon cord. Tied the loose end to the leg of the heavy workbench. He moved a wooden keg over so Ozzie could sit.

Maybe while Thorn was gone, Ozzie would reflect on what he'd done. Recognize his sinfulness. Ask for forgiveness. Find grace. And when Thorn returned for him, the shed might be suffused with heavenly light.

But probably not. It looked like the redneck was just going to pass out.

Thorn headed for Darcy's trailer. His left arm was hanging dead. He passed a grandmother walking her white poodle. Nodded hello to her. She gasped, and her dog stood on its hind legs and performed a pirouette for Thorn. He looked down and saw he was clutching the knife in his right hand, blood to his forearm.

"Been cleaning a barracuda," he said. "Got more to do."

Darcy's door was unlocked. It took only a minute to find the Browning Baby in her bedside table. He could hear the whoops and trills of a Bugs Bunny cartoon coming from the trailer next door. It was almost nine. Saturday.

He slipped the Browning into his front pocket. And jogged back across the trailer park to Ozzie's house, where he found Papa John's white pickup. The keys were in the ignition. Ozzie's pirate hat on the passenger seat. His guitar, a blue bandanna, a rubber buccaneer's sword. And two more handguns. A .357 magnum. And a ten-millimeter Colt.

When Thorn arrived at his house, Jack Higby was running the Lakowski planer. He looked up from the machine and did a double take. Garfunkel loped over as Thorn was getting down from the truck. The dog wedged its nose into Thorn's crotch, lifted.

"The hell happened to you, boy?" Jack had hustled over and taken Thorn by the right arm, trying to help him walk. But Thorn shrugged him off.

"Call Sugarman," he said. "Tell him to meet me at Benny Cousins's house."

Jack was staring at the three pistols Thorn carried in his hand. The other one wedged in his belt.

"I just saw Sugar out on the highway," Jack said, absently. "Out there with every cop and state trooper in the county. Blocking off half the road for the parade."

"Then call the station, Jack," Thorn said as he boarded the *Heart Pounder.* "Have them radio Sugar. Do it quick."

He went down into the cabin, heard Jack's pickup start up as he pulled open his tackle drawer and scooped out a handful of plugs. Careful of the treble hooks, he deposited a half dozen of them in the right pocket of his leather flight jacket. He put the jacket on. Four pistols and a pocketful of plugs. He guessed that was enough firepower.

Thorn walked back across the yard to Papa John's truck. Got Ozzie's pirate stuff out of it and took it over to the ice cream truck, unplugged the compressor, got in. He hauled Gaeton's body out of the cooler box. Got his good shoulder under him and hefted him up to the front. Working with just that one arm, he turned Gaeton and settled him into the passenger seat.

He brushed away a frosting of ice crystals from Gaeton's forehead and started up the truck. He looked over at his friend as he was pulling out on the highway. Gaeton's hands were extended as if he were about to settle them onto the keys of a piano. Play a dirge.

He tailgated a rented convertible, playing the tape of "Three Blind Mice" loud from the overhead speaker. Traffic was ten miles an hour, all of it funneled into the two southbound lanes.

He pulled off at Hibiscus Lane and stopped in front of a group of black men leaning against a gutted Buick. He asked them where W.B. lived, and they pointed at a sagging white house on the corner of the next block. Thorn drove down there, parked out front, set the pistols on the passenger seat. He kept the motor running and loped over to the door.

A woman came to the screen wearing pink curlers, a yellow housecoat, and terry-cloth slippers.

He said he wanted to see W.B.

"He's not here," she said. "Whatta you want with him?"

"I need the keys to the John Deere he runs down in Islamorada."

"Well, they ain't here," she said. Kids were beginning to assemble behind her housecoat.

"Where are they?"

"He's got them keys with him."

"Where?"

"Down there, running that machine. They call him up five o'clock this morning, wake us all up, liked to never get the babies back to sleep. Wanting him to plant a tree first thing this morning. Now whatta them folks want a tree planted so early on a Saturday morning for?"

Thorn could've told her. But she probably wouldn't have believed him. He could hardly believe it himself.

Black pennants waved from all the flagpoles at Waldorf Plaza, a silver pirate on each one. Daggers in their mouths. Kids' crude posters of skulls and crossbones were nailed to the telephone poles along the five-mile parade route. Thorn got a good look at them. Traffic stalled.

People were beginning to collect along the shoulders of the road. Some of them with their bandanna kerchiefs, swords, eye-patches. He didn't see anybody with a pistol in his waistband. Not a single ten millimeter or Browning or .38 with a silencer.

A lot of these smiling people were his friends. A sprinkling of their children. Bartenders, waitresses, checkout clerks, shrimpers, maids, diesel mechanics. These children of wreckers and rumrunners, hardscrabble pioneers. Men who had come there to the outer fringe of America to nourish their rugged individualism.

Plenty of Januarys Thorn had stood out there with them, warming himself with Bacardi, waiting to celebrate the colorful lives of their granddaddies. He'd gotten his best history lessons out there beside that four lane, listening to the old-timers' grim memories.

And he'd been as rowdy as any of them by parade time. Hooting and cussing, as those polyester Chamber of Commerce pirates rode their floats, slashing their rubber swords. It had always seemed harmless, that cotton-candy history. A past created by wax museums and gaudy T-shirts.

But not today. Not with Benny Cousins leading the way.

Thorn edged the ice cream truck onto the narrow shoulder of the road, honking, flashing his lights. He rammed the shifter into second, then third. Passing on the right the stalled line of cars. They all ran after the farmer's wife.

In the parking lot of Tavernier Towne, the American Legion honor guard and Coast Guard Auxiliary were practicing their march steps, M-14s on their shoulders. The Shriners had begun to arrive on their mopeds, wearing eye patches and red vests and fezzes. A couple of the floats were there already. And half a dozen go-carts revving up. Peewee swashbucklers doing drag race starts in the McDonald's lot.

He made it to Benny's by nine-thirty. W.B. was tamping the earth in around the base of the latest royal palm when he pulled the ice cream truck into the drive.

He wedged the silenced .38 into his waistband and got out and walked over. W.B. was thumping the earth hard around the new tree, using a blunt steel rod. Raising it over his head, then driving it down against the fresh dirt.

Thorn called out his name as he approached, and W.B. turned and smiled. Wiped his forehead on his shirt sleeve, leaned the tamper against the tree.

"God Almighty, Thorn," said W.B., reaching out toward his torn shoulder. "You stick your hand in the wrong lobster hole?"

"You seen Benny this morning?" Thorn said.

"Him and his Elks and Rotisserie buddies up at the house getting soused for the shenanigans. Now that's a passel of fools."

Thorn nodded over at the John Deere. He said, "Mind if I use your equipment a minute or two?"

"You all right, Thorn?" W.B. said, eyeing the pistol. "You

ain't got the distemper, do you, boy?"

"Something like that," he said, and went over to the machine.

He climbed up the fender, hauling himself up with his good arm. He got settled in the seat and shifted the pistol so it didn't poke.

He ran his eyes over the levers, reminding himself. Then he started it up, put it in gear, and lowered the front-end bucket as he turned the wheel. He drove toward the newest tree.

"Thorn! What the hell you doing!" W.B. stood in the path of the machine, waving his hands.

Thorn plowed ahead, aiming the edge of the bucket at a place a third of the way up the trunk. W.B. whooped and jumped aside.

Thorn kept it in low gear as he rammed the tree, revving the engine. He pushed the palm backwards, the deep-grooved tractor wheels biting, turning in the grass. He knew the root balls on those trees were just three feet deep, set under a foot of dirt. It'd be months before the roots sprouted, took hold in that coral. Months before those trees could stand up to a good gale.

He backed off. The tree was leaning at a hard angle.

W.B. had drawn close and seemed to be about to make a lunge for the keys.

Thorn drew out the .38 and let him admire its sleek lines. W.B. smiled, showing Thorn his palms, moving away backwards.

"Hey, it's your world, Thorn. I'm just walking through."

Thorn put the pistol back in his belt and took aim again with the bucket and got some speed behind this run. He hit the tree lower down and sent it lurching backwards. It fell, and its fronds settled into the grass.

He lowered the scoop to the hole, tipped the bucket down,

and drove forward. Levered the bucket up and got the root ball into the scoop. He kept lifting it, powering the machine forward till he had the root a few feet away from the hole. He dumped it.

"Nice work," W.B. called. He was sitting on a mound of dirt a few feet away. "You ain't applying for my job, are you?"

Thorn brought the scooper back over the hole. Out of the edge of his vision he saw something moving at the house. But he kept his attention on the bucket, digging it a couple of feet down into the loose earth.

"They coming for you," W.B. called. "I spect they want a rematch. Two out of three falls."

He emptied the dirt near the hole, brought the bucket back for another scoop. This was the delicate moment. But there wasn't time to get down in the hole and do this reverently by hand. Dead was dead. If he mangled her body with the scoop in the interests of speed and justice, Darcy would've understood. Done the same.

A brown Mercedes pulled up to the edge of the John Deere, and Joey got out of the driver's door. He was wearing black tights, a red T-shirt, black bandanna around his neck. He huffed. Closed his eyes and shook his head. Drew out his long-barrel .38.

Thorn lowered the scooper into the hole again, as Joey called out to him to shut the goddamn thing off. He assumed Joey had his pistol aimed and cocked by now. But that didn't matter. Thorn'd been shot before. It wasn't as bad as everyone made it out.

He ran the bucket down one edge of the hole, turned it with the lever, and dug in. He pulled back carefully and raised it. Dirt spilled from the sides of the scoop. And a rubber thong.

Thorn swung the John Deere around so it was headed toward Benny's house. He brought it forward a couple of feet and stopped. Settled the bucket over some thick Bermuda grass, rocked it over. And onto the grass spilled a naked body. A rubber thong landing on his gut. Roger.

Not Darcy. Roger.

Thorn looked over at Joey. Yeah, his gun was out. Probably a much better shot than Ozzie. He had that look about him, as if he hadn't missed many things he really wanted to hit. His pistol lowering as Joey walked over, staring at the body on the grass.

He came up to the body, turned it over with the toe of his tennis shoe. A single shot through the forehead. The tough guy Joey brought a hand to his belly then. Couldn't handle a simple corpse before breakfast.

W.B. had walked over to Thorn. He said, "I been gravedigging. Is that what you're trying to tell me?"

Thorn nodded and said, "When Benny called last night, was it only for this one tree?"

"He said to put this one in," W.B. said, "and dig the hole for another."

Thorn took a long breath.

"Get down from there now," Joey said. "Hands high, fucker."

Thorn got down, keeping his good hand in the air. Joey pressed the barrel to the back of his neck.

He reached around and stripped the pistol out of Thorn's belt, slung it onto the ground. He patted the left pocket of Thorn's jacket. Then the right. Felt the bulge in there.

"You asshole," Joey said. "You're finished playing games in this time zone, man."

He dug his hand into Thorn's right pocket and got a palm full of torpedo plugs. Barbed steel hooks designed to slide in easy, and stay. When he got his breath back, he screamed.

And Thorn mashed Joey's hand inside the pocket, swiveling then and driving his elbow into Joey's gut. Joey sat back hard on the ground. Several of the plugs snagged to his hand. A couple had ripped free and were still hanging from Thorn's jacket pocket.

Thorn picked up the silenced .38. And Joey's donation to his collection. He carried them over to the ice cream truck and climbed back in. Set them on the floor with the others in front of Gaeton. When this was over, he'd have to rent that auger, run it as deep as it went, fill the hole with pistols. And tamp them in. His own time capsule, his meager message down the ages. These were our weapons. They made killing easier than it should be. So some of us began to bury them.

Now he should sit out here and wait for Sugar to arrive. The sensible thing. The lawful thing.

He glanced back. Joey was sitting on the mound of dirt, staring at the plugs dangling from his palm. His hand slick with his blood. And W.B. was standing beside the empty hole, examining a T-shirt, the rubber thongs.

Thorn yelled at him to come over. W.B. hesitated. Thorn yelled that he needed him. He needed him bad. And W.B. dropped the T-shirt and thongs and came over.

It took a minute more of convincing to get him to stand on the steps next to Gaeton's body. But W.B. did it, closing his eyes, took a breath, turned his head away, and held on.

Thorn cranked up the ice cream truck, switched on the tape. It was "Old MacDonald" now. With a quack-quack here and a quack-quack there. He headed on up to the house.

34

With a here quack, there quack, everywhere a quack-quack.

Thorn parked the ice cream truck beneath a poinciana tree. There were fifteen, twenty men dressed in pirate regalia horsing around the pool and the yard. Drinking from plastic cups, talking, a couple of mock sword fights going on. Gusts of laughter.

W.B. stayed by the truck while Thorn walked out to the pool area, nodding at a few people he recognized. Saying hi there. Beautiful day for it, isn't it? Getting a couple of odd looks at his bloodstained shirt, the pistol in his belt. But he made no serious waves as he moved to the pool deck and found the chair he remembered sitting in that first day with Benny. A white thing with cast-iron vines and leaves curling around iron grillwork.

He lugged it back to the ice cream truck and positioned it so it would be visible from any of the front windows when the truck was moved. In the shade of a coconut palm.

A few yards away the galleon float was parked under a large sea grape tree. It was Captain Kidd's four-masted schooner with papier-mâché cannons. Its hull was chicken wire and crepe paper.

With a moo-moo here and a quack-quack there. Here quack. There quack.

Charlie Boilini, sipping from a plastic cup, came walking over, nodding hello to Thorn. Owner of Boilini Liquors, past president of the Chamber of Commerce, the Elks, Rotary. He came up to the ice cream truck as Thorn was about to step back aboard. He smiled prosperously. In red tunic, white flounced shirt, long black boots, a red hat cocked sideways.

"I didn't know you were selling ice cream these days."

"I'm not," Thorn said.

Boilini stared at Thorn's shoulder wound. He reached out, but Thorn edged away.

"That's an interesting costume," Boilini said. "Not historical, but it's got a good realistic feel to it."

"It does have that," Thorn said.

Some of Boilini's Rotary buddies were dueling in the shade near the float, half pints showing from a few pockets.

Thorn glanced up at the house, asked Boilini where Benny was.

"Upstairs, putting the finishing touches on, I guess," he said. "Later than shit, too." He was staring at Gaeton now. Blinking. Quietly, he said, "I didn't know you knew Mr. Cousins."

Thorn said yes, they went way back. Way back.

Three or four of Benny's men were standing by the hot tub, watching the Rotary guys duel, the contest growing to five combatants, all of them huffing hard as they clacked swords. Some rum guzzling behind the float. Belly laughs. Out beyond them, the shallows were a blue sheen. The sky cloudless.

Thorn motioned for W.B., and the two of them walked around to the passenger door. Charlie followed. With a moo-moo here and a moo-moo there. Here moo. There moo.

"Let's carry him over to the chair," Thorn said to W.B.

"Touch him?"

"It's the only way," Thorn said.

W.B. shook his head. No, sir.

Boilini squinted at the corpse, then at Thorn. He stepped up one step, touched Gaeton's right hand.

"Holy shit." He stepped back down. He looked ready to swoon. "Holy shit, holy shit. Is that for real? Gaeton Richards dead."

Thorn said it was, it was for real.

"Come on, Thorn. This is a goddamn practical joke."

"No, Charlie," he said.

"Oh, Jesus, this is gonna fuck up things, Thorn. The parade, everything."

"Yeah," Thorn said. "It's a shame."

Boilini stumbled backwards, moving his eyes between Thorn and Gaeton.

Well, hell. He would just have to do it alone then. Thorn stepped up into the truck and put his shoulder into Gaeton's gut, lifted, almost lost it going backwards down the steps. Recovered and turned, staggering. W.B. pitched in then, took charge of Gaeton's legs, and together they made it the five yards across the grass. They swiveled the body and settled Gaeton into the chair. Thorn looked back to see if all of this was screened from the house by the ice cream truck. Yes. Yes.

"When you see me or anybody else come to a window up there, W.B.," Thorn said, nodding at the house, "you move the truck. Drive it back out front and park it."

W.B. was swallowing, breathing funny.

"Can you do that for me, W.B.?"

W.B. nodded that he would.

"Keep your eyes on the window."

He nodded again, sweating. A fuzzy half-smile.

Thorn got Ozzie's pirate paraphernalia from the ice cream truck. He went back over and started to get Gaeton ready for the festival.

He stretched the bandanna tight across Gaeton's forehead, hiding most of the wound. And he wedged Gaeton's hard, rubbery fingers through the plastic guard of the fake sword. The flesh was thawing fast. But the sword stayed there, catching a slip of breeze and wavering.

Thorn stood back to see how he'd done. Boilini was leading some of his buddies over toward him. Here oink, there oink. It wasn't a bad job. From twenty, thirty yards away you could barely tell.

Boilini and his friends drew around him.

"Charlie," Thorn said, turning to the group, "when you're finished gawking here, there's more bodies out front, by the road. I'm not shitting you either, go take a look."

Charlie groaned. And as the first few of them came close to the chair, reaching out for a touch, Thorn edged away to the house. When Norman Thompson stumbled back from the body and hollered for the others to get their asses over there and see this, Thorn mounted the front steps. As the rest of the civic leaders and Benny's boys were crowding around the chair, Thorn opened the front door, went inside.

The house was quiet.

He took the stairs three at a time. Halted at the landing. Listened. There was nothing but the voices outside. He dug his hand into his pocket. Next to the knife was the gold conch shell. He made a fist around it, squeezed.

He tried each door. Two empty guest rooms. The third one with an outside bolt. It was unbolted. Thorn paused. The quack-quacking and oink-oinking were still going on.

He turned the knob slowly and stepped a foot into the room.

He felt the whoosh of air before he saw the blur coming for his head. Ducked to a crouch and rolled sideways across the wood floor. And the blade of a long sword swished past his ear. Definitely not rubber.

"The boy's got some reflexes on him, doesn't he?" Benny

said. He aimed the sword at Thorn. He was dressed in a black cinched jacket with wide shoulders, gold epaulets. Black knickers and ballet slippers. A braided silver cord crossed his cummerbund and frilly white shirt. The samurai sword in his right hand.

A stainless .357 in his left.

Darcy lay on the bed. She had dark blue mumps. Lips puffy. There was a ragged three-inch gash on her cheek. But her eyes were bright. She gave him a look to live for.

Benny said, "I been waiting and waiting. I was beginning to think you'd chickenshitted right out of things. Just going to sacrifice Nancy Drew to save your own ass."

"I wouldn't have missed this," Thorn said.

Benny said, "You've been fucking up my picnic, Thorn. You been doing it and doing it. And now it's going to stop."

Benny's eyes went to the pistol at Thorn's belt, and he sighted the .357 at Thorn and told him to take that pistol out real slow, put it on the leather wing chair. Thorn drew it out of his belt, held it by the silencer in front of him with thumb and first finger as if he had a rat by its tail.

"Now, smart guy," Benny said. "Put it on the chair."

Thorn kept his face easy, his eyes floating between Benny and Darcy. Benny looking at him from down a long tunnel of hatred. A twist in his mouth, quick-draw eyes.

"So you had to kill Roger, huh?" Thorn said, still holding the pistol. "Why was that? He finally draw the line somewhere?"

Darcy said, "He tried to protect me."

"Shut up, bitch," Benny said. He waved the pistol at her, keeping his eyes on Thorn. "OK, hot rod. Put that fucking pistol down, or I start shooting right now."

Thorn set the .38 on the chair. He moved to the window. His back to it. He heard the truck start down below. Heard the here quack, there quack drifting away. He glanced over his shoulder. The gang of pirates was marching out the drive.

Benny said, "Now move away from there."

But Thorn turned his back to Benny. He looked out at Gaeton. His friend's face was mottled with light. A trickle of wind twisted the sword in his hand as if he were trying to sever the threads that still held him in this plane.

He seemed at ease there in that chair. Receding into some distant place. He'd done all that he could in this world and now he was off toward the endless meadow of hazy light, or whatever it was that Gaeton had imagined as heaven. Going there now. Going and going.

Benny cocked the pistol, told Thorn to turn the fuck around. Get the fuck away from that window.

But Thorn continued to stare. At the light and wind playing on his, friend. This man whose boyhood had mingled with Thorn's boyhood. This man with his cryptic smile. Eyes so detached now. The wind stirring his bandanna. His face bathed in sunlight and shade.

Benny jammed the barrel into the hollow at the base of Thorn's skull. The sword clattered to the floor behind them, and Benny seized Thorn's hair, dragged him back a step.

"Chain jerking, Thorn? That's all you can do, isn't it, boy? Coming in here thinking you can chain-jerk your way through it all. Jesus. You really thought I'd buy that shit?"

Benny dragged Thorn a few steps to the front of the dressing table. He held him in front of the mirror and glared over his shoulder. Thorn could see Darcy behind them, still on the bed. Her eyes cutting to the floor, back to Thorn's eyes.

Benny said, "You hold a pistol to somebody's head like this, and fire it, hey, the gases alone will kill you. It could be a blank, the ammo could be old or damp, and it'd still kill you dead. You think I don't know anything about ballistics? You really think I believed it for a second. Huh? Is that who you thought you were dealing with, mondo dorko?"

Thorn made a noise in his throat, as close to speech as he could get with his head tilted back so far.

"I'll tell you what," Benny said. "We'll try an experiment. We'll test this out, whatta you say? I'll squeeze off a round into your skull, see if you get up and run five miles tomorrow."

Thorn tossed the earring underhanded onto the glass top of the dressing table. Benny yanked his hair hard, dug the barrel in deeper.

"Now what, chain jerker?"

Benny pivoted Thorn, angling for a look. Out of the edge of his eye Thorn saw Darcy focused on the sword. Benny was panting. In a sudden explosion he shoved Thorn away to the foot of the bed.

"The fuck is this!"

Benny had the earring in his left hand. The pistol wavering at Thorn. Covering him from chest to crotch.

"Something you lost," Thorn said. "Something Gaeton spit up."

"The hell you say."

"Ask him."

"Stop it! Fucking stop it!"

"Ask him," Thorn said quietly. "He's out there. Waiting for you." He pointed at the window.

Benny battled with it for a few moments, his eyes shifting back and forth between Thorn and Darcy. Then he edged to the window. A twist of veins was pulsating in his temple. He stood facing them and tested a quick look over his shoulder.

"Look, if it makes you more comfortable, I'll stand over

here," Thorn said. He moved around the bed, his good hand at his shoulder. Darcy took a breath, gave Thorn a you-better-know-what-the-hell-you're-doing frown. Thorn stood next to a small writing table.

Benny's throat was working. He snorted. He shook his head. The stainless .357 was still aimed at Thorn. Benny measured the distance across the room, seemed to be calculating how long a look he could take. He snorted again.

"You know, Thorn, I was wrong about you. You *do* have balls. It's godamn brains you're missing."

He turned and looked out there.

"Oh, Jesus Mother of God," he said. He groaned.

"I wouldn't lie to you, Benny," Thorn said.

Benny turned and aimed the .357 at Thorn, then Darcy. His hand rattling. He looked down at the leather chair, picked up the silenced .38, looked it over.

"This fucking gun, too?"

"Yeah," Thorn said. "That, too."

Benny turned, grappled with the window for a moment, a pistol in each hand, got it unlocked, and hauled it open. He stuck his head out and made a quick sweep of the area. Stepped away, brought the silenced .38 up, and aimed down there. He squeezed off three quiet rounds. Four, five.

When the firing pin clicked on air, Thorn was behind him, got his forearm around Benny's throat, cranked his arm tight. Benny swallowed against the hold. Thorn clenched tighter, lifting this small, hard man off his feet until Benny's strength dimmed and both pistols fell to the floor. Thorn turned him away from the window, and a button fired from his fancy shirt.

"Tell me when he turns blue," Thorn said.

Darcy had picked up the sword. She was standing in front of Benny. She seemed calm, faintly amused. She cocked her head and examined his face, having her own silent transaction with this man. Then drew back the sword, aiming it at his gut.

Thorn told her to stop. Hold it.

"I'm not going to kill him. I wouldn't do that."

Benny was slack now, but Thorn kept the pressure on.

She said, "I just want to slide this inside there, reroute his intestines a little."

But Thorn kept shaking his head and she didn't move. He turned Benny toward the door, forced him through. He dragged him to the head of the stairway. The man was heavy. Probably feed a pack of wolves for a month.

A siren wailed along millionaire's alley.

Thorn got Benny out of the bedroom and down the stairs. His forearm was tight against that thick throat. He heard Darcy following. On the landing, he could see through the foyer windows the Rotarians and Benny's men clustered just beyond the porch, watching the siren approach.

"Thorn?" Darcy said.

He stopped at the entranceway and half turned to her.

She drew back and stuck the sword into Benny's side. Into the flab at his waist, not deep, not dangerous. But Benny roared, wriggled in Thorn's grip, then slumped, almost dragged them both to the floor.

"I had to do it," she said as she drew the blade out. "I know it's not right." She dropped the sword on the marble floor. "But goddamn, was it satisfying."

Sugarman was standing outside his patrol car speaking into his microphone, calling for more ambulances. Needed fifteen, maybe more, probably have to send some down from Miami.

Benny handcuffed behind his back, was in the back seat, chin on his chest.

Two slugs had hit Gaeton and knocked him out of the chair. Thorn had lifted him up, carried him back inside the truck, and settled him again into the cooler.

Thorn and Darcy were leaning against the ice cream truck.

She said, "I was doing just fine, Thorn. I really didn't need the muscle man thing. Kicking the door down. All that."

He turned to her.

"I had him talking to me," she said. "He told me about his mother. The woman used to boil his toys, Thorn. Keep everything purified around the house. He had a rubber duck, she boiled it, and it melted. It was just too Freudian. All of it."

He looked at her.

"You're being deadpan," he said.

She looked out at the flats, where all this had begun for her.

"Droll," she said. "I'm being very dry."

"I hear it now," he said. "But I wasn't sure for a minute."

As Sugarman talked on his radio, a white Ford Fairlane with blackened windows rolled into the yard, pulled up alongside the patrol car. A man with a fresh haircut got out. White shirt, red tie, dark pants, shiny shoes. He waited till Sugarman was finished on the radio, then flashed some ID inside a leather folder.

"The first string has arrived," Thorn said.

"In the nick of time," she said. Darcy wasn't leaning on the ice cream truck anymore. She had taken a few steps in the direction of the cars.

Sugarman shook his head at the man, having none of it. The man nodded back, an unequivocal yes. By the time Thorn and Darcy got to the car, the man had Benny out of the back seat of the patrol car and Sugarman was unlocking his handcuffs. He gave Thorn a disgusted look.

Benny, shirtless and bandaged around the belly, smiled up at Sugarman. Then at Thorn. And gave Darcy an especially ugly one.

"Bye, guys," he said. "And don't fire your pallbearers just yet."

The man held the door while Benny ducked into the back seat of the Fairlane. He slid in next to a woman in a big hat and big sunglasses. She kept her face turned away. The man with the haircut slammed the door and turned to Sugarman.

"You can go now," he said.

"And those bodies out front?" Sugarman said.

"They're being taken care of," the man said as he got back into the car. "You or the sheriff have any other questions, give us a call at this number." The man handed Sugarman a card. "And by the way, you did reasonably good work, considering," he said. He nodded at them all. Polite, reasonable.

"Who are you?" Thorn said, moving close, blocking the door. He was considering hauling Benny out of there, run a quick and dirty biopsy on that sneer, see if it was terminal.

"Just a public servant," the man said. "Your measly tax dollars at work."

"You're not my goddamn government," Thorn said.

"Or anybody else's around here," said Darcy.

The man smiled mildly at Thorn giving him a few seconds more to try something. Or to invent an insult the man hadn't heard before.

But Thorn stood still, got his pulse back to earth. He closed the man's door carefully. There were more important things to be done. A friend to put in the ground. Love to nourish. A house to build. An ocean full of wary fish to fool.

35

Ozzie limped over to the jukebox and fed it another quarter. "Not Johnny Cash," Bonnie said. "Anything but him."

She was hanging a stained glass red tulip up in one of the bar windows. There'd been a Hamm's beer sign in there before. She'd hung a stained glass thing in every window now. A rose, a unicorn, a sunset, and two tulips, one green and one red. Ozzie had to admit, the place was more colorful. But it was getting awful close to looking like the inside of a church.

There was a little price tag twirling on a string on each of them. When he saw her putting on those tags, Ozzie had said he wasn't running any goddamn boutique; but Bonnie had just gone on and done it, and he hadn't fought it that hard. Then, in that first week, they'd sold five of them. Seven dollars and fifty cents apiece. Drunks stumbling in saying, is this the place where the unicorns are? And Ozzie just nodded his head. Liquor people up, and there was no end to what they'd spend their money on.

Ozzie punched the numbers for Jimmy Buffet. "Margaritaville" for the seven hundredth time that week.

"Living on sponge cake," Bonnie sang as she got the tulip lined up just right in the window.

Ozzie limped back behind the bar and bought himself a beer. Didn't put a nickel in the till either.

"That makes five this afternoon," Bonnie said. "You're gonna get yourself a beer gut, you aren't careful."

"I know how many it is," said Ozzie. "I can count just fine."

"Blew out my flip-flop," Bonnie sang.

She was doing that now. Singing. Having her second goddamn childhood. Ever since he hadn't shot her out on the boat.
Ever since they'd rolled Papa John's body over the side with the
anchor around him. Ever since they'd come back to the bar and
sat around and waited to see what was going to happen. And
nothing had, except that yesterday a couple of twenty-dollar
haircuts in blue suits had come in asking where Papa John was
and Ozzie had said what he'd rehearsed. That John'd gone down
to Key West for a little while, lowering his voice like he was
being cozy with them, suggesting that Papa John was maybe
moving some contraband or something.

The two blue suits looked at each other with disgusted faces
and went outside, got in their white Ford, and left. And all that
Ozzie had been expecting to happen, the handcuffs, the judge,
the trial, the trip back to Loxahatchee Correctional, all of it
whooshed right out of his mind.

Darcy was lying in the hammock near the dock, reading what
was left of that Ashbery book. Every few minutes she'd smile
and turn a page, look over at Thorn, and wink, as though fire-
works of understanding were going off inside her. He wasn't
sure. Maybe she was just in love.

Her jaw was wired shut. It would be six weeks before she could
take solid food. Thorn had bought an electric blender at the K
Mart and had it plugged in next to the sawmill. He'd heard
about blenders before, of course, but never seen one up close.
They were fascinating things.

Jack Higby had finished turning the lignum vitae sink and was
fussing now with the siding. He'd decided he wanted to match
the wood grains, so the veins of Indonesian narra blended in
with the dark twists of mahogany and tamarind. It might take a

little longer to make it all mesh, but come on, what was the hurry? The house was going to stand there for a hundred years, what difference did an extra month or two now make? So, Thorn had said, fine, sure, whatever you think, Jack. A wonderful plan.

Thorn and Sugarman were sitting on the dock. No shirts. Both in cut offs. A few minutes earlier Sugarman had been snorkeling and had found a hermit crab living in a translucent blue jar. Darcy had informed them that it was a Noxzema skin cream jar. Sugarman brought it over to show the others, and now the crab was strutting the length of the dock, carrying that blue jar.

"It's embarrassed," Thorn said. "Probably ostracized by all the other hermit crabs."

"It isn't smart enough to be embarrassed," Darcy said in her teeth-clamped tongue. "The crab's just doing what it has to do. Working with what's available. Maybe it's even proud. A one-of-a-kind guy."

"What's your vote, Sugar?"

Sugarman shrugged. Not playing today.

Thorn watched him kick at the water, the ripples he was sending out.

"Could you go back, Sugar," Darcy said, "if you told them you'd changed your mind?"

"No," he said.

"You said things? You told people off?"

"I told them how I felt is all," Sugarman said. "How I'd lost faith."

"Well," Thorn said, rolling onto his stomach. "How does it feel?"

"I feel weird," Sugarman said. "I was always a cop. It's all I ever wanted to be."

Darcy looked up and smiled. She said, "Don't worry, Thorn'll give you unemployment lessons."

"That's what I'm afraid of," Sugarman said.

"It grows on you, Sugar." He stopped the hermit crab at the edge of the dock and aimed it back down the center.

Sugarman said, "I think I'll just take a couple of weeks. Relax. Then maybe I'll take my savings, buy into a tackle shop or something."

"Need a shrimp dipper?" Darcy said.

"I need somebody," Thorn said. "To put suntan oil on my back."

Darcy sat up in the hammock.

"Any volunteers?" Thorn said.

She came over.

"What'd you do before I showed up?" Darcy said.

"Some important places just went untouched," he said.

Sugarman kicked at the water with his bare feet. He said, "Or maybe a detective agency."

"I like the tackle shop plan better," Darcy said. "Less of a gore factor." She slid her hands across Thorn's back. He closed his eyes, made a noise in his throat.

"You do that very well," he said.

"You're just easily pleased, Thorn."

He hummed his agreement.

When Sugarman's beeper went off, Darcy's hands flinched against Thorn's back.

"Oh, God, another insight," said Thorn.

"That, or she's out of toilet paper," Sugar said.

Sugarman looked at the beeper for a moment, then nudged it off the edge of the dock and it splashed into the shallow water.

"There's a law against that," Darcy said. "Isn't there? Beeper abuse or something."

"Call a cop," Sugarman said.

Thorn tipped his head back, surrendering himself to Darcy's

hands and watching the clouds on their lazy voyages. That last cold front had scrubbed the atmosphere clean and left a crystalline ping in the air. That Arctic wind had cruised for a week at thirty thousand feet, blue-white virginal air with a piney hint, and had swooped down and flooded over them. Now everyone around the island seemed a little daffy from all that oxygen. Smiling, jabbering things that didn't quite make sense. A little happier than they'd been a few days before.

And people seemed to be making decisions. Standing up, dusting themselves off, stretching fingers to toe, and heading off in new directions. Take Sugar, take Darcy. Take even Thorn. Blenders. Suntan oil.

And though Thorn knew the carbon dioxide fumes and the methane and the ozone and all the rest of it had not been blown very far away, and though he was certain the pollution was already beginning to mount up again, still, for a while, the sky would be fresh. And for those few days he and Darcy and Sugarman and Jack and the rest of them would be able to feast on that good rich air, breathing again the way they were always meant to breathe.